D1349685

Enid Blyton

THE EXCITING ADVENTURES OF
THE FAMOUS FIVE

Enid Blyton

THE EXCITING ADVENTURES OF
THE FAMOUS FIVE

TREASURE PRESS

First published in this format in 1984
under the title *Enid Blyton's Adventures with the Famous 5*

This edition published in 1987 by
Treasure Press
Michelin House
81 Fulham Road
London SW3 6RB
by arrangement with Hodder and Stoughton Children's Books

Reprinted 1988, 1989, 1990

ISBN 1 85051 248 5

Printed in Italy by OFSA, Milan

CONTENTS

Enid Blyton

FIVE ON A TREASURE ISLAND

ILLUSTRATED BY JOLYNE KNOX

1

A great surprise

'Mother, have you heard about our summer holidays yet?' said Julian, at the breakfast-table. 'Can we go to Polseath as usual?'

'I'm afraid not,' said his mother. 'They are quite full up this year.'

The three children at the breakfast-table looked at one another in great disappointment. They did so love the house at Polseath. The beach was so lovely there, too, and the bathing was fine.

'Cheer up,' said Daddy. 'I dare say we'll find somewhere else just as good for you. And anyway, Mother and I won't be able to go with you this year. Has Mother told you?'

'No!' said Anne. 'Oh, Mother — is it true? Can't you really come with us on our holidays? You always do.'

'Well, this time Daddy wants me to go to Scotland

with him,' said Mother. 'All by ourselves! And as you
are really getting big enough to look after yourselves
now, we thought it would be rather fun for you to
have a holiday on your own too. But now that you
can't go to Polseath, I don't really quite know where
to send you.'

'What about Quentin's?' suddenly said Daddy.
Quentin was his brother, the children's uncle. They
had only seen him once, and had been rather
frightened of him. He was a very tall, frowning man,
a clever scientist who spent all his time studying. He
lived by the sea — but that was about all that the
children knew of him!

'Quentin?' said Mother, pursing her lips. 'Whatever made you think of him? I shouldn't think he'd
want the children messing about in his little house.'

'Well,' said Daddy, 'I had to see Quentin's wife in
town the other day, about a business matter — and I
don't think things are going too well for them. Fanny
said that she would be quite glad if she could hear of
one or two people to live with her for a while, to bring
a little money in. Their house is by the sea, you know.
It might be just the thing for the children. Fanny is
very nice — she would look after them well.'

'Yes — and she has a child of her own too, hasn't
she?' said the children's mother. 'Let me see —
what's her name — something funny — yes,
Georgina! How old would she be? About eleven, I
should think.'

'Same age as me,' said Dick. 'Fancy having a
cousin we've never seen! She must be jolly lonely all

10

by herself. I've got Julian and Anne to play with — but Georgina is just one on her own. I should think she'd be glad to see us.'

'Well, your Aunt Fanny said that her Georgina would love a bit of company,' said Daddy. 'You know, I really think that would solve our difficulty, if we telephone to Fanny and arrange for the children to go there. It would help Fanny, I'm sure, and Georgina would love to have someone to play with in the holidays. And we should know that our three were safe.'

The children began to feel rather excited. It would be fun to go to a place they had never been to before, and stay with an unknown cousin.

'Are there cliffs and rocks and sands there?' asked Anne. 'Is it a nice place?'

'I don't remember it very well,' said Daddy. 'But I feel sure it's an exciting kind of place. Anyway, you'll love it! It's called Kirrin Bay. Your Aunt Fanny has lived there all her life, and wouldn't leave it for anything.'

'Oh Daddy, do telephone to Aunt Fanny and ask her if we can go there!' cried Dick. 'I just feel as if it's the right place somehow. It sounds sort of adventurous!'

'Oh, you always say that, wherever you go!' said Daddy, with a laugh. 'All right — I'll ring up now, and see if there's any chance.'

They had all finished their breakfast, and they got up to wait for Daddy to telephone. He went out into the hall, and they heard him putting the call through.

'I hope it's all right for us!' said Julian. 'I wonder what Georgina's like. Funny name, isn't it? More like a boy's than a girl's. So she's eleven — a year younger than I am — same age as you, Dick — and a year older than you, Anne. She ought to fit in with us all right. The four of us ought to have a fine time together.'

Daddy came back in about ten minutes' time, and the children knew at once that he had fixed up everything. He smiled round at them.

'Well, that's settled,' he said. 'Your Aunt Fanny is delighted about it. She says it will be awfully good for Georgina to have company, because she's such a lonely little girl, always going off by herself. And she will love looking after you all. Only you'll have to be careful not to disturb your Uncle Quentin. He is working very hard, and he isn't very good-tempered when he is disturbed.'

'We'll be as quiet as mice in the house!' said Dick. 'Honestly we will. Oh, goody, goody — when are we going, Daddy?'

'Next week, if Mother can manage it,' said Daddy.

Mother nodded her head. 'Yes,' she said, 'there's nothing much to get ready for them — just bathing suits and jerseys and jeans. They all wear the same.'

'How lovely it will be to wear jeans again,' said Anne, dancing round. 'I'm tired of wearing school tunics. I want to wear shorts, or a bathing suit, and go bathing and climbing with the boys.'

'Well, you'll soon be doing it,' said Mother, with a laugh. 'Remember to put ready any toys or books you want, won't you? Not many, please, because there won't be a great deal of room.'

'Anne wanted to take all her fifteen dolls with her last year,' said Dick. 'Do you remember, Anne? Weren't you funny?'

'No, I wasn't,' said Anne, going red. 'I love my dolls, and I just couldn't choose which to take — so I thought I'd take them all. There's nothing funny about that.'

'And do you remember the year before, Anne wanted to take the rocking-horse?' said Dick, with a giggle.

Mother chimed in. 'You know, I remember a little boy called Dick who put aside two golliwogs, one teddy bear, three toy dogs, two toy cats and his old monkey to take down to Polseath one year,' she said.

Then it was Dick's turn to go red. He changed the subject at once.

'Daddy, are we going by train or by car?' he asked.

'By car,' said Daddy. 'We can pile everything into the boot. Well — what about Tuesday?'

'That would suit me well,' said Mother. 'Then we could take the children down, come back, and do our own packing at leisure, and start off for Scotland on the Friday. Yes — we'll arrange for Tuesday.'

So Tuesday it was. The children counted the days eagerly, and Anne marked one off the calendar each night. The week seemed a very long time in going. But at last Tuesday did come. Dick and Julian, who shared a room, woke up at about the same moment, and stared out of the near-by window.

'It's a lovely day, hurrah!' cried Julian, leaping out of bed. 'I don't know why, but it always seems very important that it should be sunny on the first day of a holiday. Let's wake Anne.'

Anne slept in the next room. Julian ran in and shook her. 'Wake up! It's Tuesday! And the sun's shining.'

Anne woke up with a jump and stared at Julian joyfully. 'It's come at last!' she said. 'I thought it never would. Oh, isn't it an exciting feeling to go away for a holiday!'

They started soon after breakfast. Their car was a big one, so it held them all very comfortably. Mother sat in front with Daddy, and the three children sat behind, their feet on two suitcases. In the luggage-place at the back of the car were all kinds of odds and ends, and one small trunk. Mother really thought they had remembered everything.

Along the crowded London roads they went, slowly at first, and then, as they left the town behind, more quickly. Soon they were right into the open country, and the car sped along fast. The children sang songs to themselves, as they always did when they were happy.

'Are we picnicking soon?' asked Anne, feeling hungry all of a sudden.

'Yes,' said Mother. 'But not yet. It's only eleven o'clock. We shan't have lunch till at least half-past twelve, Anne.'

'Oh, gracious!' said Anne. 'I know I can't last out till then!'

So her mother handed her some chocolate, and she and the boys munched happily, watching the hills, woods and fields as the car sped by.

The picnic was lovely. They had it on the top of a hill, in a sloping field that looked down into a sunny valley. Anne didn't very much like a big brown cow who came up close and stared at her, but it went away when Daddy told it to. The children ate enormously, and Mother said that instead of having a tea-picnic at half-past four they would have to go to a tea-house somewhere, because they had eaten all the tea sandwiches as well as the lunch ones!

'What time shall we be at Aunt Fanny's?' asked Julian, finishing up the very last sandwich and wishing there were more.

'About six o'clock with luck,' said Daddy. 'Now who wants to stretch their legs a bit? We've another long spell in the car, you know.'

The car seemed to eat up the miles as it purred along. Tea-time came, and then the three children began to feel excited all over again.

'We must watch out for the sea,' said Dick. 'I can smell it somewhere near!'

He was right. The car suddenly topped a hill — and there was the shining blue sea, calm and smooth in the evening sun. The three children gave a yell.

'There it is!'

'Isn't it marvellous!'

'Oh, I want to bathe this very minute!'

'We shan't be more than twenty minutes now, before we're at Kirrin Bay,' said Daddy. 'We've made good time. You'll see the bay soon — it's quite a big one — with a funny sort of island at the entrance of the bay.'

The children looked out for it as they drove along the coast. Then Julian gave a shout.

'There it is — that must be Kirrin Bay. Look, Dick — isn't it lovely and blue?'

'And look at the rocky little island guarding the entrance of the bay,' said Dick. 'I'd like to visit that.'

'Well, I've no doubt you will,' said Mother. 'Now, let's look out for Aunt Fanny's house. It's called Kirrin Cottage.'

They soon came to it. It stood on the low cliff overlooking the bay, and was a very old house indeed. It wasn't really a cottage, but quite a big house, built of old white stone. Roses climbed over the front of it, and the garden was gay with flowers.

'Here's Kirrin Cottage,' said Daddy, and he stopped the car in front of it. 'It's supposed to be about three hundred years old! Now — where's Quentin? Hallo, there's Fanny!'

2
The strange cousin

The children's aunt had been watching for the car. She came running out of the old wooden door as soon as she saw it draw up outside. The children liked the look of her at once.

'Welcome to Kirrin!' she cried. 'Hallo, all of you! It's lovely to see you. And what big children!'

There were kisses all round, and then the children went into the house. They liked it. It felt old and rather mysterious somehow, and the furniture was old and very beautiful.

'Where's Georgina?' asked Anne, looking round for her unknown cousin.

'Oh, the naughty girl! I told her to wait in the garden for you,' said her aunt. 'Now she's gone off somewhere. I must tell you, children, you may find George a bit difficult at first — she's always been one on her own, you know, and at first may not like you

being here. But you mustn't take any notice of that —
she'll be all right in a short time. I was very glad for
George's sake that you were able to come. She badly
needs other children to play with.'

'Do you call her "George"?' asked Anne, in
surprise. 'I thought her name was Georgina.'

'So it is,' said her aunt. 'But George hates being a
girl, and we have to call her George, as if she was a
boy. The naughty girl won't answer if we call her
Georgina.'

The children thought that Georgina sounded
rather exciting. They wished she would come. But
she didn't. Their Uncle Quentin suddenly appeared
instead. He was a most extraordinary looking man,
very tall, very dark, and with a rather fierce frown on
his wide forehead.

'Hallo, Quentin!' said Daddy. 'It's a long time
since I've seen you. I hope these three won't disturb
you very much in your work.'

'Quentin is working on a very difficult book,' said
Aunt Fanny. 'But I've given him a room all to himself
on the other side of the house. So I don't expect he
will be disturbed.'

Their uncle looked at the three children, and
nodded to them. The frown didn't come off his face,
and they all felt a little scared, and were glad that he
was to work in another part of the house.

'Where's George?' he said, in a deep voice.

'Gone off somewhere again,' said Aunt Fanny,
vexed. 'I told her she was to stay here and meet her
cousins.'

'She wants spanking,' said Uncle Quentin. The children couldn't quite make out whether he was joking or not. 'Well, children, I hope you have a good time here, and maybe you will knock a little common-sense into George!'

There was no room at Kirrin Cottage for Mother and Daddy to stay the night, so after a hurried supper they left to stay at a hotel in the nearest town. They would drive back to London immediately after breakfast the next day. So they said good-bye to the children that night.

Georgina still hadn't appeared. 'I'm sorry we haven't seen Georgina,' said Mother. 'Just give her our love and tell her we hope she'll enjoy playing with Dick, Julian and Anne.'

Then Mother and Daddy went. The children felt a little bit lonely as they saw the big car disappear round the corner of the road, but Aunt Fanny took them upstairs to show them their bedrooms, and they soon forgot to be sad.

The two boys were to sleep together in a room with slanting ceilings at the top of the house. It had a marvellous view of the bay. The boys were really delighted with it. Anne was to sleep with Georgina in a smaller room, whose windows looked over the moors at the back of the house. But one side-window looked over the sea, which pleased Anne very much. It was a nice room, and red roses nodded their heads in at the window.

'I do wish Georgina would come,' Anne said to her aunt. 'I want to see what she's like.'

'Well, she's a funny little girl,' said her aunt. 'She can be very rude and haughty — but she's kind at heart, very loyal and absolutely truthful. Once she makes friends with you, she will always be your friend — but she finds it very difficult indeed to make friends, which is a great pity.'

Anne suddenly yawned. The boys frowned at her, because they knew what would happen next. And it did!

'Poor Anne! How tired you are! You must all go to bed straight away, and have a good long night. Then you will wake up quite fresh tomorrow,' said Aunt Fanny.

'Anne, you *are* an idiot,' said Dick, crossly, when his aunt had gone out of the room. 'You know quite well what grown-ups think as soon as we yawn. I did want to go down on the beach for a while.'

'I'm so sorry,' said Anne. 'Somehow I couldn't help it. And anyway, *you're* yawning now, Dick — and Julian too!'

So they were. They were as sleepy as could be with their long drive. Secretly all of them longed to cuddle down into bed and shut their eyes.

'I wonder where Georgina is,' said Anne, when she said good-night to the boys, and went to her own room. 'Isn't she queer — not waiting to welcome us — and not coming in to supper — and not even in yet! After all, she's sleeping in my room — goodness knows what time she'll be in!'

All the three children were fast asleep before Georgina came up to bed! They didn't hear her open

Anne's door. They didn't hear her get undressed and clean her teeth. They didn't hear the creak of her bed as she got into it. They were so tired that they heard nothing at all until the sun awoke them in the morning.

When Anne awoke she couldn't at first think where she was. She lay in her little bed and looked up at the slanting ceiling, and at the red roses that nodded at the open window — and suddenly remembered all in a rush where she was! 'I'm at Kirrin Bay — and it's the holidays!' she said to herself, and screwed up her legs with joy.

Then she looked across at the other bed. In it lay the figure of another child, curled up under the bed-clothes. Anne could just see the top of a curly head, and that was all. When the figure stirred a little, Anne spoke.

'I say! Are you Georgina?'

The child in the opposite bed sat up and looked across at Anne. She had very short curly hair, almost as short as a boy's. Her face was burnt a dark-brown with the sun, and her very blue eyes looked as bright as forget-me-nots in her face. But her mouth was rather sulky, and she had a frown like her father's.

'No,' she said. 'I'm not Georgina.'

'Oh!' said Anne, in surprise. 'Then who are you?'

'I'm George,' said the girl. 'I shall only answer if you call me George. I hate being a girl. I won't be. I don't like doing the things that girls do. I like doing the things that boys do. I can climb better than any boy, and swim faster too. I can sail a boat as well as

any fisher-boy on this coast. You're to call me George. Then I'll speak to you. But I shan't if you don't.'

'Oh!' said Anne, thinking that her new cousin was most extraordinary. 'All right! I don't care what I call you. George is a nice name, I think. I don't much like Georgina. Anyway, you look like a boy.'

'Do I really?' said George, the frown leaving her face for a moment. 'Mother was awfully cross with me when I cut my hair short. I had hair all round my neck; it was awful.'

The two girls stared at one another for a moment. 'Don't you simply hate being a girl?' asked George.

'No, of course not,' said Anne. 'You see — I do like pretty frocks — and I love my dolls — and you can't do that if you're a boy.'

'Pooh! Fancy bothering about pretty frocks,' said George, in a scornful voice. 'And dolls! Well, you *are* a baby, that's all I can say.'

Anne felt offended. 'You're not very polite,' she said. 'You won't find that my brothers take much notice of you if you act as if you know everything. They're *real* boys, not pretend boys, like you.'

'Well, if they're going to be nasty to me I shan't take any notice of *them*,' said George, jumping out of bed. 'I didn't want any of you to come, anyway. Interfering with my life here! I'm quite happy on my own. Now I've got to put up with a silly girl who likes frocks and dolls, and two stupid boy-cousins!'

Anne felt that they had made a very bad beginning. She said no more, but got dressed herself too. She put on her grey jeans and a red jersey. George put on jeans too, and a boy's jersey. Just as they were ready the boys hammered on their door.

'Aren't you ready? Is Georgina there? Cousin Georgina, come out and see us.'

George flung open the door and marched out with her head high. She took no notice of the two surprised boys at all. She stalked downstairs. The other three children looked at one another.

'She won't answer if you call her Georgina,' explained Anne. 'She's awfully queer, I think. She says she didn't want us to come because we'll interfere with her. She laughed at me, and was rather rude.'

Julian put his arm round Anne, who looked a bit doleful. 'Cheer up!' he said. 'You've got us to stick up for you. Come on down to breakfast.'

They were all hungry. The smell of bacon and eggs was very good. They ran down the stairs and said good-morning to their aunt. She was just bringing the breakfast to the table. Their uncle was sitting at the head, reading his paper. He nodded at the children. They sat down without a word, wondering if they were allowed to speak at meals. They always were at home, but their Uncle Quentin looked rather fierce.

George was there, buttering a piece of toast. She scowled at the three children.

'Don't look like that, George,' said her mother. 'I hope you've made friends already. It will be fun for you to play together. You must take your cousins to see the bay this morning and show them the best places to bathe.'

'I'm going fishing,' said George.

Her father looked up at once.

'You are not,' he said. 'You are going to show a few good manners for a change, and take your cousins to the bay. Do you hear me?'

'Yes,' said George, with a scowl exactly like her father's.

'Oh, we can go to the bay by ourselves all right, if George is going fishing,' said Anne, at once, thinking that it would be nice not to have George if she was in a bad temper.

'George will do exactly as she's told,' said her father. 'If she doesn't, I shall deal with her.'

So, after breakfast, four children got ready to go down to the beach. An easy path led down to the bay, and they ran down happily. Even George lost her frown as she felt the warmth of the sun and saw the dancing sparkles on the blue sea.

'You go fishing if you want to,' said Anne when they were down on the beach. 'We won't tell tales of you. We don't want to interfere with you, you know. We've got ourselves for company, and if you don't want to be with us, you needn't.'

'But we'd like you, all the same, if you'd like to be with us,' said Julian, generously. He thought George was rude and ill-mannered, but he couldn't help rather liking the look of the straight-backed, short-haired little girl, with her brilliant blue eyes and sulky mouth.

26

George stared at him. 'I'll see,' she said. 'I don't make friends with people just because they're my cousins, or something silly like that. I only make friends with people if I like them.'

'So do we,' said Julian. 'We may not like *you*, of course.'

'Oh!' said George, as if that thought hadn't occurred to her. 'Well — you may not, of course. Lots of people don't like me, now I come to think of it.'

Anne was staring out over the blue bay. At the entrance to it lay a curious rocky island with what looked like an old ruined castle on the top of it.

'Isn't that a funny place?' she said. 'I wonder what it's called.'

'It's called Kirrin Island,' said George, her eyes as blue as the sea as she turned to look at it. 'It's a lovely place to go to. If I like you, I may take you there some day. But I don't promise. The only way to get there is by boat.'

'Who does the funny island belong to?' asked Julian.

George made a most surprising answer. 'It belongs to *me*,' she said. 'At least, it *will* belong to me — some day! It will be my very own island — and my very own castle!'

eer story – and a new friend

The three children stared at George in the greatest surprise.

George stared back at them.

'What do you mean?' said Dick, at last. 'Kirrin Island can't belong to you. You're just boasting.'

'No, I'm not,' said George. 'You ask Mother. If you're not going to believe what I say I won't tell you another word more. But I don't tell untruths. I think it's being a coward if you don't tell the truth — and I'm not a coward.'

Julian remembered that Aunt Fanny had said that George was absolutely truthful, and he scratched his head and looked at George again. How could she be possibly telling the truth?

'Well, of course we'll believe you if you tell us the truth,' he said. 'But it does sound a bit extraordinary, you know. Really it does. Children don't usually own islands, even funny little ones like that.'

'It *isn't* a funny little island,' said George, fiercely. 'It's lovely. There are rabbits there, as tame as can be — and the big cormorants sit on the other side — and all kinds of gulls go there. The castle is wonderful too, even if it *is* all in ruins.'

'It sounds fine,' said Dick. 'How does it belong to you, Georgina?'

George glared at him and didn't answer.

'Sorry,' said Dick, hastily. 'I didn't mean to call you Georgina. I meant to call you George.'

'Go on, George — tell us how the island belongs to you,' said Julian, slipping his arm through his sulky little cousin's.

She pulled away from him at once.

'Don't do that,' she said. 'I'm not sure that I want to make friends with you yet.'

'All right, all right,' said Julian, losing patience. 'Be enemies or anything you like. We don't care. But we like your mother awfully, and we don't want her to think we won't make friends with you.'

'Do you like my mother?' said George, her bright blue eyes softening a little. 'Yes — she's a dear, isn't she? Well — all right — I'll tell you how Kirrin Castle belongs to me. Come and sit down here in this corner where nobody can hear us.'

They all sat down in a sandy corner of the beach. George looked across at the little island in the bay.

'It's like this,' she said. 'Years ago my mother's people owned nearly all the land around here. Then they got poor, and had to sell most of it. But they could never sell that little island, because nobody thought it worth anything, especially as the castle has been ruined for years.'

'Fancy nobody wanting to buy a dear little island like that!' said Dick. 'I'd buy it at once if I had the money.'

'All that's left of what Mother's family owned is our own house, Kirrin Cottage, and a farm a little way off — and Kirrin Island,' said George. 'Mother says when I'm grown-up it will be mine. She says she doesn't want it now, either, so she's sort of given it to me. It belongs to me. It's my own private island, and I don't let anyone go there unless they get my permission.'

The three children stared at her. They believed every word George said, for it was quite plain that the girl was speaking the truth. Fancy having an island of your very own! They thought she was very lucky indeed.

'Oh Georgina — I mean George!' said Dick. 'I do think you're lucky. It looks such a nice island. I hope you'll be friends with us and take us there one day soon. You simply can't imagine how we'd love it.'

'Well — I might,' said George, pleased at the interest she had caused. 'I'll see. I never have taken anyone there yet, though some of the boys and girls round here have begged me to. But I don't like them, so I haven't.'

There was a little silence as the four children looked out over the bay to where the island lay in the distance. The tide was going out. It almost looked as if they could wade over to the island. Dick asked if it was possible.

'No,' said George. 'I told you — it's only possible to get to it by boat. It's farther out than it looks — and the water is very, very deep. There are rocks all about too — you have to know exactly where to row a boat, or you bump into them. It's a dangerous bit of coast here. There are a lot of wrecks about.'

'Wrecks!' cried Julian, his eyes shining. 'I say! I've never seen an old wreck. Are there any to see?'

'Not now,' said George. 'They've all been cleared up. Except one, and that's the other side of the island. It's deep down in the water. You can just see the broken mast if you row over it on a calm day and look down into the water. That wreck really belongs to me too.'

This time the children really could hardly believe George. But she nodded her head firmly.

'Yes,' she said, 'it was a ship belonging to one of my great-great-great-grandfathers, or someone like that. He was bringing gold — big bars of gold — back in his ship — and it got wrecked off Kirrin Island.'

'Oooh — what happened to the gold?' asked Anne, her eyes round and big.

'Nobody knows,' said George. 'I expect it was stolen out of the ship. Divers have been down to see, of course, but they couldn't find any gold.'

'Golly — this does sound exciting,' said Julian. 'I wish I could see the wreck.'

'Well — we might perhaps go this afternoon when the tide is right down,' said George. 'the water is so calm and clear today. We could see a bit of it.'

'Oh, how wonderful!' said Anne. 'I do so want to see a real live wreck!'

The others laughed. 'Well, it won't be very alive,' said Dick. 'I say, George — what about a bathe?'

'I must go and get Timothy first,' said George. She got up.

'Who's Timothy?' said Dick.

'Can you keep a secret?' asked George. 'Nobody must know at home.'

'Well, go on, what's the secret?' asked Julian. 'You can tell us. We're not sneaks.'

'Timothy is my very greatest friend,' said George. 'I couldn't do without him. But Mother and Father don't like him, so I have to keep him in secret. I'll go and fetch him.'

She ran off up the cliff path. The others watched her go. They thought she was the queerest girl they had ever known.

'Who in the world can Timothy be?' wondered Julian. 'Some fisher-boy, I suppose, that George's parents don't approve of.'

The children lay back in the soft sand and waited. Soon they heard George's clear voice coming down from the cliff behind them.

'Come on, Timothy! Come on!'

They sat up and looked to see what Timothy was like. They saw no fisher-boy — but instead a big black and white mongrel dog with an absurdly long tail and a big wide mouth that really seemed to grin! He was bounding all round George, mad with delight. She came running down to them.

'This is Timothy,' she said. 'Don't you think he is simply perfect?'

As a dog, Timothy was far from perfect. He was the wrong shape, his head was too big, his ears were too pricked, his tail was too long and it was quite impossible to say what kind of a dog he was supposed to be. But he was such a mad, friendly, clumsy, laughable creature that every one of the children adored him at once.

'Oh, you darling!' said Anne, and got a lick on the nose.

'I say — isn't he grand!' said Dick, and gave Timothy a friendly smack that made the dog bound madly all round him.

'I wish *I* had a dog like this,' said Julian, who really loved dogs, and had always wanted one of his own. 'Oh, George — he's fine. Aren't you proud of him?'

The little girl smiled, and her face altered at once, and became sunny and pretty. She sat down on the sand and her dog cuddled up to her, licking her wherever he could find a bare piece of skin.

'I love him awfully,' she said. 'I found him out on the moors when he was just a pup, a year ago, and I took him home. At first Mother liked him, but when he grew bigger he got terribly naughty.'

'What did he do?' asked Anne.

'Well, he's an awfully chewy kind of dog,' said George. 'He chewed up everything he could — a new rug Mother had bought — her nicest hat — Father's slippers — some of his papers, and things like that.

And he barked too. I liked his bark, but Father didn't. He said it nearly drove him mad. He hit Timothy and that made me angry, so I was awfully rude to him.'

'Did you get spanked?' said Anne. 'I wouldn't like to be rude to your father. He looks fierce.'

George looked out over the bay. Her face had gone sulky again. 'Well, it doesn't matter what punishment I got,' she said, 'but the worst part of all was when Father said I couldn't keep Timothy any more, and Mother backed Father up and said Tim must go. I cried for days — and I never do cry, you know, because boys don't and I like to be like a boy.'

'Boys do cry sometimes,' began Anne, looking at Dick, who had been a bit of a cry-baby three or four years back. Dick gave her a sharp nudge, and she said no more.

George looked at Anne.

'Boys don't cry,' she said, obstinately. 'Anyway, I've never seen one, and I always try not to cry myself. It's so babyish. But I just couldn't help it when Timothy had to go. He cried too.'

The children looked with great respect at Timothy. They had not known that a dog could cry before.

'Do you mean — he cried real tears?' asked Anne.

'No, not quite,' said George. 'He's too brave for that. He cried with his voice — howled and howled and looked so miserable that he nearly broke my heart. And then I knew I couldn't possibly part with him.'

'What happened then?' asked Julian.

'I went to Alf, a fisher-boy I know,' said George, 'and I asked him if he'd keep Tim for me, if I paid him all the pocket-money I get. He said he would, and so he does. That's why I never have any money to spend — it all has to go on Tim. He seems to eat an awful lot — don't you, Tim?'

'Woof!' said Tim, and rolled over on his back, all

his shaggy legs in the air. Julian tickled him.

'How do you manage when you want any sweets or ice-creams?' said Anne, who spent most of her pocket-money on things of that sort.

'I don't manage,' said George. 'I go without, of course.'

This sounded awful to the other children, who loved ice-creams, chocolates and sweets, and had a good many of them. They stared at George.

'Well — I suppose the other children who play on the beach share their sweets and ices with you sometimes, don't they?' asked Julian.

'I don't let them,' said George. 'If I can never give them any myself it's not fair to take them. So I say no.'

The tinkle of an ice-cream man's bell was heard in the distance. Julian felt in his pocket. He jumped up and rushed off, jingling his money. In a few moments he was back again, carrying four fat chocolate ice-cream bars. He gave one to Dick, and one to Anne, and then held out one to George. She looked at it longingly, but shook her head.

'No, thanks,' she said. 'You know what I just said. I haven't any money to buy them, so I can't share mine with you, and I can't take any from you. It's mean to take from people if you can't give even a little back.'

'You can take from us,' said Julian, trying to put the ice into George's brown hand. 'We're your cousins.'

'No, thanks,' said George again. 'Though I do

think it's nice of you.'

She looked at Julian out of her blue eyes and the boy frowned as he tried to think of a way to make the obstinate little girl take the ice. Then he smiled.

'Listen,' he said, 'you've got something we badly want to share — in fact you've got a lot of things we'd like to share, if only you'd let us. You share those with us, and let us share things like ices with you. See?'

'What things have I got that you want to share?' asked George, in surprise.

'You've got a dog,' said Julian, patting the big black and white mongrel. 'We'd love to share him with you, he's such a darling. And you've got a lovely island. We'd be simply thrilled if you'd share it sometimes. And you've got a wreck. We'd like to look at it and share it too. Ices and sweets aren't so good as those things — but it would be nice to make a bargain and share with each other.'

George looked at the brown eyes that gazed steadily into hers. She couldn't help liking Julian. It wasn't her nature to share anything. She had always been an only child, a lonely, rather misunderstood little girl, fierce and hot-tempered. She had never had any friends of her own. Timothy looked up at Julian and saw that he was offering something nice and chocolatey to George. He jumped up and licked the boy with his friendly tongue.

'There you are, you see — Tim wants to be shared,' said Julian, with a laugh. 'It would be nice for him to have three new friends.'

'Yes — it would,' said George, giving in suddenly,

38

and taking the chocolate bar. 'Thank you, Julian. I will share with you. But promise you'll never tell anyone at home that I'm still keeping Timothy?'

'Of course we'll promise,' said Julian. 'But I can't imagine that your father or mother would mind, so long as Tim doesn't live in their house. How's the ice? Is it nice?'

'Ooooh — the loveliest one I've ever tasted!' said George nibbling at it. 'It's so cold. I haven't had one this year. It's simply DELICIOUS!'

Timothy tried to nibble it too. George gave him a few crumbs at the end. Then she turned and smiled at the three children.

'You're nice,' she said. 'I'm glad you've come after all. Let's take a boat out this afternoon and row round the island to have a look at the wreck, shall we?'

'Rather!' said all three at once — and even Timothy wagged his tail as if he understood!

4

An exciting afternoon

They all had a bathe that morning, and the boys found that George was a much better swimmer than they were. She was very strong and very fast, and she could swim under water, too, holding her breath for ages.

'You're jolly good,' said Julian, admiringly. 'It's a pity Anne isn't a bit better. Anne, you'll have to practise your swimming strokes hard, or you'll never be able to swim out as far as we do.'

They were all very hungry at lunch time. They went back up the cliff-path, hoping there would be lots to eat — and there was! Cold meat and salad, plum-pie and custard, and cheese afterwards. How the children tucked in!

'What are you going to do this afternoon?' asked George's mother.

'George is going to take us out in a boat to see the

wreck on the other side of the island,' said Anne. Her aunt looked most surprised.

'*George* is going to take you!' she said. 'Why, George — what's come over you? You've never taken a single person before, though I've asked you to dozens of times!'

George said nothing, but went on eating her plum-pie. She hadn't said a word all through the meal. Her father had not appeared at the table, much to the children's relief.

'Well, George, I must say I'm pleased that you want to try and do what your father said,' began her mother again. But George shook her head.

'I'm not doing it because I've got to,' she said. 'I'm doing it because I want to. I wouldn't have taken anyone to see my wreck, not even the Queen of England, if I didn't like them.'

Her mother laughed. 'Well, it's good news that you like your cousins,' she said. 'I hope they like you!'

'Oh yes!' said Anne, eagerly, anxious to stick up for her strange cousin. 'We do like George — and we like Ti . . .'

She was just about to say that they liked Timothy too, when she got such a kick on her ankle that she cried out in pain and the tears came into her eyes. George glared at her.

'George? Why did you kick Anne like that when she was saying nice things about you?' cried her mother. 'Leave the table at once. I won't have such behaviour.'

George left the table without a word. She went out

41

into the garden. She had just taken a piece of bread and cut herself some cheese. It was all left on her plate. The other three stared at it in distress. Anne was upset. How could she have been so silly as to forget she mustn't mention Tim?

'Oh, please call George back!' she said. 'She didn't mean to kick me. It was an accident.'

But her aunt was very angry with George. 'Finish your meal,' she said to the others. 'I expect George will go into the sulks now. Dear, dear, she *is* such a difficult child!'

The others didn't mind about George going into the sulks. What they did mind was that George might refuse to take them to see the wreck now!

They finished the meal in silence. Their aunt went to see if Uncle Quentin wanted any more pie. He was having his meal in the study by himself. As soon as she had gone out of the room, Anne picked up the bread and cheese from George's plate and went out into the garden.

The boys didn't scold her. They knew that Anne's tongue very often ran away with her — but she always tried to make up for it afterwards. They thought it was very brave of her to go and find George.

George was lying on her back under a big tree in the garden. Anne went up to her. 'I'm sorry I nearly made a mistake, George,' she said. 'Here's your bread and cheese. I've brought it for you. I promise I'll never forget not to mention Tim again.'

George sat up. 'I've a good mind not to take you to

see the wreck,' she said. 'Stupid baby!'

Anne's heart sank. This was what she had feared. 'Well,' she said, 'you needn't take me, of course. But you might take the boys, George. After all, they didn't do anything silly. And anyway, you gave me an awful kick. Look at the bruise.'

George looked at it. Then she looked at Anne. 'But wouldn't you be miserable if I took Julian and Dick without you?' she asked.

'Of course,' said Anne. 'But I don't want to make them miss a treat, even if *I* have to.'

Then George did a surprising thing for her. She gave Anne a hug! Then she immediately looked most ashamed of herself, for she felt sure that no boy would have done that! And she always tried to act like a boy.

'It's all right,' she said, gruffly, taking the bread and cheese. 'You were nearly very silly — and I gave you a kick — so it's all square. Of course you can come this afternoon.'

Anne sped back to tell the boys that everything was all right — and in fifteen minutes' time four children ran down to the beach. By a boat was a brown-faced fisher-boy, about fourteen years old. He had Timothy with him.

'Boat's all ready, Master George,' he said with a grin. 'And Tim's ready, too.'

'Thanks,' said George, and told the others to get in. Timothy jumped in, too, his big tail wagging nineteen to the dozen. George pushed the boat off into the surf and then jumped in herself. She took the oars.

She rowed splendidly, and the boat shot along over the blue bay. It was a wonderful afternoon, and the children loved the movement of the boat over the water. Timothy stood at the prow and barked whenever a wave reared its head.

'He's funny on a wild day,' said George, pulling hard. 'He barks madly at the big waves, and gets so angry if they splash him. He's an awfully good swimmer.'

'Isn't it nice to have a dog with us?' said Anne, anxious to make up for her mistake. 'I do so like him.'

'Woof,' said Timothy, in his deep voice and turned round to lick Anne's ear.

'I'm sure he knew what I said,' said Anne in delight.

'Of course he did,' said George. 'He understands every single word.'

'I say — we're getting near to your island now,' said Julian, in excitement. 'It's bigger than I thought. And isn't the castle exciting?'

They drew near to the island, and the children saw that there were sharp rocks all round about it. Unless anyone knew exactly the way to take, no boat or ship could possibly land on the shore of the rocky little island. In the very middle of it, on a low hill, rose the ruined castle. It had been built of big white stones. Broken archways, tumbledown towers, ruined walls — that was all that was left of a once beautiful castle, proud and strong. Now the jackdaws nested in it and the gulls sat on the topmost stones.

'It looks awfully mysterious,' said Julian. 'How I'd

love to land there and have a look at the castle. Wouldn't it be fun to spend a night or two here!'

George stopped rowing. Her face lighted up. 'I say!' she said, in delight. 'Do you know, I never thought how lovely that would be! To spend a night on my island! To be there all alone, the four of us. To get our own meals, and pretend we really lived there. Wouldn't it be grand?'

'Yes, rather,' said Dick, looking longingly at the island. 'Do you think — do you suppose your mother would let us?'

'I don't know,' said George. 'She might. You could ask her.'

'Can't we land there this afternoon?' asked Julian.

'No, not if you want to see the wreck,' said George. 'We've got to get back for tea today, and it will take all the time to row round to the other side of Kirrin Island and back.'

'Well — I'd like to see the wreck,' said Julian, torn between the island and the wreck. 'Here, let me take the oars for a bit, George. You can't do all the rowing.'

'I can,' said George. 'But I'd quite enjoy lying back in the boat for a change! Look — I'll just take you by this rocky bit — and then you can take the oars till we come to another awkward piece. Honestly, the rocks around this bay are simply dreadful!'

George and Julian changed places in the boat. Julian rowed well, but not so strongly as George. The boat sped along rocking smoothly. They went right round the island, and saw the castle from the other side. It looked more ruined on the side that faced the sea.

'The strong winds come from the open sea,' explained George. 'There's not really much left of it this side, except piles of stones. But there's a good little harbour in a little cove, for those who know how to find it.'

George took the oars after a while, and rowed steadily out a little beyond the island. Then she stopped and looked back towards the shore.

'How do you know when you are over the wreck?' asked Julian, puzzled. 'I should never know!'

'Well, do you see that church tower on the mainland?' asked George. 'And do you see the tip of that hill over there? Well, when you get them exactly in line with one another, between the two towers of the castle on the island, you are pretty well over the wreck! I found that out ages ago.'

The children saw that the tip of the far-off hill and the church tower were practically in line, when they looked at them between the two old towers of the island castle. They looked eagerly down into the sea to see if they could spy the wreck.

The water was perfectly clear and smooth. There was hardly a wrinkle. Timothy looked down into it too, his head on one side, his ears cocked, just as if he knew what he was looking for! The children laughed at him.

'We're not exactly over it,' said George, looking down too. 'The water's so clear today that we should be able to see quite a long way down. Wait, I'll row a bit to the left.'

'Woof!' said Timothy, suddenly, and wagged his tail — and at the same moment the three children saw something deep down in the water!

'It's the wreck!' said Julian, almost falling out of the boat in his excitement. 'I can see a bit of broken mast. Look, Dick, look!'

All four children and the dog, too, gazed down earnestly into the clear water. After a little while they could make out the outlines of a dark hulk, out of which the broken mast stood.

'It's a bit on one side,' said Julian. 'Poor old ship. How it must hate lying there, gradually falling to pieces. George, I wish I could dive down and get a closer look at it.'

'Well, why don't you?' said George. 'You've got your swimming trunks on. I've often dived down. I'll come with you, if you like, if Dick can keep the boat round about here. There's a current that is trying to take it out to sea. Dick, you'll have to keep working a bit with this oar to keep the boat in one spot.'

The girl stripped off her jeans and jersey and Julian did the same. They both had on bathing costumes underneath. George took a beautiful header off the end of the boat, deep down into the water. The others watched her swimming strongly downwards, holding her breath.

After a bit she came up, almost bursting for breath. 'Well, I went almost down to the wreck,' she said. 'It's just the same as it always is — seaweedy and covered with limpets and things. I wish I could get right into the ship itself. But I never have enough breath for that. You go down now, Julian.'

So down Julian went — but he was not so good at swimming deep under water as George was, and he couldn't go down so far. He knew how to open his eyes under water, so he was able to take a good look at the deck of the wreck. It looked very forlorn and strange. Julian didn't really like it very much. It gave him rather a sad sort of feeling. He was glad to go to the top of the water again, and take deep breaths of air, and feel the warm sunshine on his shoulders.

He climbed into the boat. 'Most exciting,' he said. 'Golly, wouldn't I just love to see that wreck properly — you know — go down under the deck into the cabins and look around. And oh, suppose we could really find the boxes of gold!'

'That's impossible,' said George. 'I told you proper divers have already gone down and found nothing. What's the time? I say, we'll be late if we don't hurry back now!'

They did hurry back, and managed to be only about five minutes late for tea. Afterwards they went for a walk over the moors, with Timothy at their heels, and by the time that bedtime came they were all so sleepy that they could hardly keep their eyes open.

'Well, good-night, George,' said Anne, snuggling down into her bed. 'We've had a lovely day — thanks to you!'

'And *I've* had a lovely day, too,' said George, rather

gruffly. 'Thanks to *you*. I'm glad you all came. We're going to have fun. And won't you love my castle and my little island!'

'Oooh, yes,' said Anne, and fell asleep to dream of wrecks and castles and islands by the hundred. Oh, when would George take them to her little island?

5

A visit to the island

The children's aunt arranged a picnic for them the next day, and they all went off to a little cove not far off where they could bathe and paddle to their hearts' content. They had a wonderful day, but secretly Julian, Dick and Anne wished they could have visited George's island. They would rather have done that than anything!

George didn't want to go for the picnic, not because she disliked picnics, but because she couldn't take her dog. Her mother went with the children, and George had to pass a whole day without her beloved Timothy.

'Bad luck!' said Julian, who guessed what she was brooding about. 'I can't think why you don't tell your mother about old Tim. I'm sure she wouldn't mind you letting someone else keep him for you. I know my mother wouldn't mind.'

'I'm not going to tell anybody but you,' said George. 'I get into awful trouble at home always. I dare say it's my fault, but I get a bit tired of it. You see, Daddy doesn't make much money with the learned books he writes, and he's always wanting to give mother and me things he can't afford. So that makes him bad-tempered. He wants to send me away to a good school but he hasn't got the money. I'm glad. I don't want to go away to school. I like being here. I couldn't bear to part with Timothy.'

'You'd like boarding school,' said Anne. 'We all go. It's fun.'

'No, it isn't,' said George obstinately. 'It must be awful to be one of a crowd, and to have other girls all laughing and yelling round you. I should hate it.'

'No, you wouldn't,' said Anne. 'All that is great fun. It would be good for you, George, I should think.'

'If you start telling me what is good for me, I shall hate you,' said George, suddenly looking very fierce. 'Mother and Father are always saying that things are good for me — and they are always the things I don't like.'

'All right, all right,' said Julian, beginning to laugh. 'My goodness, how you do go up in smoke! Honestly, I believe anyone could light a cigarette from the sparks that fly from your eyes!'

That made George laugh, though she didn't want to. It was really impossible to sulk with good-tempered Julian.

They went off to bathe in the sea for the fifth time

that day. Soon they were all splashing about happily, and George found time to help Anne to swim. The little girl hadn't got the right stroke, and George felt really proud when she had taught her.

'Oh, thanks,' said Anne, struggling along. 'I'll never be as good as you — but I'd like to be as good as the boys.'

As they were going home, George spoke to Julian. 'Could you say that you want to go and buy a stamp or something?' she said. 'Then I could go with you, and just have a peep at old Tim. He'll be wondering why I haven't taken him out today.'

'Right!' said Julian. 'I don't want stamps, but I *could* do with an ice. Dick and Anne can go home with your mother and carry the things. I'll just go and tell Aunt Fanny.'

He ran up to his aunt. 'Do you mind if I go and buy some ice-creams?' he asked. 'We haven't had one today. I won't be long. Can George go with me?'

'I don't expect she will want to,' said his aunt. 'But you can ask her.'

'George, come with me!' yelled Julian, setting off to the little village at a great pace. George gave a sudden grin and ran after him. She soon caught him up and smiled gratefully at him.

'Thanks,' she said. 'You go and get the ice-creams, and I'll have a look at Tim.'

They parted, Julian bought four ice-creams, and turned to go home. He waited about for George, who came running up after a few minutes. Her face was glowing.

'He's all right,' she said. 'And you can't imagine
how pleased he was to see me! He nearly jumped over
my head! I say — another ice-cream for me. You
really are a sport, Julian. I'll have to share something
with you quickly. What about going to my island
tomorrow?'

'Golly!' said Julian, his eyes shining. 'That would
be marvellous. Will you really take us tomorrow?
Come on, let's tell the others!'

The four children sat in the garden eating their
ices. Julian told them what George had said. They all
felt excited. George was pleased. She had always felt
quite important before when she had haughtily
refused to take any of the other children to see Kirrin
Island — but it felt much nicer somehow to have
consented to row her cousins there.

'I used to think it was much, much nicer always to
do things on my own,' she thought, as she sucked the
last bits of her ice. 'But it's going to be fun doing
things with Julian and the others.'

The children were sent to wash themselves and to
get tidy before supper. They talked eagerly about the
visit to the island next day. Their aunt heard them
and smiled.

'Well, I really must say I'm pleased that George is
going to share something with you,' she said. 'Would
you like to take your dinner there, and spend the day?
It's hardly worth while rowing all the way there and
landing unless you are going to spend some hours
there.'

'Oh, Aunt Fanny! It would be marvellous to take

our dinner!' cried Anne.

George looked up. 'Are you coming too, Mother?' she asked.

'You don't sound at all as if you want me to,' said her mother, in a hurt tone. 'You looked cross yesterday, too, when you found I was coming. No — I shan't come tomorrow — but I'm sure your cousins must think you are a queer girl never to want your mother to go with you.'

George said nothing. She hardly ever did say a word when she was scolded. The other children said nothing too. They knew perfectly well that it wasn't that George didn't want her mother to go — it was just that she wanted Timothy with her!

'Anyway, I couldn't come,' went on Aunt Fanny. 'I've some gardening to do. You'll be quite safe with George. She can handle a boat like a man.'

The three children looked eagerly at the weather the next day when they got up. The sun was shining, and everything seemed splendid.

'Isn't it a marvellous day?' said Anne to George, as they dressed. 'I'm so looking forward to going to the island.'

'Well, honestly, I think really we oughtn't to go,' said George, unexpectedly.

'Oh, but why?' cried Anne, in dismay.

'I think there's going to be a storm or something,' said George, looking out to the south-west.

'But, George, why do you say that?' said Anne, impatiently. 'Look at the sun — and there's hardly a cloud in the sky!'

56

'The wind is wrong,' said George. 'And can't you see the little white tops of the waves out there by my island? That's always a bad sign.'

'Oh, George — it will be the biggest disappointment of our lives if we don't go today,' said Anne, who couldn't bear any disappointment, big or small. 'And besides,' she added, artfully, 'if we hang about the house, afraid of a storm, we shan't be able to have dear old Tim with us.'

'Yes, that's true,' said George. 'All right — we'll go. But mind — if a storm does come, you're not to be a baby. You're to try and enjoy it and not be frightened.'

'Well, I don't much like storms,' began Anne, but stopped when she saw George's scornful look. They went down to breakfast, and George asked her mother if they could take their dinner as they had planned.

'Yes,' said her mother. 'You and Anne can help to make the sandwiches. You boys can go into the garden and pick some ripe plums to take with you. Julian, you can go down to the village when you've done that and buy some bottles of lemonade or ginger-beer, whichever you like.'

'Ginger-pop for me, thanks!' said Julian, and everyone else said the same. They all felt very happy. It would be marvellous to visit the queer little island. George felt happy because she would be with Tim all day.

They set off at last, the food in two kit-bags. The first thing they did was to fetch Tim. He was tied up in the fisher-boy's back yard. The boy himself was there, and grinned at George.

''Morning, Master George,' he said. It seemed so queer to the other children to hear Georgina called 'Master George'! 'Tim's been barking his head off for you. I guess he knew you were coming for him today.'

'Of course he did,' said George, untying him. He at once went completely mad, and tore round and round the children, his tail down and his ears flat.

'He'd win any race if only he was a greyhound,' said Julian, admiringly. 'You can hardly see him for dust. Tim! Hie, Tim! Come and say "Good-morning".'

Tim leapt up and licked Julian's left ear as he passed on his whirlwind way. Then he sobered down and ran lovingly by George as they all made their way to the beach. He licked George's bare legs every now and again, and she pulled at his ears gently.

They got into the boat, and George pushed off. The fisher-boy waved to them. 'You won't be very long, will you?' he called. 'There's a storm blowing up. Bad one it'll be, too.'

'I know,' shouted back George. 'But maybe we'll get back before it begins. It's pretty far off yet.'

George rowed all the way to the island. Tim stood at each end of the boat in turn, barking when the waves reared up at him. The children watched the island coming closer and closer. It looked even more exciting than it had the other day.

'George, where are you going to land?' asked Julian. 'I simply can't imagine how you know your way in and out of these awful rocks. I'm afraid every moment we'll bump into them!'

'I'm going to land at the little cove I told you about the other day,' said George. 'There's only one way to it, but I know it very well. It's hidden away on the east side of the island.'

The girl cleverly worked her boat in and out of the rocks, and suddenly, as it rounded a low wall of sharp rocks, the children saw the cove she had spoken of. It was like a natural little harbour, and was a smooth inlet of water running up to a stretch of sand, sheltered between high rocks. The boat slid into the inlet, and at once stopped rocking, for here the water was like glass, and had hardly a wrinkle.

'I say — this is fine!' said Julian, his eyes shining with delight. George looked at him and her eyes shone too, as bright as the sea itself. It was the first time she had ever taken anyone to her precious island, and she was enjoying it.

They landed on the smooth yellow sand. 'We're really on the island!' said Anne, and she capered about, Tim joining her and looking as mad as she did. The others laughed. George pulled the boat high up on the sand.

'Why so far up?' said Julian, helping her. 'The tide's almost in, isn't it? Surely it won't come as high as this.'

'I told you I thought a storm was coming,' said, George. 'If one does, the waves simply tear up this inlet and we don't want to lose our boat, do we?'

'Let's explore the island, let's explore the island!'

yelled Anne, who was now at the top of the little natural harbour, climbing up the rocks there. 'Oh do come on!'

They all followed her. It really was a most exciting place. Rabbits were everywhere! They scuttled about as the children appeared, but did not go into their holes.

'Aren't they awfully tame?' said Julian, in surprise.

'Well, nobody ever comes here but me,' said George, 'and I don't frighten them. Tim! Tim, if you go after the rabbits, I'll spank you.'

Tim turned big sorrowful eyes on to George. He and George agreed about every single thing except

rabbits. To Tim rabbits were made for one thing —
to chase! He never could understand why George
wouldn't let him do this. But he held himself in and
walked solemnly by the children, his eyes watching
the lolloping rabbits longingly.

'I believe they would almost eat out of my hand,'
said Julian.

But George shook her head.

'No, I've tried that with them,' she said. 'They
won't. Look at those baby ones. Aren't they lovely?'

'Woof!' said Tim, agreeing, and he took a few steps
towards them. George made a warning noise in her
throat, and Tim walked back, his tail down.

'There's the castle!' said Julian. 'Shall we explore
that now? I do want to.'

'Yes, we will,' said George. 'Look — that is where
the entrance used to be — through that big broken
archway.'

The children gazed at the enormous old archway,
now half-broken down. Behind it were ruined stone
steps leading towards the centre of the castle.

'It had strong walls all round it, with two towers,'
said George. 'One tower is almost gone, as you can
see, but the other is not so bad. The jackdaws build in
that every year. They've almost filled it up with their
sticks!'

As they came near to the better tower of the two the
jackdaws circled round them with loud cries of
'Chack, chack, chack!' Tim leapt into the air as if he
thought he could get them, but they only called
mockingly to him.

'This is the centre of the castle,' said George, as they entered through a ruined doorway into what looked like a great yard, whose stone floor was now overgrown with grass and other weeds. 'Here is where the people used to live. You can see where the rooms were — look, there's one almost whole there. Go through that little door and you'll see it.'

They trooped through a doorway and found themselves in a dark, stone-walled, stone-roofed room, with a space at one end where a fire-place must have been. Two slit-like windows lighted the room. It felt very queer and mysterious.

'What a pity it's all broken down,' said Julian, wandering out again. 'That room seems to be the only one quite whole. There are some others here — but all of them seem to have either no roof, or one or other of the walls gone. That room is the only liveable one. Was there an upstairs to the castle, George?'

'Of course,' said George. 'But the steps that led up are gone. Look! You can see part of an upstairs room there, by the jackdaw tower. You can't get up to it, though, because I've tried. I nearly broke my neck trying to get up. The stones crumble away so.'

'Were there any dungeons?' asked Dick.

'I don't know,' said George. 'I expect so. But nobody could find them now — everywhere is so overgrown.'

It was indeed overgrown. Big blackberry bushes grew here and there, and a few gorse bushes forced their way into gaps and corners. The coarse green grass sprang everywhere, and pink thrift grew its cushions in holes and crannies.

'Well, I think it's a perfectly lovely place,' said Anne. 'Perfectly and absolutely lovely!'

'Do you really?' said George, pleased. 'I'm so glad. Look! We're right on the other side of the island now, facing the sea. Do you see those rocks, with those queer big birds sitting there?'

The children looked. They saw some rocks sticking up, with great black shining birds sitting on them in queer positions.

'They are cormorants,' said George. 'They've caught plenty of fish for their dinner, and they're sitting there digesting it. Hallo — they're all flying away. I wonder why!'

She soon knew — for, from the south-west there suddenly came an ominous rumble.

'Thunder!' said George. 'That's the storm. It's coming sooner than I thought!'

6

What the storm did

The four children stared out to sea. They had all been so interested in exploring the exciting old castle that not one of them had noticed the sudden change in the weather.

Another rumble came. It sounded like a big dog growling in the sky. Tim heard it and growled back, sounding like a small roll of thunder himself.

'My goodness, we're in for it now,' said George, half-alarmed. 'We can't get back in time, that's certain. It's blowing up at top speed. Did ever you see such a change in the sky?'

The sky had been blue when they started. Now it was overcast, and the clouds seemed to hang very low indeed. They scudded along as if someone was chasing them — and the wind howled round in such a mournful way that Anne felt quite frightened.

'It's beginning to rain,' said Julian, feeling an

enormous drop spatter on his outstretched hand. 'We had better shelter, hadn't we, George? We shall get wet through.'

'Yes, we will in a minute,' said George. 'I say, just look at these big waves coming! My word, it really *is* going to be a storm. Golly — what a flash of lightning!'

The waves were certainly beginning to run very high indeed. It was queer to see what a change had come over them. They swelled up, turned over as soon as they came to rocks, and then rushed up the beach of the island with a great roar.

'I think we'd better pull our boat up higher still,' said George suddenly. 'It's going to be a very bad storm indeed. Sometimes these sudden summer storms are worse than a winter one.'

She and Julian ran to the other side of the island where they had left the boat. It was a good thing they went, for great waves were already racing right up to it. The two children pulled the boat up almost to the top of the low cliff and George tied it to a stout gorse bush growing there.

By now the rain was simply pelting down, and George and Julian were soaked. 'I hope the others have been sensible enough to shelter in that room that has a roof and walls,' said George.

They were there all right, looking rather cold and scared. It was very dark there, for the only light came through the two slits of windows and the small doorway.

'Could we light a fire to make things a bit more

cheerful?' said Julian, looking round. 'I wonder where we can find some nice dry sticks?'

Almost as if they were answering the question a small crowd of jackdaws cried out wildly as they circled in the storm. 'Chack, chack, chack!'

'Of course! There are plenty of sticks on the ground below the tower!' cried Julian. 'You know — where the jackdaws nest. They've dropped lots of sticks there.'

He dashed out into the rain and ran to the tower. He picked up an armful of sticks and ran back.

'Good,' said George. 'We'll be able to make a nice fire with those. Anyone got any paper to start it — or matches?'

'I've got some matches,' said Julian. 'But nobody's got paper.'

'Yes,' said Anne, suddenly. 'The sandwiches are wrapped in paper. Let's undo them, and then we can use the paper for the fire.'

'Good idea,' said George. So they undid the sandwiches, and put them neatly on a broken stone, rubbing it clean first. Then they built up a fire, with the paper underneath and the sticks arranged criss-cross on top.

It was fun when they lighted the paper. It flared up and the sticks at once caught fire, for they were very old and dry. Soon there was a fine cracking fire going and the little ruined room was lighted by dancing flames. It was very dark outside now, for the clouds hung almost low enough to touch the top of the castle tower! And how they raced by! The wind sent them

66

off to the north-east, roaring behind them with a noise like the sea itself.

'I've never, never heard the sea making such an awful noise,' said Anne. 'Never! It really sounds as if it's shouting at the top of its voice.'

What with the howling of the wind and the crashing of the great waves all round the little island, the children could hardly hear themselves speak! They had to shout at one another.

'Let's have our dinner!' yelled Dick, who was feeling terribly hungry as usual. 'We can't do anything much while this storm lasts.'

'Yes, let's,' said Anne, looking longingly at the ham sandwiches. 'It will be fun to have a picnic round the fire in this dark old room. I wonder how long ago other people had a meal here? I wish I could see them.'

'Well, I don't' said Dick, looking round half-scared as if he expected to see the old-time people walk in to share their picnic. 'It's quite a queer enough day without wanting things like that to happen.'

They all felt better when they were eating the sandwiches and drinking the ginger-beer. The fire flared up as more and more sticks caught, and gave out quite a pleasant warmth, for now that the wind had got up so strongly, the day had become cold.

'We'll take it in turn to fetch sticks,' said George. But Anne didn't want to go alone. She was trying her best not to show that she was afraid of the storm — but it was more than she could do to go out of the cosy room into the rain and thunder by herself.

Tim didn't seem to like the storm either. He sat close by George, his ears cocked, and growled whenever the thunder rumbled. The children fed him with titbits and he ate them eagerly, for he was hungry too.

All the children had four biscuits each. 'I think I shall give all mine to Tim,' said George. 'I didn't bring him any of his own biscuits, and he does seem so hungry.'

'No, don't do that,' said Julian. 'We'll each give him a biscuit — that will be four for him — and we'll still have three left each. That will be plenty for us.'

'You are really nice,' said George. 'Tim, don't you think they are nice?'

Tim did. He licked everyone and made them laugh. Then he rolled over on his back and let Julian tickle him underneath.

The children fed the fire and finished their picnic. When it came to Julian's turn to get more sticks, he disappeared out of the room into the storm. He stood and looked around, the rain wetting his bare head.

The storm seemed to be right overhead now. The lightning flashed and the thunder crashed at the same moment. Julian was not a bit afraid of storms, but he couldn't help feeling rather over-awed at this one. It was so magnificent. The lightning tore the sky in half almost every minute, and the thunder crashed so loudly that it sounded almost as if mountains were falling down all around!

The sea's voice could be heard as soon as the thunder stopped — and that was magnificent to hear too. The spray flew so high into the air that it wetted Julian as he stood in the centre of the ruined castle.

'I really must see what the waves are like,' thought the boy. 'If the spray flies right over me here, they must be simply enormous!'

He made his way out of the castle and climbed up on to part of the ruined wall that had once run all round the castle. He stood up there, looking out to the open sea. And what a sight met his eyes!

The waves were like great walls of grey-green! They dashed over the rocks that lay all around the island, and spray flew from them, gleaming white in the stormy sky. They rolled up to the island and dashed themselves against it with such terrific force that Julian could feel the wall beneath his feet tremble with the shock.

The boy looked out to sea, marvelling at the really great sight he saw. For half a moment he wondered if the sea might come right over the island itself! Then he knew that couldn't happen, for it would have happened before. He stared at the great waves coming in — and then he saw something rather queer.

There was something else out on the sea by the rocks besides the waves — something dark, something big, something that seemed to lurch out of the waves and settle down again. What could it be?

'It can't be a ship,' said Julian to himself, his heart beginning to beat fast as he strained his eyes to see through the rain and the spray. 'And yet it looks more like a ship than anything else. I hope it isn't a ship.

There wouldn't be anyone saved from it on this dreadful day!'

He stood and watched for a while. The dark shape heaved into sight again and then sank away once more. Julian decided to go and tell the others. He ran back to the firelit room.

'George! Dick! There's something queer out on the rocks beyond the island!' he shouted, at the top of his voice. 'It looks like a ship — and yet it can't possibly be. Come and see!'

The others stared at him in surprise, and jumped to their feet. George hurriedly flung some more sticks on the fire to keep it going, and then she and the others quickly followed Julian out into the rain.

The storm seemed to be passing over a little now. The rain was not pelting down quite so hard. The thunder was rolling a little farther off, and the lightning did not flash so often. Julian led the way to the wall on which he had climbed to watch the sea.

Everyone climbed up to gaze out to sea. They saw a great tumbled, heaving mass of grey-green water, with waves rearing up everywhere. Their tops broke over the rocks and they rushed up to the island as if they would gobble it whole. Anne slipped her arm through Julian's. She felt rather small and scared.

'You're all right, Anne,' said Julian, loudly. 'Now just watch — you'll see something queer in a minute.'

They all watched. At first they saw nothing, for the waves reared up so high that they hid everything a little way out. Then suddenly George saw what Julian meant.

'Gracious!' she shouted. 'It *is* a ship! Yes, it is! Is it being wrecked? It's a big ship — not a sailing-boat, or fishing-smack!'

'Oh, is anyone in it?' wailed Anne.

The four children watched and Tim began to bark as he saw the queer dark shape lurching here and there in the enormous waves. The sea was bringing the ship nearer to shore.

'It will be dashed on to those rocks,' said Julian, suddenly. 'Look — there it goes!'

As he spoke there came a tremendous crashing, splintering sound, and the dark shape of the ship settled down on to the sharp teeth of the dangerous rocks on the south-west side of the island. It stayed there, shifting only slightly as the big waves ran under it and lifted it a little.

'She's stuck there,' said Julian. 'She won't move now. The sea will soon be going down a bit, and then the ship will find herself held by those rocks.'

As he spoke, a ray of pale sunshine came wavering out between a gap in the thinning clouds. It was gone almost at once. 'Good!' said Dick, looking upwards. 'The sun will be out again soon. We can warm ourselves then and get dry — and maybe we can find out what that poor ship is. Oh, Julian — I do so hope there was nobody in it. I hope they've all taken to boats and got safely to land.'

The clouds thinned out a little more. The wind stopped roaring and dropped to a steady breeze. The sun shone out again for a longer time, and the children felt its welcome warmth. They all stared at the ship on the rocks. The sun shone on it and lighted it up.

'There's something queer about it somehow,' said Julian, slowly. 'Something awfully queer. I've never seen a ship quite like it.'

George was staring at it with a strange look in her eyes. She turned to face the three children, and they were astonished to see the bright gleam in her blue eyes. The girl looked almost too excited to speak.

'What is it?' asked Julian, catching hold of her hand.

'Julian — oh, Julian — it's my wreck!' she cried, in a high excited voice. 'Don't you see what's happened? The storm has lifted the ship up from the bottom of the sea, and has lodged it on those rocks. It's my wreck!'

The others saw at once that she was right. It was the old wrecked ship! No wonder it looked queer. No wonder it looked so old and dark, and such a strange shape. It was the wreck, lifted high out of its sleeping-place and put on the rocks near by.

'George! We shall be able to row out and get into the wreck now!' shouted Julian. 'We shall be able to explore it from end to end. We may find the boxes of gold. Oh, *George!*'

7

Back to Kirrin Cottage

The four children were so tremendously surprised
and excited that for a minute or two they didn't say a
word. They just stared at the dark hulk of the old
wreck, imagining what they might find. Then Julian
clutched George's arm and pressed it tightly.

'Isn't this wonderful?' he said. 'Oh, George, isn't it
an extraordinary thing to happen?'

Still George said nothing, but stared at the wreck,
all kinds of thoughts racing through her mind. Then
she turned to Julian.

'If only the wreck is still mine now it's thrown up
like this!' she said. 'I don't know if wrecks belong to
the queen or anyone, like lost treasure does. But after
all, the ship did belong to our family. Nobody
bothered much about it when it was down under the
sea — but do you suppose people will still let me have
it for my own now it's thrown up?'

75

'Well, don't let's tell anyone!' said Dick.

'Don't be silly,' said George. 'One of the fishermen is sure to see it when his ship goes slipping out of the bay. The news will soon be out.'

'Well, then, we'd better explore it thoroughly ourselves before anyone else does!' said Dick, eagerly. 'No one knows about it yet. Only us. Can't we explore it as soon as the waves go down a bit?'

'We can't wade out to the rocks, if that's what you mean,' said George. 'We might get there by boat — but we couldn't possibly risk it now, while the waves are so big. They won't go down today, that's certain. The wind is still too strong.'

'Well, what about tomorrow morning, early?' said Julian. 'Before anyone has got to know about it? I bet if only *we* can get into the ship first, we can find anything there is to find!'

'Yes, I expect we could,' said George. 'I told you divers had been down and explored the ship as thoroughly as they could — but of course it is difficult to do that properly under water. We might find something they've missed. Oh, this is like a dream. I can't believe it's true that my old wreck has come up from the bottom of the sea like that!'

The sun was now properly out, and the children's wet clothes dried in its hot rays. They steamed in the sun, and even Tim's coat sent up a mist too. He didn't seem to like the wreck at all, but growled deeply at it.

'You are funny, Tim,' said George, patting him. 'It won't hurt you! What do you think it is?'

76

'He probably thinks it's a whale,' said Anne with a laugh. 'Oh, George — this is the most exciting day of my life! Oh, can't we possibly take the boat and see if we can get to the wreck?'

'No, we can't,' said George. 'I only wish we could. But it's quite impossible, Anne. For one thing I don't think the wreck has quite settled down on the rocks yet, and maybe it won't till the tide has gone down. I can see it lifting a little still when an extra big wave comes. It would be dangerous to go into it yet. And for another thing I don't want my boat smashed to bits on the rocks, and us thrown into that wild water! That's what would happen. We must wait till tomorrow. It's a good idea to come early. I expect lots of grown-ups will think it's their business to explore it.'

The children watched the old wreck for a little time longer and then went all round the island again. It was certainly not very large, but it really was exciting, with its rocky little coast, its quiet inlet where their boat was, the ruined castle, the circling jackdaws, and the scampering rabbits everywhere.

'I do love it,' said Anne. 'I really do. It's just small enough to *feel* like an island. Most islands are too big to feel like islands. I mean, Britain is an island, but nobody living on it could possibly know it unless they were told. Now this island really *feels* like one because wherever you are you can see to the other side of it. I love it.'

George felt very happy. She had often been on her island before, but always alone except for Tim. She had always vowed that she never, never would take anyone there, because it would spoil her island for her. But it hadn't been spoilt. It had made it much nicer. For the first time George began to understand that sharing pleasures doubles their joy.

'We'll wait till the waves go down a bit then we'll go back home,' she said. 'I rather think there's some more rain coming, and we'll only get soaked through. We shan't be back till tea-time as it is, because we'll have a long pull against the out-going tide.'

All the children felt a little tired after the excitements of the morning. They said very little as they rowed home. Everyone took turns at rowing except Anne, who was not strong enough with the oars to row against the tide. They looked back at the island as they left it. They couldn't see the wreck because that was on the opposite side, facing the open sea.

'It's just as well it's there,' said Julian. 'No one can see it yet. Only when a boat goes out to fish will it be seen. And we shall be there as early as any boat goes out! I vote we get up at dawn.'

'Well, that's pretty early,' said George. 'Can you wake up? I'm often out at dawn, but you're not used to it.'

'Of course we can wake up,' said Julian. 'Well — here we are back at the beach again — and I'm jolly glad. My arms are awfully tired and I'm so hungry I could eat a whole larderful of things.'

'Woof,' said Tim, quite agreeing.

'I'll have to take Tim to Alf,' said George, jumping

out of the boat. 'You get the boat in, Julian. I'll join you in a few minutes.'

It wasn't long before all four were sitting down to a good tea. Aunt Fanny had baked new scones for them, and had made a ginger cake with black treacle. It was dark brown and sticky to eat. The children finished it all up and said it was the nicest they had ever tasted.

'Did you have an exciting day?' asked their aunt.

'Oh yes!' said Anne, eagerly. 'The storm was grand. It threw up . . .'

Julian and Dick both kicked her under the table. George couldn't reach her or she would most certainly have kicked her too. Anne stared at the boys angrily, with tears in her eyes.

'Now what's the matter?' asked Aunt Fanny. 'Did somebody kick you, Anne? Well, really, this kicking under the table has got to stop. Poor Anne will be covered with bruises. What did the sea throw up, dear?'

'It threw up the most enormous waves,' said Anne, looking defiantly at the others. She knew they had thought she was going to say that the sea had thrown up the wreck — but they were wrong! They had kicked her for nothing!

'Sorry for kicking you, Anne,' said Julian. 'My foot sort of slipped.'

'So did mine,' said Dick. 'Yes, Aunt Fanny, it was a magnificent sight on the island. The waves raced up that little inlet, and we had to take our boat almost up to the top of the low cliff there.'

'I wasn't really afraid of the storm,' said Anne. 'In fact, I wasn't really as afraid of it as Ti . . .'

Everyone knew perfectly well that Anne was going to mention Timothy, and they all interrupted her at once, speaking very loudly. Julian managed to get a kick in again.

'Oooh!' said Anne.

'The rabbits were so tame,' said Julian, loudly.

'We watched the cormorants,' said Dick and George joined in too, talking at the same time.

'The jackdaws made such a noise, they said "Chack, chack, chack," all the time.'

'Well, really, you sound like jackdaws yourselves, talking all at once like this!' said Aunt Fanny, with a laugh. 'Now, have you all finished? Very well, then, go and wash your sticky hands — yes, George, I know they're sticky, because *I* made that ginger-bread, and you've had three slices! Then you had better go and play quietly in the other room, because it's raining, and you can't go out. But don't disturb your father, George. He's very busy.'

The children went to wash. 'Idiot!' said Julian to Anne. 'Nearly gave us away twice!'

'I didn't mean what you thought I meant the first time!' began Anne indignantly.

George interrupted her.

'I'd rather you gave the secret of the wreck away than my secret about Tim,' she said. 'I do think you've got a careless tongue.'

'Yes, I have,' said Anne, sorrowfully. 'I think I'd better not talk at meal-times any more. I love Tim so

much I just can't seem to help wanting to talk about him.'

They all went to play in the other room. Julian turned a table upside down with a crash. 'We'll play at wrecks,' he said. 'This is the wreck. Now we're going to explore it.'

The door flew open and an angry, frowning face looked in. It was George's father!

'What was that noise?' he said. 'George! Did you overturn that table?'

'I did,' said Julian. 'I'm sorry, sir. I quite forgot you were working.'

'Any more noise like that and I shall keep you all in bed tomorrow!' said his Uncle Quentin. 'Georgina, keep your cousins quiet.'

The door shut and Uncle Quentin went out. The children looked at one another.

'Your father's awfully fierce, isn't he?' said Julian. 'I'm sorry I made that row. I didn't think.'

'We'd better do something really quiet,' said George. 'Or he'll keep his word — and we'll find ourselves in bed tomorrow just when we want to explore the wreck.'

This was a terrible thought. Anne went to get one of her dolls to play with. She had managed to bring quite a number after all. Julian fetched a book. George took up a beautiful little boat she was carving out of a piece of wood. Dick lay back on a chair and thought of the exciting wreck. The rain poured down steadily, and everyone hoped it would have stopped by the morning.

'We'll have to be up most awfully early,' said Dick, yawning. 'What about going to bed in good time tonight? I'm tired with all that rowing.'

In the ordinary way none of the children liked going to bed early — but with such an exciting thing to look forward to, early bed seemed different that night.

'It will make the time go quickly,' said Anne, putting down her doll. 'Shall we go now?'

'Whatever do you suppose Mother would say if we went just after tea?' said George. 'She'd think we were all ill. No, let's go after supper. We'll just say we're tired with rowing — which is perfectly true — and we'll get a good night's sleep, and be ready for our adventure tomorrow morning. And it *is* an adventure, you know. It isn't many people that have the chance of exploring an old, old wreck like that, which has always been at the bottom of the sea!'

So, by eight o'clock, all the children were in bed, rather to Aunt Fanny's surprise. Anne fell asleep at once. Julian and Dick were not long — but George lay awake for some time, thinking of her island, her wreck — and, of course, her beloved dog!

'I must take Tim too,' she thought, as she fell asleep. 'We can't leave old Tim out of this. He shall share in the adventure too!'

8

Exploring the wreck

Julian woke first the next morning. He awoke just as the sun was slipping over the horizon in the east, and filling the sky with gold. Julian stared at the ceiling for a moment, and then, in a rush, he remembered all that had happened the day before. He sat up straight in bed and whispered as loudly as he could.

'Dick! Wake up! We're going to see the wreck! Do wake up!'

Dick woke and grinned at Julian. A feeling of happiness crept over him. They were going on an adventure. He leapt out of bed and ran quietly to the girls' room. He opened the door. Both the girls were fast asleep, Anne curled up like a dormouse under the sheet.

Dick shook George and then dug Anne in the back. They awoke and sat up. 'Buck up!' whispered Dick. 'The sun is just rising. We'll have to hurry.'

George's blue eyes shone as she dressed. Anne skipped about quietly, finding her few clothes — just a bathing suit, jeans and jersey — and rubber shoes for her feet. It wasn't many minutes before they were all ready.

'Now, not a creak on the stairs — not a cough or a giggle!' warned Julian, as they stood together on the landing. Anne was a dreadful giggler, and had often given secret plans away by her sudden explosive choke. But this time the little girl was as solemn as the others, and as careful. They crept down the stairs and undid the little front door. Not a sound was made. They shut the door quietly and made their way down the garden path to the gate. The gate always creaked, so they climbed over it instead of opening it.

The sun was now shining brightly, though it was still low in the eastern sky. It felt warm already. The sky was so beautifully blue that Anne couldn't help feeling it had been freshly washed! 'It looks just as if it had come back from the laundry,' she told the others.

They squealed with laughter at her. She did say odd things at times. But they knew what she meant. The day had a lovely new feeling about it — the clouds were so pink in the bright blue sky, and the sea looked so smooth and fresh. It was impossible to imagine that it had been so rough the day before.

George got her boat. Then she went to get Tim, while the boys hauled the boat down to the sea. Alf, the fisher-boy, was surprised to see George so early. He was about to go with his father, fishing. He grinned at George.

'You going fishing, too?' he said to her. 'My, wasn't that a storm yesterday! I thought you'd be caught in it.'

'We were,' said George. 'Come on, Tim! Come on!'

Tim was very pleased to see George so early. He capered round her as she ran back to the others, almost tripping her up as she went. He leapt into the boat as soon as he saw it, and stood at the stern, his red tongue out, his tail wagging violently.

'I wonder his tail keeps on,' said Anne, looking at it. 'One day, Timothy, you'll wag it right off.'

They set off to the island. It was easy to row now, because the sea was so calm. They came to the island, and rowed around it to the other side.

And there was the wreck, piled high on some sharp rocks! It had settled down now and did not stir as waves slid under it. It lay a little to one side, and the broken mast, now shorter than before, stuck out at an angle.

'There she is,' said Julian, in excitement. 'Poor old wreck! I guess she's a bit more battered now. What a noise she made when she went crashing on to those rocks yesterday!'

'How do we get to her?' asked Anne, looking at the mass of ugly, sharp rocks all around. But George was not at all dismayed. She knew almost every inch of the coast around her little island. She pulled steadily at the oars and soon came near to the rocks in which the great wreck rested.

The children looked at the wreck from their boat. It was big, much bigger than they had imagined when they had peered at it from the top of the water. It was encrusted with shellfish of some kind, and strands of brown and green seaweed hung down. It smelt queer. It had great holes in its sides, showing where it had battered against rocks. There were holes in the deck too. Altogether, it looked a sad and forlorn old ship — but to the four children it was the most exciting thing in the whole world.

They rowed to the rocks on which the wreck lay. The tide washed over them. George took a look round.

'We'll tie our boat up to the wreck itself,' she said. 'And we'll get on to the deck quite easily by climbing up the side. Look, Julian! — throw this loop of rope over that broken bit of wood there, sticking out from the side.'

Julian did as he was told. The rope tightened and the boat was held in position. Then George clambered up the side of the wreck like a monkey. She was a marvel at climbing. Julian and Dick followed her, but Anne had to be helped up. Soon all four were standing on the slanting deck. It was slippery with seaweed, and the smell was very strong indeed. Anne didn't like it.

'Well, this was the deck,' said George, 'and that's where the men got up and down.' She pointed to a large hole. They went to it and looked down. The remains of an iron ladder were still there. George looked at it.

'I think it's still strong enough to hold us,' she said. 'I'll go first. Anyone got a torch? It looks pretty dark down there.'

Julian had a torch. He handed it to George. The children became rather quiet. It was mysterious somehow to look down into the dark inside of the big ship. What would they find? George switched on the torch and then swung herself down the ladder. The others followed.

The light from the torch showed a very queer sight. The under-parts of the ship were low-ceilinged, made of thick oak. The children had to bend their heads to get about. It seemed as if there were places that might have been cabins, though it was difficult to tell now, for everything was so battered, sea-drenched and seaweedy. The smell was really horrid, though it was mostly of drying seaweed.

The children slipped about on the seaweed as they went round the inside of the ship. It didn't seem so big inside after all. There was a big hold under the cabins, which the children saw by the light of their torch.

'That's where the boxes of gold would have been kept, I expect,' said Julian. But there was nothing in the hold except water and fish! The children couldn't go down because the water was too deep. One or two barrels floated in the water, but they had burst open and were quite empty.

'I expect they were water-barrels, or barrels of pork or biscuit,' said George. 'Let's go round the other part of the ship again — where the cabins are. Isn't it strange to see bunks there that sailors have slept in? — and look at that old wooden chair. Fancy

it still being here after all these years! Look at the things on those hooks too — they are all rusty now, and covered with seaweedy stuff — but they must have been the cook's pans and dishes!'

It was a very queer trip round the old wreck. The children were all on the look-out for boxes which might contain bars of gold — but there didn't seem to be one single box of any kind anywhere!

They came to a rather bigger cabin than the others. It had a bunk in one corner, in which a large crab rested. An old bit of furniture looking rather like a table with two legs, all encrusted with greyish shells, lay against the bunk. Wooden shelves, festooned with grey-green seaweed, hung crookedly on the walls of the cabin.

'This must have been the captain's own cabin,' said Julian. 'It's the biggest one. Look, what's that in the corner?'

'An old cup!' said Anne, picking it up. 'And here's half of a saucer. I expect the captain was sitting here having a cup of tea when the ship went down.'

This made the children feel rather queer. It was dark and smelly in the little cabin, and the floor was wet and slippery to their feet. George began to feel that her wreck was really more pleasant sunk under the water than raised above it!

'Let's go,' she said, with a shiver. 'I don't like it much. It *is* exciting, I know — but it's a bit frightening too.'

They turned to go. Julian flashed his torch round the little cabin for the last time. He was about to switch it off and follow the others up to the deck above when he caught sight of something that made him stop. He flashed his torch on to it, and then called to the others.

'I say! Wait a bit. There's a cupboard here in the wall. Let's see if there's anything in it!'

The others turned back and looked. They saw what looked like a small cupboard let in level with the wall of the cabin. What had caught Julian's eye was the keyhole. There was no key there, though.

'There just *might* be something inside,' said Julian. He tried to prise open the wooden door with his fingers, but it wouldn't move. 'It's locked,' he said. 'Of course it would be!'

'I expect the lock is rotten by now,' said George, and she tried too. Then she took out her big strong pocket-knife and inserted it between the cupboard door and the cabin-wall. She forced back the blade — and the lock of the cupboard suddenly snapped! As she had said, it was quite rotten. The door swung open, and the children saw a shelf inside with a few curious things on it.

There was a wooden box, swollen with the wet sea-water in which it had lain for years. There were two or three things that looked like old, pulpy books. There was some sort of glass drinking-vessel, cracked in half — and two or three funny objects so spoilt by sea-water that no one could possibly say what they were.

'Nothing very interesting — except the box,' said Julian, and he picked it up. 'Anyway, I expect that whatever is inside is ruined. But we may as well try and open it.'

He and George tried their best to force the lock of the old wooden box. On the top of it were stamped initials — H. J. K.

'I expect those were the captain's initials,' said Dick.

'No, they were the initials of my great-great-great-grandfather!' said George, her eyes shining suddenly. 'I've heard all about him. His name was Henry John Kirrin. This was his ship, you know. This must have been his very-private box in which he kept his old papers or diaries. Oh — we simply *must* open it!'

But it was quite impossible to force the lid up with the tools they had there. They soon gave it up, and Julian picked up the box to carry it to the boat.

'We'll open it at home,' he said, his voice sounding rather excited. 'We'll get a hammer or something, and get it open somehow. Oh, George — this really is a find!'

They all of them felt that they really had something mysterious in their possession. Was there anything inside the box — and if so, what would it be? They longed to get home and open it!

They went up on deck, climbing the old iron ladder. As soon as they got there they saw that others besides themselves had discovered that the wreck had been thrown up from the bottom of the sea!

'Golly! Half the fishing-smacks of the bay have discovered it!' cried Julian, looking round at the fishing-boats that had come as near as they dared to the wreck. The fishermen were looking at the wreck in wonder. When they saw the children on board they halloo-ed loudly.

'Ahoy there! What's that ship?'

'It's the old wreck!' yelled back Julian. 'She was thrown up yesterday in the storm!'

'Don't say any more,' said George, frowning. 'It's *my* wreck. I don't want sightseers on it!'

So no more was said, and the four children got into their boat and rowed home as fast as they could. It was past their breakfast-time. They might get a good scolding. They might even be sent to bed by George's fierce father — but what did they care? They had explored the wreck — and had come away with a box which *might* contain — well, if not bars of gold, one *small* bar, perhaps!

They did get a scolding. They had to go without half their breakfast, too, because Uncle Quentin said that children who came in so late didn't deserve hot bacon and eggs — only toast and marmalade. It was very sad.

They hid the box under the bed in the boys' room. Tim had been left with the fisher-boy — or rather, had been tied up in his back yard, for Alf had gone out fishing, and was even now gazing from his father's boat at the strange wreck.

'We can make a bit of money taking sightseers out to this wreck,' said Alf. And before the day was out scores of interested people had seen the old wreck from the decks of motor-boats and fishing-smacks.

George was furious about it. But she couldn't do anything. After all, as Julian said, anybody could have a look!

9

The box from the wreck

The first thing that the children did after breakfast was to fetch the precious box and take it out to the tool-shed in the garden. They were simply longing to force it open. All of them secretly felt certain that it would hold treasure of some sort.

Julian looked round for a tool. He found a chisel and decided that would be just the thing to force the box open. He tried, but the tool slipped and jabbed his fingers. Then he tried other things, but the box obstinately refused to open. The children stared at it crossly.

'I know what to do,' said Anne at last. 'Let's take it to the top of the house and throw it down to the ground. It would burst open then, I expect.'

The others thought over the idea. 'It might be worth trying,' said Julian. 'The only thing is — it might break or spoil anything inside the box.'

But there didn't seem any other way to open the box, so Julian carried it up to the top of the house. He went to the attic and opened the window there. The others were down below, waiting. Julian hurled the box out of the window as violently as he could. It flew through the air and landed with a terrific crash on the crazy paving below.

At once the french window there opened and their Uncle Quentin came out like a bullet from a gun.

'Whatever are you doing?' he cried. 'Surely you aren't throwing things at each other out of the window? What's this on the ground?'

The children looked at the box. It had burst open, and lay on the ground, showing a tin lining that was waterproof. Whatever was in the box would not be spoilt! It would be quite dry!

Dick ran to pick it up.

'I said, what's this on the ground?' shouted his uncle and moved towards him.

'It — it's something that belongs to us,' said Dick, going red.

'Well, I shall take it away from you,' said his uncle. 'Disturbing me like this! Give it to me. Where did you get it?'

Nobody answered. Uncle Quentin frowned till his glasses nearly fell off. 'Where did you get it?' he barked, glaring at poor Anne, who was nearest.

'Out of the wreck,' stammered the little girl, scared.

'Out of the *wreck*!' said her uncle, in surprise. 'The

old wreck that was thrown up yesterday? I heard about that. Do you mean to say you've been in it?'

'Yes,' said Dick. Julian joined them at that moment, looking worried. It would be too awful if his uncle took the box just as they got it open. But that was exactly what he did do!

'Well, this box may contain something important,' he said, and he took it from Dick's hands. 'You've no right to go prying about in that old wreck. You might take something that mattered.'

'Well, it's my wreck,' said George, in a defiant tone. 'Please, Father, let us have the box. We'd just got it opened. We thought it might hold — a gold bar — or something like that!'

'A gold bar!' said her father, with a snort. 'What a baby you are! This small box would never hold a thing like that! It's much more likely to contain particulars of what happened to the bars! I have always thought that the gold was safely delivered somewhere — and that the ship, empty of its valuable cargo, got wrecked as it left the bay!'

'Oh, Father — please, please let us have our box,' begged George, almost in tears. She suddenly felt certain that it did contain papers that might tell them what had happened to the gold. But without another word her father turned and went into the house, carrying the box, burst open and cracked, its tin lining showing through under his arm.

Anne burst into tears. 'Don't blame me for telling him we got it from the wreck,' she sobbed. 'Please don't. He glared at me so. I just had to tell him.'

'All right, Baby,' said Julian, putting his arm round Anne. He looked furious. He thought it was very unfair of his uncle to take the box like that. 'Listen — I'm not going to stand this. We'll get hold of that box somehow and look into it. I'm sure your father won't bother himself with it, George — he'll start writing his book again and forget all about it. I'll wait my chance and slip into his study and get it, even if it means a spanking if I'm discovered!'

'Good!' said George. 'We'll all keep a watch and see if Father goes out.'

So they took it in turns to keep watch, but most annoyingly their Uncle Quentin remained in his study all the morning. Aunt Fanny was surprised to see one or two children always about the garden that day, instead of down on the beach.

'Why don't you all keep together and bathe or do something?' she said. 'Have you quarrelled with one another?'

'No,' said Dick. 'Of course not.' But he didn't say why they were in the garden!

'Doesn't your father *ever* go out?' he said to George, when it was her turn to keep watch. 'I don't think he leads a very healthy life.'

'Scientists never do,' said George, as if she knew all about them. 'But I tell you what — he may go to sleep this afternoon! He sometimes does!'

Julian was left behind in the garden that afternoon. He sat down under a tree and opened a book. Soon he heard a curious noise that made him look up. He knew at once what it was!

'That's Uncle Quentin snoring!' he said in excitement. 'It is! Oh — I wonder if I could possibly creep in at the french window and get our box!'

He stole to the windows and looked in. One was a little way open and Julian opened it a little more. He saw his uncle lying back in a comfortable arm-chair, his mouth a little open, his eyes closed, fast asleep! Every time he took a breath, he snored.

'Well, he really does look sound asleep,' thought the boy. 'And there's the box, just behind him, on that table. I'll risk it. I bet I'll get an awful spanking if I'm caught, but I can't help that!'

He stole in. His uncle still snored. He tiptoed by him to the table behind his uncle's chair. He took hold of the box.

And then a bit of the broken wood of the box fell to the floor with a thud! His uncle stirred in his chair and opened his eyes. Quick as lightning the boy crouched down behind his uncle's chair, hardly breathing.

'What's that?' he heard his uncle say. Julian didn't move. Then his uncle settled down again and shut his eyes. Soon there was the sound of his rhythmic snoring!

'Hurrah!' thought Julian. 'He's off again!'

Quietly he stood up, holding the box. On tiptoe he crept to the french window. He slipped out and ran softly down the garden path. He didn't think of hiding the box. All he wanted to do was to get to the other children and show them what he had done!

He ran to the beach where the others were lying in

the sun. 'Hi!' he yelled. 'Hi! I've got it! I've got it!'

They all sat up with a jerk, thrilled to see the box in Julian's arms. They forgot all about the other people on the beach. Julian dropped down on the sand and grinned.

'Your father went to sleep,' he said to George. 'Tim, don't lick me like that! And George, I went in — and a bit of the box dropped on the floor — and it woke him up!'

'Golly!' said George. 'What happened?'

'I crouched down behind his chair till he went to sleep again,' said Julian. 'Then I fled. Now — let's see what's in here. I don't believe your father's even tried to see!'

He hadn't. The tin lining was intact. It had rusted with the years of lying in the wet, and the lid was so tightly fitted down that it was almost impossible to move it.

But once George began to work at it with her pocket-knife, scraping away the rust, it began to loosen — and in about a quarter-of-an-hour it came off!

The children bent eagerly over it. Inside lay some old papers and a book of some kind with a black cover. Nothing else at all. No bar of gold. No treasure. Everyone felt a little bit disappointed.

'It's all quite dry,' said Julian, surprised. 'Not a bit damp. The tin lining kept everything perfect.'

He picked up the book and opened it. 'It's a diary your great-great-great-grandfather kept of the ship's voyages,' he said. 'I can hardly read the writing. It's so small and funny.'

George picked up one of the papers. It was made of thick parchment, quite yellow with age. She spread it out on the sand and looked at it. The others glanced at it too, but they couldn't make out what it was at all. It seemed to be a kind of map.

'Perhaps it's a map of some place he had to go to,' said Julian. But suddenly George's hands began to shake as she held the map, and her eyes gleamed brilliantly as she looked up at the others. She opened her mouth but didn't speak.

'What's the matter?' said Julian, curiously. 'What's up? Have you lost your tongue?'

George shook her head and then began to speak with a rush. 'Julian! Do you know what this is? It's a map of my old castle — of Kirrin Castle — when it wasn't a ruin. And it shows the dungeons! And look — just look what's written in this corner of the dungeons!'

She put a trembling finger on one part of the map. The others leaned over to see what it was — and, printed in old-fashioned letters was a curious word.

INGOTS

'Ingots!' said Anne, puzzled. 'What does that mean? I've never heard that word before.'

But the two boys had. 'Ingots!' cried Dick. 'Why — that must be the bars of gold. They were called ingots.'

'Most bars of metal are called ingots,' said Julian, going red with excitement. 'But as we know there is gold missing from that ship, then it really looks as if ingots here meant bars of gold. Oh golly! To think they may still be hidden somewhere under Kirrin Castle. George! George! Isn't it terribly, awfully exciting?'

George nodded. She was trembling all over with excitement. 'If only we could find it!' she whispered. 'If only we could!'

'We'll have a jolly good hunt for it,' said Julian. 'It will be awfully difficult because the castle is in ruins now, and so overgrown. But somehow or other we'll find those ingots. What a lovely word. Ingots! Ingots! Ingots!'

It sounded somehow more exciting than the word gold. Nobody spoke about gold any more. They talked about the Ingots. Tim couldn't make out what the excitement was at all. He wagged his tail and tried hard to lick first one and then another of the children, but for once in a way not one of them paid any attention to him! He simply couldn't understand it, and after a while he went and sat down by himself with his back to the children, and his ears down.

'Oh, do look at poor Timothy!' said George. 'He can't understand our excitement. Tim! Tim, darling, it's all right, you're not in disgrace or anything. Oh, Tim, we've got the most wonderful secret in the whole world.'

Tim bounded up, his tail wagging, pleased to be taken notice of once more. He put his big paw on the precious map, and the four children shouted at him at once.

'Golly! We can't have that torn!' said Julian. Then he looked at the others and frowned. 'What are we going to do about the box?' he said. 'I mean — George's father will be sure to miss it, won't he? We'll have to give it back.'

'Well, can't we take out the map and keep it?' said Dick. 'He won't know it was there if he hasn't looked in the box. And it's pretty certain he hasn't. The other things don't matter much — they are only that old diary and a few letters.'

'To be on the safe side, let's take a copy of the map,' said Dick. 'Then we can put the real map back and replace the box.'

They all voted that a very good idea. They went back to Kirrin Cottage and traced out the map carefully. They did it in the tool-shed because they didn't want anyone to see them. It was a queer map. It was in three parts.

'This part shows the dungeons under the castle,' said Julian. 'And this shows a plan of the ground floor of the castle — and this shows the top part. My word, it was a fine place in those days! The dungeons run all under the castle. I bet they were pretty awful places. I wonder how people got down to them.'

'We'll have to study the map a bit more and see,' said George. 'It all looks rather muddled to us at present — but once we take the map over to the castle and study it there, we may be able to make out how to get down to the hidden dungeons. Ooooh! I don't expect any children ever had such an adventure as this.'

Julian put the traced map carefully into his jeans pocket. He didn't mean it to leave him. It was very precious. Then he put the real map back into the box and looked towards the house. 'What about putting it back now?' he said. 'Maybe your father is still asleep, George.'

But he wasn't. He was awake. Luckily he hadn't missed the box! He came into the dining-room to have tea with the family, and Julian took his chance. He muttered an excuse, slipped away from the table, and replaced the box on the table behind his uncle's chair!

He winked at the others when he came back. They felt relieved. They were all scared of Uncle Quentin, and were not at all anxious to be in his bad books. Anne didn't say one word during the whole of the meal. She was so terribly afraid she might give something away, either about Tim or the box. The others spoke very little too. While they were at tea the telephone rang and Aunt Fanny went to answer it.

She soon came back. 'It's for you, Quentin,' she said. 'Apparently the old wreck has caused quite a lot of excitement, and there are men from a London paper who want to ask you questions about it.'

'Tell them I'll see them at six,' said Uncle Quentin. The children looked at one another in alarm. They hoped that their uncle wouldn't show the box to the newspaper men. Then the secret of the hidden gold might come out!

'What a mercy we took a tracing of the map!' said Julian, after tea. 'But I'm jolly sorry now we left the real map in the box. Someone else may guess our secret!'

10

An astonishing offer

The next morning the papers were full of the extraordinary way in which the old wreck had been thrown up out of the sea. The newspaper men had got out of the children's uncle the tale of the wreck and the lost gold, and some of them even managed to land on Kirrin Island and take pictures of the old ruined castle.

George was furious. 'It's *my* castle!' she stormed to her mother. 'It's *my* island. You said it could be mine. You did, you did!'

'I know, George dear,' said her mother. 'But you really must be sensible. It can't hurt the island to be landed on, and it can't hurt the castle to be photographed.'

'But I don't want it to be,' said George, her face dark and sulky. 'It's mine. And the wreck is mine. You said so.'

'Well, I didn't know it was going to be thrown up like that,' said her mother. 'Do be sensible, George. What can it possibly matter if people go to look at the wreck? You can't stop them.'

George couldn't stop them, but that didn't make her any the less angry about it. The children were astonished at the interest that the cast-up wreck caused, and because of that, Kirrin Island became an object of great interest too. Sightseers from the places all around came to see it, and the fishermen managed to find the little inlet and land the people there. George sobbed with rage, and Julian tried to comfort her.

'Listen, George! No one knows our secret yet. We'll wait till this excitement has died down, and then we'll go to Kirrin Castle and find the ingots.'

'If someone doesn't find them first,' said George, drying her eyes. She was furious with herself for crying, but she really couldn't help it.

'How could they?' said Julian. 'No one has seen inside the box yet! I'm going to wait my chance and get that map out before anyone sees it!'

But he didn't have a chance, because something dreadful happened. Uncle Quentin sold the old box to a man who bought antique things! He came out from his study, beaming, a day or two after the excitement began, and told Aunt Fanny and the children.

'I've struck a very good bargain with that man,' he said to his wife. 'You know that old tin-lined box from the wreck? Well, this fellow collects curious things like that, and he gave me a very good price for it. Very good indeed. More even than I could expect for the writing of my book! As soon as he saw the old map there and the old diary he said at once that he would buy the whole collection.'

The children stared at him in horror. The box was sold! Now someone would study that map and perhaps jump to what 'ingots' meant. The story of the lost gold had been put into all the newspapers now. Nobody could fail to know what the map showed if they studied it carefully.

The children did not dare to tell Uncle Quentin what they knew. It was true he was all smiles now, and was promising to buy them new shrimping-nets, and a raft for themselves — but he was such a changeable person. He might fly into a furious temper if he heard that Julian had taken the box and opened it himself, while his uncle was sleeping.

When they were alone the children discussed the whole matter. It seemed very serious indeed to them. They half-wondered if they should let Aunt Fanny into the secret — but it was such a precious secret, and so marvellous, that they felt they didn't want to give it away to anyone at all.

'Now listen!' said Julian, at last. 'We'll ask Aunt Fanny if we can go to Kirrin Island and spend a day or two there — sleep there at night too, I mean. That will give us a little time to poke round and see what we can find. The sightseers won't come after a day or two, I'm sure. Maybe we'll get in before anyone tumbles to our secret. After all, the man who bought the box may not even guess that the map shows Kirrin Castle.'

They felt more cheerful. It was so awful to do nothing. As soon as they had planned to act, they felt better. They decided to ask their aunt the next day if they might go and spend the week-end at the castle. The weather was gloriously fine, and it would be great fun. They could take plenty of food with them.

When they went to ask Aunt Fanny, Uncle Quentin was with her. He was all smiles again, and even clapped Julian on the back. 'Well!' he said. 'What's this deputation for?'

'We just wanted to ask Aunt Fanny something,' said Julian, politely. 'Aunt Fanny, as the weather is so fine, do you think you would let us go for the week-end to Kirrin Castle, please, and spend a day or two there on the island? You can't think how we would love to!'

'Well — what do you think, Quentin?' asked their aunt, turning to her husband.

'If they want to, they can,' said Uncle Quentin. 'They won't have a chance to, soon. My dears, we have had a marvellous offer for Kirrin Island! A man wants to buy it, rebuild the castle as a hotel, and make it into a proper holiday place! What do you think of that?'

All four children stared at the smiling man, shocked and horrified. Somebody was going to buy the island! Had their secret been discovered? Did the man want to buy the castle because he had read the map, and knew there was plenty of gold hidden there?

George gave a curious choke. Her eyes burned as if they were on fire. 'Mother! You can't sell my island! You can't sell my castle! I won't let them be sold.'

Her father frowned. 'Don't be silly, Georgina,' he said. 'It isn't really yours. You know that. It belongs to your mother, and naturally she would like to sell it if she could. We need the money very badly. You will be able to have a great many nice things once we sell the island.'

'I don't want nice things!' cried poor George. 'My castle and my island are the nicest things I could ever have. Mother! Mother! You know you said I could have them. You know you did! I believed you.'

'George dear, I did mean you to have them to play on, when I thought they couldn't possibly be worth anything,' said her mother, looking distressed. 'But now things are different. Your father has been offered quite a good sum, far more than we ever thought of getting — and we really can't afford to turn it down.'

'So you only gave me the island when you thought it wasn't worth anything,' said George, her face white and angry. 'As soon as it is worth money you take it away again. I think that's horrid. It — it isn't honourable.'

'That's enough, Georgina,' said her father, angrily. 'Your mother is guided by me. You're only a child. Your mother didn't really mean what she said — it was only to please you. But you know well enough you will share in the money we get and have anything you want.'

112

'I won't touch a penny!' said George, in a low, choking voice. 'You'll be sorry you sold it.'

The girl turned and stumbled out of the room. The others felt very sorry for her. They knew what she was feeling. She took things so very seriously. Julian thought she didn't understand grown-ups very well. It wasn't a bit of good fighting grown-ups. They could do exactly as they liked. If they wanted to take away George's island and castle, they could. If they wanted to sell it, they could! But what Uncle Quentin didn't know was the fact that there might be a store of gold ingots there! Julian stared at his uncle and wondered whether to warn him. Then he decided not to. There was just a chance that the four children could find the gold first!

'When are you selling the island, Uncle?' he asked quietly.

'The deeds will be signed in about a week's time,' was the answer. 'So if you really want to spend a day or two there, you'd better do so quickly, for after that you may not get permission from the new owners.'

'Was it the man who bought the old box who wants to buy the island?' asked Julian.

'Yes', said his uncle. 'I was a little surprised myself, for I thought he was just a buyer of old things. It was astonishing to me that he should get the idea of buying the island to rebuild the castle as a hotel. Still, I dare say there will be big money in running an hotel there — very romantic, staying on a little island like that — people will like it. I'm no businessman myself, and I certainly shouldn't care to invest my money in

114

a place like Kirrin Island. But I should think he knows what he is doing all right.'

'Yes, he certainly does,' thought Julian to himself, as he went out of the room with Dick and Anne. 'He's read that map — and has jumped to the same idea that we did — the store of hidden ingots is somewhere on that island — and he's going to get it! He doesn't want to build an hotel! He's after the treasure! I expect he's offered Uncle Quentin some silly low price that poor old uncle thinks is marvellous! Oh dear — this is a horrible thing to happen.'

He went to find George. She was in the tool-shed, looking quite green. She said she felt sick.

'It's only because you're so upset,' said Julian. He slipped his arm round her. For once George didn't push it away. She felt comforted. Tears came into her eyes, and she angrily tried to blink them away.

'Listen, George!' said Julian. 'We mustn't give up hope. We'll go to Kirrin Island tomorrow, and we'll do our very, very best to get down into the dungeons somehow and find the ingots. We'll jolly well stay there till we do. See? Now cheer up, because we'll want your help in planning everything. Thank goodness we took a tracing of the map.'

George cheered up a little. She still felt angry with her father and mother, but the thought of going to Kirrin Island for a day or two, and taking Timothy too, certainly seemed rather good.

'I do think my father and mother are unkind,' she said.

'Well, they're not really,' said Julian, wisely. 'After

all, if they need money badly, they would be silly not to part with something they think is quite useless. And you know, your father did say you could have anything you want. I know what I would ask for, if I were you!'

'What?' asked George.

'Timothy, of course!' said Julian. And that made George smile and cheer up tremendously!

11

Off to Kirrin Island

Julian and George went to find Dick and Anne. They were waiting for them in the garden, looking rather upset. They were glad to see Julian and George and ran to meet them.

Anne took George's hands. 'I'm awfully sorry about your island, George,' she said.

'So am I,' said Dick. 'Bad luck, old girl — I mean, old boy!'

George managed to smile. 'I've been behaving like a girl,' she said, half-ashamed. 'But I did get an awful shock.'

Julian told the others what they had planned. 'We'll go tomorrow morning,' he said. 'We'll make out a list of all the things we shall need. Let's begin now.'

He took out a pencil and notebook. The others looked at him.

'Things to eat,' said Dick at once. 'Plenty because we'll be hungry.'

'Something to drink,' said George. 'There's no water on the island — though I believe there was a well or something, years ago, that went right down below the level of the sea, and was fresh water. Anyway, I've never found it.'

'Food,' wrote down Julian, 'and drink.' He looked at the others.

'Spades,' he said solemnly, and scribbled the word down.

Anne stared in surprise.

'What for?' she asked.

'Well, we'll want to dig about when we're hunting for a way down to the dungeons,' said Julian.

'Ropes,' said Dick. 'We may want those too.'

'And torches,' said George. 'It'll be dark in the dungeons.'

'Oooh!' said Anne, feeling a pleasant shiver go down her back at the thought. She had no idea what dungeons were like, but they sounded thrilling.

'Rugs,' said Dick. 'We'll be cold at night if we sleep in that little old room.'

Julian wrote them down. 'Mugs to drink from,' he said. 'And we'll take a few tools too — we may perhaps need them. You never know.'

At the end of half an hour they had quite a nice long list, and everyone felt pleased and excited. George was beginning to recover from her rage and disappointment. If she had been alone, and had brooded over everything, she would have been in an even worse sulk and temper — but somehow the others were so calm and sensible and cheerful. It was impossible to sulk for long if she was with them.

'I think I'd have been much nicer if I hadn't been on my own so much,' thought George to herself, as she looked at Julian's bent head. 'Talking about things to other people does help a lot. They don't seem so dreadful then; they seem more bearable and ordinary. I like my three cousins awfully. I like them because they talk and laugh and are always cheerful and kind. I wish I was like them. I'm sulky and bad-tempered and fierce, and no wonder Father doesn't like me and scolds me so often. Mother's a dear, but I understand now why she says I am difficult. I'm different from my cousins — they're easy to understand, and everyone likes them. I'm glad they came. They are making me more like I ought to be.'

This was a long thought to think, and George looked very serious while she was thinking it. Julian looked up and caught her blue eyes fixed on him. He smiled.

'Penny for your thoughts!' he said.

'They're not worth a penny,' said George, going red. 'I was just thinking how nice you all are — and how I wished I could be like you.'

'You're an awfully nice person,' said Julian, surprisingly. 'You can't help being an only child. They're always a bit queer, you know, unless they're mighty careful. You're a most interesting person, I think.'

119

George flushed red again, and felt pleased. 'Let's go and take Timothy for a walk,' she said. 'He'll be wondering what's happened to us today.'

They all went off together, and Timothy greeted them at the top of his voice. They told him all about their plans for the next day, and he wagged his tail and looked up at them out of his soft brown eyes as if he understood every single word they said!

'He must feel pleased to think he's going to be with us for two or three days,' said Anne.

It was very exciting the next morning, setting off in the boat with all their things packed neatly at one end. Julian checked them all by reading out aloud from his list. It didn't seem as if they had forgotten anything.

'Got the map?' said Dick, suddenly.

Julian nodded.

'I put on clean jeans this morning,' he said, 'but you may be sure I remembered to pop the map into my pocket. Here it is!'

He took it out — and the wind at once blew it right out of his hands! It fell into the sea and bobbed there in the wind. All four children gave a cry of utter dismay. Their precious map!

'Quick! Row after it!' cried George, and swung the boat round. But someone was quicker then she was! Tim had seen the paper fly from Julian's hand, and had heard and understood the cries of dismay. With an enormous splash he leapt into the water and swam valiantly after the map.

He could swim well for a dog, for he was strong and

powerful. He soon had the map in his mouth and was swimming back to the boat. The children thought he was simply marvellous!

George hauled him into the boat and took the map from his mouth. There was hardly the mark of his teeth on it! He had carried it so carefully. It was wet, and the children looked anxiously at it to see if the tracing had been spoilt. But Julian had traced it very strongly, and it was quite all right. He placed it on a seat to dry, and told Dick to hold it there in the sun.

'That was a narrow squeak!' he said, and the others agreed.

George took the oars again, and they set off once more to the island, getting a perfect shower-bath from Timothy when he stood up and shook his wet coat. He was given a big biscuit as a reward, and crunched it up with great enjoyment.

George made her way through the reefs of rocks with a sure hand. It was marvellous to the others how she could slide the boat in between the dangerous rocks and never get a scratch. They thought she was really wonderful. She brought them safely to the little inlet, and they jumped out on to the sand. They pulled the boat high up, in case the tide came far up the tiny cove, and then began to unload their goods.

'We'll carry all the things to that little stone room,' said Julian. 'They will be safe there and won't get wet if it rains. I hope nobody comes to the island while we are here, George.'

'I shouldn't think they would,' said George. 'Father said it would be about a week before the deeds were signed, making over the island to that man. It won't be his till then. We've got a week, anyhow.'

'Well, we don't need to keep a watch in case anyone else arrives then,' said Julian, who had half thought that it would be a good idea to make someone stay on guard at the inlet, to give a warning to the others in case anyone else arrived. 'Come on! You take the spades, Dick. I'll take the food and drink with George. And Anne can take the little things.'

The food and drink were in a big box, for the children did not mean to starve while they were on the island! They had brought loaves of bread, butter, biscuits, jam, tins of fruit, ripe plums, bottles of ginger-beer, a kettle to make tea, and anything else they could think of! George and Julian staggered up the cliff with the heavy box. They had to put it down once or twice to give themselves a rest!

They put everything into the little room. Then they went back to get the collection of blankets and rugs from the boat. They arranged them in the corners of the little room, and thought that it would be most exciting to spend the night there.

'The two girls can sleep together on this pile of rugs,' said Julian. 'And we two boys will have this pile.'

George looked as if she didn't want to be put with Anne, and classed as a girl. But Anne didn't wish to sleep alone in her corner, and she looked so beseechingly at George that the bigger girl smiled at

her and made no objection. Anne thought that
George was getting nicer and nicer!

'Well, now we'll get down to business,' said Julian,
and he pulled out his map. 'We must study this really
carefully, and find out exactly under what spot the
entrances to the dungeons are. Now — come around
and let's do our best to find out! It's up to us to use
our brains — and beat that man who's bought the
island!'

They all bent over the traced map. It was quite dry
now, and the children looked at it earnestly. It was
plain that in the old days the castle had been a very
fine place.

'Now look,' said Julian, putting his finger on the
plan of the dungeons. 'These seem to run all along
under the castle — and here — and — here — are the
marks that seem to be meant to represent steps or
stairs.'

'Yes,' said George. 'I should think they are. Well, if
so, there appear to be two ways of getting down into
the dungeons. One lot of steps seems to begin
somewhere near this little room — and the other
seems to start under the tower there. And what do
you suppose this thing is here, Julian?'

She put her finger on a round hole that was shown
not only in the plan of the dungeons, but also in the
plan of the ground floor of the castle.

'I can't imagine what that is,' said Julian, puzzled.
'Oh yes, I know what it might be! You said there was
an old well somewhere, do you remember? Well, that
may be it, I should think. It would have to be very

deep to get fresh water right under the sea — so it probably goes down through the dungeons too. Isn't this thrilling?'

Everyone thought it was. They felt happy and excited. There was something to discover — something they could and must discover within the next day or two.

They looked at one another. 'Well,' said Dick, 'what are we going to start on? Shall we try to find the entrance to the dungeons — the one that seems to start round about this little room? For all we know there may be a big stone we can lift that opens above the dungeon steps!'

This was a thrilling thought, and the children jumped up at once. Julian folded up the precious map and put it into his pocket. He looked round. The stone floor of the little room was overgrown with creeping weeds. They must be cleared away before it was possible to see if there were any stones that looked as if they might be moved.

'We'd better set to work,' said Julian, and he picked up a spade. 'Let's clear away these weeds with our spades — scrape them off, look, like this — and then examine every single stone!'

They all picked up spades and soon the little stone room was full of a scraping sound as the four of them chiselled away at the close-growing weeds with their spades. It wasn't very difficult to get the stones clear of them, and the children worked with a will.

Tim got most excited about everything. He hadn't any idea at all what they were doing, but he joined in valiantly. He scraped away at the floor with his four paws, sending earth and plants flying high into the air!

'Hi, Tim!' said Julian, shaking a clod of earth out of his hair. 'You're being a bit too vigorous. My word, you'll send the stones flying into the air too, in a minute. George, isn't Tim marvellous the way he joins in everything?'

How they all worked! How they all longed to find the entrance to the underground dungeons! What a thrill that would be.

12

Exciting discoveries

Soon the stones of the little room were clear of earth, sand and weeds. The children saw that they were all the same size — big and square, fitted well together. They went over them carefully with their torches, trying to find one that might move or lift.

'We should probably find one with an iron ring handle sunk into it,' said Julian. But they didn't. All the stones looked exactly the same. It was most disappointing.

Julian tried inserting his spade into the cracks between the various stones, to see if by any chance he could move one. But they couldn't be moved. It seemed as if they were all set in the solid ground. After about three hours' hard work the children sat down to eat a meal.

They were very hungry indeed, and felt glad to think there were so many things to eat. As they ate they discussed the problem they were trying to solve.

'It looks as if the entrance to the dungeons was not under this little room after all,' said Julian. 'It's disappointing — but somehow I don't think now that the steps down to the dungeon started from here. Let's measure the map and see if we can make out exactly where the steps do start. It may be, of course, that the measurements aren't correct and won't be any help to us at all. But we can try.'

So they measured as best they could, to try and find out in exactly what place the dungeon steps seemed to begin. It was impossible to tell, for the plans of the three floors seemed to be done to different scales. Julian stared at the map, puzzled. It seemed rather hopeless. Surely they wouldn't have to hunt all over the ground floor of the castle! It would take ages.

'Look,' said George, suddenly, putting her finger on the hole that they all thought must be meant to represent the well. 'The entrance to the dungeons seems to be not very far off the well. If only we could find the well, we could hunt around a bit for the beginning of the dungeon steps. The well is shown in both maps. It seems to be somewhere about the middle of the castle.'

'That's a good idea of yours,' said Julian, pleased. 'Let's go out into the middle of the castle — we can more or less guess where the old well ought to be, because it definitely seems to be about the middle of the old yard out there.'

Out they all went into the sunshine. They felt very important and serious. It was marvellous to be looking for lost ingots of gold. They all felt perfectly certain that they really were somewhere beneath their feet. It didn't occur to any of the children that the treasure might not be there.

They stood in the ruined courtyard that had once been the centre of the castle. They paced out the middle of the yard and then stood there, looking around in vain for anything that might perhaps have been the opening of an old well. It was all so overgrown. Sand had blown in from the shore, and weeds and bushes of all kinds grew there. The stones that had once formed the floor of the big courtyard were now cracked and were no longer lying flat. Most of them were covered with sand or weeds.

'Look! There's a rabbit!' cried Dick, as a big sandy rabbit lollopped slowly across the yard. It disappeared into a hole on the other side. Then another rabbit appeared, sat up and looked at the children, and then vanished too. The children were thrilled. They had never seen such tame rabbits before.

A third rabbit appeared. It was a small one with absurdly big ears, and the tiniest white bob of a tail. It didn't even look at the children. It bounded about in a playful way, and then, to the children's enormous delight, it sat up on its hind legs, and began to wash its big ears, pulling down first one and then the other.

But this was too much for Timothy. He had watched the other two bound across the yard and then disappear without so much as barking at them. But to see this youngster actually sitting there washing its ears under his very nose was really too much for any dog. He gave an excited yelp and rushed full-tilt at the surprised rabbit.

For a moment the little thing didn't move. It had never been frightened or chased before, and it stared with big eyes at the rushing dog. Then it turned itself about and tore off at top speed, its white bobtail going up and down as it bounded away. It disappeared under a gorse bush near the children. Timothy went after it, vanishing under the big bush too.

Then a shower of sand and earth was thrown up as Tim tried to go down the hole after the rabbit and scraped and scrabbled with his strong front paws as fast as he could. He yelped and whined in excitement, not seeming to hear George's voice calling to him. He meant to get that rabbit! He went almost mad as he scraped at the hole, making it bigger and bigger.

'Tim! Do you hear me! Come out of there!' shouted George. 'You're not to chase the rabbits here. You know you mustn't. You're very naughty. Come out!'

But Tim didn't come out. He just went on and on scraping away madly. George went to fetch him. Just as she got up to the gorse bush the scraping suddenly stopped. There came a scared yelp — and no more noise was heard. George peered under the prickly bush in astonishment.

Tim had disappeared! He just simply wasn't there any more. There was the big rabbit-hole, made enormous by Tim — but there was no Tim.

'I say, Julian — Tim's gone,' said George in a scared voice. 'He surely can't have gone down the rabbit's hole, can he? I mean — he's such a big dog!'

The children crowded round the big gorse bush. There came the sound of a muffled whine from somewhere below it. Julian looked astonished.

'He *is* down the hole!' he said. 'How queer! I never heard of a dog really going down a rabbit-hole before. However are we going to get him out?'

'We'll have to dig up the gorse bush, to begin with,' said George, in a determined voice. She would have dug up the whole of Kirrin Castle to get Tim back, that was certain! 'I can't have poor old Tim whining for help down there and not do what we can to help him.'

The bush was far too big and prickly to creep underneath. Julian was glad they had brought tools of all kinds. He went to fetch an axe. They had brought a small one with them and it would do to chop away the prickly branches and trunk of the gorse bush. The children slashed at it and soon the poor bush began to look a sorry sight.

It took a long time to destroy it, for it was prickly, sturdy and stout. Every child's hands were scratched by the time the bush had been reduced to a mere stump. Then they could see the hole quite well. Julian shone his torch down it.

He gave a shout of surprise. 'I know what's happened! The old well is here! The rabbits had a hole at the side of it — and Tim scraped away to make it bigger and uncovered a bit of the well-hole — and he's fallen down the well!'

'Oh no, oh no,' cried George, in panic. 'Oh Tim,

131

Tim, are you all right?'

A distant whine came to their ears. Evidently Tim was there somewhere. The children looked at one another.

'Well, there's only one thing to do,' said Julian. 'We must get out spades now and dig out the hole of the well. Then maybe we can let a rope down or something and get Tim.'

They set to work with their spades. It was not really difficult to uncover the hole, which had been blocked only by the spreading roots of the big gorse bush, some fallen masonry, earth, sand and small stones. Apparently a big slab had fallen from part of the tower across the well-hole, and partly closed it. The weather and the growing gorse bush had done the rest.

It took all the children together to move the slab. Underneath was a very rotten wooden cover, which had plainly been used in the old days to protect the well. It had rotted so much that when Tim's weight had been pressed on it, it had given just there and made a hole for Tim to fall through.

Julian removed the old wooden cover and then the children could see down the well-hole. It was very deep and very dark. They could not possibly see the bottom. Julian took a stone and dropped it down. They all listened for the splash. But there was no splash. Either there was no longer any water there, or the well was too deep even to hear the splash!

'I think it's too deep for us to hear anything,' said Julian. 'Now — where's Tim?'

He shone his torch down — and there was Tim! Many years before a big slab had fallen down the well itself and had stuck a little way down, across the well-hole — and on this old cracked slab sat Tim, his big eyes staring up in fright. He simply could not imagine what had happened to him.

There was an old iron ladder fastened to the side of the well. George was on it before anyone else could get there! Down she went, not caring if the ladder held or not, and reached Tim. Somehow she got him on to her shoulder and, holding him there with one hand, she climbed slowly up again. The other three hauled her out and Tim jumped round her, barking and licking for all he was worth!

'Well, Tim!' said Dick, 'you shouldn't chase rabbits — but you've certainly done us a good turn, because you've found the well for us! Now we've only got to look around a little to find the dungeon entrance!'

They set to work again to hunt for the dungeon entrance. They dug about with their spades under all the bushes. They pulled up crooked stones and dug their spades into the earth below, hoping that they might suddenly find them going through into space! It was really very thrilling.

And then Anne found the entrance! It was quite by accident. She was tired and sat down to rest. She lay on her front and scrabbled about in the sand. Suddenly her fingers touched something hard and cold in the sand. She uncovered it — and lo and behold, it was an iron ring! She gave a shout and the others looked up.

'There's a stone with an iron ring in it here!' yelled Anne, excitedly. They all rushed over to her. Julian dug about with his spade and uncovered the whole stone. Sure enough, it did have a ring in it — and rings are only let into stones that need to be moved! Surely this stone must be the one that covered the dungeon entrance!

All the children took turns at pulling on the iron ring, but the stone did not move. Then Julian tied two or three turns of rope through it and the four children put out their full strength and pulled for all they were worth.

The stone moved. The children distinctly felt it stir. 'All together again!' cried Julian. And all together they pulled. The stone stirred again and then suddenly gave way. It moved upwards — and the children fell over on top of one another like a row of dominoes suddenly pushed down! Tim darted to the hole and barked madly down it as if all the rabbits of the world lived there!

Julian and George shot to their feet and rushed to the opening that the moved stone had disclosed. They stood there, looking downwards, their faces shining with delight. They *had* found the entrance to the dungeons! A steep flight of steps, cut out of the rock itself, led downwards into deep darkness.

'Come on!' cried Julian, snapping on his torch. 'We've found what we wanted! Now for the dungeons!'

The steps down were slippery. Tim darted down

first, lost his foot-hold and rolled down five or six steps, yelping with fright. Julian went after him, then George, then Dick and then Anne. They were all tremendously thrilled. Indeed, they quite expected to see piles of gold and all kinds of treasure everywhere around them!

It was dark down the steep flight of steps, and smelt very musty. Anne choked a little.

'I hope the air down here is all right,' said Julian. 'Sometimes it isn't good in these underground places. If anyone feels a bit funny they'd better say so and we'll go up into the open air again.'

But however funny they might feel nobody would have said so. It was all far too exciting to worry about feeling queer.

The steps went down a long way. Then they came to an end. Julian stepped down from the last rock-stair and flashed his torch around. It was a weird sight that met his eyes.

The dungeons of Kirrin Castle were made out of the rock itself. Whether there were natural caves there, or whether they had been hollowed out by man the children could not tell. But certainly they were very mysterious, dark and full of echoing sounds. When Julian gave a sigh of excitement it fled into the rocky hollows and swelled out and echoed around as if it were a live thing. It gave all the children a very queer feeling.

'Isn't it strange?' said George, in a low voice. At once the echoes took up her words, and multiplied them and made them louder — and all the dungeon caves gave back the girl's words over and over again. 'Isn't it strange, ISN'T IT STRANGE, ISN'T IT STRANGE.'

Anne slipped her hand into Dick's. She felt scared. She didn't like the echoes at all. She knew they *were* only echoes — but they did sound exactly like the voices of scores of people hidden in the caves!

'Where do you suppose the ingots are?' said Dick. And at once the caves threw him back his words. 'INGOTS! INGOTS are! INGOTS ARE! ARE! ARE!'

Julian laughed — and his laugh was split up into dozens of different laughs that came out of the dungeons and spun round the listening children. It really was the queerest thing.

'Come on,' said Julian. 'Maybe the echoes won't be so bad a little farther in.'

'FARTHER IN,' said the echoes at once. 'FARTHER IN!'

They moved away from the end of the rocky steps and explored the nearby dungeons. They were really only rocky cellars stretching under the castle. Maybe wretched prisoners had been kept there many, many years before, but mostly they had been used for storing things.

'I wonder which dungeon was used for storing the ingots,' said Julian. He stopped and took the map out of his pocket. He flashed his torch on to it. But although it showed him quite plainly the dungeon where INGOTS were marked, he had no idea at all of the right direction.

'I say — look — there's a door here, shutting off the

next dungeon!' suddenly cried Dick. 'I bet this is the dungeon we're looking for! I bet there are ingots in here!'

13

Down in the dungeons

Four torches were flashed on to the wooden door. It was big and stout, studded with great iron nails. Julian gave a whoop of delight and rushed to it. He felt certain that behind it was the dungeon used for storing things.

But the door was fast shut. No amount of pushing or pulling would open it. It had a great key-hole — but no key there! The four children stared in exasperation at the door. Bother it! Just as they really thought they were near the ingots, this door wouldn't open!

'We'll fetch the axe,' said Julian, suddenly. 'We may be able to chop round the keyhole and smash the lock.'

'That's a good idea!' said George, delighted. 'Come on back!'

They left the big door, and tried to get back the

way they had come. But the dungeons were so big and so rambling that they lost their way. They stumbled over old broken barrels, rotting wood, empty bottles and many other things as they tried to find their way back to the big flight of rock-steps.

'This is sickening!' said Julian, at last. 'I simply haven't any idea at all where the entrance is. We keep on going into one dungeon after another, and one passage after another, and they all seem to be exactly the same — dark and smelly and mysterious.'

'Suppose we have to stay here all the rest of our lives!' said Anne, gloomily.

'Idiot!' said Dick, taking her hand. 'We shall soon find the way out. Hallo! — what's this? —'

They all stopped. They had come to what looked like a chimney shaft of brick, stretching down from the roof of the dungeon to the floor. Julian flashed his torch on to it. He was puzzled.

'I know what it is!' said George, suddenly. 'It's the well, of course! You remember it was shown in the plan of the dungeons, as well as in the plan of the ground floor. Well, that's the shaft of the well going down and down. I wonder if there's any opening in it just here — so that water could be taken into the dungeons as well as up to the ground floor.'

They went to see. On the other side of the well-shaft was a small opening big enough for one child at a time to put his head and shoulders through and look down. They shone their torches down and up. The well was so deep that it was still impossible to see the bottom of it. Julian dropped a stone down

again, but there was no sound of either a thud or a splash. He looked upwards, and could see the faint gleam of daylight that slid round the broken slab of stone lying a little way down the shaft — the slab on which Tim had sat, waiting to be rescued.

'Yes,' he said, 'this is the well all right. Isn't it queer? Well — now we've found the well we know that the entrance to the dungeons isn't very far off!'

That cheered them all up tremendously. They took hands and hunted around in the dark, their torches making bright beams of light here and there.

Anne gave a screech of excitement. 'Here's the entrance! It must be, because I can see faint daylight coming down!'

The children rounded a corner and sure enough, there was the steep, rocky flight of steps leading upwards. Julian took a quick look round so that he might know the way to go when they came down again. He didn't feel at all certain that he would find the wooden door!

They all went up into the sunshine. It was delicious to feel the warmth on their heads and shoulders after the cold air down in the dungeons. Julian looked at his watch and gave a loud exclamation.

'It's half-past six! *Half-past six!* No wonder I feel hungry. We haven't had any tea. We've been working, and wandering about those dungeons for hours.'

'Well, let's have a kind of tea-supper before we do anything else,' said Dick. 'I don't feel as if I've had

142

anything to eat for about twelve months.'

'Well, considering you ate about twice as much as anyone else at dinner-time,' began Julian, indignantly. Then he grinned. 'I feel the same as you,' he said. 'Come on! — let's get a really good meal. George, what about boiling a kettle and making some cocoa, or something? I feel cold after all that time underground.'

It was fun boiling the kettle on a fire of dry sticks. It was lovely to lie about in the warmth of the evening sun and munch bread and cheese and enjoy cake and biscuits. They all enjoyed themselves thoroughly. Tim had a good meal too. He hadn't very much liked being underground, and had followed the others very closely indeed, his tail well down. He had been very frightened, too, of the curious echoes here and there.

Once he had barked, and it had seemed to Tim as if the whole of the dungeons were full of other dogs, all barking far more loudly than he could. He hadn't even dared to whine after that! But now he was happy again, eating the tit-bits that the children gave him, and licking George whenever he was near her.

It was past eight o'clock by the time that the children had finished their meal and tidied up. Julian looked at the others. The sun was sinking, and the day was no longer so warm.

'Well,' he said, 'I don't know what you feel. But I don't somehow want to go down into those dungeons again today, not even for the sake of smashing in that door with the axe and opening it! I'm tired — and I don't like the thought of losing my way in those

143

dungeons at night.'

The others heartily agreed with him, especially Anne, who had secretly been dreading going down again with the night coming on. The little girl was almost asleep; she was so tired out with hard work and excitement.

'Come on, Anne!' said George, pulling her to her feet. 'Bed for you. We'll cuddle up together in the rugs on the floor of that little room — and in the morning when we wake we'll be simply thrilled to think of opening that big wooden door.'

All four children, with Tim close behind, went off to the little stone room. They curled up on their piles of rugs, and Tim crept in with George and Anne. He lay down on them, and felt so heavy that Anne had to push him off her legs.

He sat himself down on her again, and she groaned, half-asleep. Tim wagged his tail and thumped it hard against her ankles. Then George pulled him on to her own legs and lay there, feeling him breathe. She was very happy. She was spending the night on her island. They had almost found the ingots, she was sure. She had Tim with her, actually sleeping on her rugs. Perhaps everything would come right after all — somehow.

She fell asleep. The children felt perfectly safe with Tim on guard. They slept peacefully until the morning, when Tim saw a rabbit through the broken archway leading to the little room, and sped away to chase it. He awoke George as he got up from the rugs, and she sat up and rubbed her eyes.

'Wake up!' she cried to the others. 'Wake up, all of you! It's morning! And we're on the island!'

They all awoke. It was really thrilling to sit up and remember everything. Julian thought of the big wooden door at once. He would soon smash it in with his axe, he felt sure. And then what would they find?

They had breakfast, and ate just as much as ever. Then Julian picked up the axe they had brought and took everyone to the flight of steps. Tim went too, wagging his tail, but not really feeling very pleased at the thought of going down into the queer places where other dogs seemed to bark, and yet were not to be found. Poor Tim would never understand echoes!

They all went down underground again. And then, of course, they couldn't find the way to the wooden door! It was most tiresome.

'We shall lose our way all over again,' said George, desperately. 'These dungeons are about the most rambling spread-out maze of underground caves I've ever known! We shall lose the entrance again too!'

Julian had a bright idea. He had a piece of white chalk in his pocket, and he took it out. He went back to the steps, and marked the wall there. Then he began to put chalk-marks along the passages as they walked in the musty darkness. They came to the well, and Julian was pleased.

'Now,' he said, 'whenever we come to the well we shall at least be able to find the way back to the steps, because we can follow my chalk-marks. Now the thing is — which is the way next? We'll try and find it and I'll put chalk-marks along the walls here and

145

there — but if we go the wrong way and have to come back, we'll rub out the marks, and start again from the well another way.'

This was really a very good idea. They did go the wrong way, and had to come back, rubbing out Julian's marks. They reached the well, and set off in the opposite direction. And this time they did find the wooden door!

There it was, stout and sturdy, its old iron nails rusty and red. The children stared at it in delight. Julian lifted his axe.

Crash! He drove it into the wood and round about the keyhole. But the wood was still strong, and the axe only went in an inch or two. Julian drove it in once more. The axe hit one of the big nails and slipped a little to one side. A big splinter of wood flew out — and struck poor Dick on the cheek!

He gave a yell of pain. Julian jumped in alarm, and turned to look at him. Dick's cheek was pouring with blood!

'Something flew out of the door and hit me,' said poor Dick. 'It's a splinter, or something.'

'Golly!' said Julian, and he shone his torch on to Dick. 'Can you bear it a moment if I pull the splinter out? It's a big one, and it's still sticking into your poor cheek.'

But Dick pulled it out himself. He made a face with the pain, and then turned very white.

'You'd better get up into the open air for a bit,' said Julian. 'And we'll have to bathe your cheek and stop it bleeding somehow. Anne's got a clean hanky. We'll bathe it and dab it with that. We brought some water with us, luckily.'

'I'll go with Dick,' said Anne. 'You stay here with George. There's no need for us all to go.'

But Julian thought he would like to see Dick safely up into the open air first, and then he could leave him with Anne while he went back to George and went on with the smashing down of the door. He handed the axe to George.

'You can do a bit of chopping while I'm gone,' he said. 'It will take some time to smash that big door in. You get on with it — and I'll be down in a few minutes again. We can easily find the way to the entrance because we've only got to follow my chalk-marks.'

'Right!' said George, and she took the axe. 'Poor old Dick — you do look a sight.'

Leaving George behind with Tim, valiantly attacking the big door, Julian took Dick and Anne up to the open air. Anne dipped her hanky into the kettle of water and dabbed Dick's cheek gently. It was bleeding very much, as cheeks do, but the wound was not really very bad. Dick's colour soon came back, and he wanted to go down into the dungeons again.

'No, you'd better lie down on your back for a little,' said Julian. 'I know that's good for nose-bleeding — and maybe it's good for cheek-bleeding too. What about Anne and you going out on the rocks over there, where you can see the wreck, and staying there for half an hour or so? Come on — I'll take you both there, and leave you for a bit. You'd better not get up till your cheek's stopped bleeding, old boy.'

Julian took the two out of the castle yard and out on to the rocks on the side of the island that faced the open sea. The dark hulk of the old wreck was still there on the rocks. Dick lay down on his back and stared up into the sky, hoping that his cheek would soon stop bleeding. He didn't want to miss any of the fun!

Anne took his hand. She was very upset at the little accident, and although she didn't want to miss the fun either, she meant to stay with Dick till he felt better. Julian sat down beside them for a minute or two. Then he went back to the rocky steps and disappeared down them. He followed his chalk-marks, and soon came to where George was attacking the door.

She had smashed it well round the lock — but it simply would *not* give way. Julian took the axe from her and drove it hard into the wood.

After a blow or two something seemed to happen to the lock. It became loose, and hung a little sideways. Julian put down his axe.

'I think somehow that we can open the door now,' he said, in an excited voice. 'Get out of the way, Tim, old fellow. Now then, push, George!'

They both pushed — and the lock gave way with a grating noise. The big door opened creakingly, and the two children went inside, flashing their torches in excitement.

The room was not much more than a cave, hollowed out of the rock — but in it was something quite different from the old barrels and boxes the children had found before. At the back, in untidy piles, were curious, brick-shaped things of dull yellow-brown metal. Julian picked one up.

'George!' he cried. 'The ingots! These are real gold! Oh, I know they don't look like it — but they are, all the same. George, oh George, there's a small fortune here in this cellar — and it's yours! We've found it at last!'

14

Prisoners!

George couldn't say a word. She just stood there, staring at the pile of ingots, holding one in her hand. She could hardly believe that these strange brick-shaped things were really gold. Her heart thumped fast. What a wonderful, marvellous find!

Suddenly Tim began to bark loudly. He stood with his back to the children, his nose towards the door — and how he barked!

'Shut up, Tim!' said Julian. 'What can you hear? Is it the others coming back?'

He went to the door and yelled down the passage outside. 'Dick! Anne! Is it you? Come quickly, because we've found the ingots! WE'VE FOUND THEM! HURRY! HURRY!'

Tim stopped barking and began to growl. George looked puzzled. 'Whatever *can* be the matter with Tim?' she said. 'He surely can't be growling at Dick

150

and Anne.'

Then both children got a most tremendous shock
— for a man's voice came booming down the dark
passage, making queer echoes all around.

'Who is here? Who is down here?'

George clutched Julian in fright. Tim went on
growling, all the hairs on his neck standing up
straight. 'Do be quiet, Tim!' whispered George,
snapping off her torch. But Tim simply would *not* be
quiet. He went on growling as if he were a small
thunderstorm.

The children saw the beam of a powerful torchlight
coming round the corner of the dungeon passage.
Then the light picked them out, and the holder of the
torch came to a surprised stop.

'Well, well, well!' said a voice. 'Look who's here!
Two children in the dungeons of my castle.'

'What do you mean, *your* castle!' cried George.

'Well, my dear little girl, it *is* my castle, because
I'm in the process of buying it,' said the voice. Then
another voice spoke, more gruffly.

'What are you doing down here? What did you
mean when you shouted out "Dick" and "Anne",
and said you had found the ingots? What ingots?'

'Don't answer,' whispered Julian to George. But
the echoes took his words and made them very loud
in the passage. 'DON'T ANSWER! DON'T ANSWER!'

'Oh, so you won't answer,' said the second man,
and he stepped towards the children. Tim bared his
teeth, but the man didn't seem at all frightened of
him. The man went to the door and flashed his torch

inside the dungeon. He gave a long whistle of surprise.

'Jake! Look here!' he said. 'You were right. The gold's here all right. And how easy to take away! All in ingots — my word, this is the most amazing thing we've ever struck.'

'This gold is mine,' said George, in a fury. 'The island and the castle belong to my mother — and so does anything found here. This gold was brought here and stored by my great-great-great-grandfather before his ship got wrecked. It's not yours, and never will be. As soon as I get back home I shall tell my father and mother what we've found — and then you may be sure you won't be able to buy the castle or the island! You were very clever, finding out from the map in the old box about the gold — but just not clever enough for us. We found it first!'

The men listened in silence to George's clear and angry voice. One of them laughed. 'You're only a child,' he said. 'You surely don't think you can keep us from getting our way? We're going to buy this island — and everything in it — and we shall take the gold when the deeds are signed. And if by any chance we couldn't buy the island, we'd take the gold just the same. It would be easy enough to bring a ship here and transfer the ingots from here by boat to the ship. Don't worry — we shall get what we want all right.'

'You will not!' said George, and she stepped out of the door. 'I'm going straight home now — and I'll tell my father all you've said.'

'My dear little girl, you are not going home,' said the first man, putting his hands on George and forcing her back into the dungeon. 'And, by the way, unless you want me to shoot this unpleasant dog of yours, call him off, will you?'

George saw, to her dismay, that the man had a shining revolver in his hand. In fright she caught hold of Tim's collar and pulled him to her. 'Be quiet, Tim,' she said. 'It's all right.'

154

But Tim knew quite well that it wasn't all right. Something was very wrong. He went on growling fiercely.

'Now listen to me,' said the man, after he had had a hurried talk with his companion. 'If you are going to be sensible, nothing unpleasant will happen to you. But if you want to be obstinate, you'll be very sorry. What we are going to do is this — we're going off in our motor-boat, leaving you nicely locked up here — and we're going to get a ship and come back for the gold. We don't think it's worth while buying the island now we know where the ingots are.'

'And you are going to write a note to your companions above, telling them you've found the gold and they are to come down and look for it,' said the other man. 'Then we shall lock up all of you in this dungeon, with the ingots to play with, leaving you food and drink till we come back. Now then — here is a pencil. Write a note to Dick and Anne, whoever they are, and send your dog up with it. Come on.'

'I won't,' said George, her face furious. 'I won't. You can't make me do a thing like that. I won't get poor Dick and Anne down here to be made prisoners. And I won't let you have my gold, just when I've discovered it.'

'We shall shoot your dog if you don't do as you're told,' said the first man, suddenly. George's heart sank down and she felt cold and terrified.

'No, no,' she said in a low, desperate voice.

'Well, write the note then,' said the man, offering

her a pencil and paper. 'Go on. I'll tell you what to say.'

'I can't!' sobbed George. 'I don't want to get Dick and Anne down here to be made prisoners.'

'All right — I'll shoot the dog then,' said the man, in a cold voice and he levelled his revolver at poor Tim. George threw her arms round her dog and gave a scream.

'No, no! I'll write the note. Don't shoot Tim, don't shoot him!'

The girl took the paper and pencil in a shaking hand and looked at the man. 'Write this,' he ordered. '"Dear Dick and Anne. We've found the gold. Come on down at once and see it." Then sign your name, whatever it is.'

George wrote what the man had said. Then she signed her name. But instead of writing 'George' she put 'Georgina.' She knew that the others would feel certain she would never sign herself that — and she hoped it would warn them that something queer was up. The man took the note and fastened it to Tim's collar. The dog growled all the time, but George kept telling him not to bite.

'Now tell him to go and find your friends,' said the man.

'Find Dick and Anne,' commanded George. 'Go on, Tim. Find Dick and Anne. Give them the note.'

Tim did not want to leave George, but there was something very urgent in her voice. He took one last look at his mistress, gave her hand a lick and sped off down the passage. He knew the way now. Up the

156

rocky steps he bounded and into the open air. He stopped in the old yard, sniffing. Where were Dick and Anne?

He smelt their footsteps and ran off, his nose to the ground. He soon found the two children out on the rocks. Dick was feeling better now and was sitting up. His cheek had almost stopped bleeding.

'Hallo,' he said in surprise, when he saw Tim. 'Here's Timothy! Why, Tim, old chap, why have you come to see us? Did you get tired of being underground in the dark?'

'Look, Dick — he's got something twisted into his collar,' said Anne, her sharp eyes seeing the paper there. 'It's a note. I expect it's from the others, telling us to go down. Isn't Tim clever to bring it?'

Dick took the paper from Tim's collar. He undid it and read it.

'"Dear Dick and Anne,"' he read out aloud. '"We've found the gold. Come on down at once and see it. Georgina."'

'Oooh!' said Anne, her eyes shining. 'They've found it. Oh, Dick — are you well enough to come now? Let's hurry.'

But Dick did not get up from the rocks. He sat and stared at the note, puzzled.

'What's the matter?' said Anne, impatiently.

'Well, don't you think it's funny that George should suddenly sign herself "Georgina"?' said Dick, slowly. 'You know how she hates being a girl, and having a girl's name. You know how she will never answer if anyone calls her Georgina. And yet in this

158

note she signs herself by the name she hates. It does seem a bit funny to me. Almost as if it's a kind of warning that there's something wrong.'

'Oh, don't be so silly, Dick,' said Anne. 'What could be wrong? Do come on.'

'Anne, I'd like to pop over to that inlet of ours to make sure there's no one else come to the island,' said Dick. 'You stay here.'

But Anne didn't want to stay there alone. She ran round the coast with Dick, telling him all the time that she thought he was very silly.

But when they came to the little harbour, they saw that there was another boat there, as well as their own. It was a motor-boat! Someone else *was* on the island!

'Look,' said Dick, in a whisper. 'There *is* someone else here. And I bet it's the men who want to buy the island. I bet they've read that old map and know there's gold here. And they've found George and Julian and want to get us all together down in the dungeons so that they can keep us safe till they've stolen the gold. That's why they made George send us that note — but she signed it with a name she never uses — to warn us! Now — we must think hard. What are we going to do?'

15

Dick to the rescue!

Dick caught hold of Anne's hand and pulled her quickly away from the cove. He was afraid that whoever had come to the island might be somewhere about and see them. The boy took Anne to the little stone room where their things were and they sat down in a corner.

'Whoever has come has discovered Julian and George smashing in that door, I should think,' said Dick, in a whisper. 'I simply can't think what to do. We mustn't go down into the dungeons or we'll most certainly be caught. Hallo — where's Tim off to?'

The dog had kept with them for a while but now he ran off to the entrance of the dungeons. He disappeared down the steps. He meant to get back to George, for he knew she was in danger. Dick and Anne stared after him. They had felt comforted while he was there, and now they were sorry he had gone.

They really didn't know what to do. Then Anne had an idea. 'I know!' she said. 'We'll row back to the land in our boat and get help.'

'I'd thought of that,' said Dick, gloomily. 'But you know perfectly well we'd never know the way in and out of those awful rocks. We'd wreck the boat. I'm sure we're not strong enough either to row all the way back. Oh, dear — I do wish we could think what to do.'

They didn't need to puzzle their brains long. The men came up out of the dungeons and began to hunt for the two children! They had seen Tim when he came back and had found the note gone. So they knew the two children had taken it — and they couldn't imagine why they had not obeyed what George had said in the note, and come down to the dungeons!

Dick heard their voices. He clutched hold of Anne to make her keep quiet. He saw through the broken archway that the men were going in the opposite direction.

'Anne! I know where we can hide!' said the boy, excitedly. 'Down the old well! We can climb down the ladder a little way and hide there. I'm sure no one would ever look there!'

Anne didn't at all want to climb down the well even a little way. But Dick pulled her to her feet and hurried her off to the middle of the old courtyard. The men were hunting around the other side of the castle. There was just time to climb in. Dick slipped aside the old wooden cover of the well and helped Anne down the ladder. She was very scared. Then the boy climbed down himself and slipped the wooden cover back again over his head, as best he could.

The old stone slab that Tim had sat on when he fell down the well was still there. Dick climbed down to it and tested it. It was immovable.

'It's safe for you to sit on, Anne, if you don't want to keep clinging to the ladder,' he whispered. So Anne sat shivering on the stone slab across the well-shaft, waiting to see if they were discovered or not. They kept hearing the voices of the men, now near at hand and now far-off. Then the men began to shout for them.

'Dick! Anne! The others want you! Where are you? We've exciting news for you.'

'Well, why don't they let Julian and George come up and tell us then?' whispered Dick. 'There's something wrong, I know there is. I do wish we could get to Julian and George and find out what has happened.'

The two men came into the courtyard. They were angry. 'Where have those kids got to?' said Jake. 'Their boat is still in the cove, so they haven't got away. They must be hiding somewhere. We can't wait all day for them.'

'Well, let's take some food and drink down to the two we've locked up,' said the other man. 'There's plenty in that little stone room. I suppose it's a store the children brought over. We'll leave half in the room so that the other two kids can have it. And we'll take their boat with us so that they can't escape.'

'Right,' said Jake. 'The thing to do is to get the gold away as quickly as possible, and make sure the children are prisoners here until we've made a safe getaway. We won't bother any more about trying to buy the island. After all, it was only the idea of getting the ingots that put us up to the idea of getting Kirrin Castle and the island.'

'Well — come on,' said his companion. 'We will take the food down now, and not bother about the other kids. You stay here and see if you can spot them while I go down.'

Dick and Anne hardly dared to breathe when they heard all this. How they hoped that the men wouldn't think of looking down the well! They heard one man walk to the little stone room. It was plain that he was getting food and drink to take down to the two prisoners in the dungeons below. The other man stayed in the courtyard, whistling softly.

After what seemed a very long time to the hidden children, the first man came back. Then the two talked together, and at last went off to the cove. Dick heard the motor-boat being started up.

'It's safe to get out now, Anne,' he said. 'Isn't it cold down here? I'll be glad to get out into the sunshine.'

They climbed out and stood warming themselves in the hot summer sunshine. They could see the motor-boat streaking towards the mainland.

'Well, they're gone for the moment,' said Dick. 'And they've not taken our boat, as they said. If only we could rescue Julian and George, we could get help, because George could row us back.'

'Why *can't* we rescue them?' cried Anne, her eyes shining. 'We can go down the steps and unbolt the door, can't we?'

'No — we can't,' said Dick. 'Look!'

Anne looked to where he pointed. She saw that the two men had piled big, heavy slabs of broken stone over the dungeon entrance. It had taken all their strength to put the big stones there. Neither Dick nor Anne could hope to move them.

'It's quite impossible to get down the steps,' said Dick. 'They've made sure we shan't do that! And you know we haven't any idea where the second entrance is. We only know it was somewhere near the tower.'

'Let's see if we can find it,' said Anne eagerly. They set off to the tower on the right of the castle — but it was quite clear that whatever entrance there might have been once, it was gone now! The castle had fallen in very much just there, and there were piles of old broken stones everywhere, quite impossible to move. The children soon gave up the search.

'Blow!' said Dick. 'How I do hate to think of poor old Julian and George prisoners down below, and we can't even help them! Oh, Anne — can't *you* think of something to do?'

Anne sat down on a stone and thought hard. She was very worried. Then she brightened up a little and turned to Dick.

'Dick! I suppose — I suppose we couldn't *possibly* climb down the well, could we?' she asked. 'You know it goes past the dungeons — and there's an opening on the dungeon floor from the well-shaft, because don't you remember we were able to put in our heads and shoulders and look right up the well to the top? Could we get past that slab, do you think — the one that I sat on just now, that has fallen across the well?'

Dick thought it all over. He went to the well and peered down it. 'You know, I believe you are right, Anne,' he said at last. 'We might be able to squeeze past that slab. There's just about room. I don't know how far the iron ladder goes down though.'

'Oh, Dick — do let's try,' said Anne. 'It's our only chance of rescuing the others!'

'Well,' said Dick, 'I'll try it — but not you, Anne. I'm not going to have you falling down that well. The ladder might be broken half-way down — anything might happen. You must stay up here and I'll see what I can do.'

'You will be careful, won't you?' said Anne, anxiously. 'Take a rope with you, Dick, so that if you need one you won't have to climb all the way up again.'

'Good idea,' said Dick. He went to the little stone room and got one of the ropes they had put there. He wound it round and round his waist. Then he went back to Anne.

'Well, here goes!' he said, in a cheerful voice. 'Don't worry about me. I'll be all right.'

Anne was rather white. She was terribly afraid that Dick might fall right down to the bottom of the well. She watched him climb down the iron ladder to the slab of stone. He tried his best to squeeze by it, but it was very difficult. At last he managed it and after that Anne could see him no more. But she could hear him, for he kept calling up to her.

'Ladder's still going strong, Anne! I'm all right. Can you hear me?'

'Yes,' shouted Anne down the well, hearing her voice echo in a funny hollow manner. 'Take care, Dick. I do hope the ladder goes all the way down.'

'I think it does!' yelled back Dick. Then he gave a loud exclamation. 'Blow! It's broken just here. Broken right off. Or else it ends. I'll have to use my rope.'

There was a silence as Dick unwound the rope from his waist. He tied it firmly to the last but one rung of the ladder, which seemed quite strong.

'I'm going down the rope now!' he shouted to Anne. 'Don't worry. I'm all right. Here I go!'

Anne couldn't hear what Dick said after that, for the well-shaft made his words go crooked and she couldn't make out what they were. But she was glad to hear him shouting even though she didn't know what he said. She yelled down to him too, hoping he could hear her.

Dick slid down the rope, holding on to it with hands, knees and feet, glad that he was so good at gym at school. He wondered if he was anywhere near the dungeons. He seemed to have gone down a long way. He managed to get out his torch. He put it between his teeth after he had switched it on, so that he might have both hands free for the rope. The light from the torch showed him the walls of the well around him. He couldn't make out if he was above or below the dungeons. He didn't want to go right down to the bottom of the well!

He decided that he must have just passed the opening into the dungeon-caves. He climbed back up the rope a little way and to his delight saw that he was right. The opening on to the dungeons was just by his head. He climbed up till he was level with it and then swung himself to the side of the well where the small opening was. He managed to get hold of the bricked edge, and then tried to scramble though the opening into the dungeon.

It was difficult, but luckily Dick was not very big. He managed it at last and stood up straight with a sigh of relief. He was in the dungeons! He could now follow the chalk-marks to the room or cave where the ingots were — and where he felt sure that George and Julian were imprisoned!

He shone his torch on the wall. Yes — there were the chalk-marks. Good! He put his head into the well-opening and yelled at the top of his voice.

'Anne! I'm in the dungeons! Watch out that the men don't come back!'

Then he began to follow the white chalk-marks, his heart beating fast. After a while he came to the door of the store-room. As he had expected, it was fastened so that George and Julian couldn't get out. Big bolts had been driven home at the top and bottom, and the children inside could not possibly get out. They had tried their hardest to batter down the door, but it was no good at all.

They were sitting inside the store-cave, feeling angry and exhausted. The man had brought them food and drink, but they had not touched it. Tim was with them, lying down with his head on his paws, half-angry with George because she hadn't let him fly at the men as he had so badly wanted to. But George felt certain that Tim would be shot if he tried biting or snapping.

'Anyway, the other two had sense enough not to come down and be made prisoners too,' said George. 'They must have known there was something funny about that note when they saw I had signed myself Georgina instead of George. I wonder what they are doing. They must be hiding.'

Tim suddenly gave a growl. He leapt to his feet and went to the closed door, his head on one side. He had heard something, that was certain.

'I hope it's not those men back again already,' said George. Then she looked at Tim in surprise, flashing her torch on to him. He was wagging his tail!

A great bang at the door made them all jump out of their skins! Then came Dick's cheerful voice. 'Hi, Julian! Hi, George! Are you here?'

'Wufffff!' barked Tim joyfully, and scratched at the door.

'Dick! Open the door!' yelled Julian in delight. 'Quick, open the door!'

16

A plan – and a narrow escape

Dick unbolted the door at the top and bottom and flung it open. He rushed in and thumped George and Julian happily on the back.

'Hallo!' he said. 'How does it feel to be rescued?'

'Fine!' cried Julian, and Tim barked madly round them.

George grinned at Dick.

'Good work!' she said. 'What happened?'

Dick told them in a few words all that had happened. When he related how he had climbed down the old well, George and Julian could hardly believe their ears. Julian slipped his arm through his younger brother's.

'You're a brick!' he said. 'A real brick! Now quick — what are we going to do?'

'Well, if they've left us our boat I'm going to take us all back to the mainland as quickly as possible,' said George. 'I'm not playing about with men who brandish revolvers all the time. Come on! Up the well we go and find the boat.'

They ran to the well-shaft and squeezed through the small opening one by one. Up the rope they went, and soon found the iron ladder. Julian made them go up one by one in case the ladder wouldn't bear the weight of all three at once.

It really wasn't very long before they were all up in the open air once more, giving Anne hugs, and hearing her exclaim gladly, with tears in her eyes, how pleased she was to see them all again.

'Now come on!' said George after a minute. 'Off to the boat. Quick! Those men may be back at any time.'

They rushed to the cove. There was their boat, lying where they had pulled it, out of reach of the waves. But what a shock for them!

'They've taken the oars!' said George, in dismay. 'The beasts! They know we can't row the boat away without oars. They were afraid you and Anne might row off, Dick — so instead of bothering to tow the boat behind them, they just grabbed the oars. Now we're stuck. We can't possibly get away.'

It was a great disappointment. The children were almost ready to cry. After Dick's marvellous rescue of George and Julian, it had seemed as if everything was going right — and now suddenly things were going wrong again.

'We must think this out,' said Julian, sitting down where he could see at once if any boat came in sight.

'The men have gone off— probably to get a ship from somewhere in which they can put the ingots and sail away. They won't be back for some time, I should think, because you can't charter a ship all in a hurry — unless, of course, they've got one of their own.'

'And in the meantime we can't get off the island to get help, because they've got our oars,' said George. 'We can't even signal to any passing fishing-boat because they won't be out just now. The tide's wrong. It seems as if all we've got to do is wait here patiently till the men come back and take my gold! And we can't stop them.'

'You know — I've got a sort of plan coming into my head,' said Julian, slowly. 'Wait a bit — don't interrupt me. I'm thinking.'

The others waited in silence while Julian sat and frowned, thinking of his plan. Then he looked at the others with a smile.

'I believe it will work,' he said. 'Listen! We'll wait here in patience till the men come back. What will they do? They'll drag away those stones at the top of the dungeon entrance, and go down the steps. They'll go to the store-room, where they left us — thinking we are still there — and they will go into the room. Well, what about one of us being hidden down there ready to bolt *them* into the room? Then we can either go off in their motor-boat or our own boat if they bring back our oars — and get help.'

Anne thought it was a marvellous idea. But Dick and George did not look so certain. 'We'd have to go down and bolt that door again to make it seem as if

172

we are still prisoners there,' said George. 'And suppose the one who hides down there doesn't manage to bolt the men in? It might be very difficult to do that quickly enough. They will simply catch whoever we plan to leave down there — and come up to look for the rest of us.'

'That's true,' said Julian, thoughtfully. 'Well — we'll suppose that Dick, or whoever goes down, doesn't manage to bolt them in and make them prisoners — and the men come up here again. All right — while they are down below we'll pile big stones over the entrance, just as they did. Then they won't be able to get out.'

'What about Dick down below?' said Anne, at once.

'I could climb up the well again!' said Dick, eagerly. 'I'll be the one to go down and hide. I'll do my best to bolt the men into the room. And if I have to escape I'll climb up the well-shaft again. The men don't know about that. So even if they are not prisoners in the dungeon room, they'll be prisoners underground!'

The children talked over this plan, and decided that it was the best they could think of. Then George said she thought it would be a good thing to have a meal. They were all half-starved and, now that the worry and excitement of being rescued was over, they were feeling very hungry!

They fetched some food from the little room and ate it in the cove, keeping a sharp look-out for the return of the men. After about two hours they saw a

173

big fishing-smack appear in the distance, and heard the chug-chug-chug of a motor-boat too.

'There they are!' said Julian, in excitement, and he jumped to his feet. 'That's the ship they mean to load with the ingots, and sail away in safety — and there's the motor-boat bringing the men back! Quick, Dick, down the well you go, and hide until you hear them in the dungeons!'

Dick shot off. Julian turned to the others. 'We'll have to hide,' he said. 'Now that the tide is out we'll hide over yonder, behind those uncovered rocks. I don't somehow think the men will do any hunting for Dick and Anne — but they might. Come on! Quick!'

They all hid themselves behind the rocks, and heard the motor-boat come chugging into the tiny harbour. They could hear men calling to one another. There sounded to be more than two men this time. Then the men left the inlet and went up the low cliff towards the ruined castle.

Julian crept behind the rocks and peeped to see what the men were doing. He felt certain they were pulling away the slabs of stone that had been piled on top of the entrance to prevent Dick and Anne going down to rescue the others.

'George! Come on!' called Julian in a low tone. 'I think the men have gone down the steps into the dungeons now. We must go and try to put those big stones back. Quick!'

George, Julian and Anne ran softly and swiftly to the old courtyard of the castle. They saw that the stones had been pulled away from the entrance to the dungeons. The men had disappeared. They had plainly gone down the steps.

The three children did their best to tug at the heavy stones to drag them back. But their strength was not the same as that of the men, and they could not manage to get any very big stones across. They put three smaller ones, and Julian hoped the men would find them too difficult to move from below. 'If only Dick has managed to bolt them into that room!' he said to the others. 'Come on, back to the well now. Dick will have to come up there, because he won't be able to get out of the entrance.'

They all went to the well. Dick had removed the old wooden cover, and it was lying on the ground. The children leaned over the hole of the well and waited anxiously. What was Dick doing? They could hear nothing from the well and they longed to know what was happening.

There was plenty happening down below! The two men, and another, had gone down into the dungeons, expecting, of course, to find Julian, George and the dog still locked up in the store-room with the ingots. They passed the well-shaft not guessing that an excited small boy was hidden there, ready to slip out of the opening as soon as they had passed.

Dick heard them pass. He slipped out of the well-opening and followed behind quietly, his feet making no sound. He could see the beams made by the men's powerful torches, and with his heart thumping loudly he crept along the smelly old passages, between great caves, until the men turned into the wide passage where the store-cave lay.

'Here it is,' Dick heard one of the men say, as he flashed his torch on to the great door. 'The gold's in there — so are the kids!'

The men unbolted the door at top and bottom. Dick was glad that he had slipped along to bolt the door, for if he hadn't done that before the men had come they would have known that Julian and George had escaped, and would have been on their guard.

The man opened the door and stepped inside. The second man followed him. Dick crept as close as he dared, waiting for the third man to go in too. Then he meant to slam the door and bolt it!

The first man swung his torch round and gave a loud exclamation. 'The children are gone! How strange! Where are they?'

Two of the men were now in the cave — and the third stepped in at that moment. Dick darted forward and slammed the door. It made a crash that went echoing round and round the caves and passages. Dick fumbled with the bolts, his hand trembling. They were stiff and rusty. The boy found it hard to shoot them home in their sockets. And meanwhile the men were not idle!

As soon as they heard the door slam they spun round. The third man put his shoulder to the door at once and heaved hard. Dick had just got one of the bolts almost into its socket. Then all three men forced their strength against the door, and the bolt gave way!

Dick stared in horror. The door was opening! He

turned and fled down the dark passage. The men flashed their torches on and saw him. They went after the boy at top speed.

Dick fled to the well-shaft. Fortunately the opening was on the opposite side, and he could clamber into it without being seen in the light of the torches. The boy only just had time to squeeze through into the shaft before the three men came running by. Not one of them guessed that the runaway was squeezed into the well-shaft they passed! Indeed, the men did not even know that there was a well there.

Trembling from head to foot, Dick began to climb the rope he had left dangling from the rungs of the iron ladder. He undid it when he reached the ladder itself, for he thought that perhaps the men might discover the old well and try to climb up later. They would not be able to do that if there was no rope dangling down.

The boy climbed up the ladder quickly, and squeezed round the stone slab near the top. The other children were there, waiting for him.

They knew at once by the look on Dick's face that he had failed in what he had tried to do. They pulled him out quickly. 'It was no good,' said Dick, panting with his climb. 'I couldn't do it. They burst the door open just as I was bolting it, and chased me. I got into the shaft just in time.'

'They're trying to get out of the entrance now!' cried Anne, suddenly. 'Quick! What shall we do? They'll catch us all!'

'To the boat!' shouted Julian, and he took Anne's

hand to help her along. 'Come along! It's our only chance. The men will perhaps be able to move those stones.'

The four children fled down the courtyard. George darted into the little stone room as they passed it, and caught up an axe. Dick wondered why she bothered to do that. Tim dashed along with them, barking madly.

They came to the cove. Their own boat lay there without oars. The motor-boat was there too. George jumped into it and gave a yell of delight.

'Here are our oars!' she shouted. 'Take them, Julian, I've got a job to do here! Get the boat down to the water, quick!'

Julian and Dick took the oars. Then they dragged their boat down to the water, wondering what George was doing. All kinds of crashing sounds came from the motor-boat!

'George! George! Buck up. The men are out!' suddenly yelled Julian. He had seen the three men running to the cliff that led down to the cove. George leapt out of the motor-boat and joined the others. They pushed their boat out on to the water, and George took the oars at once, pulling for all she was worth.

The three men ran to their motor-boat. Then they paused in the greatest dismay — for George had completely ruined it! She had chopped wildly with her axe at all the machinery she could see — and now the boat could not possibly be started! It was damaged beyond any repair the men could make

with the few tools they had.

'You wicked girl!' yelled Jake, shaking his fist at George. 'Wait till I get you!'

'I'll wait!' shouted back George, her blue eyes shining dangerously. 'And you can wait too! You won't be able to leave my island now!'

17

The end of the great adventure

The three men stood at the edge of the sea, watching George pull away strongly from the shore. They could do nothing. Their boat was quite useless.

'The fishing-smack they've got waiting out there is too big to use that little inlet,' said George, as she pulled hard at her oars. 'They'll have to stay there till someone goes in with a boat. I guess they're as wild as can be!'

Their boat had to pass fairly near to the big fishing-boat. A man hailed them as they came by.

'Ahoy there! Have you come from Kirrin Island?'

'Don't answer,' said George. 'Don't say a word.' So no one said anything at all, but looked the other way as if they hadn't heard.

'AHOY THERE!' yelled the man, angrily. 'Are you deaf? Have you come from the island?'

Still the children said nothing at all, but looked

away while George rowed steadily. The man on the ship gave it up, and looked in a worried manner towards the island. He felt sure the children had come from there — and he knew enough of his comrades' adventures to wonder if everything was right on the island.

'He may put out a boat from the smack and go and see what's happening,' said George. 'Well, he can't do much except take the men off — with a few ingots! I hardly think they'll dare to take any of the gold though, now that we've escaped to tell our tale!'

Julian looked behind at the ship. He saw after a time that the little boat it carried was being lowered into the sea. 'You're right,' he said to George. 'They're afraid something is up. They're going to rescue those three men. What a pity!'

Their little boat reached land. The children leapt out into the shallow water and dragged it up to the beach. Tim pulled at the rope too, wagging his tail. He loved to join in anything that the children were doing.

'Shall you take Tim to Alf?' asked Dick.

George shook her head. 'No,' she said, 'we haven't any time to waste. We must go and tell everything that has happened. I'll tie Tim up to the fence in the front garden.'

They made their way to Kirrin Cottage at top speed. Aunt Fanny was gardening there. She stared in surprise to see the hurrying children.

'Why,' she said, 'I thought you were not coming back till tomorrow or the next day! Has anything happened? What's the matter with Dick's cheek?'

'Nothing much,' said Dick.

The others chimed in.

'Aunt Fanny, where's Uncle Quentin? We have something important to tell him!'

'Mother, we've had such an adventure!'

'Aunt Fanny, we've an awful lot to tell you! We really have!'

Aunt Fanny looked at the untidy children in amazement. 'Whatever has happened?' she said. Then she turned towards the house and called 'Quentin! Quentin! The children have something to tell us!'

Uncle Quentin came out, looking rather cross, for he was in the middle of his work. 'What's the matter?' he asked.

'Uncle, it's about Kirrin Island,' said Julian, eagerly. 'Those men haven't bought it yet, have they?'

'Well, it's practically sold,' said his uncle. 'I've signed my part, and they are to sign their part tomorrow. Why? What's that to do with you?'

'Uncle, those men won't sign tomorrow,' said Julian. 'Do you know why they wanted to buy the island and the castle? Not because they really wanted to build an hotel or anything like that — but because they knew the lost gold was hidden there!'

'What nonsense are you talking?' said his uncle.

'It isn't nonsense, Father!' cried George indignantly. 'It's all true. The map of the old castle was in that box you sold — and in the map was shown where the ingots were hidden by my great-great-great-grandfather!'

George's father looked amazed and annoyed. He simply didn't believe a word! But his wife saw by the solemn and serious faces of the four children that something important really had happened. And then Anne suddenly burst into loud sobs! The excitement had been too much for her and she couldn't bear to think that her uncle wouldn't believe that everything was true.

'Aunt Fanny, Aunt Fanny, it's all true!' she sobbed. 'Uncle Quentin is horrid not to believe us. Oh, Aunt Fanny, the man had a revolver — and oh, he made Julian and George prisoners in the dungeons — and Dick had to climb down the well to rescue them. And George has smashed up their motor-boat to stop them escaping!'

Her aunt and uncle couldn't make head or tail of this, but Uncle Quentin suddenly seemed to think that the matter was serious and worth looking into. 'Smashed up a motor-boat!' he said. 'Whatever for? Come indoors. I shall have to hear the story from beginning to end. It seems quite unbelievable to me.'

They all trooped indoors. Anne sat on her aunt's knee and listened to George and Julian telling the whole story. They told it well and left nothing out. Aunt Fanny grew quite pale as she listened, especially when she heard about Dick climbing down the well.

'You might have been killed,' she said. 'Oh, Dick! What a brave thing to do!'

Uncle Quentin listened in the utmost amazement. He had never had much liking or admiration for any children — he always thought they were noisy, tiresome, and silly. But now, as he listened to Julian's tale, he changed his mind about these four children at once!

'You've been very clever,' he said. 'And very brave too. I'm proud of you. Yes, I'm very proud of you all. No wonder you didn't want me to sell the island, George, when you knew about the ingots! But why didn't you tell me?'

The four children stared at him and didn't answer. They couldn't very well say, 'Well, firstly, you wouldn't have believed us. Secondly, you are bad-tempered and unjust and we are frightened of you. Thirdly, we didn't trust you enough to do the right thing.'

'Why don't you answer?' said their uncle. His wife answered for them, in a gentle voice.

'Quentin, you scare the children, you know, and I don't expect they liked to go to you. But now that they have, you will be able to take matters into your own hands. The children cannot do any more. You must ring up the police and see what they have to say about all this.'

'Right,' said Uncle Quentin, and he got up at once. He patted Julian on the back. 'You have all done well,' he said. Then he ruffled George's short curly hair. 'And I'm proud of you, too, George,' he said. 'You're as good as a boy any day!'

'Oh, Father!' said George, going red with surprise

and pleasure. She smiled at him and he smiled back. The children noticed that he had a very nice face when he smiled. He and George were really very alike to look at. Both looked ugly when they sulked and frowned — and both were good to look at when they laughed or smiled!

George's father went off to telephone the police and his lawyer too. The children sat and ate biscuits and plums, telling their aunt a great many little details they had forgotten when telling the story before.

As they sat there, there came a loud and angry bark from the front garden. George looked up. 'That's Tim,' she said, with an anxious look at her mother. 'I hadn't time to take him to Alf, who keeps him for me. Mother, Tim was such a comfort to us on the island, you know. I'm sorry he's barking now — but I expect he's hungry.'

'Well, fetch him in,' said her mother, unexpectedly. 'He's quite a hero, too — we must give him a good dinner.'

George smiled in delight. She sped out of the door and went to Tim. She set him free and he came bounding indoors, wagging his long tail. He licked George's mother and cocked his ears at her.

'Good dog,' she said, and actually patted him. 'I'll get you some dinner!'

Tim trotted out to the kitchen with her. Julian grinned at George. 'Well, look at that,' he said. 'Your mother's a brick, isn't she?'

'Yes — but I don't know what Father will say

when he sees Tim in the house again,' said George, doubtfully.

Her father came back at that minute, his face grave. 'The police take a serious view of all this,' he said, 'and so does my lawyer. They all agree in thinking that you children have been remarkably clever and brave. And George — my lawyer says that the ingots definitely belong to us. Are there really a lot?'

'Father! There are hundreds!' cried George. 'Simply hundreds — all in a big pile in the dungeon. Oh, Father — shall we be rich now?'

'Yes,' said her father. 'We shall. Rich enough to give you and your mother all the things I've longed to give you for so many years and couldn't. I've worked hard enough for you — but it's not the kind of work that brings in a lot of money, and so I've become irritable and bad-tempered. But now you shall have everything you want!'

'I don't really want anything I haven't already got,' said George. 'But Father, there is one thing I'd like more than anything else in the world — and it won't cost you a penny!'

'You shall have it, my dear!' said her father, slipping his arm around George, much to her surprise. 'Just say what it is — and even if it costs a hundred pounds you shall have it!'

Just then there came the pattering of big feet down the passage to the room they were in. A big hairy head pushed itself through the door and looked inquiringly at everyone there. It was Tim, of course!

Uncle Quentin stared at him in surprise. 'Why, isn't that Tim?' he asked. 'Hallo, Tim!'

'Father! Tim is the thing I want most in all the world,' said George, squeezing her father's arm. 'You can't think what a friend he was to us on the island — and he wanted to fly at those men and fight them. Oh, Father, I don't want any other present — I only want to keep Tim and have him here for my very own. We could afford to give him a proper kennel to sleep in now, and I'd see that he didn't disturb you, I really would.'

'Well, of course you can have him!' said her father — and Tim came right into the room at once, wagging his tail, looking for all the world as if he had understood every word that had been said. He actually licked Uncle Quentin's hand! Anne thought that was very brave of him.

But Uncle Quentin was quite different now. It seemed as if a great weight had been lifted off his shoulders. They were rich now — George could go to a good school — and his wife could have the things he had so much wanted her to have — and he would be able to go on with the work he loved without feeling that he was not earning enough to keep his family in comfort. He beamed round at everyone, looking as jolly a person as anyone could wish!

George was overjoyed about Tim. She flung her arms round her father's neck and hugged him, a thing she had not done for a long time. He looked astonished but very pleased. 'Well, well,' he said, 'this is all very pleasant. Hallo — is this the police already?'

It was. They came up to the door and had a few words with Uncle Quentin. Then one stayed behind to take down the children's story in his note-book and the others went off to get a boat to the island.

The men had gone from there! The boat from the fishing-smack had fetched them away! — and now both ship and boat had disappeared! The motor-boat was still there, quite unusable. The inspector looked at it with a grin.

'Fierce young lady, isn't she, that Miss Georgina?' he said. 'Done this job pretty well — no one could get away in this boat. We'll have to get it towed into harbour.'

The police brought back with them some of the ingots of gold to show Uncle Quentin. They had sealed up the door of the dungeon so that no one else could get in until the children's uncle was ready to go and fetch the gold. Everything was being done thoroughly and properly — though far too slowly for the children! They had hoped that the men would have been caught and taken to prison — and that the police would bring back the whole of the gold at once!

They were all very tired that night and didn't make any fuss at all when their aunt said that they must go to bed early. They undressed and then the boys went to eat their supper in the girls' bedroom. Tim was there, ready to lick up any fallen crumbs.

'Well, I must say we've had a wonderful adventure,' said Julian, sleepily. 'In a way I'm sorry it's ended — though at times I didn't enjoy it very much

— especially when you and I, George, were prisoners in that dungeon. That was awful.'

George was looking very happy as she nibbled her gingerbread biscuits. She grinned at Julian.

'And to think I hated the idea of you all coming here to stay!' she said. 'I was going to be such a beast to you! I was going to make you wish you were all home again! And now the only thing that makes me sad is the idea of you going away — which you will do, of course, when the holidays end. And then, after having three friends with me, enjoying adventures like this, I'll be all on my own again. I've never been lonely before — but I know I shall be now.'

'No, you won't,' said Anne, suddenly. 'You can do something that will stop you being lonely ever again.'

'What?' said George in surprise.

'You can ask to go to the same boarding-school as I go to,' said Anne. 'It's such a lovely one — and we are allowed to keep our pets, so Tim could come too!'

'Gracious! Could he really?' said George, her eyes shining. 'Well, I'll go then. I always said I wouldn't — but I will because I see now how much better and happier it is to be with others than all by myself. And if I can have Tim, well that's simply wonderful!'

'You'd better go back to your own bedroom now, boys,' said Aunt Fanny, appearing at the doorway. 'Look at Dick, almost dropping with sleep! Well, you should all have pleasant dreams tonight, for you've had an adventure to be proud of. George — is that Tim under your bed?'

'Well, yes it is, Mother,' said George, pretending

190

to be surprised. 'Dear me! Tim, what are you doing here?'

Tim crawled out and went over to George's mother. He lay flat on his tummy and looked up at her most appealingly out of his soft brown eyes.

'Do you want to sleep in the girls' room tonight?' said George's mother, with a laugh. 'All right — just for once!'

'*Mother!*' yelled George, overjoyed. 'Oh, thank you, thank you, thank you! How did you guess that I just didn't want to be parted from Tim tonight? Oh, Mother! Tim, you can sleep on the rug over there.'

Four happy children snuggled down into their beds. Their wonderful adventure had come to a happy end. They had plenty of holidays still in front of them — and now that Uncle Quentin was no longer poor, he would give them the little presents he wanted to. George was going to school with Anne — and she had Tim for her own again! The island and castle still belonged to George — everything was marvellous!

'I'm so glad Kirrin Island wasn't sold, George,' said Anne, sleepily. 'I'm so glad it still belongs to you.'

'It belongs to three other people too,' said George. 'It belongs to me — and to you and Julian and Dick. 'I've discovered that it's fun to share things. So tomorrow I am going to draw up a deed, or whatever it's called, and put in it that I give you and the others a quarter-share each. Kirrin Island and Castle shall belong to us all!'

'Oh, George — how lovely!' said Anne, delighted. 'Won't the boys be pleased? I do feel so ha . . .'

But before she could finish, the little girl was asleep. So was George. In the other room the two boys slept, too, dreaming of ingots and dungeons and all kinds of exciting things.

Only one person was awake — and that was Tim. He had one ear up and was listening to the children's breathing. As soon as he knew they were asleep he got up quietly from his rug. He crept softly over to George's bed. He put his front paws up and sniffed at the sleeping girl.

Then, with a bound he was on the bed, and snuggled himself down into the crook of her legs. He gave a sigh, and shut his eyes. The four children might be happy — but Tim was happiest of all.

'Oh, Tim,' murmured George, half waking up as she felt him against her. 'Oh, Tim, you mustn't — but you do feel so nice. Tim — we'll have other adventures together, the five of us — won't we?'

They will — but that's another story!

Enid Blyton

FIVE GO ADVENTURING AGAIN

ILLUSTRATED BY JOLYNE KNOX

1

Christmas holidays

It was the last week of the Christmas term, and all the girls at Gaylands School were looking forward to the Christmas Holidays. Anne sat down at the breakfast-table and picked up a letter addressed to her.

'Hallo, look at this!' she said to her cousin Georgina, who was sitting beside her. 'A letter from Daddy — and I only had one from him and Mummy yesterday.'

'I hope it's not bad news,' said George. She would not allow anyone to call her Georgina, and now even the mistresses called her George. She really was very like a boy with her short curly hair, and her boyish ways. She looked anxiously at Anne as her cousin read the letter.

'Oh, George — we can't go home for the holidays!' said Anne, with tears in her eyes. 'Mummy's got scarlet fever — and Daddy is in quarantine for it — so they can't have us back. Isn't it just too bad?'

'Oh, I *am* sorry,' said George. She was just as disappointed for herself as for Anne, because Anne's mother had invited George, and her dog Timothy, to stay for the Christmas holidays with them. She had been promised many things she had never seen before — the pantomime, and the circus — and a big party with a fine Christmas tree! Now it wouldn't happen.

'Whatever will the two boys say?' said Anne,

thinking of Julian and Dick, her two brothers. 'They won't be able to go home either.'

'Well — what are you going to do for the holidays then?' asked George. 'Won't you come and stay at Kirrin Cottage with *me*? I'm sure my mother would love to have you again. We had such fun when you came to stay for the summer hols.'

'Wait a minute — let me finish the letter and see what Daddy says,' said Anne, picking up the note again. 'Poor Mummy — I do hope she isn't feeling very ill.'

She read a few more lines and then gave such a delighted exclamation that George and the other girls waited impatiently for her to explain.

'George! We *are* to come to you again — but oh blow, blow, blow! — we've got to have a tutor for the hols, partly to look after us so that your mother doesn't have too much bother with us, and partly because both Julian and Dick have been ill with 'flu twice this term, and have got behind in their work.'

'A tutor! How sickening! That means I'll have to do lessons too, I'll bet!' said George, in dismay. 'When my mother and father see my report I guess they'll find out how little I know. After all, this is the first time I've ever been to a proper school, and there are heaps of things I don't know.'

'What horrid hols they'll be, if we have a tutor running after us all the time,' said Anne, gloomily. 'I expect I'll have quite a good report, because I've done well in the exams — but it won't be any fun for me not doing lessons with you three in the hols.

Though, of course, I could go off with Timothy, I suppose. *He* won't be doing lessons!'

'Yes, he will,' said George, at once. She could not bear the idea of her beloved dog Timothy going off each morning with Anne, while she, George, sat and worked hard with Julian and Dick.

'Timothy can't do lessons, don't be silly, George,' said Anne.

'He can sit under my feet while *I'm* doing them,' said George. 'It will be a great help to feel him there. For goodness' sake eat up your sausages, Anne. We've all nearly finished. The bell will be going in a minute and you won't have had any breakfast.'

'I am glad Mummy isn't very bad,' said Anne, hurriedly finishing her letter. 'Daddy says he's written to Dick and Julian — and to your father to ask him to engage a tutor for us. Oh dash — this is an awful disappointment, isn't it? I don't mean I shan't enjoy going to Kirrin Cottage again — and seeing Kirrin Island — but after all there are no pantomimes or circuses or parties to look forward to at Kirrin.'

The end of the term came quickly. Anne and George packed up their trunks, and put on the labels, enjoying the noise and excitement of the last two days. The big school coaches rolled up to the door, and the girls clambered in.

'Off to Kirrin again!' said Anne. 'Come on, Timothy darling, you can sit between me and George.'

Gaylands School allowed the children to keep their

own pets, and Timothy, George's big mongrel dog, had been a great success. Except for the time when he had run after the dustman, and dragged the dustbin away from him, all the way up the school grounds and into George's classroom, he had really behaved extremely well.

'I'm sure *you'll* have a good report, Tim,' said George, giving the dog a hug. 'We're going home again. Will you like that?'

'Woof,' said Tim, in his deep voice. He stood up, wagging his tail, and there was a squeal from the seat behind.

'George! Make Tim sit down. He's wagging my hat off!'

It was not very long before the two girls and Timothy were in London, being put into the train for Kirrin.

'I do wish the boys broke up today too,' sighed Anne. 'Then we could all have gone down to Kirrin together. That would have been fun.'

Julian and Dick broke up the next day and were to join the girls then at Kirrin Cottage. Anne was very much looking forward to seeing them again. A term was a long time to be away from one another. She had been glad to have her cousin George with her. The three of them had stayed with George in the summer, and had had some exciting adventures together on the little island off the coast. An old castle stood on the island and in the dungeons the children had made all kinds of wonderful discoveries.

'It will be lovely to go across to Kirrin Island

again, George,' said Anne, as the train sped off towards the west.

'We shan't be able to,' said George. 'The sea is terribly rough round the island in the winter. It would be too dangerous to try and row there.'

'Oh, what a pity,' said Anne disappointed. 'I was looking forward to some more adventures there.'

'There won't be any adventures at Kirrin in the winter,' said George. 'It's cold down there — and when it snows we sometimes get frozen up completely — can't even walk to the village because the sea-wind blows the snow-drifts so high.'

'Oooh — that sounds rather exciting!' said Anne.

'Well, it isn't really,' said George. 'It's awfully boring — nothing to do but sit at home all day, or turn out with a spade and dig the snow away.'

It was a long time before the train reached the little station that served Kirrin. But at last it was there pulling in slowly and stopping at the tiny platform. The two girls jumped out eagerly, and looked to see if anyone had met them. Yes — there was George's mother!

'Hallo, George darling — hallo, Anne!' said George's mother, and gave both children a hug. 'Anne, I'm so sorry about your mother, but she's getting on all right, you'll be glad to know.'

'Oh, good!' said Anne. 'It's nice of you to have us, Aunt Fanny. We'll try and be good! What about Uncle Quentin? Will he mind having four children in the house in the winter-time? We won't be able to go out and leave him in peace as often as we did in the summer!'

George's father was a scientist, a very clever man, but rather frightening. He had little patience with children, and the four of them had felt very much afraid of him at times in the summer.

'Oh, your uncle is still working very hard at his book,' said Aunt Fanny. 'You know, he has been working out a secret theory — a secret idea — and putting it all into his book. He says that once it is all explained and finished, he is to take it to some high authority, and then his idea will be used for the good of the country.'

'Oh, Aunt Fanny — it does sound exciting,' said Anne. 'What's the secret?'

'I can't tell you that, silly child,' said her aunt, laughing. 'Why, even I myself don't know it. Come along, now — it's cold standing here. Timothy looks very fat and well, George dear.'

'Oh Mother, he's had a marvellous time at school,' said George. 'He really has. He chewed up the cook's old slippers . . .'

'And he chased the cat that lives in the stables every time he saw her,' said Anne.

'And he once got into the larder and ate a whole steak pie,' said George; 'and once . . .'

'Good gracious, George, I should think the school will refuse to have Timothy next term,' said her mother, in horror. 'Wasn't he well punished? I hope he was.'

'No — he wasn't,' said George, going rather red. 'You see, Mother, we are responsible for our pets and

203

their behaviour ourselves — so if ever Timothy does anything bad *I'm* punished for it, because I haven't shut him up properly, or something like that.'

'Well, you must have had quite a lot of punishments then,' said her mother, as she drove the little pony-trap along the frosty roads. 'I really think that's rather a good idea!' There was a twinkle in her eyes, as she spoke. 'I think I'll keep on with the same idea — punish you every time Timothy misbehaves himself!'

The girls laughed. They felt happy and excited. Holidays were fun. Going back to Kirrin was lovely. Tomorrow the boys would come — and then Christmas would be there!

'Good old Kirrin Cottage!' said Anne, as they came in sight of the pretty old house. 'Oh — look, there's Kirrin Island!' The two looked out to sea, where the old ruined castle stood on the little island of Kirrin — what adventures they had had there in the summer!

The girls went into the house. 'Quentin!' called George's mother. 'Quentin! The girls are here.'

Uncle Quentin came out of his study at the other side of the house. Anne thought he looked taller and darker than ever. 'And frownier!' she said to herself. Uncle Quentin might be very clever, but Anne preferred someone jolly and smiling like her own father. She shook hands with her uncle politely, and watched George kiss him.

'Well!' said Uncle Quentin to Anne. 'I hear I've got to get a tutor for you! At least, for the two boys. My word, you *will* have to behave yourself with a tutor, I can tell you!'

This was meant to be a joke, but it didn't sound very nice to Anne and George. People you had to behave well with were usually very strict and tiresome. Both girls were glad when George's father had gone back into his study.

'Your father has been working far too hard lately,' said George's mother to her. 'He is tired out. Thank goodness his book is nearly finished. He had hoped to finish it by Christmas so that he could join in the fun and games — but now he says he can't.'

'What a pity,' said Anne, politely, though secretly she thought it was a good thing. It wouldn't be much fun having Uncle Quentin to play charades and things like that! 'Oh, Aunt Fanny, I'm so looking forward to seeing Julian and Dick — and won't they be pleased to see Tim and George? Aunt Fanny, nobody calls George Georgina at school, not even our Form mistress. I was rather hoping they would, because I wanted to see what would happen when she refused to answer to Georgina! George, you liked school, didn't you?'

'Yes,' said George, 'I did. I thought I'd hate being with a lot of others, but it's fun, after all. But Mother, you won't find my report very good, I'm afraid. There were such a lot of things I was bad at because I'd never done them before.'

'Well, you'd never been to school before!' said her mother. 'I'll explain it to your father if he gets upset. Now go along and get ready for a late tea. You must be very hungry.'

The girls went upstairs to their little room. 'I'm glad I'm not spending my hols by myself,' said George. 'I've had much more fun since I've known you and the boys. Hi, Timothy, where have you gone?'

'He's gone to smell all round the house to make sure it's his proper home!' said Anne, with a giggle. 'He wants to know if the kitchen smells the same — and the bathroom — and his basket. It must be just as exciting for him to come home for the holidays as it is for us!'

Anne was right. Timothy was thrilled to be back again. He ran round George's mother, sniffing at her legs in friendliness, pleased to see her again. He ran into the kitchen but soon came out again because someone new was there — Joanna the cook — a fat, panting person who eyed him with suspicion.

'You can come into this kitchen once a day for your dinner,' said Joanna. 'And that's all. I'm not having meat and sausages and chicken disappearing under my nose if I can help it. I know what dogs are, I do!'

Timothy ran into the scullery and sniffed round there. He ran into the dining-room and the sitting-room, and was pleased to find they had the same old smell. He put his nose to the door of the study where George's father worked, and sniffed very cautiously. He didn't mean to go in. Timothy was just as wary of George's father as the others were!

He ran upstairs to the girls' bedroom again. Where was his basket? Ah, there it was by the window-seat. Good! That meant he was to sleep in the girls' bedroom once more. He curled himself up in his basket, and thumped loudly with his tail.

'Glad to be back,' said his tail, 'glad — to — be — back!'

2

All together again

The next day the boys came back. Anne and George went to meet them with Timothy. George drove the pony-trap, and Tim sat beside her. Anne could hardly wait for the train to stop at the station. She ran along the platform, looking for Julian and Dick in the carriages that passed.

Then she saw them. They were looking out of a window at the back of the train, waving and yelling.

'Anne! Anne! Here we are! Hallo, George! Oh, there's Timothy!'

'Julian! Dick!' yelled Anne. Timothy began to bark and leap about. It was most exciting.

'Oh, Julian! It's lovely to see you both again!' cried Anne, giving her two brothers a hug each. Timothy leapt up and licked them both. He was beside himself with joy. Now he had all the children around him that he loved.

The three children and the dog stood happily together, all talking at once while the porter got the luggage out of the train. Anne suddenly remembered George. She looked round her. She was nowhere to be seen, although she had come on the station platform with Anne.

'Where's old George?' said Julian. 'I saw her here when I waved out of the window.'

'She must have gone back to the pony-trap,' said Anne. 'Tell the porter to bring your trunks out to the trap, Julian. Come along! We'll go and find George.'

George was standing by the pony, holding his head. She looked rather gloomy, Anne thought. The boys went up to her.

'Hallo, George, old thing!' cried Julian, and gave her a hug. Dick did the same.

'What's up?' asked Anne, wondering at George's sudden silence.

'I believe George felt left-out!' said Julian with a grin. 'Funny old Georgina!'

'*Don't* call me Georgina!' said the little girl fiercely. The boys laughed.

'Ah, it's the same fierce old George, all right,' said Dick, and gave the girl a friendly slap on the shoulder. 'Oh, George — it's good to see you again. Do you remember our marvellous adventures in the summer?'

George felt her awkwardness slipping away from her. She *had* felt left-out when she had seen the great welcome that the two boys gave to their small sister — but no one could sulk for long with Julian and

Dick. They just wouldn't let anyone feel left-out or awkward or sulky.

The four children climbed into the trap. The porter heaved in the two trunks. There was only just room for them. Timothy sat on top of the trunks, his tail wagging nineteen to the dozen, and his tongue hanging out because he was panting with delight.

'You two girls were lucky to be able to take Tim to school with you,' said Dick, patting the big dog lovingly. 'No pets are allowed at our school. Awfully hard on those fellows who like live things.'

'Thompson Minor kept white mice,' said Julian. 'And one day they escaped and met Matron round a corner of the passage. She squealed the place down.'

The girls laughed. The boys always had funny tales to tell when they got home.

'And Kennedy keeps snails,' said Dick. 'You know, snails sleep for the winter — but Kennedy kept his in far too warm a place, and they all crawled out of their box and went up the walls. You should have heard how we laughed when the geography master asked Thompson to point out Cape Town on the map — and there was one of the snails in the very place!'

Everyone laughed again. It was so good to be all together once more. They were very much of an age — Julian was twelve, George and Dick were eleven, and Anne was ten. Holidays and Christmas time were in front of them. No wonder they laughed at everything, even the silliest little joke!

'It's good that Mummy is getting on all right, isn't it?' said Dick, as the pony went along the road at a

210

spanking trot. 'I was disappointed not to go home, I must say — I did want to go to see Aladdin and the Lamp, and the Circus — but still, it's good to be back at Kirrin Cottage again. I wish we could have some more exciting adventures. Not a hope of that this time, though.'

'There's one snag about these hols,' said Julian. 'And that's the tutor. I hear we've got to have one because Dick and I missed so much school this term, and we've got to take important exams next summer.'

'Yes,' said Anne. 'I wonder what he'll be like. I do hope he will be a sport. Uncle Quentin is going to choose one today.'

Julian and Dick made faces at one another. They felt sure that any tutor chosen by Uncle Quentin would be anything but a sport. Uncle Quentin's idea of a tutor would be somebody strict and gloomy and forbidding.

Never mind! He wouldn't come for a day or two. And he *might* be fun. The boys cheered up and pulled Timothy's thick coat. The dog pretended to growl and bite. *He* wasn't worried about tutors. Lucky Timothy!

They all arrived at Kirrin Cottage. The boys were really pleased to see their aunt, and rather relieved when she said that their uncle had not yet come back.

'He's gone to see two or three men who have answered the advertisement for a tutor,' she said. 'He won't be long before he's back.'

'Mother, I haven't got to do lessons in the hols too,

have I?' asked George. Nothing had yet been said to her about this, and she longed to know.

'Oh yes, George,' said her mother. 'Your father has seen your report, and although it isn't really a bad one, and we certainly didn't expect a marvellous one, still it does show that you are behind your age in some things. A little extra coaching will soon help you along.'

George looked gloomy. She had expected this but it was tiresome all the same. 'Anne's the only one who won't have to do lessons,' she said.

'I'll do some too,' promised Anne. 'Perhaps not always, George, if it's a very fine day, for instance — but sometimes, just to keep you company.'

'Thanks,' said George. 'But you needn't. I shall have Timmy.'

George's mother looked doubtful about this. 'We'll have to see what the tutor says about that,' she said.

'Mother! If the tutor says I can't have Timothy in the room, I jolly well won't do holiday lessons!' began George, fiercely.

Her mother laughed. 'Well, well — here's our fierce, hot-tempered George again!' she said. 'Go along, you two boys, and wash your hands and do your hair. You seem to have collected all the grime on the railway.'

The children and Timothy went upstairs. It was such fun to be five again. They always counted Tim as one of themselves. He went everywhere with them, and really seemed to understand every single word they said.

212

'I wonder what sort of a tutor Uncle Quentin will choose,' said Dick, as he scrubbed his nails. 'If only he would choose the right kind — someone jolly and full of fun, who knows that holiday lessons are sickening to have, and tries to make up for them by being a sport out of lesson-time. I suppose we'll have to work every morning.'

'Hurry up. I want my tea,' said Julian. 'Come on down, Dick. We'll know about the tutor soon enough!'

They all went down together, and sat round the table. Joanna the cook had made a lovely lot of buns and a great big cake. There was not much left of either by the time the four children had finished!

Uncle Quentin returned just as they were finishing. He seemed rather pleased with himself. He shook hands with the two boys and asked them if they had had a good term.

'Did you get a tutor, Uncle Quentin?' asked Anne, who could see that everyone was simply bursting to know this.

'Ah — yes, I did,' said her uncle. He sat down, while Aunt Fanny poured him out a cup of tea. 'I interviewed three applicants, and had almost chosen the last one, when another fellow came in, all in a hurry. Said he had only just seen the advertisement, and hoped he wasn't too late.'

'Did you choose him?' asked Dick.

'I did,' said his uncle. 'He seemed a most intelligent fellow. Even knew about me and my work! And he had the most wonderful letters of recommendation.'

'I don't think the children need to know all these details,' murmured Aunt Fanny. 'Anyway — you asked him to come?'

'Oh yes,' said Uncle Quentin. 'He's a good bit older than the others — they were rather young

214

fellows — this one seems very responsible and intelligent. I'm sure you'll like him, Fanny. He'll fit in here very well. I feel I would like to have him to talk to me sometimes in the evening.'

The children couldn't help feeling that the new tutor sounded rather alarming. Their uncle smiled at the gloomy faces.

'You'll like Mr Roland,' he said. 'He knows how to handle youngsters — knows he's got to be very firm, and to see that you know a good bit more at the end of the holidays than you did at the beginning.'

This sounded even more alarming. All four children wished heartily that Aunt Fanny had been to choose the tutor, and not Uncle Quentin.

'When is he coming?' asked George.

'Tomorrow,' said her father. 'You can all go to meet him at the station. That will make a nice welcome for him.'

'We *had* thought of taking the bus and going to do a bit of Christmas shopping,' said Julian, seeing Anne looked very disappointed.

'Oh, no, you must certainly go and meet Mr Roland,' said his uncle. 'I told him you would. And mind you, you four — no nonsense with him! You've to do as you're told, and you must work hard with him, because your father is paying very high fees for his coaching. I'm paying a third, because I want him to coach George a little too — so George, you must do your best.'

'I'll try,' said George. 'If he's nice, I'll do my very best.'

'You'll do your best whether you think him nice or

215

not!' said her father, frowning. 'He will arrive by the ten-thirty train. Be sure to be there in time.'

'I do hope he won't be too strict,' said Dick, that evening, when the five of them were alone for a minute or two. 'It's going to spoil the hols, if we have someone down on us all the time. And I do hope he'll like Timothy.'

George looked up at once. 'Like Timothy!' she said. 'Of course he'll like Timothy! How couldn't he?'

'Well — your father didn't like Timothy very much last summer,' said Dick. 'I don't see how anyone could *dislike* darling Tim — but there are people who don't like dogs, you know, George.'

'If Mr Roland doesn't like Timothy, I'll not do a single thing for him,' said George. 'Not one single thing!'

'She's gone all fierce again!' said Dick, with a laugh. 'My word — the sparks will fly if Mr Roland dares to dislike our Timothy!'

3
The new tutor

Next morning the sun was out, all the sea-mist that had hung about for the last two days had disappeared, and Kirrin Island showed plainly at the mouth of Kirrin Bay. The children stared longingly at the ruined castle on it.

'I do wish we could get over to the castle,' said Dick. 'It looks quite calm enough, George.'

'It's very rough by the island,' said George. 'It always is at this time of year. I know Mother wouldn't let us go.'

'It's a lovely island, and it's all our own!' said Anne. 'You said you would share it with us for ever and ever, didn't you, George?'

'Yes, I did,' said George. 'And so I will, dungeons and all. Come on — we must get the trap out. We shall be late meeting the train if we stand here all day looking at the island.'

They got the pony and trap and set off down the hard lanes. Kirrin Island disappeared behind the cliffs as they turned inland to the station.

'Did all this land round about belong to your family once upon a time?' asked Julian.

'Yes, all of it,' said George. 'Now we don't own anything except Kirrin Island, our own house — and that farm away over there — Kirrin Farm.'

She pointed with her whip. The children saw a fine old farm-house standing on a hill a good way off, over the heather-clad common.

'Who lives there?' asked Julian.

'Oh, an old farmer and his wife,' said George. 'They were nice to me when I was smaller. We'll go over there one day, if you like. Mother says they don't make the farm pay any more, and in the summertime they take in people who want a holiday.'

'Hark! That's the train whistling in the tunnel!' said Julian, suddenly. 'Buck up, for goodness' sake, George. We shan't be there in time!'

The four children and Timothy looked at the train coming out of the tunnel and drawing in at the station. The pony cantered along swiftly. They would be just in time.

'Who's going on to the platform to meet him?' asked George, as they drew into the little station yard. 'I'm not. I must look after Tim and the pony.'

'I don't want to,' said Anne. 'I'll stay with George.'

'Well, we'd better go, then,' said Julian, and he and Dick leapt out of the trap. They ran on to the platform just as the train pulled up.

Not many people got out. A woman clambered out
with a basket. A young man leapt out, whistling, the
son of the baker in the village. An old man climbed
down with difficulty. The tutor could be none of
those!

Then, right at the front of the train, rather a queer-looking man got out. He was short and burly, and he had a beard rather like a sailor. His eyes were piercingly blue, and his thick hair was sprinkled with grey. He glanced up and down the platform, and then beckoned to the porter.

'That must be Mr Roland,' said Julian to Dick. 'Come on — let's ask him. There's no one else it could be.'

The boys went up to the bearded man. 'Are you Mr Roland, sir?' he asked.

'I am,' said the man. 'I suppose you are Julian and Dick?'

'Yes, sir,' answered the boys together. 'We brought the pony-trap for your luggage.'

'Oh, fine,' said Mr Roland. His bright blue eyes looked the boys up and down, and he smiled. Julian and Dick liked him. He seemed sensible and jolly.

'Are the other two here as well?' said Mr Roland, walking down the platform, with the porter trailing behind with his luggage.

'Yes — George and Anne are outside with the trap,' said Julian.

'George and Anne,' said Mr Roland, in a puzzled voice. 'I thought the others were girls. I didn't know there was a third boy.'

'Oh, George is a girl,' said Dick, with a laugh. 'Her real name is Georgina.'

'And a very nice name too,' said Mr Roland.

'George doesn't think so,' said Julian. 'She won't answer if she's called Georgina. You'd better call her

George, sir!'

'Really?' said Mr Roland, in rather a chilly tone. Julian took a glance at him.

'Not quite so jolly as he looks!' thought the boy.

'Tim's out there too,' said Dick.

'Oh — and is Tim a boy or a girl?' inquired Mr Roland, cautiously.

'A dog, sir!' said Dick, with a grin.

Mr Roland seemed rather taken aback. 'A dog?' he said. 'I didn't know there was a dog in the household. Your uncle said nothing to me about a dog.'

'Don't you like dogs?' asked Julian, in surprise.

'No,' said Mr Roland, shortly. 'But I dare say your dog won't worry me much. Hallo, hallo — so here are the little girls! How do you do?'

George was not very pleased at being called a little girl. For one thing she hated to be spoken of as little, and for another thing she always tried to be a boy. She held out her hand to Mr Roland and said nothing. Anne smiled at him, and Mr Roland thought she was much the nicer of the two.

'Tim! Shake hands with Mr Roland!' said Julian to Timothy. This was one of Tim's really good tricks. He could hold out his right paw in a very polite manner. Mr Roland looked down at the big dog, and Tim looked back at him.

Then, very slowly and deliberately, Timothy turned his back on Mr Roland and climbed up into the pony-trap! Usually he put out his paw at once when told to, and the children stared at him in amazement.

221

'Timothy! What's come over you?' cried Dick. Tim put his ears down and did not move.

'He doesn't like you,' said George, looking at Mr Roland. 'That's very queer. He usually likes people. But perhaps you don't like dogs?'

'No, I don't, as a matter of fact,' said Mr Roland. 'I was once very badly bitten as a boy, and somehow or other I've never managed to like dogs since. But I dare say your Tim will take to me sooner or later.'

They all got into the trap. It was a tight squeeze. Timothy looked at Mr Roland's ankles as if he would rather like to nibble them. Anne laughed.

'Tim *is* behaving queerly!' she said. 'It's a good thing you haven't come to teach him, Mr Roland!' She smiled up at the tutor, and he smiled back, showing very white teeth. His eyes were as brilliant a blue as George's.

Anne liked him. He joked with the boys as they drove him, and both of them began to feel that their Uncle Quentin hadn't made such a bad choice after all.

Only George said nothing. She sensed that the tutor disliked Timothy, and George was not prepared to like anyone who didn't take to Timothy at first sight. She thought it was very queer too, that Tim would not shake paws with the tutor. 'He's a clever dog,' she thought. 'He knows Mr Roland doesn't like him, so he won't shake hands. I don't blame you, Tim darling, I wouldn't shake hands with anyone who didn't like *me*!'

Mr Roland was shown up to his room when he

222

arrived. Aunt Fanny came down and spoke to the children. 'Well! He seems very nice, youngish and jolly.'

'Youngish!' exclaimed Julian. 'Why, he's awfully old! Must be forty at the very least!'

Aunt Fanny laughed. 'Does he seem so old to you?' she said. 'Well, old or not, he'll be quite nice to you, I'm sure.'

'Aunt Fanny, we shan't begin lessons until after Christmas, shall we?' asked Julian, anxiously.

'Of course you will!' said his aunt. 'It is almost a week till Christmas — you don't suppose we have asked Mr Roland to come and do nothing till Christmas is over, do you?'

The children groaned. 'We wanted to do some Christmas shopping,' said Anne.

'Well, you can do that in the afternoons,' said her aunt. 'You will only do lessons in the morning, for three hours. That won't hurt any of you!'

The new tutor came downstairs at that moment, and Aunt Fanny took him to see Uncle Quentin. She came out after a while, looking very pleased.

'Mr Roland will be nice company for your uncle,' she said to Julian. 'I think they will get on very well together. Mr Roland seems to understand quite a bit about your uncle's work.'

'Let's hope he spends most of his time with him then!' said George, in a low voice.

'Come on out for a walk,' said Dick. 'It's so fine today. We shan't have lessons this morning, shall we, Aunt Fanny?'

'Oh, no,' said his aunt. 'You'll begin tomorrow. Go for a walk now, all of you — we shan't often get sunny days like this!'

'Let's go over to Kirrin Farm,' said Julian. 'It looks such a nice place. Show us the way, George.'

'Right!' said George. She whistled to Timothy, and he came bounding up. The five of them set off together, going down the lane, and then on to a rough road over the common that led to the farm on the distant hill.

It was lovely walking in the December sun. Their feet rang on the frosty path, and Tim's blunt claws made quite a noise as he pattered up and down, overjoyed at being with his four friends again.

After a good long walk across the common the children came to the farm-house. It was built of white stone, and stood strong and lovely on the hillside. George opened the farm-gate and went into the farm-yard. She kept her hand on Tim's collar for there were two farm-dogs somewhere about.

Someone clattered round the barn near by. It was an old man, and George hailed him loudly.

'Hallo, Mr Sanders! How are you?'

'Why, if it isn't Master George!' said the old fellow with a grin. George grinned too. She loved being called Master instead of Miss.

'These are my cousins,' shouted George. She turned to the others. 'He's deaf,' she said. 'You'll have to shout to make him hear.'

'I'm Julian,' said Julian in a loud voice and the others said their names too. The farmer beamed at them.

224

'You come along in and see the Missis,' he said.
'She'll be rare pleased to see you all. We've known
Master George since she was a baby, and we knew
her mother when *she* was a baby too, and we knew her
granny as well.'

'You must be very, very old,' said Anne.

The farmer smiled down at her.

'As old as my tongue and a little older than my
teeth!' he said, chuckling. 'Come away in now.'

They all went into the big, warm farm-house
kitchen, where a little old woman, as lively as a
bantam hen, was bustling about. She was just as
pleased to see the four children as her husband was.

'Well, there now!' she said. 'I haven't seen you for
months, Master George. I did hear that you'd gone
away to school.'

'Yes, I did,' said George. 'But I'm home for the
holidays now. Does it matter if I let Timothy loose,
Mrs Sanders? I think he'll be friendly if your dogs
are, too.'

'Yes, you let him loose,' said the old lady. 'He'll
have a fine time in the farm-yard with Ben and Rikky.
Now what would you like to drink? Hot milk? Cocoa?
Coffee? And I've some new shortbread baked
yesterday. You shall have some of that.'

'Ah, the wife's very busy this week, cooking up all
sorts of things,' said the old farmer, as his wife
bustled off to the larder. 'We've company this
Christmas!'

'Have you?' said George, surprised, for she knew
that the old pair had never had any children of their
own. 'Who is coming? Anyone I know?'

225

'Two artists from London Town!' said the old
farmer: 'Wrote and asked us to take them for three
weeks over Christmas — and offered us good money

too. So the old wife's as busy as a bee.'

'Are they going to paint pictures?' asked Julian, who rather fancied himself as an artist, too. 'I wonder if I could come and talk to them some day. I'm rather good at pictures myself. They might give me a few hints.'

'You come along whenever you like,' said old Mrs Sanders, making cocoa in a big jug. She set out a plate of most delicious-looking shortbreads, and the children ate them hungrily.

'I should think the two artists will be rather lonely down here, in the depths of the country at Christmas-time,' said George. 'Do they know anyone?'

'They say they don't know a soul,' said Mrs Sanders. 'But there — artists are queer folk. I've had some here before. They seemed to like mooning about all alone. These two will be happy enough, I'll be bound.'

'They should be, with all the good things you're cooking up for them,' said her old husband. 'Well, I must be out after the sheep. Good-day to you, youngsters. Come again and see us sometimes.'

He went out. Old Mrs Sanders chattered on to the children as she bustled about the big kitchen. Timothy ran in and settled down on the rug by the fire.

He suddenly saw a tabby cat slinking along by the wall, all her hairs on end with fear of the strange dog. He gave a delighted wuff and sprang at the cat. She fled out of the kitchen into the old panelled hall. Tim flew after her, taking no notice at all of George's stern shout.

The cat tried to leap on top of an old grandfather

228

clock in the hall. With a joyous bark Tim sprang too. He flung himself against a polished panel — and then a most extraordinary thing happened!

The panel disappeared — and a dark hole showed in the old wall! George, who had followed Tim out into the hall, gave a loud cry of surprise. 'Look! Mrs Sanders, come and look!'

4

An exciting discovery

Old Mrs Sanders and the other three children rushed out into the hall when they heard George's shout.

'What's up?' cried Julian. 'What's happened?'

'Tim sprang at the cat, missed her, and fell hard against the panelled wall,' said George, 'and the panel moved, and look — there's a hole in the wall!'

'It's a secret panel!' cried Dick, in excitement, peering into the hole. 'Golly! Did you know there was one here, Mrs Sanders?'

'Oh yes,' said the old lady. 'This house is full of funny things like that. I'm very careful when I polish that panel, because if I rub too hard in the top corner, it always slides back.'

'What's behind the panel?' asked Julian. The hole was only about the width of his head, and when he stuck his head inside, he could see only darkness. The wall itself was about eight inches behind the panelling, and was of stone.

'Get a candle, do get a candle!' said Anne, thrilled. 'You haven't got a torch, have you, Mrs Sanders?'

'No,' said the old woman. 'But you can get a candle if you like. There's one on the kitchen mantelpiece.'

Anne shot off to get it. Julian lighted it and put it into the hole behind the panel. The others pushed against him to try and peep inside.

'Don't,' said Julian, impatiently. 'Wait your turn, sillies! Let me have a look.'

He had a good look, but there didn't really seem anything to see. It was all darkness behind, and stone wall. He gave the candle to Dick, and then each of the children had a turn at peeping. Old Mrs Sanders had gone back to the kitchen. She was used to the sliding panel!

'She said this house was full of queer things like that,' said Anne. 'What other things are there, do you think? Let's ask her.'

They slid the panel back into place and went to find Mrs Sanders. 'Mrs Sanders, what other funny things are there in Kirrin Farmhouse?' asked Julian.

'There's a cupboard upstairs with a false back,' said Mrs Sanders. 'Don't look so excited! There's nothing in it at all! And there's a big stone over there by the fireplace that pulls up to show a hidey-hole. I suppose in the old days people wanted good hiding-places for things.'

The children ran to the stone she pointed out. It had an iron ring in it, and was easily pulled up. Below was a hollowed-out place, big enough to take a small box. It was empty now, but all the same it looked exciting.

'Where's the cupboard?' asked Julian.

'My old legs are too tired to go traipsing upstairs this morning,' said the farmer's wife. 'But you can go yourselves. Up the stairs, turn to the right, and go into the second door you see. The cupboard is at the farther end. Open the door and feel about at the bottom till you come across a dent in the wood. Press it hard, and the false back slides to the side.'

The four children and Timothy ran upstairs as fast as they could, munching shortbread as they went. This really was a very exciting morning!

They found the cupboard and opened the door. All four went down on hands and knees to press round the bottom of the cupboard to find the dented place. Anne found it.

'I've got it!' she cried. She pressed hard, but her little fingers were not strong enough to work the mechanism of the sliding back. Julian had to help her.

There was a creaking noise, and the children saw the false back of the cupboard sliding sideways. A big space showed behind, large enough to take a fairly thin man.

'A jolly good hiding-place,' said Julian. 'Anyone could hide there and no one would ever know!'

'I'll get in and you shut me up,' said Dick. 'It would be exciting.'

He got into the space. Julian slid the back across, and Dick could no longer be seen!

232

'Bit of a tight fit!' he called. 'And awfully dark! Let me out again.'

The children all took turns at going into the space behind the back of the cupboard and being shut up. Anne didn't like it very much.

They went down to the warm kitchen again. 'It's a most exciting cupboard, Mrs Sanders,' said Julian. 'I do wish we lived in a house like this, full of secrets!'

'Can we come and play in that cupboard again?' asked George.

'No, I'm afraid you can't, Master George,' said Mrs Sanders. 'That room where the cupboard is, is one the two gentlemen are going to have.'

'Oh!' said Julian, disappointed. 'Shall you tell them about the sliding back, Mrs Sanders?'

'I don't expect so,' said the old lady. 'It's only you children that get excited about things like that, bless you. Two gentlemen wouldn't think twice about it.'

'How funny grown-ups are!' said Anne, puzzled. 'I'm quite certain I shall be thrilled to see a sliding panel or a trap-door even when I'm a hundred.'

'Same here,' said Dick. 'Could I just go and look into the sliding panel in the hall once more, Mrs Sanders? I'll take the candle.'

Dick never knew why he suddenly wanted to have another look. It was just an idea he had. The others didn't bother to go with him, for there really was nothing to see behind the panelling except the old stone wall.

Dick took the candle and went into the hall. He pressed on the panel at the top and it slid back. He put the candle inside and had another good look. There was nothing at all to be seen. Dick took out his head and put in his arm, stretching along the wall as far as his hand would reach. He was just about to take it back when his fingers found a hole in the wall.

'Funny!' said Dick. 'Why should there be a hole in the stone wall just there?'

He stuck in his finger and thumb and worked them about. He felt a little ridge inside the wall, rather like a bird's perch, and was able to get hold of it. He wriggled his fingers about the perch, but nothing happened. Then he got a good hold and pulled.

The stone came right out! Dick was so surprised that he let go the heavy stone and it fell to the ground behind the panelling with a crash!

The noise brought the others out into the hall. 'Whatever are you doing, Dick?' said Julian. 'Have you broken something?'

'No,' said Dick, his face reddening with excitement. 'I say — I put my hand in here — and found a hole in one of the stones the wall is made of — and I got hold of a sort of ridge with my finger and thumb and pulled. The stone came right out, and I got such a surprise I let go. It fell, and that's what you heard!'

'Golly!' said Julian, trying to push Dick away from the open panel. 'Let me see.'

'No, Julian,' said Dick, pushing him away. 'This is *my* discovery. Wait till I see if I can feel anything in the hole. It's difficult to get at!'

The others waited impatiently. Julian could hardly prevent himself from pushing Dick right

234

away. Dick put his arm in as far as he could, and curved his hand round to get into the space behind where the stone had been. His fingers felt about and he closed them round something that felt like a book. Cautiously and carefully he brought it out.

'An old book!' he said.

'What's in it?' cried Anne.

They turned the pages carefully. They were so dry and brittle that some of them fell into dust.

'I think it's a book of recipes,' said Anne, as her sharp eyes read a few words in the old brown, faded handwriting. 'Let's take it to Mrs. Sanders.'

The children carried the book to the old lady. She laughed at their beaming faces. She took the book and looked at it, not at all excited.

'Yes,' she said. 'It's a book of recipes, that's all it is. See the name in the front — Alice Mary Sanders — that must have been my great-grandmother. She was famous for her medicines, I know. It was said she could cure any ill in man or animal, no matter what it was.'

'It's a pity it's so hard to read her writing,' said Julian, disappointed. 'The whole book is falling to pieces too. It must be very old.'

'Do you think there's anything else in that hidey-hole?' asked Anne. 'Julian, you go and put *your* arm in, it's longer than Dick's.'

'There didn't seem to be anything else at all,' said Dick. 'It's a very small place — just a few inches of hollow space behind that brick or stone that fell down.'

236

'Well, I'll just put my hand in and see,' said Julian. They all went back into the hall. Julian put his arm into the open panel, and slid it along the wall to where the stone had fallen out. His hand went into the space there, and his long fingers groped about, feeling for anything else that might be there.

There was something else, something soft and flat that felt like leather. Eagerly the boy's fingers closed over it and he drew it out carefully, half afraid that it might fall to pieces with age.

'I've got something!' he said, his eyes gleaming brightly. 'Look — what is it?'

The others crowded round. 'It's rather like Daddy's tobacco pouch,' said Anne, feeling it. 'The same shape. Is there anything inside?'

It was a tobacco pouch, very dark brown, made of soft leather and very much worn. Carefully Julian undid the flap, and unrolled the leather.

A few bits of black tobacco were still in the pouch — but there was something else, too! Tightly rolled up in the last bit of pouch was a piece of linen. Julian took it out and unrolled it. He put it flat on the hall-table.

The children stared at it. There were marks and signs on the linen, done in black ink that had hardly faded. But the four of them could not make head or tail of the marks.

'It's not a map,' said Julian. 'It seems a sort of code, or something. I do wonder what it means. I wish we could make it out. It must be some sort of secret.'

The children stared at the piece of linen, very thrilled. It was so old — and contained some kind of secret. Whatever could it be?

They ran to show it to Mrs Sanders. She was studying the old recipe book, and her face glowed with pleasure as she raised it to look at the excited children.

'This book's a wonder!' she said. 'I can hardly read the writing, but here's a recipe for backache. I shall try it myself. My back aches so much at the end of the day. Now, you listen . . .'

But the children didn't want to listen to recipes for backache. They pushed the piece of linen on to Mrs Sanders's lap.

'Look! What's this about, Mrs Sanders? Do you know? We found it in a kind of tobacco pouch in that place behind the panel.'

Mrs Sanders took off her glasses, polished them, and put them on again. She looked carefully at the piece of linen with its strange marks.

She shook her head. 'No — this doesn't make any sense to me. And what's this now? — it looks like an old tobacco pouch. Ah, my John would like that, I guess. He's got such an old one that it won't hold his tobacco any more! This is old too — but there's a lot of wear in it yet.'

'Mrs Sanders, do you want this piece of linen too?' asked Julian, anxiously. He was longing to take it home and study it. He felt certain there was some kind of exciting secret hidden there, and he could not bear the thought of leaving it with Mrs Sanders.

'You take it, Master Julian, if you want it,' said Mrs Sanders, with a laugh. 'I'll keep the recipes for myself, and John shall have the pouch. You can have the old rag if you want it, though it beats me why you set such store by it! Ah, here's John!'

She raised her voice and shouted to the deaf old man. 'Hey, John, here's a tobacco pouch for you. The children found it somewhere behind that panel that opens in the hall.'

John took it and fingered it. 'It's a queer one,' he said, 'but better than mine. Well, youngsters, I don't want to hurry you, but it's one o'clock now, and you'd best be going if it's near your dinner-time!'

'Gracious!' said Julian. 'We shall be late! Good-bye, Mrs Sanders, and thanks awfully for the shortbread and this old rag. We'll try our best to make out what's on it and tell you. Hurry, everyone! Where's Tim? Come on, Timothy, we're late!'

The five of them ran off quickly. They really were late, and had to run most of the way, which meant that it was difficult to talk. But they were so excited about their morning that they panted remarks to one another as they went.

'I wonder what this old rag says!' panted Julian. 'I mean to find out. I'm sure it's something mysterious.'

'Shall we tell anyone?' asked Dick.

'No!' said George. 'Let's keep it a secret.'

'If Anne starts to give away anything, kick her under the table, like we did last summer,' said Julian, with a grin. Poor Anne always found it difficult to keep a secret, and often had to be nudged or kicked when she began to give things away.

'I won't say a word,' said Anne, indignantly. 'And don't you dare to kick me. It only makes me cry out and then the grown-ups want to know why.'

'We'll have a good old puzzle over this piece of linen after dinner,' said Julian. 'I bet we'll find out what it says, if we really make up our minds to!'

'Here we are,' said George. 'Not too late. Hallo, Mother! We won't be a minute washing our hands! We've had a lovely time.'

5

An unpleasant walk

After dinner the four children went upstairs to the
boys' bedroom and spread out the bit of linen on a
table there. There were words here and there,
scrawled in rough printing. There was the sign of a
compass, with E marked clearly for East. There were
eight rough squares, and in one of them, right in the
middle, was a cross. It was all very mysterious.

'You know, I believe these words are Latin,' said
Julian, trying to make them out. 'But I can't read
them properly. And I expect if I *could* read them, I
wouldn't know what they meant. I wish we knew
someone who could read Latin like this.'

'Could your father, George?' asked Anne.

'I expect so,' said George. But nobody wanted to
ask George's father. He might take the curious old
rag away. He might forget all about it, he might even
burn it. Scientists were such queer people.

'What about Mr Roland?' said Dick. 'He's a tutor. He knows Latin.'

'We won't ask him till we know a bit more about him,' said Julian, cautiously. 'He *seems* jolly and nice — but you never know. Oh, blow — I wish we could make this out, I really do.'

'There are two words at the top,' said Dick, and he tried to spell them out. 'VIA OCCULTA.' 'What do you think they could mean, Julian?'

'Well — the only thing I can think of that they can mean is — Secret Way, or something like that,' said Julian, screwing up his forehead into a frown.

'Secret Way!' said Anne, her eyes shining. 'Oh, I hope it's that! Secret Way! How exciting. What sort of secret way would it be, Julian?'

'How do I know, Anne, silly?' said Julian. 'I don't even know that the words are meant to mean "Secret Way". It's really a guess on my part.'

'If they did mean that — the linen might have directions to find the Secret Way, whatever it is,' said Dick. 'Oh Julian — isn't it exasperating that we can't read it? Do, do try. You know more Latin than I do.'

'It's so hard to read the funny old letters,' said Julian, trying again. 'No — it's no good at all. I can't make them out.'

Steps came up the stairs, and the door opened. Mr Roland looked in.

'Hallo, hallo!' he said. 'I wondered where you all were. What about a walk over the cliffs?'

'We'll come,' said Julian, rolling up the old rag.

'What have you got there? Anything interesting?'

242

asked Mr Roland.

'It's a —' began Anne, and at once all the others began to talk, afraid that Anne was going to give the secret away.

'It's a wonderful afternoon for a walk.'

'Come on, let's get our things on!'

'Tim, Tim, where are you?' George gave a piercing whistle. Tim was under the bed and came bounding out. Anne went red as she guessed why all the others had interrupted her so quickly.

'Idiot,' said Julian, under his breath. 'Baby.'

Fortunately Mr Roland said no more about the piece of linen he had seen Julian rolling up. He was looking at Tim.

'I suppose he must come,' he said. George stared at him in indignation.

'Of course he must!' she said. 'We never never go anywhere without Timothy.'

Mr Roland went downstairs, and the children got ready to go out. George was scowling. The very idea of leaving Tim behind made her angry.

'You nearly gave our secret away, you silly,' said Dick to Anne.

'I didn't think,' said the little girl, looking ashamed of herself. 'Anyway, Mr Roland seems very nice. I think we might ask him if he could help us to understand those funny words.'

'You leave that to me to decide,' said Julian, crossly. 'Now don't you dare to say a word.'

They all set out, Timothy too. Mr Roland need not have worried about the dog, for Timothy would not

go near him. It was very queer, really. He kept away
from the tutor, and took not the slightest notice of
him even when Mr Roland spoke to him.

'He's not usually like that,' said Dick. 'He's a most
friendly dog, really.'

'Well, as I've got to live in the same house with
him, I must try and make him friends with me,' said
the tutor. 'Hi, Timothy! Come here! I've got a biscuit
in my pocket.'

Timothy pricked up his ears at the word 'biscuit',
but did not even look towards Mr Roland. He put his
tail down and went to George. She patted him.

'If he doesn't like anyone, not even a biscuit or a
bone will make him go to them when he is called,' she
said.

Mr Roland gave it up. He put the biscuit back into
his pocket. 'He's a queer-looking dog, isn't he?' he
said. 'A terrible mongrel! I must say I prefer
well-bred dogs.'

George went purple in the face. 'He's *not* queer-
looking!' she spluttered. 'He's not nearly so queer-
looking as you! He's not a terrible mongrel. He's the
best dog in the world!'

'I think you are being a little rude,' said Mr
Roland, stiffly. 'I don't allow my pupils to be cheeky,
Georgina.'

Calling her Georgina made George still more
furious. She lagged behind with Tim, looking as
black as a thundercloud. The others felt uncomfortable. They knew what tempers George got into, and
how difficult she could be. She had been so much

better and happier since the summer, when they had come to stay for the first time. They did hope she wasn't going to be silly and get into rows. It would spoil the Christmas holidays.

Mr Roland took no more notice of George. He did not speak to her, but strode on ahead with the others, doing his best to be jolly. He could really be very funny, and the boys began to laugh at him. He took Anne's hand, and the little girl jumped along beside him, enjoying the walk.

Julian felt sorry for George. It wasn't nice to be left out of things, and he knew how George hated anything like that. He wondered if he dared to put in a good word for her. It might make things easier.

'Mr Roland, sir,' he began. 'Could you call my cousin by the name she likes — George — she simply hates Georgina. And she's very fond of Tim. She can't bear anyone to say horrid things about him.'

Mr Roland looked surprised. 'My dear boy, I am sure you mean well,' he said, in rather a dry sort of voice, 'but I hardly think I want your advice about any of my pupils. I shall follow my own wishes in my treatment of Georgina, not yours. I want to be friends with you all, and I am sure we shall be — but Georgina has got to be sensible, as you three are.'

Julian felt rather squashed. He went red and looked at Dick. Dick gave him a squeeze on his arm. The boys knew George could be silly and difficult, especially if anyone didn't like her beloved dog — but they thought Mr Roland might try to be a bit more understanding too. Dick slipped behind and walked with George.

'You needn't walk with me,' said George at once, her blue eyes glinting. 'Walk with your friend Mr Roland.'

246

'He isn't my friend,' said Dick. 'Don't be silly.'

'I'm not silly,' said George, in a tight sort of voice. 'I heard you all laughing and joking with him. You go on and have a good laugh again. I've got Timothy.'

'George, it's Christmas holidays,' said Dick. 'Do let's all be friends. Do. Don't let's spoil Christmas.'

'I can't like anyone who doesn't like Tim,' said George, obstinately.

'Well, after all, Mr Roland did offer him a biscuit,' said Dick, trying to make peace as hard as he could.

George said nothing. Her small face looked fierce. Dick tried again.

'George! Promise to try and be nice till Christmas is over, anyway. Don't let's spoil Christmas, for goodness' sake! Come on, George.'

'All right,' said George, at last. 'I'll try.'

'Come and walk with us then,' said Dick. So George caught up the others, and tried not to look too sulky. Mr Roland guessed that Dick had been trying to make George behave, and he included her in his talk. He could not make her laugh, but she did at least answer politely.

'Is that Kirrin Farmhouse?' asked Mr Roland, as they came in sight of the farm.

'Yes. Do you know it?' asked Julian, in surprise.

'No, no,' said Mr Roland, at once, 'I've heard of it, and wondered if that was the place.'

'We went there this morning,' said Anne. 'It's an exciting place.' She looked at the others, wondering if they would mind if she said anything about the things they had seen that morning. Julian thought for a

247

moment. After all, it couldn't matter telling him about the stone in the kitchen and the false back to the cupboard. Mrs Sanders would tell anyone that. He could speak about the sliding panel in the hall too, and say they had found an old recipe book there. He did not need to say anything about the old bit of marked linen.

So he told their tutor about the exciting things there had been at the old farm-house, but said nothing at all about the linen and its strange markings. Mr Roland listened with the greatest interest.

'This is all very remarkable,' he said. 'Very remarkable indeed. Most interesting. You say the old couple live there quite alone?'

'Well, they are having two people to stay over Christmas,' said Dick. 'Artists. Julian thought he would go over and talk to them. He can paint awfully well, you know.'

'Can he really?' said Mr Roland. 'Well, he must show me some of his pictures. But I don't think he'd better go and worry the artists at the farmhouse. They might not like it.'

This remark made Julian feel obstinate. He made up his mind at once that he *would* go and talk to the two artists when he got the chance!

It was quite a pleasant walk on the whole except that George was quiet, and Timothy would not go anywhere near Mr Roland. When they came to a frozen pond Dick threw sticks on it for Tim to fetch. It was so funny to see him go slithering about on his long legs, trying to run properly!

Everyone threw sticks for the dog, and Tim fetched all the sticks except Mr Roland's. When the tutor threw a stick the dog looked at it and took no more notice. It was almost as if he had said, 'What, *your* stick! No, thank you!'

'Now, home we go,' said Mr Roland, trying not to look annoyed with Tim. 'We shall just be in time for tea!'

6

Lessons with Mr Roland

Next morning the children felt a little gloomy.
Lessons! How horrid in the holidays! Still, Mr
Roland wasn't so bad. The children had not had him
with them in the sitting-room the night before,
because he had gone to talk to their uncle. So they
were able to get out the mysterious bit of linen again
and pore over it.

But it wasn't a bit of good. Nobody could make
anything of it at all. Secret Way! What did it mean?
Was it really directions for a Secret Way? And where
was the way, and why was it secret? It was most
exasperating not to be able to find out.

'I really feel we'll have to ask someone soon,'
Julian had said with a sigh. 'I can't bear this mystery
much longer. I keep on and on thinking of it.'

He had dreamt of it too that night, and now it was
morning, with lessons ahead. He wondered what

lesson Mr Roland would take — Latin perhaps. Then he could ask him what the words 'VIA OCCULTA' meant.

Mr Roland had seen all their reports and had noted the subjects they were weak in. One was Latin, and another was French. Maths were very weak in both Dick's report and George's. Both children must be helped on in those. Geometry was Julian's weakest spot.

Anne was not supposed to need any coaching. 'But if you like to come along and join us, I'll give you some painting to do,' said Mr Roland, his blue eyes twinkling at her. He liked Anne. She was not difficult and sulky like George.

Anne loved painting. 'Oh, yes,' she said, happily, 'I'd love to do some painting. I can paint flowers, Mr Roland. I'll paint you some red poppies and blue cornflowers out of my head.'

'We will start at half-past nine,' said Mr Roland. 'We are to work in the sitting-room. Take your school-books there, and be ready punctually.'

So all the children were there, sitting round a table, their books in front of them, at half-past nine. Anne had some painting water and her painting-box. The others looked at her enviously. Lucky Anne, to be doing painting while they worked hard at difficult things like Latin and Maths!

'Where's Timothy?' asked Julian in a low voice, as they waited for their tutor to come in.

'Under the table,' said George, defiantly. 'I'm sure he'll lie still. Don't any of you say anything about

251

him. I want him there. I'm not going to do lessons without Tim here.'

'I don't see why he shouldn't be here with us,' said Dick. 'He's very very good. Sh! Here comes Mr Roland.'

The tutor came in, his black beard bristling round his mouth and chin. His eyes looked very piercing in the pale winter sunlight that filtered into the room. He told the children to sit down.

'I'll have a look at your exercise books first,' he said, 'and see what you were doing last term. You come first, Julian.'

Soon the little class were working quietly together. Anne was very busy painting a bright picture of poppies and cornflowers. Mr Roland admired it very much. Anne thought he really was very nice.

Suddenly there was a huge sigh from under the table. It was Tim, tired of lying so still. Mr Roland looked up, surprised. George at once sighed heavily, hoping that Mr Roland would think it was she who had sighed before.

'You sound tired, Georgina,' said Mr Roland. 'You shall all have a little break at eleven.'

George frowned. She hated being called Georgina. She put her foot cautiously on Timothy to warn him not to make any more noises. Tim licked her foot.

After a while, just when the class was at its very quietest, Tim felt a great wish to scratch himself very hard on his back. He got up. He sat down again with a thump, gave a grunt, and began to scratch himself furiously. The children all began to make noises to hide the sounds that Tim was making.

George clattered her feet on the floor. Julian began to cough, and let one of his books slip to the ground. Dick jiggled the table and spoke to Mr Roland.

'Oh dear, this sum is so hard; it really is! I keep doing it and doing it, and it simply *won't* come right!'

'Why all this sudden noise?' said Mr Roland in surprise. 'Stop tapping the floor with your feet, Georgina.'

Tim settled down quietly again. The children gave a sigh of relief. They became quiet, and Mr Roland told Dick to come to him with his Maths book.

The tutor took it, and stretched his legs out under the table, leaning back to speak to Dick. To his enormous surprise his feet struck something soft and warm — and then something nipped him sharply on the ankle! He drew in his feet with a cry of pain.

The children stared at him. He bent down and looked under the table. 'It's that dog,' he said, in disgust. 'The brute snapped at my ankles. He has made a hole in my trousers. Take him out, Georgina.'

Georgina said nothing. She sat as though she had not heard.

'She won't answer if you call her Georgina,' Julian reminded him.

'She'll answer me whatever I call her,' said Mr Roland, in a low and angry voice. 'I won't have that dog in here. If you don't take him out this very minute, Georgina, I will go to your father.'

George looked at him. She knew perfectly well that if she didn't take Tim out, and Mr Roland went to her father, he would order Timothy to live in the garden kennel, and that would be dreadful. There was absolutely nothing to be done but obey. Red in the face, a huge frown almost hiding her eyes, she got up and spoke to Tim.

'Come on, Tim! I'm not surprised you bit him. I would, too, if I were a dog!'

'There is no need to be rude, Georgina,' said Mr Roland, angrily.

The others stared at George. They wondered how she dared to say things like that. When she got fierce it seemed as if she didn't care for anyone at all!

'Come back as soon as you have put the dog out,' said Mr Roland.

George scowled, but came back in a few minutes. She felt caught. Her father was friendly with Mr Roland, and knew how difficult George was — if she behaved as badly as she felt she would like to, it would be Tim who would suffer, for he would certainly be banished from the house. So for Tim's sake George obeyed the tutor — but from that moment she disliked him and resented him bitterly with all her fierce little heart.

The others were sorry for George and Timothy, but they did not share the little girl's intense dislike of the new tutor. He often made them laugh. He was patient with their mistakes. He was willing to show them how to make paper darts and ships, and to do funny little tricks. Julian and Dick thought these were fun, and stored them up to try on the other boys when they went back to school.

After lessons that morning the children went out for half an hour in the frosty sunshine. George called Tim.

'Poor old boy!' she said. 'What a shame to turn you out of the room! Whatever did you snap at Mr Roland for? I think it was a very good idea, Tim — but I really don't know what made you!'

'George, you can't play about with Mr Roland,' said Julian. 'You'll only get into trouble. He's tough. He won't stand much from any of us. But I think he'll be quite a good sport if we get on the right side of him.'

'Well, get on the right side of him if you like,' said George, in rather a sneering voice. 'I'm not going to. If I don't like a person, I don't — and I don't like *him*.'

'Why? Just because he doesn't like Tim?' asked Dick.

'Mostly because of that — but because he makes me feel prickly down my back,' said George. 'I don't like his nasty mouth.'

'But you can't see it,' said Julian. 'It's covered with his moustache and beard.'

'I've seen his lips through them,' said George, obstinately. 'They're thin and cruel. You look and see. I don't like thin-lipped people. They are always spiteful and hard. And I don't like his cold eyes either. You can suck up to him all you like. *I* shan't.'

Julian refused to get angry with the stubborn little girl. He laughed at her. 'We're not going to suck up to him,' he said. 'We're just going to be sensible, that's

255

all. You be sensible too, George, old thing.'

But once George had made up her mind about something nothing would alter her. She cheered up when she heard that they were all to go Christmas shopping on the bus that afternoon — without Mr Roland! He was going to watch an experiment that her father was going to show him.

'I will take you into the nearest town and you shall shop to your hearts' content,' said Aunt Fanny to the children. 'Then we will have tea in a tea-shop and catch the six o'clock bus home.'

This was fun. They caught the afternoon bus and rumbled along the deep country lanes till they got to the town. The shops looked very gay and bright. The children had brought their money with them, and were very busy indeed, buying all kinds of things. There were so many people to get presents for!

'I suppose we'd better get something for Mr Roland, hadn't we?' said Julian.

'I'm going to,' said Anne. 'I'm going to buy him a packet of cigarettes. I know the kind he smokes.'

'Fancy buying Mr *Roland* a present!' said George, in her scornful voice.

'Why shouldn't she, George?' asked her mother, in surprise. 'Oh dear, I hope you are going to be sensible about him, and not take a violent dislike to the poor man. I don't want him to complain to your father about you.'

'What are you going to buy for Tim, George?' asked Julian, changing the subject quickly.

'The largest bone the butcher has got,' said

George. 'What are *you* going to buy him?'

'I guess if Tim had money, he would buy us each a present,' said Anne, taking hold of the thick hair round Tim's neck, and pulling it lovingly. 'He's the best dog in the world!'

George forgave Anne for saying she would buy Mr Roland a present, when the little girl said that about Tim! She cheered up again and began to plan what she would buy for everyone.

They had a fine tea, and caught the six o'clock bus back. Aunt Fanny went to see if the cook had given the two men their tea. She came out of the study beaming.

'Really, I've never seen your uncle so jolly,' she said to Julian and Dick. 'He and Mr Roland are getting on like a house on fire. He has been showing your tutor quite a lot of his experiments. It's nice for him to have someone to talk to that knows a little about these things.'

Mr Roland played games with the children that evening. Tim was in the room, and the tutor tried again to make friends with him, but the dog refused to take any notice of him.

'As sulky as his little mistress!' said the tutor, with a laughing look at George, who was watching Tim refuse to go to Mr Roland, and looking rather pleased about it. She gave the tutor a scowl and said nothing.

'Shall we ask him whether "VIA OCCULTA" really does mean "Secret Way" or not, tomorrow?' said Julian to Dick, as they undressed that night. 'I'm just longing to know if it does. What do you think of Mr

Roland, Dick?'

'I don't really quite know,' said Dick. 'I like lots of things about him, but then I suddenly don't like him at all. I don't like his eyes. And George is quite right about his lips. They are so thin there's hardly anything of them at all.'

'I think he's all right,' said Julian. 'He won't stand any nonsense, that's all. I wouldn't mind showing him the whole piece of rag and asking him to make out its meaning for us.'

'I thought you said it was to be a proper secret,' said Dick.

'I know — but what's the use of a secret we don't know the meaning of ourselves?' said Julian. 'I'll tell you what we *could* do — ask him to explain the words to us, and not show him the bit of linen.'

'But we can't read some of the words ourselves,' said Dick. 'So that's no use. You'd have to show him the whole thing, and tell him where we got it.'

'Well, I'll see,' said Julian, getting into bed.

The next day there were lessons again from half-past nine to half-past twelve. George appeared without Tim. She was angry at having to do this, but it was no good being defiant and refusing to come to lessons without Tim. Now that he had snapped at Mr Roland, he had definitely put himself in the wrong, and the tutor had every right to refuse to allow him to come. But George looked very sulky indeed.

In the Latin lesson Julian took the chance of asking what he wanted to know. 'Please, Mr Roland,' he said, 'could you tell me what "VIA OCCULTA means?'

'"VIA OCCULTA"?' said Roland, frowning. 'Yes — it means "Secret Path" or, "Secret Road". A hidden way — something like that. Why do you want to know?'

All the children were listening eagerly. Their hearts thumped with excitement. So Julian had been right. That funny bit of rag contained directions for some hidden way, some secret path — but where to! Where did it begin, and end?

'Oh — I just wanted to know,' said Julian. 'Thank you, sir.'

He winked at the others. He was as excited as they were. If only they could make out the rest of the markings, they might be able to solve the mystery. Well — perhaps he would ask Mr Roland in a day or two. The secret must be solved somehow.

'"The Secret Way",' said Julian to himself, as he worked out a problem in geometry. 'The "Secret Way". I'll find it somehow.'

7

Directions for the Secret Way

For the next day or two the four children did not really have much time to think about the Secret Way, because Christmas was coming near, and there was a good deal to do.

There were Christmas cards to draw and paint for their mothers and fathers and friends. There was the house to decorate. They went out with Mr Roland to find sprays of holly, and came home laden.

'You look like a Christmas card yourselves,' said Aunt Fanny, as they walked up the garden path, carrying the red-berried holly over their shoulders. Mr Roland had found a group of trees with tufts of mistletoe growing from the top branches, and they had brought some of that too. Its berries shone like pale green pearls.

'Mr Roland had to climb the tree to get this,' said Anne. 'He's a good climber — as good as a monkey.'

Everyone laughed except George. She never laughed at anything to do with the tutor. They all dumped their loads down in the porch, and went to wash. They were to decorate the house that evening.

'Is Uncle going to let his study be decorated too?' asked Anne. There were all kinds of strange instruments and glass tubes in the study now, and the children looked at them with wonder whenever they ventured into the study, which was very seldom.

'No, my study is certainly not to be messed about,' said Uncle Quentin, at once. 'I wouldn't hear of it.'

'Uncle, why do you have all these funny things in your study?' asked Anne, looking round with wide eyes.

Uncle Quentin laughed. 'I'm looking for a secret formula!' he said.

'What's that?' said Anne.

'You wouldn't understand,' said her uncle. 'All these "funny things" as you call them, help me in my experiments, and I put down in my book what they tell me — and from all I learn I work out a secret formula, that will be of great use when it is finished.'

'You want to know a secret formula, and we want to know a secret way,' said Anne, quite forgetting that she was not supposed to talk about this.

Julian was standing by the door. He frowned at Anne. Luckily Uncle Quentin was not paying any more attention to the little girl's chatter. Julian pulled her out of the room.

'Anne, the only way to stop you giving away secrets is to sew up your mouth, like Brer Rabbit

262

wanted to do to Mister Dog!' he said.

Joanna the cook was busy baking Christmas cakes. An enormous turkey had been sent over from Kirrin Farm, and was hanging up in the larder. Timothy thought it smelt glorious, and Joanna was always shooing him out of the kitchen.

There were boxes of crackers on the shelf in the sitting-room, and mysterious parcels everywhere. It was very, very Christmassy! The children were happy and excited.

Mr Roland went out and dug up a little spruce fir tree. 'We must have a Christmas tree,' he said. 'Have you any tree-ornaments, children?'

'No,' said Julian, seeing George shake her head.

'I'll go into the town this afternoon and get some for you,' promised the tutor. 'It will be fun dressing the tree. We'll put it in the hall, and light candles on it on Christmas Day after tea. Who's coming with me to get the candles and the ornaments?'

'I am!' cried three children. But the fourth said nothing. That was George. Not even to buy tree-ornaments would the obstinate little girl go with Mr Roland. She had never had a Christmas tree before, and she was very much looking forward to it — but it was spoilt for her because Mr Roland bought the things that made it so beautiful.

Now it stood in the hall, with coloured candles in holders clipped to the branches, and gay shining ornaments hanging from top to bottom. Silver strands of frosted string hung down from the branches like icicles, and Anne had put bits of white

263

cotton-wool here and there to look like snow. It really was a lovely sight to see.

'Beautiful!' said Uncle Quentin, as he passed through the hall, and saw Mr Roland hanging the last ornaments on the tree. 'I say — look at the fairy doll on the top! Who's that for? A good girl?'

Anne secretly hoped that Mr Roland would give her the doll. She was sure it wasn't for George — and anyway, George wouldn't accept it. It was such a pretty doll, with its gauzy frock and silvery wings.

Julian, Dick and Anne had quite accepted the tutor now as teacher and friend. In fact, everyone had, their uncle and aunt too, and even Joanna the cook. George, of course, was the only exception, and she and Timothy kept away from Mr Roland, each looking as sulky as the other whenever the tutor was in the room.

'You know, I never knew a dog could look so sulky!' said Julian, watching Timothy. 'Really, he scowls almost like George.'

'And I always feel as if George puts her tail down like Tim, when Mr Roland is in the room,' giggled Anne.

'Laugh all you like,' said George, in a low tone. 'I think you're beastly to me. I know I'm right about Mr Roland. I've got a feeling about him. And so has Tim.'

'You're silly, George,' said Dick. 'You haven't *really* got a Feeling — it's only that Mr Roland will keep calling you Georgina and putting you in your place, and that he doesn't like Tim. I dare say he can't help disliking dogs. After all, there was once a famous man called Lord Roberts who couldn't bear cats.'

'Oh well, cats are different,' said George. 'If a person doesn't like dogs, especially a dog like our Timothy, then there really *must* be something wrong with him.'

'It's no use arguing with George,' said Julian. 'Once she's made up her mind about something, she won't budge!'

George went out of the room in a huff. The others thought she was behaving rather stupidly.

'I'm surprised really,' said Anne. 'She was so jolly last term at school. Now she's gone all queer, rather like she was when we first knew her last summer.'

'I do think Mr Roland has been decent digging up the Christmas tree and everything,' said Dick. 'I still don't like him awfully much sometimes, but I think he's a sport. What about asking him if he can read that old linen rag for us — I don't think I'd mind him sharing our secret, really.'

'I would *love* him to share it,' said Anne, who was busy doing a marvellous Christmas card for the tutor. 'He's most awfully clever. I'm sure he could tell us what the Secret Way is. Do let's ask him.'

'All right,' said Julian. 'I'll show him the piece of linen. It's Christmas Eve tonight. He will be with us in the sitting-room, because Aunt Fanny is going into the study with Uncle Quentin to wrap up presents for all of us!'

So, that evening, before Mr Roland came in to sit

with them, Julian took out the little roll of linen and stroked it out flat on the table. George looked at it in surprise.

'Mr Roland will be here in a minute,' she said. 'You'd better put it away quickly.'

'We're going to ask him if he can tell us what the old Latin words mean,' said Julian.

'You're not!' cried George, in dismay. 'Ask him to share our secret! However can you?'

'Well, we want to know what the secret is, don't we?' said Julian. 'We don't need to tell him where we got this or anything about it except that we want to know what the markings mean. We're not exactly sharing the secret with him — only asking him to use his brains to help us.'

'Well, I never thought you'd ask *him*,' said George. 'And he'll want to know simply everything about it, you just see if he won't! He's terribly snoopy.'

'Whatever do you mean?' said Julian, in surprise. 'I don't think he's a bit snoopy.'

'I saw him yesterday snooping round the study when no one was there,' said George. 'He didn't see me outside the window with Tim. He was having a real poke round.'

'You know how interested he is in your father's work,' said Julian. 'Why shouldn't he look at it? Your father likes him too. You're just seeing what horrid things you can find to say about Mr Roland.'

'Oh shut up, you two,' said Dick. 'It's Christmas Eve. Don't let's argue or quarrel or say beastly things.'

266

Just at that moment the tutor came into the room. 'All as busy as bees?' he said, he mouth smiling beneath its moustache. 'Too busy to have a game of cards, I suppose?'

'Mr Roland, sir,' began Julian, 'could you help us with something? We've got an old bit of linen here with odd markings on it. The words seem to be in some sort of Latin and we can't make them out.'

George gave an angry exclamation as she saw Julian push the piece of linen over towards the tutor. She went out of the room and shut the door with a bang. Tim was with her.

'Our sweet-tempered Georgina doesn't seem to be very friendly tonight,' remarked Mr Roland, pulling the bit of linen towards him. 'Where in the world did you get this? What an odd thing!'

Nobody answered. Mr Roland studied the roll of linen, and then gave an exclamation. 'Ah — I see why you wanted to know the meaning of those Latin words the other day — the ones that meant "hidden path", you remember. They are at the top of this linen roll.'

'Yes,' said Dick. All the children leaned over towards Mr Roland, hoping he would be able to unravel a little of the mystery for them.

'We just want to know the meaning of the words, sir,' said Julian.

'This is really very interesting,' said the tutor, puzzling over the linen. 'Apparently there are directions here for finding the opening or entrance of a secret path or road.'

267

'That's what we thought!' cried Julian, excitedly. 'That's exactly what we thought. Oh sir, do read the directions and see what you make of them.'

'Well, these eight squares are meant to represent wooden boards or panels, I think,' said the tutor, pointing to the eight rough squares drawn on the linen. 'Wait a minute — I can hardly read some of the words. This is most fascinating. *Solum lapideum — paries ligneus* — and what's this? — *cellula* — yes, *cellula!*'

The children hung on his words. 'Wooden panels!' That must mean panels somewhere at Kirrin Farmhouse.

Mr Roland frowned down at the old printed words. Then he sent Anne to borrow a magnifying glass from her uncle. She came back with it, and the four of them looked through the glass, seeing the words three times as clearly now.

'Well,' said the tutor at last, 'as far as I can make out the directions mean this: a room facing east; eight wooden panels, with an opening somewhere to be found in that marked one; a stone floor — yes, I think that's right, a stone floor; and a cupboard. It all sounds most extraordinary and very thrilling. Where *did* you get this from?'

'We just found it,' said Julian, after a pause. 'Oh Mr Roland, thanks awfully. We could never have made it out by ourselves. I suppose the entrance to the Secret Way is in a room facing east then.'

'It looks like it,' said Mr Roland, poring over the linen roll again. 'Where did you say you found this?'

268

'We didn't say,' said Dick. 'It's a secret really, you see.'

'I think you might tell me,' said the tutor, looking at Dick with his brilliant blue eyes. 'I can be trusted with secrets. You've no idea how many queer secrets I know.'

'Well,' said Julian, 'I don't really see why you shouldn't know where we found this, Mr Roland. We found it at Kirrin Farmhouse, in an old tobacco pouch. I suppose the Secret Way begins somewhere there! I wonder where and wherever can it lead to?'

'You found it at Kirrin Farmhouse!' exclaimed Mr Roland. 'Well, well — I must say that seems to be an interesting old place. I shall have to go over there one day.'

Julian rolled up the piece of linen and put it into his pocket. 'Well, thank you, sir,' he said. 'You've solved a bit of the mystery for us but set another puzzle! We must look for the entrance of the Secret Way after Christmas, when we can walk over to Kirrin Farmhouse.'

'I'll come with you,' said Mr Roland. 'I may be able to help a little. That is — if you don't mind me having a little share in this exciting secret.'

'Well — you've been such a help in telling us what the words mean,' said Julian; 'we'd like you to come if you want to, sir.'

'Yes, we *would*,' said Anne.

'We'll go and look for the Secret Way, then,' said Mr Roland. 'What fun we shall have, tapping round the panels, waiting for a mysterious dark entrance to appear!'

'I don't suppose George will go,' Dick murmured to Julian. 'You shouldn't have said Mr Roland could go with us, Ju. That means that old George will have to be left out of it. You know how she hates that.'

'I know,' said Julian, feeling uncomfortable. 'Don't let's worry about that now though. George may feel different after Christmas. She can't keep up this kind of behaviour for ever!'

8

What happened on Christmas night

It was great fun on Christmas morning. The children awoke early and tumbled out of bed to look at the presents that were stacked on chairs near by. Squeals and yells of delight came from everyone.

'Oh! a railway station! Just what I wanted! Who gave me this marvellous station?'

'A new doll — with eyes that shut! I shall call her Betsy-May. She looks just like a Betsy-May!'

'I say — what a whopping great book — all about aeroplanes. From Aunt Fanny! How decent of her!'

'Timothy! Look what Julian has given you — a collar with big brass studs all round — you *will* be grand. Go and lick him to say thank you!'

'Who's this from? I say, who gave me this? Where's the label? Oh — from Mr Roland. How decent of him! Look, Julian, a pocket-knife with three blades!'

So the cries and exclamations went on, and the

four excited children and the equally-excited dog spent a glorious hour before a late Christmas breakfast, opening all kinds and shapes of parcels. The bedrooms were in a fine mess when the children had finished!

'Who gave you that book about dogs, George?' asked Julian, seeing rather a nice dog-book lying on George's pile.

'Mr Roland,' said George, rather shortly. Julian wondered if George was going to accept it. He rather thought she wouldn't. But the little girl, defiant and obstinate as she was, had made up her mind not to spoil Christmas Day by being 'difficult'. So, when the others thanked the tutor for their things she too added her thanks, though in rather a stiff little voice.

George had not given the tutor anything, but the others had, and Mr Roland thanked them all very heartily, appearing to be very pleased indeed. He told Anne that her Christmas card was the nicest he had ever had, and she beamed at him with joy.

'Well, I must say it's nice to be here for Christmas!' said Mr Roland, when he and the others were sitting round a loaded Christmas table, at the mid-day dinner. 'Shall I carve for you, Mr Quentin? I'm good at that!'

Uncle Quentin handed him the carving knife and fork gladly. 'It's nice to have you here,' he said warmly. 'I must say you've settled in well — I'm sure we all feel as if we've known you for ages!'

It really was a jolly Christmas Day. There were no lessons, of course, and there were to be none the next day either. The children gave themselves up to the enjoyment of eating a great deal, sucking sweets, and looking forward to the lighting of the Christmas tree.

It looked beautiful when the candles were lighted. They twinkled in the darkness of the hall, and the bright ornaments shone and glowed. Tim sat and looked at it, quite entranced.

'He likes it as much as we do,' said George. And indeed Tim had enjoyed the day just as much as any of them.

They were all tired out when they went to bed. 'I shan't be long before I'm asleep,' yawned Anne. 'Oh, George — it's been fun, hasn't it? I did like the Christmas tree.'

'Yes, it's been lovely,' said George, jumping into bed. 'Here comes Mother to say good night. Basket, Tim, basket!'

Tim leapt into his basket by the window. He was always there when George's mother came into say good-night to the girls but as soon as she had gone downstairs, the dog took a flying leap and landed on George's bed. There he slept, his head curled round her feet.

'Don't you think Tim ought to sleep downstairs tonight?' said George's mother. 'Joanna says he ate such an enormous meal in the kitchen that she is sure he will be sick.'

'Oh *no*, Mother!' said George, at once. 'Make Tim sleep downstairs on Christmas night? Whatever would he think?'

'Oh, very well,' said her mother, with a laugh. 'I

273

might have known it was useless to suggest it. Now to sleep quickly, Anne and George — it's late and you are all tired.'

She went into the boys' room and said good-night to them too. They were almost asleep.

Two hours later everyone else was in bed. The house was still and dark. George and Anne slept peacefully in their small beds. Timothy slept too, lying heavily on George's feet.

Suddenly George awoke with a jump. Tim was

growling softly! He had raised his big shaggy head and George knew that he was listening.

'What it it, Tim?' she whispered. Anne did not wake. Tim went on growling softly. George sat up and put her hand on his collar to stop him. She knew that if he awoke her father, he would be cross.

Timothy stopped growling now that he had roused George. The girl sat and wondered what to do. It wasn't any good waking Anne. The little girl would be frightened. Why was Tim growling? He never did that at night!

'Perhaps I'd better go and see if everything is all right,' thought George. She was quite fearless, and the thought of creeping through the still, dark house did not disturb her at all. Besides she had Tim! Who could be afraid with Tim beside them!

She slipped on her dressing-gown. 'Perhaps a log has fallen out of one of the fire-places and a rug is burning,' she thought, sniffing as she went down the stairs. 'It would be just like Tim to smell it and warn us!'

With her hand on Tim's head to warn him to be quite quiet, George crept softly through the hall to the sitting-room. The fire was quite all right there, just a red glow. In the kitchen all was peace too. Tim's feet made a noise there, as his claws rattled against the linoleum.

A slight sound came from the other side of the house.

Tim growled quite loudly, and the hairs on the back of his neck rose up. George stood still. Could it possibly be burglars?

Suddenly Timothy shook himself free from her fingers and leapt across the hall, down a passage, and into the study beyond! There was the sound of an exclamation, and a noise as if someone was falling over.

'It *is* a burglar!' said George, and she ran to the study. She saw a torch shining on the floor, dropped by someone who was even now struggling with Tim.

George switched on the light, and then looked with the greatest astonishment into the study. Mr Roland was there in his dressing-gown, rolling on the floor, trying to get away from Timothy, who, although not biting him, was holding him firmly by his dressing-gown.

'Oh — it's you, George! Call your beastly dog off!' said Mr Roland, in a low and angry voice. 'Do you want to rouse all the household?'

'Why are you creeping about with a torch?' demanded George.

'I heard a noise down here, and came to see what it was,' said Mr Roland, sitting up and trying to fend off the angry dog. 'For goodness' sake, call your beast off.'

'Why didn't you put on the light?' asked George, not attempting to take Tim away. She was very much enjoying the sight of an angry and frightened Mr Roland.

'I couldn't find it,' said the tutor. 'It's on the wrong side of the door, as you see.'

This was true. The switch was an awkward one to find if you didn't know it. Mr Roland tried to push Tim away again, and the dog suddenly barked.

'Well — he'll wake everyone!' said the tutor, angrily. 'I didn't want to rouse the house. I thought I could find out for myself if there was anyone about — a burglar perhaps. Here comes your father!'

278

George's father appeared, carrying a large poker. He stood still in astonishment when he saw Mr Roland on the ground and Timothy standing over him.

'What's all this?' he exclaimed. Mr Roland tried to get up, but Tim would not let him. George's father called to him sternly.

'Tim! Come here, sir!'

Timothy glanced at George to see if his mistress agreed with her father's command. She said nothing. So Timothy took no notice of the order and merely made a snap at Mr Roland's ankles.

'That dog's mad!' said Mr Roland, from the floor. 'He's already bitten me once before, and now he's trying to do it again!'

'Tim! Will you come here, sir!' shouted George's father. 'George, that dog is really disobedient. Call him off at once.'

'Come here, Tim!' said George, in a low voice. The dog at once came to her, standing by her side with the hairs on his neck still rising up stiffly. He growled softly as if to say, 'Be careful, Mr Roland, be careful!'

The tutor got up. He was very angry indeed. He spoke to George's father.

'I heard some sort of noise and came down with my torch to see what it was,' he said. 'I thought it came from your study, and knowing you kept your valuable books and instruments here, I wondered if some thief was about. I had just got down, and into the room, when that dog appeared from somewhere and got me down on the ground! George came along

279

too, and would not call him off.'

'I can't understand your behaviour, George; I really can't,' said her father, angrily. 'I hope you are not going to behave stupidly, as you used to behave before your cousins came last summer. And what is this I hear about Tim biting Mr Roland before?'

'George had him under the table during lessons,' said Mr Roland. 'I didn't know that, and when I stretched out my legs, they touched Tim, and he bit me. I didn't tell you before, sir, because I didn't want to trouble you. Both George and the dog have tried to annoy me ever since I have been here.'

'Well, Tim must go outside and live in the kennel,' said George's father. 'I won't have him in the house. It will be a punishment for him, and a punishment for you too, George. I will not have this kind of behaviour. Mr Roland has been extremely kind to you all.'

'I won't let Tim live outside,' said George furiously. 'It's such cold weather, and it would simply break his heart.'

'Well, his heart must be broken then,' said her father. 'It will depend entirely on your behaviour from now on whether Tim is allowed in the house at all these holidays. I shall ask Mr Roland each day how you have behaved. If you have a bad report, then Tim stays outside. Now you know! Go back to bed but first apologise to Mr Roland!'

'I won't!' said George, and choked by feelings of anger and dismay, she tore out of the room and up the stairs. The two men stared after her.

280

'Let her be,' said Mr Roland. 'She's a very difficult child — and has made up her mind not to like me, that's quite plain. But I shall be very glad, sir, to know that that dog isn't in the house. I'm not at all certain that Georgina wouldn't set him on me, if she could!'

'I'm sorry about all this,' said George's father. 'I wonder what the noise was that you heard? — a log falling in the grate I expect. Now — what am I to do about that tiresome dog tonight? Go and take him outside, I suppose!'

'Leave him tonight,' said Mr Roland. 'I can hear noises upstairs — the others are awake by now! Don't let's make any more disturbance tonight.'

'Perhaps you are right,' said George's father, thankfully. He didn't at all want to tackle a defiant little girl and an angry big dog in the middle of a cold night!

The two men went to bed and slept. George did not sleep. The others had been awake when she got upstairs, and she had told them what had happened.

'George! You really are an idiot!' said Dick. 'After all, why shouldn't Mr Roland go down if he heard a noise! *You* went down! Now we shan't have darling old Tim in the house this cold weather!'

Anne began to cry. She didn't like hearing that the tutor she liked so much had been knocked down by Tim, and she hated hearing that Tim was to be punished.

'Don't be a baby,' said George. '*I'm* not crying, and it's *my* dog!'

But, when everyone had settled down again in bed, and slept peacefully, George's pillow was very wet indeed. Tim crept up beside her and licked the salt tears off her cheek. He whined softly. Tim was always unhappy when his little mistress was sad.

9

A hunt for the Secret Way

There were no lessons the next day. George looked rather pale, and was very quiet. Tim was already out in the yard-kennel, and the children could hear him whining unhappily. They were all upset to hear him.

'Oh, George, I'm awfully sorry about it all,' said Dick. 'I wish you wouldn't get so fierce about things. You only get yourself into trouble — and poor old Tim.'

George was full of mixed feelings. She disliked Mr Roland so much now that she could hardly bear to look at him — and yet she did not dare to be openly rude and rebellious because she was afraid that if she was, the tutor would give her a bad report, and perhaps she would not be allowed even to *see* Timothy. It was very hard for a defiant nature like hers to force herself to behave properly.

Mr Roland took no notice of her at all. The other

children tried to bring George into their talks and plans, but she remained quiet and uninterested.

'George! We're going over to Kirrin Farmhouse today,' said Dick. 'Coming? We're going to try and find the entrance to the Secret Way. It must start somewhere there.'

The children had told George what Mr Roland had said about the piece of marked linen. They had all been thrilled about this, though the excitements of Christmas Day had made them forget about it for a while.

'Yes — of course I'll come,' said George, looking more cheerful. 'Timothy can come too. He wants a walk.'

But when the little girl found that Mr Roland was also going, she changed her mind at once. Not for anything would she go with the tutor! No — she would go for a walk alone with Timothy.

'But, George — think of the excitement we'll have trying to find the Secret Way,' said Julian, taking hold of her arm. George wrenched it away.

'I'm not going if Mr Roland is,' she said, obstinately, and the others knew that it was no good trying to coax her.

'I shall go alone with Tim,' said George. 'You go off together with your dear Mr Roland!'

She set out with Timothy, a lonely little figure going down the garden path. The others stared after her. This was horrid. George was being more and more left out, but what could they do about it?

'Well, children, are you ready?' asked Mr Roland.

'You start off by yourselves, will you? I'll meet you at the farmhouse later. I want to run down to the village first to get something.'

So the three children set off by themselves, wishing that George was with them. She was nowhere to be seen.

Old Mr and Mrs Sanders were pleased to see the three children, and sat them down in the big kitchen to eat ginger buns and drink hot milk.

'Well, have you come to find a few more secret things?' asked Mrs Sanders, with a smile.

'May we try?' asked Julian. 'We're looking for a room that's facing east, with a stone floor, and panelling!'

'All the rooms downstairs have stone floors,' said Mrs Sanders. 'You hunt all you like, my dears. You won't do any damage, I know. But don't go into the room upstairs with the cupboard that has a false back, will you? or the one next to it! Those are the rooms the two artists have.'

'All right,' said Julian, rather sorry that they were unable to fiddle about with the exciting cupboard again. 'Are the artists here, Mrs Sanders? I'd like to talk to them about pictures. I hope one day I'll be an artist too.'

'Dear me, is that so?' said Mrs Sanders. 'Well, well — it's always a marvel to me how people make any money at painting pictures.'

'It isn't making money that artists like, so much as the painting of the pictures,' said Julian, looking rather wise. That seemed to puzzle Mrs Sanders even more. She shook her head and laughed.

'They're queer folk!' she said. 'Ah well — you go along and have a hunt for whatever it is you want to find. You can't talk to the two artists today though, Master Julian — they're out.'

The children finished their buns and milk and then stood up, wondering where to begin their search. They must look for a room or rooms facing east. That would be the first thing to do.

'Which side of the house faces east, Mrs Sanders?' asked Julian. 'Do you know?'

'The kitchen faces due north,' said Mrs Sanders. 'So east will be over there,' she pointed to the right.

'Thanks,' said Julian. 'Come on, everyone!' The three children went out of the kitchen, and turned to the right. There were three rooms there — a kind of scullery, not much used now, a tiny room used as a den by old Mr Sanders, and a room that had once been a drawing-room, but which was now cold and unused.

'They've all got stone floors,' said Julian.

'So we'll have to hunt through all of the three rooms,' said Anne.

'No, we won't,' said Julian. 'We shan't have to look in this scullery, for one thing!'

'Why not?' asked Anne.

'Because the walls are of stone, silly, and we want panelling,' said Julian. 'Use your brains, Anne!'

'Well, that's one room we needn't bother with, then,' said Dick. 'Look — both this little room and the drawing-room have panelling, Julian. We must search in both.'

'There must be some reason for putting *eight* squares of panelling in the directions,' said Julian, looking at the roll of linen again. 'It would be a good idea to see whether there's a place with eight squares only — you know, over a window, or something.'

It was tremendously exciting to look round the two rooms! The children began with the smaller room. It was panelled all the way round in dark oak, but there was no place where only eight panels showed. So the children went into the next room.

The panelling there was different. It did not look so old, and was not so dark. The squares were rather a different size, too. The children tried each panel, tapping and pressing as they went, expecting at any moment to see one slide back as the one in the hall had done.

But they were disappointed. Nothing happened at all. They were still in the middle of trying when they heard footsteps in the hall, and voices. Somebody looked into the drawing-room. It was a man, thin and tall, wearing glasses on his long nose.

'Hallo!' he said. 'Mrs Sanders told me you were treasure-hunting, or something. How are you getting on?'

'Not very well,' said Julian, politely. He looked at the man, and saw behind him another one, younger, with rather screwed-up eyes and a big mouth. 'I suppose you are the two artists?' he asked.

'We are!' said the first man, coming into the room. 'Now, just exactly what are you looking for?'

Julian did not really want to tell him, but it was
difficult not to. 'Well — we're just seeing if there's a
sliding panel here,' he said at last. 'There's one in the
hall, you know. It's exciting to hunt round.'

'Shall we help?' said the first artist, coming into the
room. 'What are your names? Mine's Thomas, and
my friend's name is Wilton.'

The children talked politely for a minute or two, not at all wanting the two men to help. If there was anything to be found, *they* wanted to find it. It would spoil everything if grown-ups solved the puzzle!

Soon everyone was tap-tap-tapping round the wooden panels. They were in the middle of this when a voice hailed them.

'Hallo! My word, we *are* all busy!'

The children turned, and saw their tutor standing in the doorway, smiling at them. The two artists looked at him.

'Is this a friend of yours?' asked Mr Thomas.

'Yes — he's our tutor, and he's very nice!' said Anne, running to Mr Roland and putting her hand in his.

'Perhaps you will introduce me, Anne,' said Mr Roland, smiling at the little girl.

Anne knew how to introduce people. She had often seen her mother doing it. 'This is Mr Roland,' she said to the two artists. Then she turned to Mr Roland. 'This is Mr Thomas,' she said, waving her hand towards him, 'and the other one is Mr Wilton.'

The men half-bowed to one another and nodded. 'Are you staying here?' asked Mr Roland. 'A very nice old farmhouse, isn't it?'

'It isn't time to go yet, is it?' asked Julian, hearing a clock strike.

'Yes, I'm afraid it is,' said Mr Roland. 'I'm later meeting you than I expected. We must go in about five minutes — no later. I'll just give you a hand in trying to find this mysterious secret way!'

But no matter how any one of them pressed and tapped around the panels in either of the two rooms, they could not find anything exciting. It really was most disappointing.

'Well, we really must go now,' said Mr Roland. 'Come and say good-bye to Mrs Sanders.'

They all went into the warm kitchen, where Mrs Sanders was cooking something that smelt most delicious.

'Something for our lunch, Mrs Sanders?' said Mr Wilton. 'My word, you really are a wonderful cook!'

Mrs Sanders smiled. She turned to the children. 'Well, dearies, did you find what you wanted?' she asked.

'No,' said Mr Roland, answering for them. 'We haven't been able to find the secret way, after all!'

'The secret way?' said Mrs Sanders, in surprise. 'What do you know about that now? I thought it had all been forgotten — in fact, I haven't believed in that secret way for many a year!'

'Oh, Mrs Sanders — do you know about it?' cried Julian. 'Where is it?'

'I don't know, dear — the secret of it has been lost for many a day,' said the old lady. 'I remember my old grandmother telling me something about it when I was smaller than any of you. But I wasn't interested in things like that when I was little. I was all for cows and hens and sheep.'

'Oh, Mrs Sanders — do, do try and remember something!' begged Dick. 'What *was* the secret way?'

'Well, it was supposed to be a hidden way from

Kirrin Farmhouse to somewhere else,' said Mrs Sanders. 'I don't know where, I'm sure. It was used in the olden days when people wanted to hide from enemies.'

It was disappointing that Mrs Sanders knew so little. The children said good-bye and went off with their tutor, feeling that their morning had been wasted.

George was indoors when they got to Kirrin Cottage. Her cheeks were not so pale, now, and she greeted the children eagerly.

'Did you discover anything? Tell me all about it!' she said.

'There's nothing to tell,' said Dick, rather gloomily. 'We found three rooms facing east, with stone floors, but only two of them had wooden panelling, so we hunted round those, tapping and punching — but there wasn't anything to be discovered at all.'

'We saw the two artists,' said Anne. 'One was tall and thin and had a long nose with glasses on. He was called Mr Thomas. The other was younger, with little piggy eyes and an enormous mouth.'

'I met them out this morning,' said George. 'It must have been them. Mr Roland was with them, and they were all talking together. They didn't see me.'

'Oh, it couldn't have been the artists you saw,' said Anne, at once. 'Mr Roland didn't know them. I had to introduce them.'

'Well, I'm sure I heard Mr Roland call one of them Wilton,' said George, puzzled. 'He *must* have known them.'

291

'It couldn't have been the artists,' said Anne, again. 'They really didn't know Mr Roland. Mr Thomas asked if he was a friend of ours.'

'I'm sure I'm not mistaken,' said George, looking obstinate. 'If Mr Roland said he didn't know the two artists, he was telling lies.'

'Oh, you're always making out that he is doing something horrid!' cried Anne, indignantly. 'You just make up things about him!'

'Sh!' said Julian. 'Here he is.'

The door opened and the tutor came in. 'Well,' he said, 'it *was* disappointing that we couldn't find the secret way, wasn't it? Anyway, we were rather foolish to hunt about that drawing-room as we did — the panelling there wasn't really old — it must have been put in years after the other.'

'Oh — well, it's no good looking there again,' said Julian, disappointed. 'And I'm pretty sure there's nothing to be found in that other little room. We went all over it so thoroughly. Isn't it disappointing?'

'It is,' said Mr Roland. 'Well, Julian, how did you like the two artists? I was pleased to meet them — they seemed nice fellows, and I shall like to know them.'

George looked at the tutor. Could he possibly be telling untruths in such a truthful voice? The little girl was very puzzled. She felt sure it was the artists she had seen him with. But why should he pretend he didn't know them? She must be mistaken. But all the same, she felt uncomfortable about it, and made up her mind to find out the truth, if she could.

10

A shock for George and Tim

Next morning there were lessons again — and no Timothy under the table! George felt very much inclined to refuse to work, but what would be the good of that? Grown-ups were so powerful, and could dole out all kinds of punishments. She didn't care how much she was punished herself but she couldn't bear to think that Timothy might have to share in the punishments too.

So, pale and sullen, the little girl sat down at the table with the others. Anne was eager to join in the lessons — in fact she was eager to do anything to please Mr Roland, because he had given her the fairy doll from the top of the Christmas tree! Anne thought it was the prettiest doll she had ever seen.

George had scowled at the doll when Anne showed it to her. She didn't like dolls, and she certainly wasn't going to like one that Mr Roland had chosen, and given to Anne! But Anne loved it, and had made up her mind to do lessons with the others, and work as well as she could.

George did as little as she could without getting into trouble. Mr Roland took no interest in her or in her work. He praised the others, and took a lot of trouble to show Julian something he found difficult.

The children heard Tim whining outside as they worked. This troubled them very much, for Timothy was such a companion, and so dear to them all. They could not bear to think of him left out of everything, cold and miserable in the yard-kennel. When the ten minutes' break came, and Mr Roland went out of the room for a few minutes, Julian spoke to George.

'George! It's awful for us to hear poor old Tim whining out there in the cold. And I'm sure I heard him cough. Let me speak to Mr Roland about him. You must feel simply dreadful knowing that Tim is out there.'

'I thought I heard him cough, too,' said George, looking worried. 'I hope he won't get a cold. He simply doesn't understand why I have to put him there. He thinks I'm terribly unkind.'

The little girl turned her head away, afraid that tears might come into her eyes. She always boasted that she never cried — but it was very difficult to keep the tears away when she thought of Timothy out there in the cold.

Dick took her arm. 'Listen, George — you just hate Mr Roland, and I suppose you can't help it. But we can none of us bear Timothy being out there all alone

294

— and it looks like snow today, which would be awful for him. Could you be awfully, awfully good today, and forget your dislike, so that when your father asks Mr Roland for your report, he can say you were very good — and then we'll all ask Mr Roland if he wouldn't let Timmy come back into the house.'

'See?'

Timothy coughed again, out in the yard, and George's heart went cold. Suppose he got that awful illness called pneumonia — and she couldn't nurse him because he had to live in the kennel? She would die of unhappiness! She turned to Julian and Dick.

'All right,' she said. 'I do hate Mr Roland — but I love Timothy more than I hate the tutor — so for Tim's sake I'll pretend to be good and sweet and hard-working. And then you can beg him to let Timothy come back.'

'Good girl!' said Julian. 'Now here he comes — so do your best.'

To the tutor's enormous surprise, George gave him a smile when he came into the room. This was so unexpected that it puzzled him. He was even more puzzled to find that George worked harder than anyone for the rest of the morning, and she answered politely and cheerfully when he spoke to her. He gave her a word of praise.

'Well done, Georgina! I can see you've got brains.'

'Thank you,' said George, and gave him another wan smile — a very watery, poor affair, compared with the happy smiles the others had been used to — but still, it *was* a smile!

At dinner-time George looked after Mr Roland most politely — passed him the salt, offered him more bread, got up to fill his glass when it was empty! The others looked at her in admiration. George had plenty of pluck. She must be finding it very difficult to behave as if Mr Roland was a great friend, when she really disliked him so much!

Mr Roland seemed very pleased, and appeared to be quite willing to respond to George's friendliness. He made a little joke with her, and offered to lend her a book he had about a dog. George's mother was delighted to find that her difficult daughter seemed to be turning over a new leaf. Altogether things were very much happier that day.

'George, you go out of the room before your father comes in to ask Mr Roland about your behaviour tonight,' said Julian. 'Then, when the tutor gives you a splendid report, we will all ask if Timothy can come back. It will be easier if you are not there.'

'All right,' said George. She was longing for this difficult day to be over. It was very hard for her to pretend to be friendly, when she was not. She could never never do it, if it wasn't for Timothy's sake!

George disappeared out of the room just before six o'clock, when she heard her father coming. He walked into the room and nodded to Mr Roland.

'Well? Have your pupils worked well today?' he asked.

'Very well indeed,' said Mr Roland. 'Julian has really mastered something he didn't understand today. Dick has done well in Latin. Anne has written out a French exercise without a single mistake!'

'And what about George?' asked Uncle Quentin.

'I was coming to Georgina,' said Mr Roland, looking round and seeing that she was gone. 'She has worked better than anyone else today! I am really pleased with her. She has tried hard — and she has really been polite and friendly. I feel she is trying to turn over a new leaf.'

'She's been a brick today,' said Julian, warmly. 'Uncle Quentin, she has tried awfully hard, she really has. And, you know, she's terribly unhappy.'

'Why?' asked Uncle Quentin in surprise.

'Because of Timothy,' said Julian. 'He's out in the cold, you see. And he's got a dreadful cough.'

'Oh, Uncle Quentin, please do let poor Timmy come indoors,' begged Anne.

'Yes, please do,' said Dick. 'Not only for George's sake, because she loves him so, but for us too. We hate to hear him whining outside. And George does deserve a reward, Uncle — she's been marvellous today.'

'Well,' said Uncle Quentin, looking doubtfully at the three eager faces before him, 'well — I hardly know what to say. If George is going to be sensible — and the weather gets colder — well . . .'

He looked at Mr Roland, expecting to hear him say something in favour of Timothy. But the tutor said nothing. He looked annoyed.

'What do you think, Roland?' asked Uncle Quentin.

'I think you should keep to what you said and let

the dog stay outside,' said the tutor. 'George is spoilt, and needs firm handling. You should really keep to your decision about the dog. There is no reason to give way about it just because she has tried to be good for once!'

The three children stared at Mr Roland in surprise and dismay. It had never entered their heads that he would not back them up!

'Oh, Mr Roland, you *are* horrid!' cried Anne. 'Oh do, do say you'll have Timothy back.'

The tutor did not look at Anne. He pursed up his mouth beneath its thick moustache and looked straight at Uncle Quentin.

'Well,' said Uncle Quentin, 'perhaps we had better see how George behaves for a whole week. After all — just one day isn't much.'

The children stared at him in disgust. They thought he was weak and unkind. Mr Roland nodded his head.

'Yes,' he said, 'a week will be a better test. If Georgina behaves well for a whole week, we'll have another word about the dog, sir. But at present I feel it would be better to keep him outside.'

'Very well,' said Uncle Quentin, and went out of the room. He paused to look back. 'Come along into my study sometime,' he said. 'I've got a bit further with my formula. It's at a very interesting stage.'

The three children looked at one another but said nothing. How mean of the tutor to stop Uncle Quentin from having Timothy indoors again! They all felt disappointed in him. The tutor saw their faces.

298

'I'm sorry to disappoint you,' he said. 'But I think if you'd been bitten by Timothy once and snapped at all over when he got you on the floor, you would not be very keen on having him in either!'

He went out of the room. The children wondered what to say to George. She came in a moment later, her face eager. But when she saw the gloomy looks of the other three, she stopped short.

'Isn't Tim to come in?' she asked, quickly. 'What's happened? Tell me!'

They told her. The little girl's face grew dark and angry when she heard how the tutor had put his foot down about Timothy, even when her father had himself suggested that the dog might come indoors.

'Oh, what a beast he is!' she cried. 'How I do hate him! I'll pay him out for this. I will, I will, I will!'

She rushed out of the room. They heard her fumbling in the hall, and then the front door banged.

'She's gone out into the dark,' said Julian. 'I bet she's gone to Timmy. Poor old George. Now she'll be worse than ever!'

That night George could not sleep. She lay and tossed in her bed, listening for Timothy. She heard him cough. She heard him whine. He was cold, she knew he was. She had put plenty of fresh straw into his kennel and had turned it away from the cold north wind — but he must feel the bitter night terribly, after sleeping for so long on her bed!

Timothy gave such a hollow cough that George could bear it no longer. She must, she simply must, get up and go down to him. 'I shall bring him into the

house for a little while and rub his chest with some of
that stuff Mother uses for herself when she's got a
cold on her chest,' thought the girl. 'Perhaps that will
do him good.'

300

She quickly put a few clothes on and crept downstairs. The whole house was quiet. She slipped out into the yard and undid Tim's chain. He was delighted to see her and licked her hands and face lovingly.

'Come along into the warm for a little while,' whispered the little girl. 'I'll rub your poor chest with some oil I've got.'

Timmy pattered behind her into the house. She took him to the kitchen — but the fire was out and the room was cold. George went to look at the other rooms.

There was quite a nice fire still in her father's study. She and Tim went in there. She did not put on the light, because the firelight was fairly bright. She had with her the little bottle of oil from the bathroom cupboard. She put it down by the fire to warm.

Then she rubbed the dog's hairy chest with the oil, hoping it would do him good. 'Don't cough now if you can help it, Tim,' she whispered. 'If you do, someone may hear you. Lie down here by the fire, darling, and get nice and warm. Your cold will soon be better.'

Timothy lay down on the rug. He was glad to be out of his kennel and with his beloved mistress. He put his head on her knee. She stroked him and whispered to him.

The firelight glinted on the curious instruments and glass tubes that stood around on shelves in her father's study. A log shifted a little in the fire and settled lower, sending up a cloud of sparks. It was warm and peaceful there.

The little girl almost fell asleep. The big dog closed his eyes too, and rested peacefully, happy and warm. George settled down with her head on his neck.

She awoke to hear the study clock striking six! The room was cold now, and she shivered. Goodness! Six o'clock! Joanna the cook would soon be awake. She must not find Timmy and George in the study!

'Tim darling! Wake up! We must put you back into your kennel,' whispered George. 'I'm sure your cold is better, because you haven't coughed once since you've been indoors. Get up — and don't make a noise. Sh!'

Tim stood up and shook himself. He licked George's hand. He understood perfectly that he must be quite quiet. The two of them slipped out of the study, went into the hall and out of the front door.

In a minute or two Timothy was on the chain, and in his kennel, cuddled down among the straw. George wished she could cuddle there with him. She gave him a pat and slipped back indoors again.

She went up to bed, sleepy and cold. She forgot that she was partly dressed and got into bed just as she was. She was asleep in a moment!

In the morning Anne was most amazed to find that George had on vest, knickers, jeans and jersey, when she got out of bed to dress.

'Look!' she said. 'You're half-dressed! But I *saw* you undressing last night.'

'Be quiet,' said George. 'I went down and let Tim in last night. We sat in front of the study fire and I rubbed him with oil. Now don't you dare to say a word to anyone! Promise!'

Anne promised — and she faithfully kept her word. Well, well — to think that George dared to roam about like that all night — what an extraordinary girl she was!

11

Stolen papers

'George, don't behave fiercely today, will you?' said
Julian, after breakfast. 'It won't do you or Timothy
any good at all.'

'Do you suppose I'm going to behave well when I
know perfectly well that Mr Roland will never let me
have Tim indoors all these holidays?' said George.

'Well — they said a week,' said Dick. 'Can't you
try for a week?'

'No. At the end of a week Mr Roland will say I
must try for another week,' said George. 'He's got a
real dislike for poor Tim. And for me too. I'm not
surprised at that, because I know that when I try to
be horrid, I really *am* horrid. But he shouldn't hate
poor Timmy.'

'Oh George — you'll spoil the whole hols if you are
silly, and keep getting into trouble,' said Anne.

'Well, I'll spoil them then,' said George, the sulky

look coming back on her face.

'I don't see why you have to spoil them for *us*, as well as for yourself,' said Julian.

'They don't need to be spoilt for you,' said George. 'You can have all the fun you want — go for walks with your dear Mr Roland, play games with him in the evening, and laugh and talk as much as you like. You don't need to take any notice of me.'

'You are a funny girl, George,' said Julian, with a sigh. 'We like you, and we hate you to be unhappy — so how can we have fun if we know you're miserable — and Timmy too?'

'Don't worry about *me*,' said George, in rather a choky voice. 'I'm going out to Tim. I'm not coming in to lessons today.'

'George! But you must!' said Dick and Julian together.

'There's no "must" about it,' said George. 'I'm just not coming. I won't work with Mr Roland till he says I can have Timothy indoors again.'

'But you know you can't do things like that — you'll be spanked or something,' said Dick.

'I shall run away if things get too bad,' said George, in a shaky voice. 'I shall run away with Tim.'

She went out of the room and shut the door with a bang. The others stared after her. What could you do with a person like George? Anyone could rule her with kindness and understanding — but as soon as she came up against anyone who disliked her, or whom she disliked, she shied away like a frightened horse — and kicked like a frightened horse, too!

305

Mr Roland came into the sitting-room, his books in his hand. He smiled at the three children.

'Well? All ready for me, I see. Where's Georgina?'

Nobody answered. Nobody was going to give George away!

'Don't you know where she is?' asked Mr Roland in surprise. He looked at Julian.

'No, sir,' said Julian, truthfully. 'I've no idea where she is.'

'Well — perhaps she will come along in a few minutes,' said Mr Roland. 'Gone to feed that dog of hers, I suppose.'

They all settled down to work. The time went on and George did not come in. Mr Roland glanced at the clock and made an impatient clicking noise with his tongue.

'Really, it's too bad of Georgina to be so late! Anne, go and see if you can find her.'

Anne went. She looked in the bedroom. There was no George there. She looked in the kitchen. Joanna was there, making cakes. She gave the little girl a hot piece to eat. She had no idea where George was.

Anne couldn't find her anywhere. She went back and told Mr Roland. He looked angry.

'I shall have to report this to her father,' he said. 'I have never had to deal with such a rebellious child before. She seems to do everything she possibly can to get herself into trouble.'

Lessons went on. Break came, and still George did not appear. Julian slipped out and saw that the yard-kennel was empty. So George had gone out with

Timmy! What a row she would get into when she got back!

No sooner had the children settled down after break to do the rest of the morning's lessons, than a big disturbance came.

Uncle Quentin burst in looking upset and worried.

'Have any of you children been into my study?' he asked.

'No, Uncle Quentin,' they all answered.

'You said we weren't to,' said Julian.

'Why, sir? Has something been broken?' asked Mr Roland.

'Yes — the test-tubes I set yesterday for an experiment have been broken — and what is worse, three most important pages of my book have gone,' said Uncle Quentin. 'I can write them out again, but only after a great deal of work. I can't understand it. Are you *sure*, children, that none of you has been meddling with things in my study?'

'Quite sure,' they answered. Anne went very red — she suddenly remembered what George had told her. George said she had taken Timmy into Uncle Quentin's study last night, and rubbed his chest with oil! But George couldn't possibly have broken the test-tubes, and taken pages from her father's book!

Mr Roland noticed that Anne had gone red.

'Do you know anything about this, Anne?' he asked.

'No, Mr Roland,' said Anne, blushing even redder, and looking very uncomfortable indeed.

'Where's George?' suddenly said Uncle Quentin.

The children said nothing, and it was Mr Roland who answered:

'We don't know. She didn't come to lessons this morning.'

'Didn't come to lessons! Why not?' demanded Uncle Quentin, beginning to frown.

'She didn't say,' said Mr Roland dryly. 'I imagine she was upset because we were firm about Timothy last night, sir — and this is her way of being defiant.'

'The naughty girl!' said George's father, angrily. 'I don't know what's come over her lately. Fanny! Come here! Did you know that George hasn't been in to her lessons today?'

Aunt Fanny came into the room. She looked very worried. She had a little bottle in her hand. The children wondered what it was.

'Didn't come in to lessons!' repeated Aunt Fanny. 'How extraordinary! Then where is she?'

'I don't think you need to worry about her,' said Mr Roland, smoothly. 'She's probably gone off with Timothy in a fit of temper. What is very much more important, sir, is the fact that your work appears to have been spoilt by someone. I only hope it is not George, who has been spiteful enough to pay you out for not allowing her to have her dog in the house.'

'Of *course* it wasn't George!' cried Dick, angry that anyone should even think such a thing of his cousin.

'George would never, never do a thing like that,' said Julian.

'No, she never would,' said Anne, sticking up valiantly for her cousin, although a horrid doubt was

308

in her mind. After all — George *had* been in the study last night!

'Quentin, I am sure George would not even *think* of such a thing,' said Aunt Fanny. 'You will find those pages somewhere — and as for the test-tubes that were broken, well, perhaps the wind blew the curtain against them, or something! When did you last see those pages?'

'Last night,' said Uncle Quentin. 'I read them over again, and checked my figures to make sure they were right. Those pages contain the very heart of my formula! If they got into anyone else's hands, they could use my secret. This is a terrible thing for me! I *must* know what has happened to them.'

'I found this in your study, Quentin,' said Aunt Fanny, and she held up the little bottle she carried. 'Did you put it there? It was in the fender.'

Uncle Quentin took the bottle and stared at it. 'Camphorated oil!' he said. 'Of course I didn't take it there. Why should I?'

'Well — who took it there, then?' asked Aunt Fanny, puzzled. 'None of the children has a cold — and anyway, they wouldn't think of the camphorated oil, and take it into the study to use! It's most extraordinary!'

Everyone was astonished. Why should a bottle of camphorated oil appear in the study fender?

Only one person could think why. It suddenly came into Anne's mind in a flash. George had said she had taken Timmy into the study, and rubbed him with oil! He had had a cough, that was why. And she had left the oil in the study. Oh dear, oh dear — now what would happen? What a pity George had forgotten the oil!

Anne went very red again as she looked at the oil. Mr Roland, whose eyes seemed very sharp this morning, looked hard at the little girl.

'Anne! You know something about that oil!' he said suddenly. 'What do you know? Did you put it there?'

'No,' said Anne. 'I haven't been into the study. I said I hadn't.'

'Do you know anything about the oil?' said Mr Roland, again. 'You *do* know something.'

Everyone stared at Anne. She stared back. This was simply dreadful. She could not give George away. She could *not*. George was in quite enough trouble as it was, without getting into any more. She pursed up her little mouth and did not answer.

'Anne!' said Mr Roland, sternly. 'Answer when you are spoken to.'

Anne said nothing. The two boys stared at her, guessing that it was something to do with George. They did not know that George had brought Timothy in the night before.

'Anne, dear,' said her aunt, gently. 'Tell us if you know something. It might help us to find out what has happened to Uncle Quentin's papers. It is very, very, important.'

Still Anne said nothing. Her eyes filled with tears. Julian squeezed her arm.

'Don't bother Anne,' he said to the grown-ups. 'If

she thinks she can't tell you, she's got some very good reason.'

'I think she's shielding George,' said Mr Roland. 'Is that it, Anne?'

Anne burst into tears. Julian put his arms round his little sister, and spoke again to the three grown-ups.

'*Don't* bother Anne! Can't you see she's upset?'

'We'll let George speak for herself, when she thinks she will come in,' said Mr Roland. 'I'm sure she knows how that bottle got there — and if she put it there herself she must have been into the study — and she's the only person that *has* been there.'

The boys could not think for one moment that George would do such a thing as spoil her father's work. Anne feared it, and it upset her. She sobbed in Julian's arms.

'When George comes in, send her to me in my study,' said Uncle Quentin, irritably. 'How can a man work when these upsets go on? I was always against having children in the house.'

He stamped out, tall, cross and frowning. The children were glad to see him go. Mr Roland shut the books on the table with a snap.

'We can't do any more lessons this morning,' he said. 'Put on your things and go out for a walk till dinner-time.'

'Yes, do,' said Aunt Fanny, looking white and worried. 'That's a good idea.'

Mr Roland and their aunt went out of the room. 'I don't know if Mr Roland thinks he's coming out with us,' said Julian, in a low voice, 'but we've got to get out first and give him the slip. We've got to find George and warn her what's up.'

'Right!' said Dick. 'Dry your eyes, Anne darling. Hurry and get your things. We'll slip out of the garden door before Mr Roland comes down. I bet George has gone for her favourite walk over the cliffs. We'll meet her!' The three children threw on their outdoor things and crept out of the garden door quietly. They raced down the garden path, and out of the gate before Mr Roland even knew they were gone! They made their way to the cliffs, and looked to see if George was coming.

'There she is — and Timothy, too!' cried Julian, pointing. 'George! George! Quick, we've got something to tell you!'

12

George in trouble

'What's the matter?' asked George, as the three children tore up to her. 'Has something happened?'

'Yes, George. Someone has taken three most important pages out of your father's book!' panted Julian. 'And broken the test-tubes he was making an experiment with. Mr Roland thinks you might have had something to do with it!'

'The beast!' said George, her blue eyes deepening with anger. 'As if I'd do a thing like that! Why should he think it's me, anyway?'

'Well, George, you left that bottle of oil in the study fender,' said Anne. 'I haven't told anyone at all what you told me happened last night — but somehow Mr Roland guessed you had something to do with the bottle of oil.'

'Didn't you tell the boys how I got Timmy indoors?' asked George. 'Well, there's nothing much to tell, Julian. I just heard poor old Tim coughing in the night, and I half-dressed, went down, and took him into the study, where there was a fire. Mother keeps a bottle of oil that she used to rub her chest with when she has a cough — so I thought it might do Timmy's cold good, too. I got the oil and rubbed him well — and we both fell asleep by the fire till six o'clock. I was sleepy when I woke up, and forgot the oil. That's all.'

'And you didn't take any pages from the book Uncle Quentin is writing, and you didn't break anything in the study, did you?' said Anne.

'Of course not, silly,' said George, indignantly. 'How can you ask me a thing like that? You must be mad.'

George never told a lie, and the others always believed her, whatever she said. They stared at her, and she stared back.

'I wonder who could have taken those pages then?' said Julian. 'Maybe your father will come across them, after all. I expect he put them into some safe place and then forgot all about them. And the test-tubes might easily have over-balanced and broken themselves. Some of them look very shaky to me.'

'I suppose I shall get into trouble now for taking Tim into the study,' said George.

'And for not coming into lessons this morning,' said Dick. 'You really are an idiot, George. I never knew anyone like you for walking right into trouble.'

'Hadn't you better stay out a bit longer, till

everyone has calmed down a bit?' said Anne.

'No,' said George at once. 'If I'm going to get into a row, I'll get into it now! *I'm* not afraid!'

She marched over the cliff path, with Timmy running round her as usual. The others followed. It wasn't nice to think that George was going to get into such trouble.

They came to the house and went up the path.

Mr Roland saw them from the window and opened the door. He glanced at George.

'Your father wants to see you in the study,' said the tutor. Then he turned to the others, looking annoyed.

'Why did you go out without me? I meant to go with you.'

'Oh did you, sir? I'm sorry,' said Julian, politely, not looking at Mr Roland. 'We just went out on the cliff a little way.'

'Georgina, did you go into the study last night?' asked Mr Roland, watching George as she took off her hat and coat.

'I'll answer my father's questions, not yours,' said George.

'What you want is a good spanking,' said Mr Roland. 'And if I were your father I'd give it to you!'

'You're not my father,' answered George. She went to the study door and opened it. There was no one there.

'Father isn't here,' said George.

'He'll be there in a minute,' said Mr Roland. 'Go in and wait. And you others, go up and wash for lunch.'

The other three children felt almost as if they were

deserting George as they went up the stairs. They could hear Timmy whining from the yard outside. He knew his little mistress was in trouble, and he wanted to be with her.

George sat down on a chair, and gazed at the fire, remembering how she had sat on the rug there with Tim last night, rubbing his hairy chest. How silly of her to have forgotten the bottle of oil!

Her father came into the room, frowning and angry. He looked sternly at George.

'Were you in here last night, George?' he asked.

'Yes, I was,' answered George at once.

'What were you doing in here?' asked her father. 'You know you children are forbidden to come into my study.'

'I know,' said George. 'But you see Timmy had a dreadful cough, and I couldn't bear it. So I crept down about one o'clock and let him in. This was the only room that was really warm, so I sat here and rubbed his chest with the oil Mother uses when she has a cold.'

'Rubbed the dog's chest with camphorated oil!' exclaimed her father, in amazement. 'What a mad thing to do! As if it would do him any good.'

'It didn't seem mad to me,' said George. 'It seemed sensible. And Timmy's cough is much better today. I'm sorry for coming into the study. I didn't touch a thing, of course.'

'George, something very serious has happened,' said her father, looking gravely at her. 'Some of my test-tubes with which I was doing an important experiment, have been broken — and, worse than that, three pages of my book have gone. Tell me on your honour that you know nothing of these things.'

'I know nothing of them,' said George, looking her father straight in the eyes. Her own eyes shone very blue and clear as she gazed at him. He felt quite certain that George was speaking the truth. She could know nothing of the damage done. Then where were those pages?

'George, last night when I went to bed at eleven o'clock, everything was in order,' he said. 'I read over those three important pages and checked them once more myself. This morning they are gone.'

'Then they must have been taken between eleven o'clock and one o'clock,' said George. 'I was here from that time until six.'

'But *who* could have taken them?' said her father. 'The window was fastened, as far as I know. And nobody knows that those three pages were so important but myself. It is most extraordinary.'

'Mr Roland probably knew,' said George, slowly.

'Don't be absurd,' said her father. 'Even if he did realise they were important, he would not have taken them. He's a very decent fellow. And that reminds me — why were you not at lessons this morning, George?'

'I'm not going to do lessons any more with Mr Roland,' said George. 'I simply hate him!'

'George! I will *not* have you talking like this!' said her father. 'Do you want me to say you are to lose Tim altogether?'

'No,' said George, feeling shaky about the knees. 'And I don't think it's fair to keep trying to force me to do things by threatening me with losing Timothy. If — if — you do a thing like that — I'll — I'll run away or something!'

There were no tears in George's eyes. She sat bolt upright on her chair, gazing defiantly at her father. How difficult she was! Her father sighed, and remembered that he too in his own childhood had been called 'difficult'. Perhaps George took after him. She could be so good and sweet — and here she was being perfectly impossible!

Her father did not know what to do with George. He thought he had better have a word with his wife. He got up and went to the door.

'Stay here. I shall be back in a moment. I want to speak to your mother about you.'

'Don't speak to Mr Roland about me, will you?' said George, who felt quite certain that the tutor would urge terrible punishments for her and Timmy. 'Oh, Father, if only Timothy had been in the house last night, sleeping in my room as usual, he would have heard whoever it was that stole your secret — and he would have barked and roused the house!'

Her father said nothing, but he knew that what George had said was true. Timmy wouldn't have let anyone get into the study. It was funny he hadn't barked in the night, if anyone from outside had climbed in at the study window. Still, it was the other side of the house. Maybe he had heard nothing.

The door closed. George sat still on her chair,

319

gazing up at the mantelpiece, where a clock ticked away the time. She felt very miserable. Everything was going wrong, every single thing!

As she gazed at the panelled overmantel, she counted the wooden panels. There were eight. Now, where had she heard of eight panels before? Of course — in that Secret Way. There were eight panels marked on the roll of linen. What a pity there had not been eight panels in a wooden over-mantel at Kirrin Farmhouse!

George glanced out of the window, and wondered if it faced east. She looked to see where the sun was — it was not shining into the room — but it did in the early morning — so it must face east. Fancy — here was a room facing east and with eight wooden panels. She wondered if it had a stone floor.

The floor was covered with a large thick carpet. George got up and went to the wall. She pulled up the edge of the carpet there — and saw that the floor underneath was made of large flat stones. The study had a stone floor too!

She sat down again and gazed at the wooden panels, trying to remember which one in the roll of linen was marked with a cross. But of course it couldn't be a room in Kirrin Cottage — it must be in Kirrin Farmhouse where the Secret Way began.

But just suppose it *was* Kirrin Cottage! Certainly the directions had been found in Kirrin Farmhouse — but that was not to say that the Secret Way had to begin there, even though Mrs Sanders seemed to think it did.

320

George was feeling excited. 'I must tap round about those eight panels and try to find the one that is marked on the linen roll,' she thought. 'It may slide back or something, and I shall suddenly see the entrance opening!'

She got up to try her luck — but at that moment the door opened again and her father came in looking very grave.

'I have been talking to your mother,' he said. 'She agrees with me that you have been very disobedient, rude and defiant. We can't let behaviour like that pass, George. You will have to be punished.'

George looked anxiously at her father. If only her punishment had nothing to do with Timothy! But, of course, it had.

'You will go to bed for the rest of the day, and you will not see Timothy for three days,' said her father. 'I will get Julian to feed him and take him for a walk. If you persist in being defiant, Timothy will have to go away altogether. I am afraid, queer as it may seem, that that dog has a bad influence on you.'

'He hasn't, he hasn't!' cried George. 'Oh, he'll be so miserable if I don't see him for three whole days.'

'There's nothing more to be said,' said her father. 'Go straight upstairs to bed, and think over all I have said to you, George. I am very disappointed in your behaviour these holidays. I really did think the influence of your three cousins had made you into a normal, sensible girl. Now you are worse than you have ever been.'

He held open the door and George walked out,

holding her head high. She heard the others having their dinner in the dining-room. She went straight upstairs and undressed. She got into bed and thought miserably of not seeing Tim for three days. She couldn't bear it! Nobody could possibly know how much she loved Timothy!

Joanna came up with a tray of dinner. 'Well, Miss, it's a pity to see you in bed,' she said cheerfully. 'Now you be a sensible girl and behave properly and you'll soon be downstairs again.'

George picked at her dinner. She did not feel at all hungry. She lay back on the bed, thinking of Tim and thinking of the eight panels over the mantelpiece. Could they possibly be the ones shown in the Secret Way directions? She gazed out of the window and thought hard.

'Golly, it's snowing!' she said suddenly, sitting up. 'I thought it would when I saw that leaden sky this morning. It's snowing hard! It will be quite thick by tonight — inches deep. Oh, poor Timothy. I hope Julian will see that his kennel is kept clear of the drifting snow.'

George had plenty of time to think as she lay in bed. Joanna came and took the tray away. No one else came to see her. George felt sure the other children had been forbidden to go up and speak to her. She felt lonely and left-out.

She thought of her father's lost pages. Could Mr Roland have taken them? After all, he was very interested in her father's work and seemed to understand it. The thief must have been someone who knew which were the important pages. Surely Timothy would have barked if a thief had come in from outside, even though the study was the other side of the house. Timmy had such sharp ears.

'I think it must have been someone *in*side the house,' said George. 'None of us children, that's certain — and not Mother or Joanna. So that only leaves Mr Roland. And I did find him in the study that other night when Timmy woke me by growling.'

She sat up in bed suddenly. 'I believe Mr Roland had Timothy put out of the house because he wanted to go poking round the study again and was afraid Tim would bark!' she thought. 'He was so very insistent that Tim should go out of doors — even when everyone else begged for me to have him indoors. I believe — I really do believe — that Mr Roland is the thief!'

The little girl felt very excited. Could it be that the tutor had stolen the pages — and broken those important test-tubes? How she wished that the others would come and see her, so that she could talk things over with them!

13

Julian has a surprise

The three children downstairs felt very sorry for George. Uncle Quentin had forbidden them to go up and see her.

'A little time for thinking out things all alone may do George good,' he said.

'Poor old George,' said Julian. 'It's too bad, isn't it? I say — look at the snow!'

The snow was falling very thickly. Julian went to the window and looked out. 'I shall have to go and see that Timmy's kennel is all right,' he said. 'We don't want the poor old fellow to be snowed up! I expect he is wondering what the snow is!'

Timothy was certainly very puzzled to see everywhere covered with soft white stuff. He sat in his kennel and stared out at the falling flakes, his big brown eyes following them as they fell to the ground. He was puzzled and unhappy. Why was he living out here by himself in the cold? Why didn't George come to him? Didn't she love him any more? The big dog was very miserable, as miserable as George!

He was delighted to see Julian. He jumped up at the boy and licked his face. 'Good old Tim!' said Julian. 'Are you all right? Let me sweep away some of this snow and swing your kennel round a bit so that no flakes fly inside. There — that's better. No, we're not going for a walk, old thing — not now.'

The boy patted the dog and fussed him a bit, then went indoors. The others met him at the sitting-room door.

'Julian! Mr Roland is going out for a walk by himself. Aunt Fanny is lying down, and Uncle Quentin is in his study. Can't we go up and see George?'

'We were forbidden to,' said Julian, doubtfully.

'I know,' said Dick. 'But I don't mind risking it for the sake of making George feel a bit happier. It must be so awful for her, lying up there all alone, knowing she can't see Tim for days.'

'Well — let me go up, as I'm the eldest,' said Julian. 'You two stay down here in the sitting-room and talk. Then Uncle Quentin will think we're all here. I'll slip up and see George for a few minutes.'

'All right,' said Dick. 'Give her our love and tell her we'll look after Timmy.'

Julian slipped quietly up the stairs. He opened George's door and crept inside. He shut the door, and saw George sitting up in bed, looking at him in delight.

326

'Sh!' said Julian. 'I'm not supposed to be here!'

'Oh Julian!' said George joyfully. 'How good of you to come. I was so lonely. Come this side of the bed. Then if anyone comes in suddenly, you can duck down and hide.'

Julian went to the other side of the bed. George began to pour out to him all she had been thinking of.

'I believe Mr Roland is the thief, I really do!' she said. 'I'm not saying that because I hate him, Julian, really I'm not. After all, I *did* find him snooping round the study one afternoon — and again in the middle of the night. He may have got to hear of my father's work, and come to see if he could steal it. It was just lucky for him that we needed a tutor. I'm sure he stole those pages, and I'm sure he wanted Timmy out of the house so that he could do his stealing without Tim hearing him and growling.'

'Oh, George — I don't think so,' said Julian, who really could not approve of the idea of the tutor doing such a thing. 'It all sounds so far-fetched and unbelievable.'

'Lots of unbelievable things happen,' said George. 'Lots. And this is one of them.'

'Well, if Mr Roland *did* steal the pages, they must be somewhere in the house,' said Julian. 'He hasn't been out all day. They must be somewhere in his bedroom.'

'Of course!' said George, looking thrilled. 'I wish he'd go out! Then I'd search his room.'

'George, you can't do things like that,' said Julian, quite shocked.

328

'You simply don't know what things I can do, if I really want to,' said George, setting her mouth in a firm line. 'Oh — what's that noise?'

There was the bang of a door. Julian went cautiously to the window and peeped out. The snow had stopped falling for a time, and Mr Roland had taken the chance of going out.

'It's Mr Roland,' said Julian.

'Oooh — I could search his room now, if you'll keep watch at the window and tell me if he comes back,' said George, throwing back the bedclothes at once.

'No, George, don't,' said Julian. 'Honestly and truly, it's awful to search somebody's room like that. And anyway, I dare say he's got the pages with him. He may even be going to give them to somebody!'

'I never thought of that,' said George, and she looked at Julian with wide eyes. 'Isn't that sickening? Of course he may be doing that. He knows those two artists at Kirrin Farmhouse, for instance. They may be in the plot too.'

'Oh, George, don't be silly,' said Julian. 'You are making a mountain out of a mole-hill, talking of plots and goodness knows what! Anyone would think we were in the middle of a big adventure.'

'Well, I think we are,' said George, unexpectedly, and she looked rather solemn. 'I sort of feel it all round me — a Big Adventure!'

Julian stared at his cousin thoughtfully. Could there possibly be anything in what she said?

'Julian, will you do something for me?' said George.

330

'Of course,' said the boy, at once.

'Go out and follow Mr Roland,' said George. 'Don't let him see you. There's a white macintosh cloak in the hall cupboard. Put it on and you won't be easily seen against the snow. Follow him and see if he meets anyone and gives them anything that looks like the pages of my father's book — you know those big pages he writes on. They're very large.'

'All right,' said Julian. 'But if I do, promise you won't go and search his room. You can't do things like that, George.'

'I can,' said George. 'But I won't, if you'll just follow Mr Roland for me. I'm sure he's going to hand over what he has stolen to others who are in the plot! And I bet those others will be the two artists at Kirrin Farmhouse that he pretended not to know!'

'You'll find you're quite wrong,' said Julian, going to the door. 'I'm sure I shan't be able to follow Mr Roland, anyway — he's been gone five minutes now!'

'Yes, you will, silly — he'll have left his footmarks in the snow,' said George. 'And oh, Julian — I quite forgot to tell you something else exciting. Oh dear, there isn't time now. I'll tell you when you come back, if you can come up again then. It's about the Secret Way.'

'Really?' said Julian, in delight. It had been a great disappointment to him that all their hunting and searching had come to nothing. 'All right — I'll try and creep up again later. If I don't come, you'll know I can't, and you must wait till bed-time.'

He disappeared and shut the door quietly. He slipped downstairs, popped his head into the sitting-room and whispered to the others that he was going out after the tutor.

'Tell you why, later,' he said. He put the white

macintosh cloak around him and went out into the garden. Snow was beginning to fall again, but not yet heavily enough to hide Mr Roland's deep footsteps.

He had had big Wellington boots on, and the footmarks showed up well in the six-inch-deep snow.

The boy followed them quickly. The countryside was very wintry-looking now. The sky was low and leaden, and he could see there was much more snow to come. He hurried on after Mr Roland, though he could not see a sign of the tutor.

Down the lane and over the path that led across the common went the double row of footmarks. Julian stumbled on, his eyes glued to the foot-prints. Suddenly he heard the sound of voices and stopped. A big gorse bush lay to the right and the voices came from there. The boy went nearer to the bush. He heard his tutor's voice, talking in low tones. He could not hear a word that was said.

'Whoever can he be talking to?' he wondered. He crept up closer to the bush. There was a hollow space inside. Julian thought he could creep right into it, though it would be very prickly, and peer out of the other side. Carefully the boy crept into the prickly hollow, where the branches were bare and brown.

He parted the prickly branches slowly and cautiously — and to his amazement he saw Mr Roland talking to the two artists from Kirrin Farmhouse — Mr Thomas and Mr Wilton! So George was right. The tutor had met them — and, as Julian watched, Mr Roland handed over to Mr Thomas a doubled-up sheaf of papers.

'They look just like pages from Uncle Quentin's book,' said Julian to himself. 'I say — this is mighty queer. It does begin to look like a plot — with Mr

Roland as the centre of it!'

Mr Thomas put the papers into the pocket of his overcoat. The men muttered a few more words, which even Julian's sharp ears could not catch, and then parted. The artists went off towards Kirrin Farmhouse, and Mr Roland took the path back over the common. Julian crouched down in the hollow of the prickly gorse bush, hoping the tutor would not turn and see him. Luckily he didn't. He went straight on and disappeared into the snow, which was now falling thickly. It was also beginning to get dark and Julian, unable to see the path very clearly, hurried after Mr Roland, half-afraid of being lost in the snow-storm.

Mr Roland was not anxious to be out longer than he could help, either. He almost ran back to Kirrin Cottage. He came to the gate at last, and Julian watched him go into the house. He gave him a little time to take off his things and then, giving Timothy a pat as he went by, he went to the garden door. He took off his macintosh cloak, changed his boots, and slipped into the sitting-room before Mr Roland had come down from his bedroom.

'What's happened?' asked Dick and Anne, seeing that Julian was in a great state of excitement. But he could not tell them, for just then Joanna came in to lay the tea.

Much to Julian's disappointment, he could not say a word to the others all that evening, because one or other of the grown-ups was always in the room. Neither could he go up to see George. He could hardly wait to tell his news, but it was no good, he had to.

'Is it still snowing, Aunt Fanny?' asked Anne.

Her aunt went to the front door and looked out. The snow was piled high against the step!

'Yes,' she said, when she came back. 'It is snowing fast and thickly. If it goes on like this we shall be completely snowed up, as we were two winters ago! We couldn't get out of the house for five days then. The milkman couldn't get to us, nor the baker. Fortunately we had plenty of tinned milk, and I can bake my own bread. You poor children — you will not be able to go out tomorrow — the snow will be too thick!'

'Will Kirrin Farmhouse be snowed up too?' asked Mr Roland.

'Oh yes — worse than we shall be,' said Aunt Fanny. 'But they won't mind! They have plenty of food there. They will be prisoners just as much, and more, as we shall.'

Julian wondered why Mr Roland had asked that question. Was he afraid that his friends would not be able to send those pages away by the post — or take them anywhere by bus or car? The boy felt certain this was the reason for the question. How he longed to be able to talk over everything with the others.

'I'm tired!' he said, about eight o'clock. 'Let's go to bed.'

Dick and Anne stared at him in astonishment. Usually, as he was the eldest, he went to bed last of all. Tonight he was actually *asking* to go! Julian winked quickly at them, and they backed him up at once.

Dick yawned widely, and so did Anne. Their aunt put down the sewing she was doing. 'You *do* sound tired!' she said. 'I think you'd better all go to bed.'

'Could I just go out and see if Timmy is all right?' asked Julian. His aunt nodded. The boy put on his rubber boots and coat, and slipped out through the garden door into the yard. It was very deep in snow, too. Tim's kennel was half-hidden in it. The dog had trampled a space in front of the kennel door, and stood there, looking for Julian as he came out of the house.

'Poor old boy, out here in the snow all alone,' said Julian. He patted the dog, and Timmy whined. He was asking to go back with the boy.

'I wish I *could* take you back with me,' said Julian. 'Never mind, Timothy. I'll come and see you tomorrow.'

He went indoors again. The children said good-night to their aunt and Mr Roland, and went upstairs.

'Undress quickly, put on dressing-gowns and meet in George's room,' whispered Julian to the others. 'Don't make a sound or we'll have Aunt Fanny up. Quick now!'

In less than three minutes the children were undressed, and were sitting on George's bed. She was very pleased to see them. Anne slipped into bed with her, because her feet were cold.

'Julian! Did you follow Mr Roland all right?'

whispered George.

'Why did he follow him?' asked Dick, who had been dying to know.

Julian told them everything as quickly as he could — all that George suspected — and how he had followed the tutor — and what he had seen. When George heard how Julian had watched him giving a sheaf of papers to the two artists, her eyes gleamed angrily.

'The thief! They must have been the lost pages! And to think my father has been so friendly to him. Oh, what can we do? Those men will get the papers away as quickly as they can, and the secret Father has been working on for ages will be used by someone else — for some other country, probably!'

'They can't get the papers away,' said Julian. 'You've no idea how thick the snow is now, George. We shall be prisoners here for a few days, if this snow goes on, and so will the people in Kirrin Farmhouse. If they want to hide the papers, they will have to hide them in the farmhouse! If only we could get over there and hunt round!'

'Well, we can't,' said Dick. 'That's quite certain. We'd be up to our necks in snow!'

The four children looked gloomily at one another. Dick and Anne could hardly believe that the jolly Mr Roland was a thief — a spy perhaps, trying to steal a valuable secret from a friendly scientist. And they couldn't stop it.

'We'd better tell your father,' said Julian at last.

'No,' said Anne. 'He wouldn't believe it, would he, George?'

338

'He'd laugh at us and go straight and tell Mr Roland,' said George. 'That would warn him, and he mustn't be warned. He mustn't know that we guess anything.'

'Sh! Aunt Fanny's coming!' whispered Dick, suddenly. The boys slipped out of the room and into bed. Anne hopped across to her own little bed. All was peace and quiet when the children's aunt came into the bedroom.

She said good-night and tucked them up. As soon as she had gone down, the four children met together again in George's room.

'George, tell me now what you were going to say about the Secret Way,' said Julian.

'Oh, yes,' said George. 'Well, there may be nothing in my idea at all — but in the study downstairs, there are eight wooden panels over the mantelpiece — and the floor is of stone — and the room faces east! A bit queer, isn't it? Just what the directions said.'

'Is there a cupboard there too?' asked Julian.

'No. But there is everything else,' said George. 'And I was just wondering if by any chance the entrance to the Secret Way is in this house, not in the farmhouse. After all, they both belonged to my family at one time, you know. The people living in the farmhouse years ago must have known all about this cottage.'

'Golly, George — suppose the entrance *was* here!' said Dick. 'Wouldn't it be simply marvellous! Let's go straight down and look!'

'Don't be silly,' said Julian. 'Go down to the study when Uncle Quentin is there? I'd rather meet twenty lions than face Uncle! Especially after what has happened!'

'Well, we simply MUST find out if George's idea is right; we simply must,' said Dick, forgetting to whisper.

'Shut up, idiot!' said Julian, giving him a punch. 'Do you want to bring the whole household up here?'

'Sorry!' said Dick. 'But, oh golly, this *is* exciting. It's an Adventure again.'

'Just what I said,' said George, eagerly. 'Listen, shall we wait till midnight, and then creep down to the study when everyone is asleep, and try our luck? There may be nothing in my idea at all — but we'll have to find out now. I don't believe I could go to sleep till I've tried each one of those panels over the mantelpiece to see if something happens.'

'Well, I know I can't sleep a wink either,' said Dick. 'Listen — is that someone coming up? We'd better go. Come on, Julian! We'll meet in George's room at midnight — and creep down and try out George's idea!'

The two boys went off to their own room. Neither of them could sleep a wink. Nor could George. She lay awake, and went over and over in her mind all that had happened those holidays. 'It's like a jigsaw puzzle,' she thought. 'I couldn't understand a lot of things at first — but now they are fitting together, and making a picture.'

Anne was fast asleep. She had to be awakened at midnight. 'Come on!' whispered Julian, shaking her. 'Don't you want to share in this adventure?'

14

The Secret Way at last!

The four children crept downstairs through the dark and silent night. Nobody made a sound at all. They made their way to the study. George softly closed the door and then switched on the light.

The children stared at the eight panels over the mantelpiece. Yes — there were exactly eight, four in one row and four in the row above. Julian spread the linen roll out on the table, and the children pored over it.

'The cross is in the middle of the second panel in the top row,' said Julian, in a low voice. 'I'll try pressing it. Watch, all of you!'

He went to the fireplace. The others followed him, their hearts beating fast with excitement. Julian stood on tiptoe and began to press hard in the middle of the second panel. Nothing happened.

'Press harder! Tap it!' said Dick.

'I daren't make too much noise,' said Julian, feeling all over the panel to see if there was any roughness that might tell of a hidden spring or lever.

Suddenly, under his hands, the panel slid silently back, just as the one had done at Kirrin Farmhouse in the hall! The children stared at the space behind, thrilled.

'It's not big enough to get into,' said George. 'It can't be the entrance to the Secret Way.'

Julian got out his torch from his dressing-gown pocket. He put it inside the opening, and gave a low exclamation.

'There's a sort of handle here — with strong wire or something attached to it. I'll pull it and see what happens.'

He pulled — but he was not strong enough to move the handle that seemed to be embedded in the wall. Dick put his hand in and the two boys then pulled together.

'It's moving — it's giving way a bit,' panted Julian. 'Go on, Dick, pull hard!'

The handle suddenly came away from the wall, and behind it came thick wire, rusty and old. At the same time a curious grating noise came from below the hearthrug in front of the fireplace, and Anne almost fell.

'Julian! Something is moving under the rug!' she said, frightened. 'I felt it. Under the rug, quick!'

The handle could not be pulled out any farther. The boys let go, and looked down. To the right of the fireplace, under the rug, something had moved. There was no doubt of that. The rug sagged down instead of being flat and straight.

'A stone has moved in the floor,' said Julian, his voice shaking with excitement. 'This handle works a lever, which is attached to this wire. Quick — pull up the rug, and roll back the carpet.'

With trembling hands the children pulled back the rug and the carpet — and then stood staring at a very strange thing. A big flat stone laid in the floor had slipped downwards, pulled in some manner by the wire attached to the handle hidden behind the panel! There was now a black space where the stone had been.

'Look at that!' said George, in a thrilling whisper. 'The entrance to the Secret Way!'

'It's here after all!' said Julian.

'Let's go down!' said Dick.

'No!' said Anne, shivering at the thought of disappearing into the black hole.

Julian flashed his torch into the black space. The stone had slid down and then sideways. Below was a space just big enough to take a man, bending down.

'I expect there's a passage or something leading from here, under the house, and out,' said Julian. 'Golly, I wonder where it leads to?'

'We simply must find out,' said George.

'Not now,' said Dick. 'It's dark and cold. I don't fancy going along the Secret Way at midnight. I don't mind just hopping down to see what it's like — but don't let's go along any passage till tomorrow.'

'Uncle Quentin will be working here tomorrow,' said Julian.

344

'He said he was going to sweep the snow away from the front door in the morning,' said George. 'We could slip into the study then. It's Saturday. There may be no lessons.'

'All right,' said Julian, who badly wanted to explore everything then and there. 'But for goodness' sake let's have a look and see if there *is* a passage down there. At present all we can see is a hole!'

'I'll help you down,' said Dick. So he gave his brother a hand and the boy dropped lightly down into the black space, holding his torch. He gave a loud exclamation.

'It's the entrance to the Secret Way all right! There's a passage leading from here under the house — awfully low and narrow — but I can see it's a passage. I do wonder where it leads to!'

He shivered. It was cold and damp down there. 'Give me a hand up, Dick,' he said. He was soon out of the hole and in the warm study again.

The children looked at one another in the greatest joy and excitement. This *was* an Adventure, a real Adventure. It was a pity they couldn't go on with it now.

'We'll try and take Timmy with us tomorrow,' said George. 'Oh, I say — how are we going to shut the entrance up?'

'We can't leave the rug and carpet sagging over that hole,' said Dick. 'Nor can we leave the panel open.'

'We'll see if we can get the stone back,' said Julian.

He stood on tiptoe and felt about inside the panel. His hand closed on a kind of knob, set deep in a stone. He pulled it, and at once the handle slid back, pulled by the wire. At the same time the sunk stone glided to the surface of the floor again, making a slight grating sound as it did so.

'Well, it's like magic!' said Dick. 'It really is! Fancy the mechanism working so smoothly after years of not being used. This is the most exciting thing I've ever seen!'

There was a noise in the bedroom above. The children stood still and listened.

'It's Mr Roland!' whispered Dick. 'He's heard us. Quick, slip upstairs before he comes down.'

They switched out the light and opened the study door softly. Up the stairs they fled, as quietly as Indians, their hearts thumping so loudly that it seemed as if everyone in the house must hear the beat.

The girls got safely to their rooms and Dick was able to slip into his. But Julian was seen by Mr Roland as he came out of his room with a torch.

'What are you doing, Julian!' asked the tutor, in surprise. 'Did you hear a noise downstairs? I thought I did.'

'Yes — I heard quite a lot of noise downstairs,' said Julian, truthfully. 'But perhaps it's snow falling off the roof, landing with a plop on the ground, sir. Do you think that's it?'

'I don't know,' said the tutor doubtfully. 'We'll go down and see.'

They went down, but of course there was nothing to be seen. Julian was glad they had been able to shut the panel and make the stone come back to its proper place again. Mr Roland was the very last persón he wanted to tell his secret to.

They went upstairs and Julian slipped into his room. 'Is it all right?' whispered Dick.

'Yes,' said Julian. 'Don't let's talk. Mr Roland's awake, and I don't want him to suspect anything.'

The boys fell asleep. When they awoke in the morning, there was a completely white world outside. Snow covered everything and covered it deeply. Timothy's kennel could not be seen! But there were footmarks round about it.

George gave a squeal when she saw how deep the snow was. 'Poor Timothy! I'm going to get him in. I don't care what anyone says! I won't let him be buried in the snow!'

She dressed and tore downstairs. She went out to the kennel, floundering knee deep in the snow. But there was no Timmy there!

A loud bark from the kitchen made her jump. Joanna the cook knocked on the kitchen window. 'It's all right! I couldn't bear the dog out there in the snow, so I fetched him in, poor thing. Your mother says I can have him in the kitchen but you're not to come and see him.'

'Oh, good — Timmy's in the warmth!' said George, gladly. She yelled to Joanna, 'Thanks awfully! You *are* kind!'

She went indoors and told the others. They were

very glad. 'And *I've* got a bit of news for *you*,' said Dick. 'Mr Roland is in bed with a bad cold, so there are to be no lessons today. Cheers!'

'Golly, that *is* good news,' said George, cheering up tremendously. 'Timmy in the warm kitchen and Mr Roland kept in bed. I do feel pleased!'

'We shall be able to explore the Secret Way safely now,' said Julian. 'Aunt Fanny is going to do something in the kitchen this morning with Joanna, and Uncle is going to tackle the snow. I vote we say we'll do lessons by ourselves in the sitting-room, and then, when everything is safe, we'll explore the Secret Way!'

'But why must we do lessons?' asked George in dismay.

'Because if we don't, silly, we'll have to help your father dig away the snow,' said Julian.

So, to his uncle's surprise, Julian suggested that the four children should do lessons by themselves in the sitting-room. 'Well, I thought you'd like to come and help dig away the snow,' said Uncle Quentin. 'But perhaps you had better get on with your work.'

The children sat themselves down as good as gold in the sitting-room, their books before them. They heard Mr Roland coughing in his room. They heard their aunt go into the kitchen and talk to Joanna. They heard Timmy scratching at the kitchen door — then paws pattering down the passage — then a big, inquiring nose came round the door, and there was old Timmy, looking anxiously for his beloved mistress!

'Timmy!' squealed George, and ran to him. She flung her arms round his neck and hugged him.

'You act as if you hadn't seen Tim for a year,' said Julian.

'It seems like a year,' said George. 'I say, there's my father digging away like mad. Can't we go to the study now? We ought to be safe for a good while.'

They left the sitting-room and went to the study. Julian was soon pulling the handle behind the secret panel. George had already turned back the rug and the carpet. The stone slid downward and sideways. The Secret Way was open!

'Come on!' said Julian. 'Hurry!'

He jumped down into the hole. Dick followed, then Anne, then George. Julian pushed them all into the narrow, low passage. Then he looked up. Perhaps he had better pull the carpet and rug over the hole, in case anyone came into the room and looked around. It took him a few seconds to do it. Then he bent down and joined the others in the passage. They were going to explore the Secret Way at last!

15

An exciting journey and hunt

Timothy had leapt down into the hole when George had jumped. He now ran ahead of the children, puzzled at their wanting to explore such a cold, dark place. Both Julian and Dick had torches, which threw broad beams before them.

There was not much to be seen. The Secret Way under the old house was narrow and low, so that the children were forced to go in single file, and to stoop almost double. It was a great relief to them when the passage became a little wider, and the room a little higher. It was very tiring to stoop all the time.

'Have you any idea where the Secret Way is going?' Dick asked Julian. 'I mean — is it going towards the sea, or away from it?'

'Oh, not towards the sea!' said Julian, who had a very good sense of direction. 'As far as I can make out the passage is going towards the common. Look at the walls — they are rather sandy in places, and we know the common has sandy soil. I hope we shan't find that the passage has fallen in anywhere.'

They went on and on. The Secret Way was very straight, though occasionally it would round a rocky part in a curve.

'Isn't it dark and cold?' said Anne, shivering. 'I wish I had put on a coat. How many miles have we come, Julian?'

'Not even one, silly!' said Julian. 'Hallo — look here — the passage has fallen in a bit there!'

Two bright torches shone in front of them and the children saw that the sandy roof had fallen in. Julian kicked at the pile of sandy soil with his foot.

'It's all right,' he said. 'We can force our way through easily. It isn't much of a fall, and it's mostly sand. I'll do a bit of kicking!'

After some trampling and kicking, the roof-fall no longer blocked the way. There was now enough room for the children to climb over it, bending their heads low to avoid knocking them against the top of the passage. Julian shone his torch forward, and saw that the way was clear.

'The Secret Way is very wide just here!' he said suddenly, and flashed his torch around to show the others.

'It's been widened out to make a sort of little room,' said George. 'Look, there's a kind of bench at the back, made out of the rock. I believe it's a resting-place.'

George was right. It was very tiring to creep along the narrow passage for so long. The little wide place with its rocky bench made a very good resting-place. The four tired children, cold but excited, huddled together on the queer seat and took a welcome rest. Timmy put his head on George's knee. He was delighted to be with her again.

'Well, come on,' said Julian, after a few minutes. 'I'm getting awfully cold. I do wonder where this passage comes out!'

'Julian — do you think it could come out at Kirrin Farmhouse?' asked George, suddenly. 'You know what Mrs Sanders said — that there was a secret passage leading from the Farmhouse somewhere. Well, this may be the one — and it leads to Kirrin Cottage!'

'George, I believe you're right!' said Julian. 'Yes — the two houses belonged to your family years ago! And in the old days there were often secret passages joining houses, so it's quite plain this secret way joins them up together! Why didn't I think of that before?'

'I say!' squealed Anne, in a high, excited voice, 'I say! I've thought of something too!'

'What?' asked everyone.

'Well — if those two artists have got Uncle's papers, we may be able to get them away before the men can send them off by post, or take them away themselves!' squealed Anne, so thrilled with her idea that she could hardly get the words out quickly

enough. 'They're prisoners at the Farmhouse because of the snow, just as we were at the Cottage.'

'*Anne!* You're right!' said Julian.

'Clever girl!' said Dick.

'I *say* — if we *could* get those papers again — how wonderful it would be!' said George. Timmy joined in the general excitement, and jumped up and down in joy. Something had pleased the children, so he was pleased too!

'Come on!' said Julian, taking Anne's hand. 'This is thrilling. If George is right, and this Secret Way comes out at Kirrin Farmhouse somewhere, we'll somehow hunt through those men's rooms and find the papers.'

'You said that searching people's rooms was a shocking thing to do,' said George.

'Well, I didn't know then all I know now,' said Julian. 'We're doing this for your father — and maybe for our country too, if his secret formula is valuable. We've got to set our wits to work now, to outwit dangerous enemies.'

'Do you really think they are dangerous?' asked Anne rather afraid.

'Yes, I should think so,' said Julian. 'But you needn't worry, Anne, you've got me and Dick and Tim to protect you.'

'I can protect her too,' said George, indignantly. 'I'm as good as a boy any day!'

'Yes, you are, really,' said Dick. 'In fact, you're fiercer than any boy I know!'

'Come on,' said Julian, impatiently. 'I'm longing to get to the end of this passage.'

They all went on again, Anne following behind Julian, and Dick behind George. Timmy ran up and down the line, squeezing by them whenever he wanted to. He thought it was a very peculiar way to spend a morning!

Julian stopped suddenly, after they had gone a good way. 'What's up?' asked Dick, from the back. 'Not another roof-fall, I hope!'

'No — but I think we've come to the end of the passage!' said Julian, thrilled. The others crowded as close to him as they could. The passage certainly had come to an end. There was a rocky wall in front of them, and set firmly in it were iron staples intended for footholds. These went up the wall and when Julian turned his torch upwards, the children saw that there was a square opening in the roof of the passage.

'We have to climb up this rocky wall now,' said Julian, 'go through that dark hole there, keep on climbing — and goodness knows where we come out! I'll go first. You wait here, everyone, and I'll come back and tell you what I've seen.'

The boy put his torch between his teeth, and then pulled himself up by the iron staples set in the wall. He set his feet on them, and then climbed up through the square dark hole, feeling for the staples as he went.

He went up for a good way. It was almost like

going up a chimney shaft, he thought. It was cold and smelt musty.

Suddenly he came to a ledge, and he stepped on to it. He took his torch from his teeth and flashed it around him.

There was a stone wall behind him, at the side of him and stone above him. The black hole up which he had come, yawned by his feet. Julian shone his torch in front of him, and a shock of surprise went through him.

There was no stone wall in front of him, but a big wooden door, made of black oak. A handle was set about waist-high; Julian turned it with trembling fingers. What was he going to see?

The door opened outwards, over the ledge, and it was difficult to get round it without falling back into the hole. Julian managed to open it wide, squeezed round it without losing his footing, and stepped beyond it, expecting to find himself in a room.

But his hand felt more wood in front of him! He shone his torch round, and found that he was up against what looked like yet another door. Under his searching fingers it suddenly moved sideways, and slid silently away!

And then Julian knew where he was! 'I'm in the cupboard at Kirrin Farmhouse — the one that has a false back!' he thought. 'The Secret Way comes up behind it! How clever! Little did we know when we played about in this cupboard that not only did it have a sliding back, but that it was the entrance to the

Secret Way, hidden behind it!'

The cupboard was now full of clothes belonging to the artists. Julian stood and listened. There was no sound of anyone in the room. Should he just take a quick look round, and see if those lost papers were anywhere about?

Then he remembered the other four, waiting patiently below in the cold. He had better go and tell them what had happened. They could all come and help in the search.

He stepped into the space behind the sliding back. The sliding door slipped across again, and Julian was left standing on the narrow ledge, with the old oak door wide open to one side of him. He did not bother to shut it. He felt about his feet, and found the iron staples in the hole below him. Down he went, clinging with his hands and feet, his torch in his teeth again.

'Julian! What a time you've been! Quick, tell us all about it!' cried George.

'It's most terribly thrilling,' said Julian. 'Absolutely super! Where do you suppose all this leads to? Into the cupboard at Kirrin Farmhouse — the one that's got a false back!'

'Golly!' said Dick.

'I *say*!' said George.

'Did you go into the room?' cried Anne.

'I climbed as far as I could and came to a big oak door,' said Julian. 'It has a handle this side, so I swung it wide open. Then I saw another wooden door in front of me — at least, I thought it was a door, I didn't know it was just the false back of that cupboard. It was quite easy to slide back and I stepped through, and found myself among a whole lot of clothes hanging in the cupboard! Then I hurried back to tell you.'

'Julian! We can hunt for those papers now,' said George, eagerly. 'Was there anyone in the room?'

'I couldn't *hear* anyone,' said Julian. 'Now what I propose is this — we'll all go up, and have a hunt round those two rooms. The men have the room next to the cupboard one too.'

'Oh good!' said Dick, thrilled at the thought of such an adventure. 'Let's go now. You go first, Ju. Then Anne, then George and then me.'

'What about Tim?' asked George.

'He can't climb, silly,' said Julian. 'He's a simply marvellous dog, but he certainly can't climb, George. We'll have to leave him down here.'

'He won't like that,' said George.

'Well, we can't carry him up,' said Dick. 'You won't mind staying here for a bit, will you, Tim, old fellow?'

Tim wagged his tail. But, as he saw the four children mysteriously disappearing up the wall, he put his big tail down at once. What! Going without him? How could they?

He jumped up at the wall, and fell back. He jumped again and whined. George called down in a low voice.

'Be quiet, Tim dear! We shan't be long.'

Tim stopped whining. He lay down at the bottom of the wall, his ears well-cocked. This adventure was becoming more and more peculiar!

Soon the children were on the narrow ledge. The old oak door was still wide open. Julian shone his torch and the others saw the false back of the cupboard. Julian put his hands on it and it slid silently sideways. Then the torch shone on coats and dressing-gowns!

The children stood quite still, listening. There was no sound from the room. 'I'll open the cupboard door and peep into the room,' whispered Julian. 'Don't make a sound!'

The boy pushed between the clothes and felt for the outer cupboard door with his hand. He found it, and pushed it slightly. It opened a little and a shaft of daylight came into the cupboard. He peeped cautiously into the room.

There was no one there at all. That was good. 'Come on!' he whispered to the others. 'The room's empty!'

One by one the children crept out of the clothes cupboard and into the room. There was a big bed there, a wash-stand, chest of drawers, small table and two chairs. Nothing else. It would be easy to search the whole room.

'Look, Julian, there's a door between the two rooms,' said George, suddenly. 'Two of us can go and hunt there and two here — and we can lock the doors that lead on to the landing, so that no one can come in and catch us!'

'Good idea!' said Julian, who was afraid that at any moment someone might come in and catch them in their search. 'Anne and I will go into the next room, and you and Dick can search this one. Lock the door that opens on to the landing, Dick, and I'll lock the one in the other room. We'll leave the connecting-door open, so that we can whisper to one another.'

Quietly the boy and girl slipped through the connecting-door into the second room, which was very like the first. That was empty too. Julian went over to the door that led to the landing, and turned the key in the lock. He heard Dick doing the same to the door in the other room. He heaved a big sigh. Now he felt safe!

'Anne, turn up the rugs and see if any papers are hidden there,' he said. 'Then look under the chair-cushions and strip the bed to see if anything is hidden under the mattress.'

Anne set to work, and Julian began to hunt too. He started on the chest of drawers, which he thought would be a very likely place to hide things in. The children's hands were shaking, as they felt here and there for the lost papers. It was so terribly exciting.

They wondered where the two men were. Down in the warm kitchen, perhaps. It was cold up here in the bedrooms, and they would not want to be away from the warmth. They could not go out because the snow was piled in great drifts round Kirrin Farmhouse!

Dick and George were searching hard in the other room. They looked in every drawer. They stripped the bed. They turned up rugs and carpet. They even put their hands up the big chimney-place!

'Julian? Have you found anything?' asked Dick in a low voice, appearing at the door between the two rooms.

'Not a thing,' said Julian, rather gloomily. 'They've hidden the papers well! I only hope they haven't got them on them — in their pockets, or something!'

Dick stared at him in dismay. He hadn't thought of that. 'That *would* be sickening!' he said.

'You go back and hunt *everywhere* — simply *everywhere!*' ordered Julian. 'Punch the pillows to see if they've stuck them under the pillow-case!'

Dick disappeared. Rather a lot of noise came from his room. It sounded as if he were doing a good deal of punching!

Anne and Julian went on hunting too. There was simply nowhere that they did not look. They even turned the pictures round to see if the papers had been stuck behind one of them. But there was nothing to be found. It was bitterly disappointing.

'We can't go without finding them,' said Julian, in desperation. 'It was such a bit of luck to get here like this, down the Secret Way — right into the bedrooms! We simply *must* find those papers!'

'I say,' said Dick, appearing again, 'I can hear

voices! Listen!'

All four children listened. Yes — there were men's voices — just outside the bedroom doors!

16

The children are discovered

'What shall we do?' whispered George. They had all tiptoed to the first room, and were standing together, listening.

'We'd better go down the Secret Way again,' said Julian.

'Oh no, we . . .' began George, when she heard the handle of the door being turned. Whoever was trying to get in, could not open the door. There was an angry exclamation, and then the children heard Mr Wilton's voice. 'Thomas! My door seems to have stuck. Do you mind if I come through your bedroom and see what's the matter with this handle?'

'Come right along!' came the voice of Mr Thomas. There was the sound of footsteps going to the outer door of the second room. Then there was the noise of a handle being turned and shaken.

'What's this!' said Mr Wilton, in exasperation. 'This won't open, either. Can the doors be locked?'

'It looks like it!' said Mr Thomas.

There was a pause. Then the children distinctly heard a few words uttered in a low voice. 'Are the papers safe? Is anyone after them?'

'They're in your room, aren't they?' said Mr Thomas. There was another pause. The children looked at one another. So the men *had* got the papers — and what was more, they *were* in the room! The very room the children stood in! They looked round it eagerly, racking their brains to think of some place they had not yet explored.

'Quick! Hunt round again while we've time,' whispered Julian. 'Don't make a noise.'

On tiptoe the children began a thorough hunt once more. How they searched! They even opened the pages of the books on the table, thinking that the papers might have been slipped in there. But they could find nothing.

'Hi, Mrs Sanders!' came Mr Wilton's voice. 'Have you by any chance locked these two doors? We can't get in!'

'Dear me!' said the voice of Mrs Sanders from the stairs. 'I'll come along and see. I certainly haven't locked any doors!'

Once again the handles were turned, but the doors would not open. The men began to get very impatient.

'Do you suppose anyone is in our rooms?' Mr

Wilton asked Mrs Sanders.

She laughed.

'Well now, sir, who would be in your rooms? There's only me and Mr Sanders in the house, and you know as well as I do that no one can come in from outside, for we're quite snowed up. I don't understand it — the locks of the doors must have slipped.'

Anne was lifting up the wash-stand jug to look underneath, at that moment. It was heavier than she thought, and she had to let it down again suddenly. It struck the marble wash-stand with a crash, and water slopped out all over the place!

Everyone outside the door heard the noise. Mr Wilton banged on the door and rattled the handle.

'Who's there? Let us in or you'll be sorry! What are you doing in there?'

'Idiot, Anne!' said Dick. 'Now they'll break the door down!'

That was exactly what the two men intended to do! Afraid that someone was mysteriously in their room, trying to find the stolen papers, they went quite mad, and began to put their shoulders to the door, and heave hard. The door shook and creaked.

'Now you be careful what you're doing!' cried the indignant voice of Mrs Sanders. The men took no notice. There came a crash as they both tried out their double strength on the door.

'Quick! We must go!' said Julian. 'We mustn't let the men know how we got here, or we shan't be able to come and hunt another time. Anne,

George, Dick — get back to the cupboard quickly!'

The children raced for the clothes cupboard. 'I'll go first and help you down,' said Julian. He got out on to the narrow ledge and found the iron foot-holds with his feet. Down he went, torch held between his teeth as usual.

'Anne, come next,' he called. 'And Dick, you come third, and give a hand to Anne if she wants it. George is a good climber — she can easily get down herself.'

Anne was slow at climbing down. She was terribly excited, rather frightened, and so afraid of falling that she hardly dared to feel for each iron staple as she went down.

'Buck up, Anne!' whispered Dick, above her. 'The men have almost got the door down!'

There were tremendous sounds coming from the bedroom door. At any moment now it might break down, and the men would come racing in. Dick was thankful when he could begin to climb down the wall! Once they were all out, George could shut the big oak door, and they would be safe.

George was hidden among the clothes in the cupboard, waiting her turn to climb down. As she stood there, trying in vain to go over any likely hiding-place in her mind, her hands felt something rustly in the pocket of a coat she was standing against. It was a macintosh coat, with big pockets. The little girl's heart gave a leap.

Suppose the papers had been left in the pocket of the coat the man had on when he took them from Mr

Roland? That was the only place the children had not searched — the pockets of the coats in the cupboard! With trembling fingers the girl felt in the pocket where the rustling was.

She drew out a sheaf of papers. It was dark in the cupboard, and she could not see if they were the ones she was hunting for, or not — but how she hoped they were! She stuffed them up the front of her jersey, for she had no big pocket, and whispered to Dick:

'Can I come now?'

CRASH! The door fell in with a terrific noise, and the two men leapt into the room. They looked round. It was empty! But there was the water spilt on the wash-stand and on the floor. Someone must be there somewhere!

'Look in the cupboard!' said Mr Thomas.

George crept out of the clothes cupboard and on to the narrow ledge, beyond the place where the false back of the cupboard used to be. It was still hidden sideways in the wall. The girl climbed down the hole a few steps and then shut the oak door which was now above her head. She had not enough strength to close it completely, but she hoped that now she was safe!

The men went to the cupboard and felt about in the clothes for anyone who might possibly be hiding there. Mr Wilton gave a loud cry.

'The papers are gone! They were in this pocket! There's not a sign of them. Quick, Thomas, we must find the thief and get them back!'

The men did not notice that the cupboard seemed

to go farther back than usual. They stepped away from it now that they were sure no one was there, and began to hunt round the room.

By now all the children except George were at the bottom of the hole, standing in the Secret Way, waiting impatiently for George to come down. Poor George was in such a hurry to get down that she caught her clothing on one of the staples, and had to stand in a very dangerous position trying to disentangle it.

'Come on, George, for goodness' sake!' said Julian.

Timothy jumped up at the wall. He could feel the fear and excitement of the waiting children, and it upset him. He wanted George. Why didn't she come? Why was she up that dark hole? Tim was unhappy about her.

He threw back his head and gave such a loud and mournful howl that all the children jumped violently.

'Shut up, Tim!' said Julian.

Tim howled again, and the weird sound echoed round and about in a queer manner. Anne was terrified, and she began to cry. Timothy howled again and again. Once he began to howl it was difficult to stop him.

The men in the bedroom above heard the extraordinary noise, and stopped in amazement.

'Whatever's that?' said one.

'Sounds like a dog howling in the depths of the earth,' said the other.

'Funny!' said Mr Wilton. 'It seems to be coming

from the direction of that cupboard.'

He went over to it and opened the door. Tim chose that moment to give a specially mournful howl, and Mr Wilton jumped. He got into the cupboard and felt about at the back. The oak door there gave way beneath his hand, and he felt it open.

'Thomas! There's something queer here,' called Mr Wilton. 'Bring my torch off the table.'

Tim howled again and the noise made Mr Wilton shiver! Tim had a peculiarly horrible howl. It came echoing up the hole, and burst out into the cupboard.

Mr Thomas got the torch. The men shone it at the back of the cupboard, and gave an exclamation.

'Look at that! There's a door here! Where does it lead to?'

Mrs Sanders, who had been watching everything in surprise and indignation, angry that her door should have been broken down, came up to the cupboard.

'My!' she said. 'I knew there was a false back to that cupboard — but I didn't know there was another door behind it too! That must be the entrance to the Secret Way that people used in the old days.'

'Where does it lead to?' rapped out Mr Wilton.

'Goodness knows!' said Mrs Sanders. 'I never took much interest in such things.'

'Come on, Thomas — we must go down,' said Mr Wilton, shining his torch into the square black hole, and seeing the iron foot-holds set in the stone. 'This is where the thief went. He can't have got far. We'll go after him. We've got to get those papers back!'

It was not long before the two men had swung themselves over the narrow ledge and down into the hole, feeling with their feet for the iron staples. Down they went and down, wondering where they were coming to. There was no sound below them. Clearly the thief had got away!

George had got down at last. Tim almost knocked her over in his joy. She put her hand on his head. 'You old silly!' she said. 'I believe you've given our secret away! Quick, Ju — we must go, because those men will be after us in a minute. They could easily hear Tim's howling!'

Julian took Anne's hand. 'Come along, Anne,' he said. 'You must run as fast as you can. Hurry now! Dick, keep with George.'

The four of them hurried down the dark, narrow passage. What a long way they had to go home! If only the passage wasn't such a long one! The children's hearts were beating painfully as they made haste, stumbling as they went.

Julian shone his light steadily in front of him, and Dick shone his at the back. Half-leading, half-dragging Anne, Julian hurried along. Behind them they heard a shout.

'Look! There's a light ahead! That's the thief! Come on, we'll soon get him!'

17

Good old Tim!

'Hurry, Anne. Do hurry!' shouted Dick, who was just behind.

Poor Anne was finding it very difficult to get along quickly. Pulled by Julian and pushed by Dick, she almost fell two or three times. Her breath came in loud pants, and she felt as if she would burst.

'Let me have a rest!' she panted. But there was no time for that, with the two men hurrying after them! They came to the piece that was widened out, where the rocky bench was, and Anne looked longingly at it. But the boys hurried her on.

Suddenly the little girl caught her foot on a stone and fell heavily, almost dragging Julian down with her. She tried to get up, and began to cry.

'I've hurt my foot! I've twisted it! Oh, Julian, it hurts me to walk.'

'Well, you've just *got* to come along, darling,' said Julian, sorry for his little sister, but knowing that they would all be caught if he was not firm. 'Hurry as much as you can.'

But now it was impossible for Anne to go fast. She cried with pain as her foot hurt her, and hobbled along so slowly that Dick almost fell over her. Dick cast a look behind him and saw the light of the men's torches coming nearer and nearer. Whatever were they to do?

'I'll stay here with Tim and keep them off,' said George, suddenly. 'Here, take these papers, Dick! I believe they're the ones we want, but I'm not sure till we get a good light to see them. I found them in a pocket of one of the coats in the cupboard.'

'Golly!' said Dick, surprised. He took the sheaf of papers and stuffed them up his jersey, just as George had stuffed them up hers. They were too big to go into his trousers pockets. 'I'll stay with you, George, and let the other two go on ahead.'

'No. I want the papers taken to safety, in case they are my father's,' said George. 'Go on, Dick! I'll be all right here with Tim. I shall stay here just where the passage curves round this rocky bit. I'll make Tim bark like mad.'

'Suppose the men have got revolvers?' said Dick, doubtfully. 'They might shoot him.'

'I bet they haven't,' said George. '*Do* go, Dick! The men are almost here. There's the light of their torch.'

Dick sped after the stumbling Anne. He told Julian

what George had suggested. 'Good for George!' said Julian. 'She really is marvellous — not afraid of anything! She will keep the men off till I get poor old Anne back.'

George was crouching behind the rocky bit, her hand on Tim's collar, waiting. 'Now, Tim!' she whispered. 'Bark your loudest. Now!'

Timothy had been growling up till now, but at George's command he opened his big mouth and barked. How he barked! He had a simply enormous voice, and the barks went echoing all down the dark and narrow passage. The hurrying men, who were near the rocky piece of the passage, stopped.

'If you come round this bend, I'll set my dog on you!' cried George.

'It's a child shouting,' said one man to another. 'Only a child! Come on!'

Timothy barked again, and pulled at his collar. He was longing to get at the men. The light of their torch shone round the bend. George let Tim go, and the big dog sprang joyfully round the curve to meet his enemies.

They suddenly saw him by the light of their torch, and he was a very terrifying sight! To begin with, he was a big dog, and now that he was angry all the hairs on the back of his neck had risen up, making him look even more enormous. His teeth were bared and glinted in the torch-light.

The men did not like the look of him at all. 'If you move one step nearer I'll tell my dog to fly at you!'

shouted George. 'Wait, Tim, wait! Stand there till I give the word.'

The dog stood in the light of the torch, growling deeply. He looked an extremely fierce animal. The men looked at him doubtfully. One man took a step forward and George heard him. At once she shouted to Tim.

'Go for him, Tim, go for him!'

Tim leapt at the man's throat. He took him completely by surprise and the man fell to the ground with a thud, trying to beat off the dog. The other man helped.

'Call off your dog or we'll hurt him!' cried the second man.

'It's much more likely he'll hurt *you*!' said George, coming out from behind the rock and enjoying the fun. 'Tim, come off.'

Tim came away from the man he was worrying, looking up at his mistress as if to say, 'I was having *such* a good time! Why did you spoil it?'

'Who are you?' said the man on the ground.

'I'm not answering any of your questions,' said George. 'Go back to Kirrin Farmhouse, that's my advice to you. If you dare to come along this passage I'll set my dog on to you again — and next time he'll do more damage.'

The men turned and went back the way they had come. They neither of them wanted to face Tim again. George waited until she could no longer see the light of their torch, then she bent down and

375

patted Timothy.

'Brave, good dog!' she said. 'I love you, darling Tim, and you don't know how proud I am of you! Come along — we'll hurry after the others now. I expect those two men will explore this passage some time tonight, and won't they get a shock when they find out where it leads to, and see who is waiting for them!'

George hurried along the rest of the long passage, with Tim running beside her. She had Dick's torch, and it did not take her long to catch the others up. She panted out to them what had happened, and even poor Anne chuckled in delight when she heard how Tim had flung Mr Wilton to the ground.

'Here we are,' said Julian, as the passage came to a stop below the hole in the study floor. 'Hallo — what's this?'

A bright light was shining down the hole, and the rug and carpet, so carefully pulled over the hole by Julian, were now pulled back again. The children gazed up in surprise.

Uncle Quentin was there, and Aunt Fanny, and when they saw the children's faces looking up at them from the hole, they were so astonished that they very nearly fell down the hole too!

'Julian! Anne! What in the wide world are you doing down there?' cried Uncle Quentin. He gave them each a hand up, and the four children and Timothy were at last safe in the warm study. How good it was to feel warm again! They got as near the fire as they could.

'Children — what *is* the meaning of this?' asked Aunt Fanny. She looked white and worried. 'I came into the study to do some dusting, and when I stood on that bit of the rug, it seemed to give way beneath me. When I pulled it up and turned back the carpet, I saw that hole — and the hole in the panelling too! And then I found that all of you had disappeared, and went to fetch your uncle. What *has* been happening — and where does that hole lead to?'

Dick took the sheaf of papers from under his jersey and gave them to George. She took them and handed them to her father. 'Are these the missing pages?' she asked.

Her father fell on them as if they had been worth more than a hundred times their weight in gold. 'Yes! Yes! They're the pages — all three of them! Thank goodness they're back. They took me three years to bring to perfection, and contained the heart of my secret formula. George, where did you get them?'

'It's a very long story,' said George. 'You tell it all, Julian, I feel tired.'

Julian began to tell the tale. He left out nothing. He told how George had found Mr Roland snooping about the study — how she had felt sure that the tutor had not wanted Timmy in the house because the dog gave warning of his movements at night — how George had seen him talking to the two artists, although he had said he did not know them. As the tale went on, Uncle Quentin and Aunt Fanny looked more and more amazed. They simply could not believe it all.

But after all, there were the missing papers, safely back. That was marvellous. Uncle Quentin hugged the papers as if they were a precious baby. He would not put them down for a moment.

George told the bit about Timmy keeping the men off the escaping children. 'So you see, although you made poor Tim live out in the cold, away from me, he really saved us all, and your papers too,' she said to her father, fixing her brilliant blue eyes on him.

Her father looked most uncomfortable. He felt very guilty for having punished George and Timothy. They had been right about Mr Roland and he had been wrong.

'Poor George,' he said, 'and poor Timmy. I'm sorry about all that.'

George did not bear malice once anyone had owned themselves to be in the wrong. She smiled at her father.

'It's all right,' she said. 'But don't you think that as I was punished unfairly, Mr Roland might be punished well and truly? He deserves it!'

'Oh, he shall be, certainly he shall be,' promised her father. 'He's up in bed with a cold, as you know. I hope he doesn't hear any of this, or he may try to escape.'

'He can't,' said George. 'We're snowed up. You could ring up the police, and arrange for them to come here as soon as ever they can manage it, when the snow has cleared. And I rather think those other two men will try to explore the Secret Way as soon as possible, to get the papers back. Could we catch them when they arrive, do you think?'

'Rather!' said Uncle Quentin, though Aunt Fanny looked as if she didn't want any more exciting things to happen! 'Now look here, you seem really frozen all of you, and you must be hungry too, because it's almost lunch-time. Go into the dining-room and sit by the fire, and Joanna shall bring us all a hot lunch. Then we'll talk about what to do.'

Nobody said a word to Mr Roland, of course. He lay in bed, coughing now and then. George had slipped up and locked his door. She wasn't going to have him wandering out and overhearing anything!

They all enjoyed their hot lunch, and became warm and cosy. It was nice to sit there together, talking over their adventure, and planning what to do.

'I will telephone to the police, of course,' said Uncle Quentin. 'And tonight we will put Timmy into the study to give the two artists a good welcome if they arrive!'

Mr Roland was most annoyed to find his door locked that afternoon when he took it into his head to dress and go downstairs. He banged on it indignantly. George grinned and went upstairs. She had told the other children how she had locked the door.

'What's the matter, Mr Roland?' she asked, in a polite voice.

379

'Oh, it's you, George, is it?' said the tutor. 'See what's the matter with my door, will you? I can't open it.'

George had pocketed the key when she had locked the door. She answered Mr Roland in a cheerful voice.

'Oh Mr Roland, there's no key in your door, so I can't unlock it. I'll see if I can find it!'

Mr Roland was angry and puzzled. He couldn't understand why his door was locked and the key gone. He did not guess that everyone knew about him now. Uncle Quentin laughed when George went down and told him about the locked door.

'He may as well be kept a prisoner,' he said. 'He can't escape now.'

That night, everyone went to bed early, and Timmy was left in the study, guarding the hole. Mr Roland had become more and more angry and puzzled when his door was not unlocked. He had shouted for Uncle Quentin, but only George had come. He could not understand it. George, of course, was enjoying herself. She made Timothy bark outside Mr Roland's door, and this puzzled him too, for he knew that George was not supposed to see Timmy for three days. Wild thoughts raced through his head. Had that fierce, impossible child locked up her father and mother and Joanna, as well as himself? He could not imagine what had happened.

In the middle of the night Timmy awoke everyone by barking madly. Uncle Quentin and the children hurried downstairs, followed by Aunt Fanny, and the amazed Joanna. A fine sight met their eyes!

Mr Wilton and Mr Thomas were in the study crouching behind the sofa, terrified of Timothy, who was barking for all he was worth! Timmy was standing by the hole in the stone floor, so that the two men could not escape down there. Artful Timmy! He had waited in silence until the men had crept up the hole into the study, and were exploring it, wondering where they were — and then the dog had leapt to the hole to guard it, preventing the men from escaping.

'Good evening, Mr Wilton, good evening, Mr Thomas,' said George, in polite voice. 'Have you come to see our tutor Mr Roland?'

'So this is where he lives!' said Mr Wilton. 'Was it you in the passage today?'

'Yes — and my cousins,' said George. 'Have you come to look for the papers you stole from my father?'

The two men were silent. They knew they were caught. Mr Wilton spoke after a moment.

'Where's Roland?'

'Shall we take these men to Mr Roland, Uncle?' asked Julian, winking at George. 'Although it's in the middle of the night I'm sure he would love to see them.'

'Yes,' said his uncle, jumping at once to what the boy meant to do. 'Take them up. Timmy, you go too.'

The men followed Julian upstairs, Timmy close at their heels. George followed too, grinning. She handed Julian the key. He unlocked the door and the men went in, just as Julian switched on the light. Mr Roland was wide awake and gave an exclamation of complete amazement when he saw his friends.

Before they had time to say a word Julian locked the door again and threw the key to George.

'A nice little bag of prisoners,' he said. 'We will leave old Tim outside the door to guard them. It's impossible to get out of that window, and anyway, we're snowed up if they could escape that way.'

Everyone went to bed again, but the children

found it difficult to sleep after such an exciting time. Anne and George whispered together and so did Julian and Dick. There was such a lot to talk about.

Next day there was a surprise for everyone. The police did arrive after all! The snow did not stop them, for somewhere or other they had got skis and had come skimming along valiantly to see the prisoners! It was a great excitement for everyone.

'We won't take the men away, sir, till the snow has gone,' said the Inspector. 'We'll just put the handcuffs on them, so that they don't try any funny tricks. You keep the door locked too, and that dog outside. They'll be safe there for a day or two. We've taken them enough food till we come back again. If they go a bit short, it will serve them right!'

The snow melted two days later, and the police took away Mr Roland and the others. The children watched.

'No more lessons *these* hols!' said Anne gleefully.

'No more shutting Timothy out of the house,' said George.

'You were right and we were wrong, George,' said Julian. 'You were fierce, weren't you? — but it's a jolly good thing you were!'

'She *is* fierce, isn't she?' said Dick, giving the girl a sudden hug. 'But I rather like her when she's fierce, don't you, Julian? Oh George, we do have marvellous adventures with you! I wonder if we'll have any more?'

They will — there isn't a doubt of that!

Enid Blyton

FIVE GO TO SMUGGLER'S TOP

ILLUSTRATED BY JOLYNE KNOX

1

Back to Kirrin Cottage

One fine day right at the beginning of the Easter holidays, four children and a dog travelled by train together.

'Soon be there now,' said Julian, a tall strong boy, with a determined face.

'Woof,' said Timothy the dog, getting excited, and trying to look out of the window too.

'Get down, Tim,' said Julian. 'Let Anne have a look.'

Anne was his younger sister. She put her head out of the window. 'We're coming into Kirrin Station!' she said. 'I do hope Aunt Fanny will be there to meet us.'

'Of course she will!' said Georgina, her cousin. She looked more like a boy than a girl, for she wore her hair very short, and it curled close about her head. She too had a determined face, like Julian. She pushed Anne away and looked out of the window.

'It's nice to be going home,' she said. 'I love school

387

— but it will be fun to be at Kirrin Cottage and perhaps sail out to Kirrin Island and visit the castle there. We haven't been since last summer.'

'Dick's turn to look out now,' said Julian, turning to his younger brother, a boy with a pleasant face, sitting reading in a corner. 'We're just coming into sight of Kirrin, Dick. Can't you stop reading for a second?'

'It's such an exciting book,' said Dick, and shut it with a clap. 'The most exciting adventure story I've ever read!'

'Pooh! I bet it's not as exciting as some of the adventures *we've* had!' said Anne, at once.

It was quite true that the five of them, counting in Timmy the dog, who always shared everything with them, had had the most amazing adventures together. But now it looked as if they were going to have nice quiet holidays, going for long walks over the cliffs, and perhaps sailing out in George's boat to their island of Kirrin.

'I've worked jolly hard at school this term,' said Julian. 'I could do with a holiday!'

'You've gone thin,' said Georgina. Nobody called her that. They all called her George. She would never answer to any other name. Julian grinned.

'Well, I'll soon get fat at Kirrin Cottage, don't you worry! Aunt Fanny will see to that. She's a great one for trying to fatten people up. It will be nice to see your mother again, George. She's an awfully good sort.'

'Yes. I hope Father will be in a good temper these hols,' said George. 'He ought to be because he has just finished some new experiments, Mother says, which have been quite successful.'

George's father was a scientist, always working out new ideas. He liked to be quiet, and sometimes he

388

flew into a temper when he could not get the peace he needed or things did not go exactly as he wanted them to. The children often thought that hot-tempered Georgina was very like her father! She too could fly into fierce tempers when things did not go right for her.

Aunt Fanny was there to meet them. The four children jumped out on the platform and rushed to hug her. George got there first. She was very fond of her gentle mother, who had so often tried to shield her when her father got angry with her. Timmy pranced round, barking in delight. He adored George's mother.

She patted him, and he tried to stand up and lick her face. 'Timmy's bigger than ever!' she said, laughing.'Down, old boy! You'll knock me over.'

Timmy was certainly a big dog. All the children loved him, for he was loyal, loving and faithful. His brown eyes looked from one to the other, enjoying the children's excitement. Timmy shared in it, as he shared in everything.

But the person he loved most, of course, was his mistress, George. She had had him since he was a small puppy. She took him to school with her each term, for she and Anne went to a boarding-school that allowed pets. Otherwise George would most certainly have refused to go!

They set off to Kirrin in the pony-trap. It was very windy and cold, and the children shivered and pulled their coats tightly round them.

'It's awfully cold,' said Anne, her teeth beginning to chatter. 'Colder than in the winter!'

'It's the wind,' said her aunt, and tucked a rug round her. 'It's been getting very strong the last day or two. The fishermen have pulled their boats high up the beach for fear of a big storm.'

The children saw the boats pulled right up as they passed the beach where they had bathed so often. They did not feel like bathing now. It made them shiver even to think of it.

The wind howled over the sea. Great scudding clouds raced overhead. The waves pounded on the beach and made a terrific noise. It excited Timmy, who began to bark.

'Be quiet, Tim,' said George, patting him. 'You will have to learn to be a good quiet dog now we are home again, or Father will be cross with you. Is Father very busy, Mother?'

'Very,' said her mother. 'But he's going to do very little work now you are coming home. He thought he would like to go for walks with you, or go out in the boat, if the weather calms down.'

The children looked at one another. Uncle Quentin was not the best of companions. He had no sense of humour, and when the children went off into fits of laughter, as they did twenty times a day or more, he could not see the joke at all.

'It looks as if these hols won't be quite so jolly if Uncle Quentin parks himself on us most of the time,' said Dick in a low voice to Julian.

'Sh,' said Julian, afraid that his aunt would hear, and be hurt. George frowned.

'Oh Mother! Father will be bored stiff if he comes with us — and we'll be bored too.'

George was very outspoken, and could never learn to keep a guard on her tongue. Her mother sighed. 'Don't talk like that, dear. I daresay your father will get tired of going with you after a bit. But it does him good to have a bit of young life about him.'

'Here we are!' said Julian, as the trap stopped outside an old house. 'Kirrin Cottage! My word, how the wind is howling round it, Aunt Fanny!'

'Yes. It made a terrible noise last night,' said his aunt. 'You take the trap round to the back, Julian, when we've got the things out. Oh, here's your uncle to help!'

Uncle Quentin came out, a tall, clever-looking man, with rather frowning eyebrows. He smiled at the children and kissed George and Anne.

'Welcome to Kirrin Cottage!' he said, 'I'm quite glad your mother and father are away, Anne, because now we shall have you all here once again!'

Soon they were sitting round the table eating a big tea. Aunt Fanny always got ready a fine meal for their first one, for she knew they were very hungry after their long journey in the train.

Even George was satisfied at last, and leaned back in her chair, wishing she could manage just one more of her mother's delicious new-made buns.

Timmy sat close to her. He was not supposed to be fed at meal-times but it was really surprising how many titbits found their way to him under the table!

The wind howled round the house. The windows rattled, the doors shook, and the mats lifted themselves up and down as the draught got under them.

'They look as if they've got snakes wriggling underneath them,' said Anne. Timmy watched them and growled. He was a clever dog, but he did not know why the mats wriggled in such a queer way.

'I hope the wind will die down tonight,' said Aunt Fanny. 'It kept me awake last night. Julian dear, you look rather thin. Have you been working hard? I must fatten you up.'

The children laughed. 'Just what we thought you'd say, Mother!' said George. 'Goodness, what's that?'

They all sat still, startled. There was a loud bumping noise on the roof, and Timmy put up his ears and growled fiercely.

'A tile off the roof,' said Uncle Quentin. 'How tiresome! We shall have to get the loose tiles seen to, Fanny, when the storm is over, or the rain will come in.'

The children rather hoped that their uncle would retire to his study after tea, as he usually did, but this time he didn't. They wanted to play a game, but it wasn't much good with Uncle Quentin there. He really wasn't any good at all, not even at such a simple game as snap.

'Do you know a boy called Pierre Lenoir?' suddenly asked Uncle Quentin, taking a letter from his pocket. 'I believe he goes to your school and Dick's, Julian.'

'Pierre Lenoir — oh you mean old Sooty,' said Julian. 'Yes — he's in Dick's form, sir. Mad as a hatter.'

'Sooty! Now why do you call him that?' said Uncle Quentin. 'It seems a silly name for a boy.'

'If you saw him you wouldn't think so,' said Dick, with a laugh. 'He's awfully dark! Hair as black as soot, eyes like bits of coal, eyebrows that look as if they've been put in with charcoal. And his name means "The black one," doesn't it? Le-noir — that's French for black.'

'Yes. Quite true. But what a name to give anyone — *Sooty*!' said Uncle Quentin. 'Well, I've been having quite a lot of correspondence with this boy's father. He and I are interested in the same scientific matters. In fact, I've asked him whether he wouldn't like to come and stay with me a few days — and bring his boy, Pierre.'

'Oh really!' said Dick, looking quite pleased. 'Well it wouldn't be bad sport to have old Sooty here, Uncle. But he's quite mad. He never does as he's told, he climbs like a monkey, and he can be awfully cheeky. I don't know if you'd like him much.'

Uncle Quentin looked sorry he had asked Sooty after he had heard what Dick had to say. He didn't like cheeky boys. Nor did he like mad ones.

'H'm,' he said, putting the letter away. 'I wish I'd asked you about the boy first, before suggesting to his father that he might bring him with him. But perhaps I can prevent him coming.'

'No, don't, Father,' said George, who rather liked the sound of Sooty Lenoir. 'Let's have him. He could come out with us and liven things up!'

'We'll see,' said her father, who had already made up his mind on no account to have the boy at Kirrin Cottage, if he was mad, climbed everywhere, and was cheeky. George was enough of a handful without a madcap of a boy egging her on!

Much to the children's relief Uncle Quentin retired to read by himself about eight o'clock. Aunt Fanny looked at the clock.

'Time for Anne to go to bed,' she said. 'And you too, George.'

'Just one good game of Slap-Down Patience, all of us playing it together, Mother!' said George. 'Come on — you play it too. It's our first evening at home. Anyway, I shan't sleep for ages, with this gale howling round! Come on, Mother — one good game, then we'll go to bed. Julian's been yawning like anything already!'

2

A shock in the night

It was nice to climb up the steep stairs to their familiar bedrooms that night. All the children were yawning widely. Their long train journey had tired them.

'If only this awful wind would stop!' said Anne, pulling the curtain aside and looking out into the night. 'There's a little moon, George. It keeps bobbing out between the scurrying clouds.'

'Let it bob!' said George, scrambling into bed. 'I'm jolly cold. Hurry, Anne, or you'll catch a chill at that window.'

'Don't the waves make a noise?' said Anne, still at the window. 'And the gale in the old ash-tree is making a whistling, howling sound, and bending it right over.'

'Timmy, hurry up and get on my bed,' commanded George, screwing up her cold toes. 'That's one good thing about being at home, Anne. I can have Timmy on my bed! He's far better than a hot water bottle.'

'You're not supposed to have him on your bed at home, any more than you're supposed to at school,' said Anne, curling up in bed. 'Aunt Fanny thinks he sleeps in his basket over there.'

'Well, I can't stop him coming on my bed at night, can I, if he doesn't want to sleep in his basket?' said George. 'That's right, Timmy darling. Make my feet warm. Where's your nose? Let me pat it. Good-night, Tim. Good-night, Anne.'

'Good-night,' said Anne, sleepily. 'I hope that Sooty boy comes, don't you? He does sound fun.'

'Yes. And anyway Father would stay in with Mr Lenoir, the boy's father, and not come out with us,' said George. 'Father doesn't mean to, but he does spoil things somehow.'

'He's not very good at laughing,' said Anne. 'He's too serious.'

A loud bang made both girls jump. 'That's the bathroom door!' said George, with a groan. 'One of the boys must have left it open. That's the sort of noise that drives Father mad! There it goes again!'

'Well, let Julian or Dick shut it,' said Anne, who was now beginning to feel nice and warm. But Julian and Dick were thinking that George or Anne might shut it, so nobody got out of bed to see to the banging door.

Very soon Uncle Quentin's voice roared up the stairs, louder than the gale.

'Shut that door, one of you! How can I work with that noise going on!'

All four children jumped out of bed like a shot. Timmy leapt off George's bed. Everyone fell over him as they rushed to the bathroom door. There was a lot of giggling and scuffling. Then Uncle Quentin's footsteps were heard on the stairs and the five fled silently to their rooms.

The gale still roared. Uncle Quentin and Aunt Fanny came up to bed. The bedroom door flew out of Uncle Quentin's hand and slammed itself shut so violently that a vase leapt off a nearby shelf.

Uncle Quentin leapt too, startled. 'This wretched gale!' he said, fiercely. 'Never known one like it all the time we've been here. If it gets much worse the fishermen's boats will be smashed up, even though they've pulled them as high up the beach as possible.'

'It will blow itself out soon, dear,' said Aunt Fanny, soothingly. 'Probably by the time morning comes it will be quite calm.'

But she was wrong. The gale did not blow itself out that night. Instead it raged round the house even more fiercely, shrieking and howling like a live thing. Nobody could sleep. Timmy kept up a continuous low growling, for he did not like the shakes and rattles and howls.

Towards dawn the wind seemed in a fury. Anne thought it sounded as if it was in a horrible temper, out to do all the harm it could. She lay and trembled, half-frightened.

Suddenly there was a strange noise. It was a loud and woeful groaning and creaking, like someone in great pain. The two girls sat up, terrified. What could it be?

The boys heard it too. Julian leapt out of bed and ran to the window. Outside stood the old ash tree, tall and black in the fitful moonlight. It was gradually bending over!

'It's the ash! It's falling!' yelled Julian, almost startling Dick out of his wits. 'It's falling, I tell you. It'll crash on the house! Quick, warn the girls!'

Shouting at the top of his voice, Julian raced out of his door on to the landing. 'Uncle! Aunt! George and Anne! Come downstairs quickly. The ash tree is falling!'

George jumped out of bed, snatched at her dressing-gown, and raced to the door, yelling to Anne. The little girl was soon with her. Timmy ran in front. At the door of Aunt Fanny's bedroom Uncle Quentin appeared, tall and amazed, wrapping his dressing-grown round him.

'What's all this noise? Julian, what's —?'

'Aunt Fanny! Come downstairs — the ash tree is falling! Listen to its terrible groans and creaks!' yelled Julian, almost beside himself with impatience. 'It'll smash in the room and the bedrooms! Listen, here it comes!'

Everyone fled downstairs, as with an appalling wail, the great ash tree hauled up its roots and fell heavily on to Kirrin Cottage. There was a terrible crash, and the sound of tiles slipping to the ground everywhere.

'Oh dear!' said poor Aunt Fanny, covering her eyes. 'I knew something would happen! Quentin, we ought to have had that ash tree topped. I knew it would fall in a great gale like this. What has it done to the roof?'

After the great crash there had come other smaller noises, sounds of things falling, thuds and little smashing noises. The children could not imagine what was happening. Timmy was thoroughly angry, and barked loudly. Uncle Quentin slapped his hand angrily on the table, and made everyone jump.

'Stop that dog barking! I'll turn him out!' But nothing would stop Timmy barking or growling that night, and George at last pushed him into the warm kitchen, and shut the door on him.

'I feel like barking or growling myself,' said Anne, who knew exactly what Timmy felt like. 'Julian, has the tree broken in the roof?'

Uncle Quentin took a powerful torch and went

carefully up the stairs to the landing to see what
damage had been done. He came down looking
rather pale.

'The tree has crashed through the attic, smashed

the roof in, and wrecked the girls' bedroom,' he said.
'A big branch has penetrated the boys' room too, but
not badly. But the girls' room is ruined! They would
have been killed if they had been in their beds.'

Everyone was silent. It was an awful thought that
George and Anne had had such a narrow escape.

'Good thing I yelled my head off to warn them,
then,' said Julian, cheerfully, seeing how white Anne
had gone. 'Cheer up, Anne — think what a tale you'll
have to tell at school next term.'

'I think some hot cocoa would do us all good,' said
Aunt Fanny, pulling herself together, though she felt
very shaken. 'I'll go and make some. Quentin, see if
the fire is still alight in your study. We want a little
warmth!'

The fire was still alight. Everyone crowded round
it. They welcomed Aunt Fanny when she came in
with some steaming milk-cocoa.

Anne looked curiously round the room as she sat
sipping her drink. This was where her uncle did his
work, his very clever work. He wrote his difficult
books here, books which Anne could not understand
at all. He drew his queer diagrams here, and made
many strange experiments.

But just at the moment Uncle Quentin did not look
very clever. He looked rather ashamed, somehow.
Anne soon knew why.

'Quentin, it is a mercy none of us was hurt or
killed,' said Aunt Fanny, looking at him rather
sternly. 'I told you a dozen times you should get that
ash tree topped. I knew it was too big and heavy to
withstand a great gale. I was always afraid it would
blow down on the house.'

'Yes, I know, my dear,' said Uncle Quentin,
stirring his cup of cocoa very vigorously. 'But I was so
busy these last months.'

400

'You always make that an excuse for not doing urgent things,' said Aunt Fanny, with a sigh. 'I shall have to manage things myself in the future. I can't risk our lives like this!'

'Well, a thing like this would only happen once in a blue moon!' cried Uncle Quentin, getting angry. Then he calmed down, seeing that Aunt Fanny was really shocked and upset, very near to tears. He put down his cocoa and slipped his arm round her.

'You've had a terrible shock,' he said. 'Don't you worry about things. Maybe they won't be so bad when morning comes.'

'Oh, Quentin — they'll be much worse!' said his wife. 'Where shall we sleep tonight, all of us, and what shall we do till the roof and upstairs rooms are repaired? The children have only just come home. The house will be full of workmen for weeks! I don't know how I'm going to manage.'

'Leave it all to me!' said Uncle Quentin. 'I'll settle everything. Don't worry. I'm sorry about this, very sorry, particularly as it's my fault. But I'll straighten things out for everyone, you just see!'

Aunt Fanny didn't really believe him, but she was grateful for his comforting. The children listened in silence, drinking their hot cocoa. Uncle Quentin was so very clever, and knew so many things — but it was so like him to neglect something urgent like cutting off the top of the old ash tree. Sometimes he didn't seem to live in this world at all!

It was no use going up to bed! The rooms upstairs were either completely ruined, or so messed up with bits and pieces, and clouds of dust, that it was impossible to sleep there. Aunt Fanny began to pile rugs on sofas. There was one in the study, a big one in the sitting-room and a smaller one in the dining-room. She found a camp bed in a cupboard and, with

Julian's help, put that up too.

'We'll just have to do the best we can,' she said. 'There isn't much left of the night, but we'll get a little sleep if we can! The gale is not nearly so wild now.'

'No — it's done all the damage it can, so it's satisfied,' said Uncle Quentin, grimly. 'Well, we'll talk things over in the morning.'

The children found it very difficult to go to sleep after such an excitement, tired though they were. Anne felt worried. How could they all stay at Kirrin Cottage now? It wouldn't be fair on Aunt Fanny. But they couldn't go home because her father and mother were both away and the house was shut up for a month.

'I hope we shan't be sent back to school,' thought Anne, trying to get comfortable on the sofa. 'It would be too awful, after having left there, and started off so gaily for the holidays.'

George was afraid of that, too. She felt sure that they would all be packed back to their schools the next morning. That would mean that she and Anne wouldn't see Julian and Dick any more those holidays, for the boys, of course, went to a different school.

Timmy was the only one who didn't worry about things. He lay on George's feet, snoring a little, quite happy. So long as he was with George he didn't really mind *where* he went!

3

Uncle Quentin has an idea

Next morning the wind was still high, but the fury of the gale was gone. The fishermen on the beach were relieved to find that their boats had suffered very little damage. But word soon went round about the accident to Kirrin Cottage, and a few sightseers came up to marvel at the sight of the great, uprooted tree, lying heavily on the little house.

The children rather enjoyed the importance of relating how nearly they had escaped with their lives. In the light of day it was surprising what damage the big tree had done. It had cracked the roof of the house like an eggshell, and the rooms upstairs were in a terrible mess.

The woman who came up from the village to help Aunt Fanny during the day exclaimed at the sight: 'Why, Mam, it'll take weeks to set that right!' she said. 'Have you got on to the builders, Mam? I'd get them up here right away and let them see what's to be done.'

'*I'm* seeing to things, Mrs Daly,' said Uncle

Quentin. 'My wife has had a great shock. She is not fit to see to things herself. The first thing to do is to decide what is to happen to the children. They can't remain here while there are no usable bedrooms.'

'They had better go back to school, poor things,' said Aunt Fanny.

'No. I've a better idea than that,' said Uncle Quentin, fishing a letter out of his pocket. 'Much better. I've had a letter from that fellow Lenoir this morning — you know, the one who's interested in the same kind of experiments as I am. He says — er, wait a minute, I'll read you the bit. Yes here it is.'

Uncle Quentin read it out: 'It is most kind of you to suggest my coming to stay with you and bringing my boy Pierre. Allow me to extend hospitality to you and your children also. I do not know how many you have, but all are welcome here in this big house. My Pierre will be glad of company, and so will his sister, Marybelle.'

Uncle Quentin looked up triumphantly at his wife. 'There you are! I call that a most generous invitation! It couldn't have come at a better time. We'll pack the whole of the children off to this fellow's house.'

'But Quentin — you can't possibly do that! Why, we don't know anything about him or his family!' said Aunt Fanny.

'His boy goes to the same school as Julian and Dick, and I know Lenoir is a remarkable, clever fellow,' said Uncle Quentin, as if that was all that really mattered. 'I'll telephone him now. What's his number?'

Aunt Fanny felt helpless in face of her husband's sudden determination to settle everything himself. He was ashamed because it was his forgetfulness that had brought on the accident to the house. Now he was going to show that he *could* see to things if he

404

liked. She heard him telephoning, and frowned. How could they possibly send off the children to a strange place like that?

Uncle Quentin put down the receiver, and went to find his wife, looking jubilant and very pleased with himself.

'It's all settled,' he said. 'Lenoir is delighted, most delighted. Says he loves children about the place, and so does his wife, and his two will be thrilled to have them. If we can hire a car today, they can go at once.'

'But Quentin — we *can't* let them go off like that to strange people! They'll hate it! I shouldn't be surprised if George refuses to go,' said his wife.

'Oh — that reminds me. She's not to take Timothy,' said Uncle Quentin. 'Apparently Lenoir doesn't like dogs.'

'Well, then, you know George won't go!' said his wife. 'That's foolish, Quentin. George won't go anywhere without Timmy.'

'She'll have to, this time,' said Uncle Quentin, quite determined that George should not upset all his marvellous plans. 'Here are the children. I'll ask them what *they* feel about going, and see what they say!'

He called them into his study. They came in, feeling sure that they were to hear bad news — probably they were all to return to school!

'You remember that boy I spoke to you about last night?' began Uncle Quentin. 'Pierre Lenoir. You had some absurd name for him.'

'Sooty,' said Dick and Julian together.

'Ah yes, Sooty. Well, his father has kindly invited you all to go and stay with him at Smuggler's Top,' said Uncle Quentin.

The children were astonished.

'*Smuggler's Top!*' said Dick, his fancy caught by the

queer name. 'What's Smuggler's Top?'

'The name of his house,' said Uncle Quentin. 'It's very old, built on the top of a queer hill surrounded by marshes over which the sea once flowed. The hill was once an island, but now it's just a tall hill rising up from the marsh. Smuggling went on there in the old days. It's a very peculiar place, so I've heard.'

All this made the children feel excited. Also Julian and Dick had always liked Sooty Lenoir. He was quite mad, but awfully good fun. They might have a first-rate time with him.

'Well — would you like to go? Or would you rather go back to school for the holidays?' asked Uncle Quentin impatiently.

'Oh *no* — not back to school!' said everyone at once.

'I'd *love* to go to Smuggler's Top,' said Dick. 'It sounds a thrilling place. And I always liked old Sooty, especially since he sawed half through one of the legs of our form-master's chair. It gave way at once when Mr Toms sat down!'

'H'm. I don't see that a trick like that is any reason for liking someone,' said Uncle Quentin, beginning to feel a little doubtful about Master Lenoir. 'Perhaps, on the whole, school would be best for you.'

'Oh no, no!' cried everyone. 'Let's go to Smuggler's Top! Do, do let's!'

'Very well,' said Uncle Quentin, pleased at their eagerness to follow his plan. 'As a matter of fact, I have already settled it. I telephoned a few minutes ago. Mr Lenoir was very kind about it all.'

'Can I take Timmy?' asked George, suddenly.

'No,' said her father. 'I'm afraid not. Mr Lenoir doesn't like dogs.'

'Then I shouldn't like *him*,' said George, sulkily. 'I won't go without Timmy.'

'You'll have to go back to school, then,' said her father, sharply. 'And take off that sulky expression, George. You know how I dislike it.'

But George wouldn't. She turned away. The others looked at her in dismay. Surely old George wasn't going to get into one of her moods, and spoil everything! It would be fun to go to Smuggler's Top. But, of course, it certainly wouldn't be so much fun without Timmy. Still — they couldn't all go back to school just because George wouldn't go anywhere without her dog.

They all went into the sitting-room. Anne put her arm through George's. George shook it off.

'George! You simply *must* come with us,' said Anne. 'I can't bear to go without you — it would be awful to see you going back to school all alone.'

'I shouldn't be all alone,' said George. 'I should have Timmy.'

The others pressed her to change her mind, but she shook them off. 'Leave me alone,' she said. 'I want to think. How are we supposed to get to Smuggler's Top, and where is it? Which road do we take?'

'We're going by car, and it's right up the coast somewhere, so I expect we'll take the coast-road,' said Julian. 'Why, George?'

'Don't ask questions,' said George. She went out with Timmy. The others didn't follow her. George was not very nice when she was cross.

Aunt Fanny began to pack for them, though it was impossible to get some of the things from the girls' room. After a time George came back, but Timmy was not with her. She looked more cheerful.

'Where's Tim?' asked Anne, at once.

'Out somewhere,' said George.

'Are you coming with us, George?' asked Julian, looking at her.

407

'Yes. I've made up my mind to,' said George, but for some reason she wouldn't look Julian in the eyes. He wondered why.

Aunt Fanny gave them all an early lunch, and then a big car came for them. They packed themselves inside. Uncle Quentin gave them all sorts of messages for Mr Lenoir, and Aunt Fanny kissed them good-bye. 'I do hope you have a nice time at Smuggler's Top,' she said. 'Mind you write at once and tell me all about it.'

'Aren't we going to say good-bye to Timmy?' said Anne, her eyes opening wide in amazement at George forgetting. 'George, surely you're not going without saying good-bye to old Timmy!'

'Can't stop now,' said Uncle Quentin, afraid that George might suddenly become awkward again. 'Right, driver! You can go off now. Don't drive too fast, please.'

Waving and shouting the children drove away from Kirrin Cottage, sad when they looked back and saw the smashed roof under the fallen tree. Never mind — they had not been sent back to school. That was the main thing. Their spirits rose as they thought of Sooty and his queerly-named home, Smuggler's Top.

'Smuggler's Top! It sounds too exciting for words!' said Anne. 'I can picture it, an old house right on the top of a hill. Fancy being an island once. I wonder why the sea went back and left marshes instead.'

George said nothing for a while, and the car sped on. The others glanced at her once or twice, but came to the conclusion that she was grieving about Timmy. Still she didn't look very sad!

The car went over a hill and sped down to the bottom. When they got there George leaned forward and touched the driver's arm.

'Would you stop a moment, please? We have to pick somebody up here.'

Julian, Dick and Anne stared at George in surprise. The driver, also rather surprised, drew the car to a standstill. George opened the car door and gave a loud whistle.

Something shot out of the hedge and hurled itself joyfully into the car. It was Timmy! He licked everyone, trod on everyone's toes, and gave the little short barks that showed he was excited and happy.

'Well,' said the driver, doubtfully, 'I don't know if you're supposed to take that dog in, Miss. Your father didn't say anything about him.'

'It's all right,' said George, her face red with joy. 'Quite all right. You needn't worry. Start the car again, please.'

'You *are* a monkey!' said Julian, half-annoyed with George, and half-pleased because Timmy was with them after all. 'Mr Lenoir may send him back, you know.'

'Well, he'll have to send *me* back too,' said George, defiantly. 'Anyhow, the main thing is, we've got Timmy after all, and I am coming with you.'

'Yes — that's fine,' said Anne, and gave first George and then Timmy a hug. '*I* didn't like going without Tim either.'

'On to Smuggler's Top!' said Dick, as the car started off again. 'On to Smuggler's Top. I wonder if we shall have any adventures there!'

4

Smuggler's Top

The car sped on, mostly along the coast, though it sometimes went inland for a few miles. But sooner or later it was in sight of the sea again. The children enjoyed the long drive. They were to stop somewhere for lunch, and the driver told them he knew of a good inn.

At half past twelve he drew up outside an old inn, and they all trooped in. Julian took charge, and ordered lunch. It was a very good one, and all the children enjoyed it. So did Timmy. The innkeeper liked dogs, and put down such a piled-up plate for Timmy that the dog hardly liked to begin on his meal in case it was not for him!

He looked up at George and she nodded to him. 'It's your dinner, Timmy. Eat it up.'

So he ate it, hoping that if they were going to stay anywhere they might be staying at the inn. Meals like this did not arrive every day for a hungry dog!

But after lunch the children got up. They went to find the driver, who was having his lunch in the kitchen with the innkeeper and his wife. They were old friends of his.

'Well, I hear you're going to Castaway,' said the innkeeper, getting up. 'You be careful there!'

'Castaway!' said Julian. 'Is that what the hill is called, where Smuggler's Top is?'

'That's its name,' said the innkeeper.

'Why is it called that?' said Anne. 'What a funny name! Were people cast away on it once, when it was an island?'

'Oh no. The old story goes that the hill was once joined to the mainland,' said the innkeeper. 'But it was the haunt of bad people, and one of the saints became angry with the place, and cast it away into the sea, where it became an island.'

'And so it was called Castaway,' said Dick. 'But perhaps it has got good again, because the sea has gone away from it, and you can walk from the mainland to the hill, can't you?'

'Yes. There's one good road you can take,' said the innkeeper. 'But you be careful of wandering away from it, if you go walking on it! The marsh will suck you down in no time if you set foot on it!'

'It does sound a most exciting place,' said George. 'Smuggler's Top on Castaway Hill! Only one road to it!'

'Time to get on,' said the driver, looking at the clock. 'You've got to be there before tea, your uncle said.'

They got into the car again, Timmy clambering over legs and feet to a comfortable place on George's lap. He was far too big and heavy to lie there but just occasionally he seemed to want to, and George never had the heart to refuse him.

They drove off once more. Anne fell asleep, and the others felt drowsy too. The car purred on and on. It

412

began to rain, and the countryside looked rather dreary.

The driver turned round after a while and spoke to Julian. 'We're coming near to Castaway Hill, sir. We'll soon be leaving the mainland, and taking the road across the marsh.'

Julian woke Anne. They all sat up expectantly. But it was very disappointing after all! The marshes were full of mist! The children could not pierce through it with their eyes, and could only see the flat road they were on, raised a little higher than the surrounding flat marsh. When the mist shifted a little now and again the children saw a dreary space of flat marsh on either side.

'Stop a minute, driver,' said Julian. 'I'd like to see what the marsh is like.'

'Well, don't step off the road,' warned the driver, stopping the car. 'And don't you let that dog out, Miss. Once he runs off the road and gets into the marsh he'll be gone for good.'

'What do you mean — gone for good?' said Anne, her eyes wide.

'He means the marsh will suck down Timmy at once,' said Julian. 'Shut him in the car, George.'

So Timmy, much to his disgust, was shut safely in the car. He pawed at the door, and tried to look out of the window. The driver turned and spoke to him. 'It's all right. They'll be back soon old fellow!'

But Timmy whined all the time the others were out of the car. He saw them go to the edge of the road. He saw Julian jump down the couple of feet that raised the road above the marsh.

There was a line of raised stones running in the marsh alongside the road. Julian stood on one of these peering at the flat marsh.

'It's mud,' he said. 'Loose, squelchy mud! Look,

when I touch it with my foot it moves! It would soon suck me down if I trod heavily on it.'

Anne didn't like it. She called to Julian. 'Come up on the road again. I'm afraid you'll fall in.'

Mists were wreathing and swirling over the salty marshes. It was a weird place, cold and damp. None of the children liked it. Timmy began to bark in the car.

'Tim will scratch the car to bits if we don't get back,' said George. So they all went back, rather silent. Julian wondered how many travellers had been lost in that strange sea-marsh.

'Oh, there's many that's never been heard of again,' said the driver, when they asked him. 'They do say there's one or two winding paths that go to the hill from the mainland, that were used before the road was built. But unless you know every inch of them you're off them in a trice, and find your feet sinking in the mud.'

'It's horrid to think about,' said Anne. 'Don't let's talk about it any more. Can we see Castaway Hill yet?'

'Yes. There it is, looming up in the mist,' said the driver. 'The top of it is out of the mist, see? Queer place, isn't it?'

The children looked in silence. Out of the slowly moving mists rose a tall, steep hill, whose rocky sides were as steep as cliffs. The hill seemed to swim in the mists, and to have no roots in the earth. It was covered with buildings which even at that distance looked old and quaint. Some of them had towers.

'That must be Smuggler's Top, right at the summit,' said Julian, pointing. 'It's like an old building of centuries ago — probably is! Look at the tower it has. What a wonderful view you'd get from it.'

The children gazed at the place where they were to stay. It looked exciting and picturesque, certainly — but it also looked rather forbidding.

'It's sort of — sort of *secret*, somehow,' said Anne, putting into words what the others were thinking. 'I mean — it looks as if it had kept all kinds of queer secrets down the centuries. I guess it could tell plenty of tales!'

The car drove on again, quite slowly, because the mists came down thickly. The road had a line of sparkling round buttons set all along the middle, and when the driver switched on his fog-lamp, they shone brightly and guided him well. Then as they neared Castaway Hill the road began to slope upwards.

'We go through a big archway soon,' said the driver. 'That used to be where the city gate once was. The whole town is surrounded by wall still, just as it used to be in olden times. It's wide enough to walk on, and if you start at a certain place, and walk long enough, you'll come round to the place you started at!'

All the children made up their minds to do this without fail. What a view they would have all round the hill, if they chose a fine day!

The road became steeper, and the driver put the engine into a lower gear. It groaned up the hill. Then it came to an archway, from which old gates were fastened back. It passed through, and the children were in Castaway.

'It's almost as if we've gone back through the centuries, and come to somewhere that existed ages ago!' said Julian, peering at the old houses and shops, with their cobbled streets, their diamond-paned windows, and stout old doors.

They went up the winding high street, and came at last to a big gateway, set with wrought-iron gates.

The driver hooted and they opened. They swept into a steep drive, and at last stopped before Smuggler's Top.

They got out, feeling suddenly shy. The big old house seemed to frown down at them. It was built of brick and timber, and its front door was as massive as that of a castle.

Queer gables jutted here and there over the diamond-paned windows. The house's one tower stood sturdily at the east side of the house, with windows all round. It was not a square tower, but a rounded one, and ended in a point.

'Smuggler's Top!' said Julian. 'It's a good name for it somehow. I suppose lots of smuggling went on here in the old days.'

Dick rang the bell. To do this he had to pull down an iron handle, and a jangling at once made itself heard in the house.

There was the sound of running feet, and the door was opened. It opened slowly, for it was heavy.

Beyond it stood two children, one a girl of about Anne's age, and the other a boy of Dick's age.

'Here you are at last!' cried the boy, his dark eyes dancing. 'I thought you were never coming!'

'This is Sooty,' said Dick to the girls, who had not met him before. They stared at him.

He was certainly very very dark. Black hair, black eyes, black eyebrows, and a brown face. In contrast to him the girl beside him looked pale and delicate. She had golden hair, blue eyes and her eyebrows were so faint they could hardly be seen.

'This is Marybelle, my sister,' said Sooty. 'I always think we look like Beauty and the Beast!'

Sooty was nice. Everyone liked him at once. George found herself twinkling at him in a way quite strange to her, for usually she was shy of strangers,

418

and would not make friends for some time. But who could help liking Sooty with his dancing black eyes and his really wicked grin?

'Come in,' said Sooty. 'Driver, you can take the car round to the next door, and Block will take in the luggage for you and give you tea.'

Suddenly Sooty's face lost its smile and grew very solemn. He had seen Timmy!

'I say! I say — that's not your dog, is it?' he said.

'He's mine,' said George, and she laid a protecting hand on Timmy's head. 'I had to bring him. I can't go anywhere without him.'

'Yes, but — no dog's allowed at Smuggler's Top,' said Sooty, still looking very worried, and glancing behind him as if he was afraid someone might come along and see Timmy. 'My stepfather won't allow any dogs here. Once I brought in a stray one and he licked me till I couldn't sit down — my stepfather licked me, I mean, not the dog.'

Anne gave a frightened little smile at the poor joke. George looked stubborn and sulky.

'I thought — I thought maybe we could hide him somewhere while we were here,' she said. 'But if that's how you feel, I'll go back home with the car. Good-bye.'

She turned and went after the car, which was backing away. Timmy went with her. Sooty stared, and then he yelled after her. 'Come back, stupid! We'll think of *something*!'

5

Sooty Lenoir

Sooty ran down the steps that led to the front door, and tore after George. The others followed. Marybelle went too, shutting the big front door behind her carefully.

There was a small door in the wall just where George was. Sooty caught hold of her and pushed her roughly through the door, holding it open for the others.

'Don't shove me like that,' began George, angrily. 'Timmy will bite you if you push me about.'

'No, he won't,' said Sooty, with a cheerful grin. 'Dogs like me. Even if I boxed your ears your dog would only wag his tail at me.'

The children found themselves in a dark passage. There was a door at the farther end. 'Wait here a minute and I'll see if the coast is clear,' said Sooty. 'I know my stepfather is in, and I tell you, if he sees that dog he'll pack you all into the car again, and send you back! And I don't want him to do that because I can't tell you how I've looked forward to having you all!'

He grinned at them, and their hearts warmed towards him again, even George's, though she still felt angry at being so roughly pushed. She kept Timmy close beside her.

All the same everyone felt a bit scared of Mr Lenoir. He sounded rather a fierce sort of person!

Sooty tiptoed to the door at the end of the passage and opened it. He peeped into the room there, and then came back to the others.

'All clear,' he said. 'We'll take the secret passage to my bedroom. No one will see us then, and once we're there we can make plans to hide the dog. Ready?'

A secret passage sounded thrilling. Feeling rather as if they were in an adventure story, the children went quietly to the door and into the room beyond. It was a dark, oak-panelled room, evidently a study of some sort, for there was a big desk there, and the walls were lined with books. There was no one there.

Sooty went to one of the oak panels in the wall, felt along it deftly, and pressed in a certain place. The panel slid softly aside. Sooty put in his hand and pulled at something. A much larger panel below slid into the wall, and left an opening big enough for the children to pass through.

'Come on,' said Sooty in a low voice. 'Don't make a row.'

Feeling excited, the children all passed through the opening. Sooty came last, and did something that shut the opening and slid the first panel back into its place again.

He switched on a small torch, for it was pitch dark where the children were standing.

They were in a narrow stone passage, so narrow that two people could not possibly have passed one another unless both were as thin as rakes. Sooty passed his torch along to Julian, who was in front.

'Keep straight on till you come to stone steps,' he said. 'Go up them, turn to the right at the top, and keep straight on till you come to a blank wall, then I'll tell you what to do.'

Julian led the way, holding up the torch for the others. The narrow passage ran straight, and came to some stone steps. It was not only very narrow but rather low, so that Anne and Marybelle were the only ones who did not have to bend their heads.

Anne didn't like it very much. She never liked being in a very narrow enclosed space. It reminded her of dreams she sometimes had of being somewhere she couldn't get away from. She was glad when Julian spoke. 'The steps are here. Up we go, everyone.'

'Don't make a row,' said Sooty, in a low voice. 'We're passing the dining-room now. There's a way into this passage from there too.'

Everyone fell silent, and tried to walk on tiptoe, though this was unexpectedly difficult when heads had to be bent and shoulders stooped.

They climbed up fourteen steps, which were quite steep, and curved round half-way. Julian turned to the right at the top. The passage ran upwards then, and was as narrow as before. Julian felt certain that a very fat person could not possibly get along it.

He went on until, with a start, he almost bumped into a blank stone wall! He flashed his torch up and down it. A low voice came from the back of the line of children.

'You've got to the blank wall, Julian. Shine your torch up to where the roof of the passage meets the wall. You will see an iron handle there. Press down on it hard.'

Julian flashed his torch up and saw the handle. He

put his torch into his left hand, and grasped the thick iron handle with his right. He pressed down as hard as he could.

And, quite silently, the great stone in the middle of the wall slid forward and sideways, leaving a gaping hole.

Julian was astonished. He let go the iron handle and flashed his torch into the hole. There was nothing but darkness there!

'It's all right. It leads into a big cupboard in my bedroom!' called Sooty from the back. 'Get through, Julian, and we'll follow. There won't be anyone in my room.'

Julian crawled through the hole and found himself in a spacious cupboard, hung with Sooty's clothes. He groped his way through them and bumped against a door. He opened it and at once daylight flooded into the cupboard, lighting up the way from the passage into the room.

One by one the others clambered through the hole, lost themselves in clothes for a moment and then went thankfully into the room through the cupboard door.

Timmy, puzzled and silent, followed close beside George. He had not liked the dark, narrow passage very much. He was glad to be in daylight again!

Sooty, coming last, carefully closed the opening into the passage by pressing the stone back. It worked easily, though Julian could not imagine how. There must be some sort of pivot, he thought.

Sooty joined the others in his bedroom, grinning. George had her hand on Timmy's collar. 'It's all right, George,' said Sooty. 'We're quite safe here. My room and Marybelle's are separate from the rest of the house. We're in a wing on our own, reached by a long passage!'

He opened the door and showed the others what he meant. There was a room next to his, which was Marybelle's. Beyond stretched a stone-floored, stone-walled passage, laid with mats. At the end of it a big window let in light. There was a door there, a great oak one, which was shut.

'See? We're quite safe here, all by ourselves,' said Sooty. 'Timmy could bark if he liked, and no one would know.'

'But doesn't anyone ever come?' said Anne surprised. 'Who keeps your rooms tidy, and cleans them?'

'Oh, Sarah comes and does that every morning,' said Sooty. 'But usually no one else comes. And anyway, I've got a way of knowing when anyone opens that door!'

He pointed to the door at the end of the passage. The others stared at him.

'How *do* you know?' said Dick.

'I've rigged up something that makes a buzzing noise here, in my room, as soon as that door is opened,' said Sooty, proudly. 'Look, I'll go along and open it, while you stay here and listen.'

He sped along the passage and opened the heavy door at the end. Immediately a low buzzing noise sounded somewhere in his room, and made everyone jump. Timmy was startled too, pricked up his ears, and growled fiercely.

Sooty shut the door and ran back. 'Did you hear the noise? It's a good idea, isn't it? I'm always thinking of things like that.'

The others thought they had come to rather a queer place! They stared round Sooty's bedroom, which was quite ordinary in its furnishings, and in its general untidiness. There was a big diamond-paned window, and Anne went to look out of it.

She gave a gasp. She had not expected to look down such a precipice! Smuggler's Top was built at the summit of the hill, and, on the side where Sooty's bedroom was, the hill fell away steeply, down and down to the marsh below!

'Oh look!' she said. 'Look how steep it is! It really gives me a very queer feeling to look down there!'

The others crowded round and looked in silence, for it certainly was strange to gaze down such a long way.

The sun was shining up on the hill-summit, but all around, as far as they could see, mists hid the marsh and the far-off sea. The only bit of the marsh that could be seen was far down below, at the bottom of the steep hill.

'When the mists are away, you can see over the flat marshes to where the sea begins,' said Sooty. 'That's quite a fine sight. You can hardly tell where the marsh ends and sea begins except when the sea is very blue. Fancy, once upon a time, the sea came right up and around this hill, and it was an island.'

'Yes. The innkeeper told us that,' said George. 'Why did the sea go back and leave it?'

'I don't know,' said Sooty. 'People say it's going back farther and farther. There's a big scheme afoot to drain the marsh, and turn it into fields, but I don't know if that will ever happen.'

'I don't like that marsh,' said Anne, with a shiver. 'It looks wicked, somehow.'

Timmy whined. George remembered that they must hide him, and make plans for him. She turned to Sooty.

'Did you mean what you said about hiding Tim?' she asked. 'Where shall we put him? And can he be fed? And how can we exercise him? He's a big dog, you know.'

'We'll plan it all,' said Sooty. 'Don't you worry. I love dogs, and I shall be thrilled to have Timmy here. But I do warn you that if my stepfather ever finds out we shall probably all get a jolly good thrashing, and you'll be sent home in disgrace.'

'But why doesn't your father like dogs?' said Anne puzzled. 'Is he afraid of them?'

'No, I don't think so. It's just that he won't have them here in the house,' said Sooty. 'I think he must have a reason for it, but I don't know what it is. He's a queer sort of man, my stepfather!'

'How is he queer?' asked Dick.

'Well — he seems full of secrets,' said Sooty. 'Queer people come here, and they come secretly without anyone knowing. I've seen lights shining in our tower on certain nights, but I don't know who puts them there or why. I've tried to find out, but I can't.'

'Do you think — do you think your father is a smuggler?' said Anne, suddenly.

'I don't think so,' said Sooty. 'We've got one smuggler here, and everyone knows him! See that house over there to the right, lower down the hill? Well, that's where he lives. He's as rich as can be. His name is Barling. Even the police know his goings-on, but they can't stop him! He is very rich and very powerful, so he does what he likes — and he won't let anyone play the same game as he plays! No one else would dare to do any smuggling in Castaway, while *he* does it!'

'This seems rather an exciting place,' said Julian. 'I have a kind of feeling there might be an adventure somewhere about!'

'Oh no,' said Sooty. 'Nothing happens, really. It's only just a feeling you get here, because the place is so old, so full of secret ways and pits and passages. Why, the whole hill is mined with passages in the rock, used by the smugglers of olden times!'

'Well,' began Julian, and stopped very suddenly. Everyone stared at Sooty. His secret buzzer had suddenly barked from its hidden corner! Someone had opened the door at the end of the passage!

6

Sooty's stepfather and mother

'Someone's coming!' said George, in a panic. 'What shall we do with Tim? Quick!'

Sooty took Timmy by the collar and shoved him into the old cupboard, and shut the door on him. 'Keep quiet!' he commanded, and Timmy stood still in the darkness, the hairs at the back of his neck standing up, his ears cocked.

'Well,' began Sooty, in a bright voice, 'perhaps I'd better show you where your bedrooms are now!'

The door opened and a man came in. He was dressed in black trousers and a white linen coat. He had a queer face. 'It's a shut face,' though Anne to herself. 'You can't tell a bit what he's like inside, because his face is all shut and secret.'

'Oh hallo, Block,' said Sooty, airily. He turned to the others. 'This is Block, my stepfather's man,' he said. 'He's deaf, so you can say what you like, but it's better not to, because though he doesn't hear he seems to sense what we say.'

429

'Anyway, I think it would be beastly to say things we wouldn't say in front of him if he wasn't deaf,' said George, who had very strict ideas about things of that sort.

Block spoke in a curiously monotonous voice. 'Your stepfather and your mother want to know why you have not brought your friends to see them,' he said. 'Why did you rush up here like this?'

Block looked all round as he spoke — almost as if he knew there was a dog, and wondered where he had gone to, George thought, in alarm. She did hope the car-driver had not mentioned Timmy.

'Oh — I was so pleased to see them I took them straight up here!' said Sooty. 'All right, Block. We'll be down in a minute.'

The man went, his face quite impassive. Not a smile, not a frown! 'I don't like him,' said Anne. 'Has he been with you long?'

'No — only about a year,' said Sooty. 'He suddenly appeared one day. Even Mother didn't know he was coming! He just came, and, without a word, changed into that white linen coat, and went to do some work in my stepfather's room. I suppose my stepfather was expecting him — but he didn't say anything to my mother, I'm sure of that. She seemed so surprised.'

'Is she your real mother, or a stepmother, too?' asked Anne.

'You don't have a stepmother *and* a stepfather!' said Sooty, scornfully. 'You only have one or the other. My mother is my real mother, and she's Marybelle's mother, too. But Marybelle and I are only half-brother and sister, because my stepfather is her *real* father.'

'It's rather muddled,' said Anne, trying to sort it out.

'Come on — we'd better go down,' said Sooty,

430

remembering. 'By the way, my stepfather is always being very affable, always smiling and joking — but it isn't real, somehow. He's quite likely to fly into a furious temper at any moment.'

'I hope we shan't see very much of him,' said Anne, uncomfortably. 'What's your mother like, Sooty?'

'Like a frightened mouse!' said Sooty. 'You'll like her, all right. She's a darling. But she doesn't like living here; she doesn't like this house, and she's terrified of my stepfather. She wouldn't say so herself, of course, but I know she is.'

Marybelle, who was too shy to have joined in any talking until then, nodded her head.

'I don't like living here, either,' she said. 'I shall be glad when I go to boarding-school, like Sooty. Except that I shall leave Mother all alone then.'

'Come on,' said Sooty, and led the way. 'We'd better leave Timmy in the cupboard till we come back, just in case Block does a bit of snooping. I'll lock the cupboard door and take the key.'

Feeling rather unhappy at leaving Timmy locked up in the cupboard, the children followed Sooty and Marybelle down the stone passage to the oak door. They went through, and found themselves at the top of a great flight of stairs, wide and shallow. They went down into a big hall.

At the right was a door, and Sooty opened it. He went in and spoke to someone.

'Here they all are,' he said. 'Sorry I rushed them off to my bedroom like that, Father, but I was so excited to see them all!'

'Your manners still need a little polishing, Pierre,' said Mr Lenoir, in a deep voice. The children looked at him. He sat in a big oak chair, a neat, clever-looking man, with fair hair brushed upwards, and eyes as blue as Marybelle's. He smiled all the time, but with his mouth, not his eyes.

'What cold eyes!' thought Anne, when she went forward to shake hands with him. His hand was cold, too. He smiled at her, and patted her on the shoulder.

'What a nice little girl!' he said. 'You will be a good companion for Marybelle. Three boys for Sooty, and one girl for Marybelle. Ha ha!'

He evidently thought George was a boy, and she did look rather like one — she was wearing jeans and jersey as usual, and her curly hair was very short.

Nobody said that George wasn't a boy. Certainly George was not going to! She, Dick and Julian shook hands with Mr Lenoir. They had not even noticed Sooty's mother!

She was there, though, sitting lost in an arm-chair, a tiny woman like a doll, with mouse-coloured hair and grey eyes. Anne turned to her.

'Oh, how small you are!' she said, before she could stop herself.

Mr Lenoir laughed. He laughed no matter what anyone said. Mrs Lenoir got up and smiled. She was only as tall as Anne, and had the smallest hands and feet that Anne had ever seen on a grown-up. Anne liked her. She shook hands, and said, 'It's so nice of you to have us all here like this. You know, I expect, that a tree fell on the roof of our house and smashed it.'

Mr Lenoir's laugh came again. He made some kind of joke, and everyone smiled politely.

'Well, I hope you'll have a good time here,' he said. 'Pierre and Marybelle will show you the old town, and, if you promise to be careful, you can walk along the road to the mainland to go the cinema there.'

'Thank you,' said everyone, and Mr Lenoir laughed his curious laugh again.

'Your father is a very clever man,' he said,

432

suddenly turning to Julian, who guessed that he had mistaken him for George. 'I am hoping he will come here to fetch you home again when you go, and then I shall have the pleasure of talking with him. He and I have been doing the same kind of experiments, but he has got further than I have.'

'Oh!' said Julian, politely. Then the doll-like Mrs Lenoir spoke in her soft voice.

'Block will give you all your meals in Marybelle's school room, then you will not disturb my husband. He does not like talk at meal-times, and that would be rather hard on six children.'

Mr Lenoir laughed again. His cold blue eyes looked intently at all the children. 'By the way, Pierre,' he said suddenly, 'I forbid you to wander about the catacombs in this hill, as I have forbidden you before, and I also forbid you to do any of your dare-devil climbing, nor will I have you acting about on the city wall now that you have others here. I will not have them taking risks. Will you promise me this?'

'I don't act about on the city wall,' protested Sooty. 'I don't take risks, either.'

'You play the fool always,' said Mr Lenoir, and the tip of his nose turned quite white. Anne looked at it with interest. She did not know that it always did this when Mr Lenoir got angry.

'Oh, sir — I was top of my form last term,' said Sooty, in a most injured tone. The others felt certain that he was trying to lead Mr Lenoir away from his request — he was not going to promise him what he had asked!

Mrs Lenoir now joined in. 'He really did do well last term,' she said. 'You must remember —'

'Enough!' snapped Mr Lenoir, and the smiles and laughs he had so freely lavished on everyone

vanished, entirely. 'Get out, all of you!'

Rather scared, Julian, Dick, Anne and George hurried from the room, followed by Marybelle and Sooty. Sooty was grinning as he shut the door.

'I didn't promise!' he said. 'He wanted to take all our fun away. This place isn't any fun if you don't explore it. I can show you heaps of queer places.'

'What are catacombs?' asked Anne, with a vague picture of cats and combs in her head.

'Winding, secret tunnels in the hill,' said Sooty. 'Nobody knows them all. You can get lost in them easily, and never get out again. Lots of people have.'

'Why are there so many secret ways and things here?' wondered George.

'Easy!' said Julian. 'It was a haunt of smugglers, and there must have been many a time when they had to hide not only their goods, but themselves! And, according to old Sooty, there still *is* a smuggler here! What did you say his name was — Barling, wasn't it?'

'Yes,' said Sooty. 'Come on upstairs and I'll show you your rooms. You've got a good view over the town.'

He took them to two rooms set side by side, on the opposite side of the big staircase from his bedroom and Marybelle's. They were small but well-furnished, and had, as Sooty said, a marvellous view over the quaint roofs and towers of Castaway Hill. They also had a remarkably good view of Mr Barling's house.

George and Anne were to sleep in one room, and Julian and Dick in the other. Evidently Mrs Lenoir had taken the trouble to remember that there were two girls and two boys, not one girl and three boys, as Mr Lenoir imagined!

'Nice cosy rooms,' said Anne. 'I like these dark oak

panels. Are there any secret passages in our rooms, Sooty?'

'You wait and see!' grinned Sooty. 'Look, there are your things, all unpacked from your suitcases. I expect Sarah did that. You'll like Sarah. She's a good sort, fat and round and jolly — not a bit like Block!'

Sooty seemed to have forgotten all about Tim. George reminded him.

'What about Timmy? He'll have to be near me, you know. And we must arrange to feed him and exercise him. Oh, I do hope he'll be all right, Sooty, I'd rather leave straight away than have Timmy unhappy.'

'He'll be all right!' said Sooty. 'I'll give him the free run of that narrow passage we came up to my bedroom by, and we'll feed him every chance we get. And we'll smuggle him out by a secret tunnel that opens half-way down the town, and give him plenty of exercise each morning. Oh, we'll have a grand time with Timmy!'

George wasn't so sure. 'Can he sleep with me at night?' she asked 'He'll howl the place down if he can't.'

'Well — we'll try and manage it,' said Sooty, rather doubtfully. 'You've got to be jolly careful, you know. We don't want to land in serious trouble. You don't know what my stepfather can be like!'

They could guess, though. Julian looked curiously at Sooty. 'Was your own father's name Lenoir, too?' he asked.

Sooty nodded. 'Yes. He was my stepfather's cousin, and was as dark as all the Lenoirs usually are. My stepfather is an exception — he's fair. People say the fair Lenoirs are no good — but don't tell my stepfather that!'

436

'As if we should!' said George. 'Gracious, he'd cut off our heads or something! Come on — let's go back to Tim.'

7

The hidden pit

The children were all very glad to think that they were going to have meals by themselves in the old schoolroom. Nobody wanted to have much to do with Mr Lenoir! They felt sorry for Marybelle because she had such a queer father.

They soon settled down at Smuggler's Top. Once George was satisfied that Timmy was safe and happy, though rather puzzled about everything, she settled down too. The only difficulty was getting Timmy to her room at night. This had to be done in darkness. Block had a most tiresome way of appearing silently and suddenly, and George was terrified of him catching a glimpse of the big dog.

Timmy had a queer sort of life the next few days! While the children were indoors, he had to stay in the narrow secret passage, where he wandered about, puzzled and lonely, pricking his ears for a sound of the whistle that meant he was to come to the cupboard and be let out.

He was fed very well, for Sooty raided the larder every night. Sarah, the cook, was amazed at the way things like soup-bones disappeared. She could not understand it. But Timmy devoured everything that was given to him.

Each morning he was given good exercise by the children. The first morning this had been really very exciting!

George had reminded Sooty of his promise to take Timmy for walks each day. 'He simply must have exercise, or he'll be terribly miserable!' she said. 'But how can we manage it? We can't possibly take him through the house and out of the front door! We'd be certain to walk into your father!'

'I told you I knew a way that came out half-way down the hill, silly,' said Sooty. 'I'll show you. We shall be quite safe once we are down there, because even if we met Block or anyone else that knew us, they wouldn't know it was our dog. They would think it was just a stray we had picked up.'

'Well — show us the way,' said George, impatiently. They were all in Sooty's bedroom, and Timmy was lying on the mat beside George. They felt really safe in Sooty's room because of the buzzer that warned them when anyone opened the door at the end of the long passage.

'We'll have to go into Marybelle's room,' said Sooty. 'You'll get a shock when you see the way that leads down the hill, I can tell you!'

He looked out of the door. The door at the end of the passage was shut. 'Marybelle, slip along and peep through the passage door,' said Sooty. 'Warn us if anyone is coming up the stairs. If not, we'll all slip quickly into your room.'

Marybelle ran to the door at the end of the passage. She opened it, and at once the warning buzzer sounded in Sooty's room, making Timmy growl fiercely. Marybelle looked through the doorway to the stairs. Then she signalled to the others that no one was coming.

They all rushed out of Sooty's room into Marybelle's, and Marybelle came to join them. She was a funny little mouse of a girl, shy and timid. Anne liked her, and once or twice teased her for being so shy.

But Marybelle did not like being teased. Her eyes filled with tears at once, and she turned away. 'She'll be better when she goes to school,' Sooty said. 'She can't help being shy, shut up all the year round in this queer house. She hardly ever sees anyone of her own age.'

They crowded into the little girl's bedroom and shut the door. Sooty turned the key in the lock. 'Just in case friend Block comes snooping,' he said with a grin.

Sooty began to move the furniture in the room to the sides, near the walls. The others watched in surprise and then helped. 'What's the idea of the furniture removal?' asked Dick, struggling with a heavy chest.

'Got to get this heavy carpet up,' panted Sooty. 'It's put there to hide the trap-door below. At least, that's what I've always thought.'

Once the furniture stood by the walls, it was easy to drag up the heavy carpet. There was a felt lining under it too, and that had to be pulled aside as well. Then the children saw a trap-door, let flat into the floor, with a ring-handle to pull it up.

They felt excited. Another secret way! This house seemed full of them. Sooty pulled at the ring and the heavy door came up quite easily. The children peered down, but they could see nothing. It was pitch-dark.

'Are there steps down?' asked Julian, holding Anne back in case she fell.

440

'No,' said Sooty, reaching out for a big torch he had brought in with him. 'Look!'

He switched on his torch, and the children gave a gasp. The trap-door led down to a pit, far, far below!

'Why! It's miles below the foundations of the house, surely!' said Julian, surprised. 'It's just a hole down to a big pit. What's it for?'

'Oh, it was probably used to hide people — or to get rid of them!' said Sooty. 'Nice little place, isn't it? If you fell down there you'd land with an awful bump!'

'But — how in the world could we get Timmy down there— or get down ourselves?' said George. '*I'm* not going to fall down it, that's certain!'

Sooty laughed. 'You won't have to,' he said. 'Look here.' He opened a cupboard and reached up to a wide shelf. He pulled something down, and the children saw that it was a rope ladder, fine but very strong.

'There you are! We can all get down by that,' he said.

'Timmy can't,' said George at once. 'He couldn't possibly climb up or down a ladder.'

'Oh, couldn't he?' said Sooty. 'He seems such a clever dog — I should have thought he could easily have done a thing like that.'

'Well, he can't,' said George, decidedly. 'That's a silly idea.'

'I know,' said Marybelle, suddenly, going red at her boldness in breaking in on the conversation. 'I think I know! We could get the laundry basket and shut Timmy in it. And we would tie it with ropes, and let him down — and pull him up the same way!'

The others stared at her. 'Now that really *is* a brainwave!' said Julian, warmly. 'Good for you, Marybelle. Timmy would be quite safe in a basket.

But it would have to be a big one.'

'There's a very big one in the kitchen,' said Marybelle. 'It's never used except when we have lots of people to stay, like now. We could borrow it.'

'Oh *yes*!' said Sooty. 'Of course we could. I'll go and get it now.'

'But what excuse will you give?' shouted Julian after him. Sooty had already unlocked the door and shot out! He was a most impatient person, and could never put off anything for a single minute.

Sooty didn't answer. He sped down the passage. Julian locked the door after him. He didn't want anyone coming in and seeing the carpet up and the yawning hole!

Sooty was back in two minutes, carrying a very heavy wicker laundry basket on his head. He banged on the door, and Julian unlocked it.

'Good!' said Julian. 'How did you get it? Did anyone mind?'

'Didn't ask them,' grinned Sooty. 'Nobody there to ask. Block's with Father, and Sarah has gone out shopping. I can always put it back if any awkward questions are asked.'

The rope-ladder was shaken out down the hole. It slipped like an uncoiling snake, down and down, and reached the pit at the bottom. Then Timmy was fetched from Sooty's room. He came in wagging his tail overjoyed at being with everyone again. George hugged him.

'Darling Timmy! I hate you being hidden away like this. But never mind, we're all going out together this morning!'

'I'll go down first,' said Sooty. 'Then you'd better let Timmy down. I'll tie his basket round with this rope. It's nice and strong, and there's plenty to let down. Better tie the other end to the end of the bed,

then when we come up again we can easily pull him up.'

Timmy was made to get inside the big basket and lie down. He was surprised and barked a little. But George put her hand over his mouth.

'Sh! You mustn't say a word, Timmy,' she said. 'I know all this is very astonishing. But never mind, you'll have a marvellous walk at the end of it.'

Timmy heard the word 'Walk' and was glad. That was what he wanted — a really nice long walk in the open air and sunshine!

He didn't at all like having the lid shut down on him, but as George seemed to think he must put up with all these queer happenings, Timmy did so, with a very good grace.

'He's really a marvellous dog,' said Marybelle. 'Sooty, get down the hole now, and be ready for when we let him down.'

Sooty disappeared down the dark hole, holding his torch between his teeth. Down and down he went, down and down. At last he stood safely at the bottom, and flashed his torch upwards. His voice came to them, sounding rather queer and far away.

'come on! Lower Timmy down!'

The laundry basket, feeling extraordinarily heavy now, was pushed to the edge of the hole. Then down it went, knocking against the sides here and there. Timmy growled. He didn't like this game!

Dick and Julian had hold of the rope between them. They lowered Timmy as smoothly as they could. He reached the bottom with a slight bump, and Sooty undid the basket. Out leapt Timmy, barking! But his bark sounded very small and distant to the watchers at the top.

'Now come on down, one by one!' shouted up Sooty waving his torch. 'Is the door locked, Julian?'

444

'Yes,' said Julian. 'Look out for Anne. She's coming now.'

Anne climbed down, a little frightened at first, but, as her feet grew use to searching for and finding the rungs of the rope-ladder, she went down quite quickly.

Then the others followed, and soon they were all standing together at the bottom of the hole, in the enormous pit. They looked round curiously. It had a musty smell, and its walls were damp and greenish. Sooty swung his torch round, and the children saw various passages leading off here and there.

'Where do they all lead to?' asked Julian, in amazement.

'Well, I told you this hill was full of tunnels,' said Sooty. 'This pit is down in the hill and these tunnels lead into the catacombs. There are miles and miles of them. No one explores them now, because so many people have been lost in them and never heard of again. There used to be an old map of them, but it's lost.'

'It's weird!' said Anne, and shivered. 'I wouldn't like to be down here alone.'

'What a place to hide smuggled goods in,' said Dick. 'No one would ever find them here.'

'I guess the old-time smugglers knew every inch of these passages,' said Sooty. 'Come on! We'll take the one that leads out of the hillside. We'll have to do a bit of climbing when we get there. I hope you don't mind.'

'Not a bit,' said Julian. 'We're all good climbers. But I say, Sooty — you're sure you know the way? We don't want to be lost for ever down here!'

''Course I know the way! Come on!' said Sooty, and, flashing his torch in front of him, he led the way into dark and narrow tunnel.

8

An exciting walk

The tunnel ran slightly downwards, and smelt nasty in places. Sometimes it opened out into pits like the one they themselves had come from. Sooty flashed his torch up them.

'That one goes into Barling's house somewhere,' he said. 'Most of the old houses hereabouts have openings into pits, like ours. Jolly well hidden some of them are, too!'

'There's daylight or something in front!' said Anne, suddenly. 'Oh good! I hate this tunnel.'

Sure enough, it was daylight, creeping in through a kind of cave-entrance in the hillside. The children crowded there, and looked out.

They were outside the hill, and outside the town, somewhere on the steep cliff-side that ran down to the marsh. Sooty climbed out on to a ledge. He put his torch into his pocket.

'We've got to get to that path down there,' he said, pointing. 'That will lead us to a place where the city wall is fairly low, and we can climb over it. Is Timmy sure-footed? We don't want him tumbling into the marsh down there!'

The marsh lay a good way below, looking ugly and flat. George sincerely hoped Timmy would never fall into it. Still, he was very sure-footed, and she didn't think he would slip. The path was steep and rocky, but quite passable.

They all went down it, clambering over rocks now and again. The path led them to the city wall, which, as Sooty had said, was fairly low just there. He climbed up to the top. He was like a cat for climbing!

'No wonder he's got such a name for climbing about everywhere at school!' said Dick to Julian. 'He's had good practice here. Do you remember how he climbed up to the roof of the school the term before last? Everyone was scared he'd slip and fall, but he didn't. He tied the Union Jack to one of the chimney-pots!'

'Come on!' called Sooty. 'The coast is clear. This is a lonely bit of the town, and no one will see us climbing up.'

Soon they were all over the wall, Timmy too. They set off for a good walk, swinging down the hill, enjoying themselves. The mist began to clear after a while, and the sun felt nice and warm.

The town was very old. Some of the houses seemed almost tumble-down, but there were people living in them, for smoke came from the chimneys. The shops were quaint, but their long narrow windows, and overhanging eaves. The children stopped to look into them.

'Look out — here's Block!' said Sooty suddenly in a low voice. 'Don't take any notice of Timmy at all. If he comes around licking us or jumping up, pretend to try and drive him off as if he was a stray.'

447

They all pretended not to see Block, but gazed earnestly into the window of a shop. Timmy feeling rather out of it, ran up to George and pawed at her, trying to make her take notice of him.

'Go away, dog!' said Sooty, and flapped at the surprised Timmy. 'Go away! Following us about like this! Go home, can't you?'

Timmy thought this was some sort of a game. He barked happily, and ran round Sooty and George, giving them an occasional lick.

'Home, dog, home!' yelled Sooty, flapping hard again.

Then Block came up to them, no expression on his face at all. 'The dog bothers you?' he said. 'I will throw a stone at him and make him go.'

'Don't you dare!' said George, immediately. 'You go home yourself! I don't mind the dog following us. He's quite a nice one.'

'Block's deaf, silly,' said Sooty. 'It's no good talking to him.' To George's horror Block picked up a big stone, meaning to throw it at Timmy. George flew at him, punched him hard on the arm, and made him drop the stone.

'How dare you throw stones at a dog!' yelled the little girl in a fury. 'I'll — I'll tell the police.'

'Now, now,' said a voice nearby. 'What's all this about? Pierre, what's the trouble?'

The children turned and saw a tall man standing near them, wearing his hair rather long. He had long, narrow eyes, a long nose and a long chin. 'He's long everywhere!' thought Anne, looking at his long thin legs and long narrow feet.

'Oh, Mr Barling! I didn't see you,' said Sooty, politely. 'Nothing's the matter, thanks. It's only that this dog is following us, and Block said he'd make it go away by chucking a stone at it. And George here is

448

fond of dogs and got angry about that.'

'I see. And who are all these children?' said Mr Barling, looking at each one of them out of his long, narrow eyes.

'They've come to stay with us because their uncle's house had an accident to it,' explained Sooty. 'George's father's house, I mean. At Kirrin.'

'Ah — at Kirrin?' said Mr Barling, and seemed to prick up his long ears. 'Surely that is where that very clever scientist friend of Mr Lenoir's lives?'

'Yes. He's my father,' said George. 'Why, do you know him?'

'I have heard of him — and of his very interesting experiments,' said Mr Barling. 'Mr Lenoir knows him well, I believe?'

'Not awfully well,' said George, puzzled. 'They just write to one another, I think. My father telephoned to Mr Lenoir to ask him if he could have us to stay while our own house in being mended.'

'And Mr Lenoir, of course, was only too delighted to have the whole company of you?' said Mr Barling. '*Such* a good, generous fellow, your father, Pierre!'

The children stared at Mr Barling, thinking that it was queer of him to say nice things in such a nasty voice. They felt uncomfortable. It was plain that Mr Barling did not like Mr Lenoir at all. Well, neither did they, but they didn't like Mr Barling any better!

Timmy saw another dog and darted happily after him. Block had now disappeared, going up the steep high street with his basket. The children said good-bye to Mr Barling, not wanting to talk to him any more.

They went after Timmy, talking eagerly as soon as they had left Mr Barling behind.

'Goodness — that was a narrow escape from

Block!' said Julian. 'Old beast — going to throw that enormous stone at Timmy. No wonder you flew at him, George! But you very nearly gave the game away, though.'

'I don't care,' said George. 'I wasn't going to have Timmy's leg broken. It was a bit of bad luck meeting Block our very first morning out.'

'We'll probably never meet him again when we take Timmy out,' said Sooty, comfortingly. 'And if we do we'll simply say the dog always joins us when it meets us. Which is perfectly true.'

They enjoyed their walk. They went into a quaint old coffee shop and had steaming cups of delicious creamy coffee and jammy buns. Timmy had two of the buns and gobbled them greedily. George went off to buy some meat for him at the butcher's, choosing a shop that Sooty said Mrs Lenoir did not go to. She did not want any butcher telling Mrs Lenoir that the children had been buying dog-meat!

They went back the same way as they had come. They made their way up the steep cliff-path, and in at the tunnel-entrance, back through the winding tunnel to the pit, and there was the rope-ladder waiting for them. Julian and Dick went up first, while George packed the surprised Timmy into the basket again and tied the rope firmly round it. Then up went the whining Timmy, bumping against the sides of the hole, until the two panting boys pulled the basket in Marybelle's room and undid it.

It was ten minutes before the dinner-hour. 'Just time to shut the trap-door, pull back the carpet and wash our hands,' said Sooty. 'And I'll put old Timmy back into the secret passage behind the cupboard in my room, George. Where is that meat you bought? I'll put that in the passage too. he can eat it when he likes.

'Did you put him a nice warm rug there, and a dish of fresh water?' asked George, anxiously, for the third or fourth time.

'You know I did. I keep telling you,' said Sooty. 'Look, we won't put back all the furniture except the chairs. We can say we want it left back because we like to play a game on the carpet. It'll be an awful bore if we have to move chests and things every time we exercise Tim.'

They were just in time for their dinner. Block was there to serve it, and so was Sarah. The children sat down hungrily, in spite of having had coffee and buns. Block and Sarah ladled out hot soup on to their plates.

'I hope you got rid of the unpleasant dog,' said Block in his monotonous voice. He gave George a rather nasty look. Evidently he had not forgotten how she had flown at him.

Sooty nodded. It was no good speaking in answer, for Block would not hear. Sarah bustled round, taking way the soup-plates and preparing to give them their second course.

The food was very good at Smuggler's Top. There was plenty of it, and the hungry visitors and Sooty ate everything put before them. Marybelle hadn't much appetite, but she was the only one. George tried to secrete tit-bits and bones whenever she could, for Timmy.

Two or three days went by, and the children fell into their new life quite happily. Timmy was taken out each morning for a long walk. The children soon got used to slipping down the rope-ladder, and making their way with Timmy to the cliff-side.

In the afternoons they went to either Sooty's room

452

or Marybelle's, and played games or read. They could have Timmy there, because the buzzer always warned them if anyone was coming.

At night it was always an excitement to get Timmy to George's room without being seen. This was usually done when Mr and Mrs Lenoir were sitting at their dinner, and Block and Sarah were serving them. The children had a light supper first, and Mr and Mrs Lenoir had their dinner an hour later. It was quite the best time to smuggle Timmy along to George's room.

Timmy seemed to enjoy the smuggling. He ran silently beside George and Sooty, stopped at every corner, and scampered gladly into George's room as soon as he got there. He lay quietly under the bed till George was in bed herself, and then he came out to lie on her feet.

George always locked their door at night. She didn't want Sarah or Mrs Lenoir coming in and finding Timmy there! But nobody came, and as night after night went by, George grew more easy about Timmy.

Taking him back to Sooty's room in the morning was a bit of nuisance, because it had to be done early, before anyone was up. But George could always wake herself at any time she chose, and each morning about half past six the little girl slipped through the house with Timmy. She went in at Sooty's door, and he jumped out of bed to deal with Timmy. He was always awakened by the buzzer that sounded when George opened the door at the end of the passage.

'I hope you are all enjoying yourselves,' Mr Lenoir said to the children, whenever they met him in the hall or on the stairs. And they always replied politely. 'Oh yes, Mr Lenoir, thank you.'

'It's quite a peaceful holiday after all,' said Julian. 'Nothing happens at all!'

And then things *did* begin to happen and once they had begun they never stopped!

9
Who is in the tower?

One night Julian was awakened by someone opening his door. He sat up at once. 'Who is it?' he said. 'Me, Sooty,' said Sooty's voice, very low. 'I say, I want you to come and see something.'

Julian woke Dick, and the two of them put on their dressing-gowns. Sooty led them quietly out of the room and took them to a queer little room, tucked away in an odd wing of the house. All kinds of things were kept here, trunks and boxes, old toys, chests of old clothes, broken vases that had never been mended, and many other worthless things.

'Look,' said Sooty, taking them to the window. They saw that the little room had a view of the tower belonging to the house. It was the only room in the house that did, for it was built at a queer angle.

The boys looked — and Julian gave an exclamation. Someone was signalling from the tower! A light there flashed every now and again. In and out — pause — flash, flash, in and out — pause. The light went regularly on and off in a certain rhythm.

'Now — who's doing that?' whispered Sooty.

'Your father?' wondered Julian.

'Don't think so,' said Sooty. 'I think I heard him snoring away in his room. We could go and find out though — see if he really is in his bedroom.'

'Well — for goodness' sake don't let's get caught,' said Julian, not at all liking the idea of prying about in his host's house.

They made their way to where Mr Lenoir had his room. It was quite plain he was there, for a regular low snoring came from behind the closed door.

'It may be Block up in the tower,' said Dick. 'He looks full of secrets. I wouldn't trust him an inch. I bet it's Block.'

'Well — shall we go to his room and see if it's empty?' whispered Sooty. 'Come on. If it's Block signalling, he's doing it without Father knowing.'

'Oh, your father might have told him to,' said Julian, who felt that he wouldn't trust Mr Lenoir much further than he would trust Block.

They went up the back-stairs to the wing where the staff slept. Sarah slept in a room there with Harriet the kitchen-maid. Block slept alone.

Sooty pushed open Block's door very softly and slowly. When he had enough room to put in his head, he did so. The room was full of moonlight. By the window was Block's bed. And Block was there! Sooty could see the humpy shape of his body, and the black round patch that was his head.

He listened, but he could not catch Block's breathing. He must sleep very quietly.

He withdrew his head, and pushed the other two boys quietly down the back-stairs.

'Was he there?' whispered Julian.

'Yes. So it can't be him, signalling up in our tower,'

said Sooty. 'Well — who can it be then? I don't like it. It couldn't possibly be Mother or Sarah or the little kitchen-maid. Is there a stranger in our house, someone we don't know, living here in secret?'

'Can't be!' said Julian, a little shiver running down his back. 'Look here — what about us going up to the tower and trying to peep through the door or something? We'd soon find out who it was then. Perhaps we ought to tell your father.'

'No. Not yet. I want to find out a whole lot more before I say anything to anyone,' said Sooty, sounding obstinate. 'Let's creep up to the tower. We shall have to be jolly careful though. You get to it by a spiral staircase, rather narrow. There's nowhere much to hide if anyone suddenly came down out of the tower.

'What's in the tower?' whispered Dick, as they made their way through the dark and silent house, thin streaks of moonlight coming in here and there between the cracks of the closed curtains.

'Nothing much. Just a table and a chair or two, and a bookcase of books,' said Sooty. 'We use it on hot summer days when the breeze gets in strongly through the windows there, and we can see a long way all round us.'

They came to a little landing. From this a winding, narrow stairway of stone went up to the rounded tower. The boys looked up. Moonlight fell on the stairway from a slit-like window in the wall.

'We'd better not all go up,' said Sooty. 'We should find it so difficult to hurry down, three of us, if the person in the tower suddenly came out. I'll go. You stay down here and wait. I'll see if I can spy anything through the crack in the door or the key-hole.'

He crept softly up the stairway, soon lost to view as

he rounded the first spiral. Julian and Dick waited in the shadows at the bottom. There was a thick curtain over one of the windows there, and they got behind it, wrapping its folds round them for warmth.

Sooty crept up to the top. The tower-room had a stout oak door, studded and barred. It was shut! It was no use trying to look through the crack, because there wasn't one. He bent down to peer through the key-hole.

But that was stuffed up with something, so he could not see through that either. He pressed his ear to it and listened.

He heard a series of little clicks. Click — click — click — click — click. Nothing else at all.

'That's the click of the light they're using,' thought Sooty. 'Still signalling like mad! What for? Who to? And who is in our tower-room, using it as a signalling-station? How I wish I knew!'

Suddenly the clicking stopped. There was the sound of someone walking across the stone floor of the tower. And almost at once the door opened!

Sooty had no time to hurry down the stairs. All he could do was to squeeze into a niche, and hope that the person would not see him or touch him as he went by. The moon went behind a cloud at that moment, and Sooty was thankful to know he was hidden in black shadow. Someone came down the stairs and actually brushed against Sooty's arm.

Sooty jumped almost out of his skin, expecting to be hauled out of his niche. But the person did not seem to notice, and went on down the spiral stairway, walking softly.

Sooty did not dare to go down after him, for he was afraid the moon would come out, and cast his shadow down for the signaller to see.

458

So he stayed squeezed in his niche, hoping that Julian and Dick were well-hidden, and would not think it was he, Sooty, who was walking down the stairs!

Julian and Dick heard the soft footsteps coming, and thought at first it was Sooty. Then, not hearing his whisper, they stiffened behind the curtains, guessing that it was the signaller himself who was walking by!

'We'd better follow him!' whispered Julian to Dick. 'Come on. Quiet, now!'

But Julian got muddled up with the great curtains, and could not seem to find his way out. Dick, however, slipped out easily enough, and padded after the disappearing person. The moon was now out again, and Dick could catch glimpses of the signaller as he went past the moonlight streaks. Keeping well in the shadows himself, he darted quiety after him. Where was he going?

He followed him across the landing to a passage. Then across another landing and up the back-stairs! But those led to the staff bedrooms. Surely the man was not going there?

Dick, to his enormous surprise, saw the person disappear silently into Block's bedroom. He crept to the door, which had been left a little ajar. There was no light in the room except that of the moon. There was no sound of talking. Nothing at all except a creak which might have come from the bed.

Dick peeped in, full of the most intense curiosity. Would he see the man waking up Block? Would he see him climbing out of the window?

He stared round the room. There was no one there at all, except Block lying in bed. The moonlight lit up the corners, and Dick could quite plainly see that the room was empty. Only Block lay there, and, as Dick watched, he heard him give a sigh and roll over in bed.

'Well! That's the queerest thing I ever saw,' thought Dick, puzzled. 'A man goes into a room and completely disappears, without a single sound! Where can he have gone?'

He went back to find the others. Sooty by this time had crept down the spiral staircase and had found Julian, who had explained that Dick had gone to follow the queer signaller.

They went to find Dick, and suddenly bumped into him, creeping along quietly in the darkness. They all jumped violently, and Julian almost cried out, but stifled his voice just in time.

'Golly! You gave me a scare, Dick!' he whispered. 'Well, did you see who it was and where he went?'

Dick told them of his queer experience. 'He simply went into Block's room and vanished,' he said. 'It there any secret passage leading out of Block's room, Sooty?'

'No, none,' said Sooty. 'That wing is much newer than the rest of the house, and hasn't any secrets in at all. I simply can't imagine what happened to the man. How very queer! Who is he, and why does he come, and where on earth does he go?'

'We really must find out,' said Julian. 'It's such a mystery! Sooty, how did you know there was signalling going on from the tower?'

'Well, some time ago I found it out, quite by accident,' said Sooty. 'I couldn't sleep, and I went along to that funny little box-room place, and ferreted about for an old book I thought I'd seen there. And suddenly I looked up at the tower, and saw a light flashing there.'

'Funny,' said Dick.

'Well, I went along there at night a good many times after that, to see if I could see the signals again,' said Sooty, 'and at last I did. The first time I had seen them there was a good moon, and the second time there was, too. So, I thought, next time there's a moon, I'll creep along to that old box-room and see if the signaller is at work again. And sure enough he was!'

'Where does that window look out on, that we saw the light flashing from?' asked Julian, thoughtfully. 'The seaward side — or the landward?'

'Seaward,' said Sooty at once. 'There's something or someone out at sea that receives those signals. Goodness knows who.'

'Some kind of smugglers, I suppose,' said Dick. 'But it can't be anything to do with your father, Sooty. I say — let's go up into the tower, shall we? We might find something there — or see something.'

They went back to the spiral staircase and climbed up to the tower-room. It was dark, for the moon was behind a cloud. But it came out after a while, and the boys looked out of the seaward window.

There was no mist at all that night. They could see the flat marshes stretching away to the sea. They gazed down in silence. Then the moon went in and darkness covered the marsh.

Suddenly Julian clutched the others, making them jump. 'I can see something!' he whispered. 'Look beyond there. What is it?'

They all looked. It seemed like a tiny line of very small dots of light. They were so far away that it was difficult to see if they stayed still or moved. Then the moon came out again, flooding everywhere with silvery light, and the boys could not see anything

462

except the moonshine.

But when the moon went in again, there was the line of tiny, pricking lights again! 'A bit nearer, surely!' whispered Sooty. 'Smugglers — coming over a secret path from the sea to Castaway Hill! Smugglers!'

10

Timmy makes a noise

The three girls were very excited the next day when the boys told them their adventure of the night before.

'Gracious!' said Anne, her eyes wide with surprise. 'Who can it be signalling like that? And wherever did he go to? Fancy him going into Block's room, with Block there in bed!'

'It's very peculiar,' said George. 'I wish you had come and told me and Anne.'

'There wasn't time — and anyway, we couldn't have Timmy about at night. He might have flown at the signaller,' said Dick.

'The man must have been signalling to the smugglers,' said Julian, thoughtfully. 'Let me see — probably they came over from France in a ship — came as near to the marsh as they could — waited for a signal to tell them that the coast was clear — probably the signal from the tower — and then waded across a path they knew through the marsh.

Each man must have carried a torch to prevent himself from leaving the path and falling into the marsh. No doubt there was someone waiting to receive the goods they brought — someone at the edge of the marsh below the hill.'

'But who?' said Dick. 'It can't have been Mr Barling, who, Sooty says, is known to be a smuggler. Because the signal lights came from *our* house, not his. It's all very puzzling.'

'Well, we'll do our best to solve the mystery,' said George. 'There's some queer game going on in this very house, without your father's knowledge, Sooty. We'll keep a jolly good lookout and see if we can find out what it is.'

They were at breakfast alone, when they discussed the night's adventure. Block came in to see if they had finished at that moment. Anne did not notice him.

'What does Mr Barling smuggle?' she asked Sooty. Immediately she got a hard kick on her ankle, and stared in pain and surprise. 'Why did you . . . ?' she began, and got another kick, harder still. Then she saw Block.

'But he's deaf,' she said. 'He can't hear anything we say.'

Block began to clear away, his face as usual showing no expression. Sooty glared at Anne. She was upset and cross, but said no more. She rubbed her bruised ankle hard. As soon as Block went out of the room she turned on Sooty.

'You mean thing! You hurt my ankle like anything! Why shouldn't I say things in front of Block? He's quite deaf!' said Anne, her face very red.

'I know he's supposed to be,' said Sooty. 'And I think he is. But I saw a funny look come over his face when you asked me what Mr Barling smuggled — almost as if he had heard what you said, and was surprised.'

'You imagined it!' said Anne, crossly, still rubbing her ankle. 'Anyway, don't kick me so hard again. A gentle push with your toe would have been enough. I won't talk in front of Block if you don't want me to, but it's quite plain he's as deaf as a post!'

'Yes, he's deaf all right,' said Dick. 'I dropped a plate off the table yesterday, by accident, just behind him, and it smashed to bits, if you remember. Well, he didn't jump or turn a hair, as he would have done if he could have heard.'

'All the same — I never trust Block, deaf or not,' said Sooty. 'I always feel he might read our lips or something. Deaf people can often do that, you know.'

'They went off to take Timmy for his usual morning walk. Timmy was quite used to being shut in the laundry basket by now, and lowered into the pit. In fact, he always jumped straight into the basket as soon as the lid was opened, and lay down.

That morning they again met Block, who stared with great interest at the dog. He plainly recognised it as the same dog as before.

'There's Block,' said Julian, in a low voice. 'Don't drive Timmy off this time. We'll pretend he's a stray who always meets us each morning.'

So they let Timmy run round them, and when Block came up, they nodded to him, and made as if to go on their way. But the man stopped them.

'That dog seems to be a friend of yours,' he said, in his curious monotone of a voice.

'Oh yes. He goes with us each morning now,' said Julian, politely. 'He quite thinks he's our dog! Nice fellow, isn't he?'

Block stared at Timmy, who growled. 'Mind you do not bring that dog into the house,' said Block. 'If you do, Mr Lenoir will have him killed.'

466

Julian saw George's face beginning to turn red with fury. He spoke hurriedly. 'Why should we bring him to the house, Block? Don't be silly!'

Block, however, did not appear to hear. He gave Timmy a nasty look, and went on his way, occasionally turning round to look at the little company of children.

'Horrid fellow!' said George, angrily. 'How dare he say things like that?'

When they got back to Marybelle's bedroom that morning, they pulled Timmy up from the pit, and let him out of the basket. 'We'll put him into the secret passage as usual,' said George, 'and I'll put some biscuits in with him. I got some nice ones for him this morning, the sort he likes, all big and crunchy.'

She went to the door — but just as she was about to unlock it and take Timmy into Sooty's room next door, Timmy gave a small growl.

George took her hand away from the door at once. She turned to look at Timmy. He was standing stiffly, the hackles on his neck rising up, and he was staring fixedly at the door. George put her hand to her lips warningly, and whispered:

'Someone's outside. Timmy knows. He's smelt them. Will you all talk loudly, and pretend to be playing a game? I'll pop Timmy into the cupboard where the rope-ladder is kept.'

At once the others began to talk to one another, while George swiftly dragged Timmy to the cupboard, patted him to make him understand he was to be quiet, and shut him in.

'My turn to deal,' said Julian loudly, and took a pack of snap cards from the top of the chest. 'You won last time, Dick. Bet I'll win this time.'

He dealt swiftly. The others, still talking loudly, saying anything that came into their heads, began to

467

play snap. They yelled 'snap' nearly all the time, pretending to be very jolly and hilarious. Anyone listening outside the door would never guess it was all pretence.

George, who was watching the door closely, saw that the handle was gradually turning, very slowly indeed. Someone meant to open the door without being heard, and come in unexpectedly. But the door was locked!

Soon the person outside, whoever it was, realised that the door was locked, and the handle slowly turned the other way again. Then it was still. There came no other sound. It was impossible to know if anyone was still outside the door or not.

But Timmy would know! Signing to the others to carry on with their shouting and laughing, George let Timmy out of the cupboard. He ran to the door of the room, and stood there, sniffing quietly. Then he turned and looked at George, his tail wagging.

'It's all right,' said George to the others. 'There's no one there now. Timmy always knows. We'd better quickly take him into your room, Sooty, while the coast is clear. Who could it have been, do you think, snooping outside?'

'Block, I should say,' said Sooty. He unlocked the door and peered out. There was no one in the passage. Sooty tiptoed to the door at the end and looked out there also. He waved to George to tell her it was all right to take Timmy into his room.

Soon Timmy was safely in the secret passage, crunching up his favourite biscuits. He had got quite used to his queer life now, and did not mind at all. He knew his way about the passage, and had explored other passages that led from it. He was quite at home in the maze of secret ways!

'Better go and have our dinner now,' said Dick.

'And mind, Anne — don't go and say anything silly in front of that horrid Block, in case he reads your lips.'

'Of course I shan't,' said Anne, indignantly. 'I wouldn't have before, but I never thought of him reading my lips. If he does, he's very clever.'

Soon they were all sitting down to lunch. Block was there, waiting to serve them. Sarah was out for the day and did not appear. Block served them with soup, and then went out.

Suddenly, to the children's intense surprise and fright, they heard Timmy barking loudly! They jumped violently.

'Listen! Hark at Timmy!' said Julian. 'He must be somewhere near here, in that secret passage. How weird it sounds, his bark coming muffled and distant like that. But anyone would know it was a dog barking.'

'Don't say anything at all about it in front of Block,' said Sooty. 'Not a word. Pretend not to hear at all, if Timmy barks again. What on earth is he barking for?'

'It's the bark he uses when he's excited and pleased,' said George. 'I expect he's chasing a rat. He always goes right off his head when he sees a rat or a rabbit. There he goes again. Oh, dear, I hope he catches the rat quickly and settles down!'

Block came back at that moment. Timmy had again just stopped barking. But, in a moment or two, his doggy voice could be heard once more, very muffled. 'Woof! Woof-woof!'

Julian was watching Block closely. The man went on serving the meat. He said nothing, but looked round at the children intently, as if he wanted to see each child's expression, or see if they said anything.

'Jolly good soup that was today,' said Julian,

cheerfully, looking round at the others. 'I must say Sarah is a wonderful cook.'

'I think her ginger buns are gorgeous,' said Anne. 'Especially when they are all hot from the oven.'

'Woof-woof,' said Timmy's voice from far away behind the walls.

'George, your mother makes the most heavenly fruit cake I ever tasted,' said Dick to George, wishing Timmy would be quiet. 'I do wonder how they're all getting on at Kirrin Cottage, and if they've started mending the roof yet.'

'Woof!' said Timmy, joyfully chasing his rat down another bit of passage.

Block served everyone and then silently disappeared. Julian went to the door to make sure he had gone and was not outside.

'I hope old Block *is* as deaf as a post!' he said. 'I could have sworn I saw a surprised look come into those cold eyes of his, when Timmy barked.'

'Well, if he *could* hear him, which I don't believe,' said George, 'he must have been jolly surprised to see us talking away and not paying any attention to a dog's barking at all!'

The others giggled. They kept a sharp ear for Block's return. They heard footsteps after a time, and began to pile their plates together for him to take away.

The schoolroom door opened. But it was not Block who came in. It was Mr Lenoir! He came in, smiling as usual, and looked round at the surprised children.

'Ah! So you are enjoying your dinner, and eating it all up, like good children,' he said. He always irritated the children because he spoke to them as if they were very small. 'Does Block wait on you properly?'

'Oh yes, sir, thank you,' said Julian, standing up

politely. 'We are having a very nice time here. We think Sarah is a wonderful cook!'

'Ah, that's good, that's good,' said Mr Lenoir. The children waited impatiently for him to go. They were so afraid that Timmy would bark again. But Mr Lenoir seemed in no hurry.

And then Timmy barked again! 'Woof, woof, woof!'

11

George is worried

Mr Lenoir cocked his head on one side almost like a startled dog, when he heard the muffled barking. He looked at the children. But they made no sign of having heard anything. Mr Lenoir listened a little while, saying nothing. Then he turned to a drawing-book, belonging to Julian, and began to look at the sketches there.

The children felt somehow that he was doing it for the sake of staying in the schoolroom a little longer. Into Julian's mind came the quick suspicion that somehow Mr Lenoir must have been told of Timmy's barking and come to investigate it for himself. It was the first time he had ever come to the schoolroom!

Timmy barked again, a little more distantly. Mr Lenoir's nose grew white at the tip. Sooty and Marybelle knew the danger-sign, and glanced at one another. That white-tipped nose usually meant a storm of temper!

'Do you hear that noise?' said Mr Lenoir, snapping out the words.

'What noise, sir?' asked Julian, politely.

Timmy barked again.

'Don't be foolish! There's the noise again!' said Mr Lenoir. At that moment a gull called outside the window, circling in the sea-breeze.

'Oh — that gull, sir? Yes, we often hear the gulls,' said Dick, brightly. 'Sometimes they seem to mew like a cat sir.'

'Pah!' said Mr Lenoir, almost spitting out the word. 'I suppose you will say they also bark like a dog?'

'Well, they might, I suppose, sir,' agreed Dick, looking faintly surprised. 'After all, if they can mew like cats, there's no reason why they shouldn't bark like dogs.'

Timmy barked again very joyfully. Mr Lenoir faced the children, in a very bad temper indeed now.

'Can't you hear that? Tell me what *that* noise is!'

The children all put their heads on one side, and pretended to listen very carefully. 'I can't hear anything,' said Dick. 'Not a thing.'

'I can hear the wind,' said Anne.

'I can hear the gulls again,' said Julian, putting his hand behind one ear.

'I can hear a door banging. Perhaps that's the noise you mean, sir!' said Sooty, with a most innocent expression. His stepfather gave him a poisonous look. He could really be very unpleasant.

'And there's a window rattling,' said Marybelle, eager to do her bit too, though she felt very frightened of her father, for she knew his sudden rages very well.

'I tell you, it's a dog, and you know it!' snapped Mr Lenoir, the tip of his nose so white now that it looked very queer indeed. 'Where's the dog? Whose is he?'

'What dog, sir?' began Julian, frowning as if he

474

were very puzzled indeed. 'There's no dog here that I can see.'

Mr Lenoir glared at him, and clenched his fingers. It was quite clear that he would have liked to box Julian's ears. 'Then listen!' he hissed. 'Listen and say what you think could make that barking, if not a dog?'

They were all forced to listen, for by now they felt scared of the angry man. But fortunately Timmy made no sound at all. Either he had let the rat escape, or was now gobbling it up. Anyway, there was not a single sound from him!

'Sorry, sir, but *really* I can't hear a dog barking,' said Julian, in rather an injured tone.

'Nor can I!' said Dick, and the others joined in, saying the same. Mr Lenoir knew that this time they were speaking the truth, for he too could not hear anything.

'When I catch that dog I will have him poisoned,' he said, very slowly and clearly. 'I will not have dogs in my house.'

He turned on his heel and went out quickly, which was a very good thing, for George was quite ready to fly into one of *her* rages, and then there would have been a real battle! Anne put her hand on George's arm to stop her shouting after Mr Lenoir.

'Don't give the game away!' she whispered. 'Don't say anything, George!'

George bit her lip. She had gone first red with rage and then white. She stamped her foot.

'How dare he, how dare he?' she burst out.

'Shut up, silly,' said Julian. 'Block will be back in a minute. We must all pretend to be awfully surprised that Mr Lenoir thought there was a dog, because, if Block can read our lips, he mustn't know the truth.'

Block came in with the pudding at that moment, his face as blank as ever. It was the most curious face the children had ever seen, for there was never any change of expression on it at all. As Anne said, it might have been a wax mask!

'Funny how Mr Lenoir thought there was a dog barking!' began Julian, and the others backed him up valiantly. If Block could indeed read their lips he would be puzzled to know whether there *had* been a dog barking or not!

The children escaped to Sooty's room afterwards, and held a council of war. 'What are we to do about Timmy?' said George. 'Does your stepfather know the secret way behind the walls of Smuggler's Top, Sooty? Could he possibly get in and find Timmy? Timmy might fly at him, you know.'

'Yes, he might,' said Sooty, thoughtfully. 'I don't know if Father does know about the secret passages. I mean, I expect he knows, but I don't know if he guessed where the entrances are. I found them out quite by accident.'

'I'm going home,' said George, suddenly. 'I'm not going to risk Timmy being poisoned.'

'You can't go home alone,' said Julian. 'It would look funny. If you do, we'd all have to, and then we won't have a chance to solve this mystery with Sooty.'

'No, for goodness' sake don't go and leave me just now,' said Sooty, looking quite alarmed. 'It would make my father furious, simply furious.'

George hesitated. She didn't want to make trouble for Sooty, whom she liked very much. But, on the other hand, she certainly was not going to risk danger to Timmy.

'Well — I'll telephone my father and say I'm homesick and want to go back,' said George. 'I'll say

476

I miss Mother. It's quite true, I do miss her. You others can stay on here and solve the mystery. It wouldn't be fair of you to try and keep me and Timmy here when you know I'd worry every moment in case someone got into the secret passage and put down poisoned meat for him to eat.'

The others hadn't thought of this. That would be terrible. Julian sighed. He would have to let George have her own way after all.

'All right. You telephone to your father,' he said. 'There's a phone downstairs. Do it now if you like. There won't be anyone about now, I don't suppose.'

George slipped down the passage, out of the door there, and down the stairs to where the telephone was enclosed in a dark little cupboard. She asked for the number she wanted.

There was a long wait. Then she heard the buzzing noise — brr — brr — brr — that told her that the telephone bell at Kirrin Cottage was ringing. She began to plan what she should say to her father. She must, she really must go home with Timmy. She didn't know how she was going to explain about Timmy — perhaps she needn't explain at all. But she meant to go home that day or the next!

'Brr — brr — brr — brr' said the bell at the other end. It went on and on, and nobody answered it. She did not hear her father's familiar voice — only the bell that went on ringing. Why did nobody answer?

The operator at the exchange spoke to her. 'I'm sorry, There's no reply.'

George put down the receiver miserably. Perhaps her parents were out? She would have to try again later on.

Poor George tried three times, but each time with the same result. No reply. As she was coming out of the telephone cupboard for the third time,

Mrs Lenoir saw her.

'Have you been trying to telephone to your home?' she said. 'Haven't you heard any news?'

'I haven't had a letter yet,' said George. 'I've tried three times to telephone Kirrin Cottage but each time there is no reply.'

'Well, we heard this morning that it is impossible to live in Kirrin Cottage while the men are hammering and knocking everywhere,' said Mrs Lenoir, in her gentle voice. 'We heard from your mother. She said that the noise was driving your father mad, and they were going away for a week or so, till things were better. But Mr Lenoir at once wrote and asked them here. We shall know tomorrow, because we have asked them to telephone a reply. We could not get them on the telephone today, of course, any more than you could, because they have gone away already.'

'Oh,' said George, surprised at all this news and wondered why her mother had not written to tell her too.

'Your mother said she had written to you,' said Mrs Lenoir. 'Maybe the letter will come by the next post. The posts are often most peculiar here. It will be a pleasure to have your parents if they can come. Mr Lenoir particularly wants to meet your clever father. He thinks he is quite a genius.'

George said no more but went back to the others, her face serious. She opened Sooty's door, and the others saw at once that she had had news of some sort.

'I can't go home with Timothy,' said George. 'Mother and Father can't stand the noise the workmen make, and they have both gone away!'

'Bad luck!' said Sooty. 'All the same, I'm glad you'll have to stay here, George. I should hate to lose you or Timmy.'

'Your mother has written to ask my mother and father to come and stay here too,' said George. 'What I shall do about Timmy I don't know! And they are sure to ask questions about him too. I can't tell a downright lie and say I left him with Alf the fisher-boy, or anything like that. I can't think *what* to do!'

'We'll think of something,' promised Sooty. 'Perhaps I can get one of the villagers to look after him for us. That would be a very good idea.'

'Oh yes!' said George, cheering up. 'Why didn't I think of that before? Let's ask someone quickly, Sooty.'

But it was impossible to do anything that day because Mrs Lenoir asked them to go down into the drawing-room after tea, and have a game with her. So none of them could go out to find someone to look after Timmy. 'Never mind,' thought George. 'He'll be safe tonight on my bed! Tomorrow will be soon enough.'

It was the first time that Mrs Lenoir had asked them down to be with her. 'You see, Mr Lenoir is out tonight on important business,' she explained. 'He has had to go to the mainland with the car. He doesn't like his evenings disturbed when he is at home, so I haven't been able to see as much of you all as I should have liked. But tonight I can.'

Julian wondered if Mr Lenoir had gone to the mainland on smuggling business! Somehow the smuggled goods must be taken across to the mainland — and if all that signalling business the other night had to do with Mr Lenoir's smuggling then maybe he had now gone to dispose of the goods!

The telephone bell rang shrilly. Mrs Lenoir got up. 'I expect that is your mother or father on the phone,' she said to George. 'Maybe I shall have news for you! Perhaps your parents will be arriving here tomorrow.'

She went out into the hall. The children waited anxiously. Would George's parents come or not?

12

Block gets a surprise

Mrs Lenoir came back after a time. She smiled at George.

'That was your father,' she said. 'He is coming tomorrow, but not your mother. They went to your aunt's, and your mother says she thinks she must stay and help her, because your aunt is not very well. But your father would like to come, because he wants to discuss his latest experiments with Mr Lenoir, who is very interested in them. It will be very nice to have him.'

The children would very much rather have had Aunt Fanny instead of Uncle Quentin, who could be very difficult at times. But still, he would probably be talking with Mr Lenoir most of the time, so that would be all right!

They finished their game with Mrs Lenoir and went up to bed. George was to get Timmy to take him to her room. Sooty went to see that the coast was clear. He could not see Block anywhere. His stepfather was still away from the house. Sarah was singing in the kitchen and the little kitchen-maid, Harriet, was knitting there in a corner.

'Block must be out,' thought Sooty, and went to tell George that the coast was clear. As he went across the landing to the long passage that led to his own room, the boy noticed two black lumps sticking out at the bottom of the thick curtains drawn across the landing window. He looked at them in surprise, and then recognised them. He grinned.

'So old Block suspects we have a dog, and he thinks it sleeps in George's room or Julian's, and he's posted himself there to watch!' he thought. 'Aha! I'll give friend Block a nasty shock!'

He ran to tell the others. George listened, alarmed. But Sooty, as usual, had a plan.

'We'll give Block an awful shock!' he said. 'I'll get a rope, and we'll all go down to the landing. I'll suddenly yell out that there's a robber hiding behind the curtains and I'll pounce on Block, and give him a few good punches. Then, with your help, Julian and Dick, I'll fold him up well in the curtains — a good jerk will bring them down on top of him as well!'

The others began to laugh. It would be fun to play a trick on Block. He really was such an unpleasant fellow. A good lesson would do him no harm.

'While all the excitement is beginning I'll slip by with Timmy,' said George. 'I only hope he won't want to join in! He might give Block a good nip!'

'Well, hold on to Timmy firmly,' said Julian. 'Get him into your room quickly. Now — are we ready?'

They were. Feeling excited they crept down the long passage that led to the door which opened out on to the landing where Block was hiding. They saw the curtains move very slightly as they came along. Block was watching.

George waited with Timmy at the passage door,

not showing herself at all. Then, with a yell from Sooty, a really blood-curdling yell that made both George and Timmy jump, things began to happen!

Sooty flung himself on the hidden Block with all his might. 'A robber! Help, a robber hiding here!' he shouted.

Block jumped, and began to struggle. Sooty got in two or three well-aimed punches. Block had often got him into trouble with his father, and now Sooty was getting a bit of his own back! Julian and Dick rushed to help.

A violent tug at the curtains brought them down on Block's head! Not only that, the curtain pole descended on him too, and knocked him sideways. Poor Block — he was completely taken by surprise, and could do nothing against the three determined boys. Even Anne gave a hand, though Marybelle stood apart, enjoying the fun though not daring to take part in it.

Just as it all began George slipped by with Timmy. But Timmy could not bear to miss the fun. He dragged behind George, and would not go with her.

She tried to forced him, her hand on his collar. But Timmy had seen a nice fat leg waving about near him, protruding from the curtain. He pounced on it.

There was an agonised yell from Block. Certainly Timmy could nip hard with his sharp white teeth. He worried at the kicking leg for a few seconds, and then had a sharp slap from George. Shocked, Timmy let go of the leg and humbly followed his mistress. She never slapped him! She must indeed be angry with him. With tail well down Timmy followed her into the bedroom and got under the bed at once. He poked his head out and looked beseechingly at George with big brown eyes.

'Oh, Timmy — I *had* to slap you!' said George, and

she knelt down by the big dog and patted his head. 'You see, you might have spoilt everything if you'd been seen. As it is I'm sure you bit Block and I don't know how we're going to explain that! Lie quietly now, old fellow. I'm going out to join the others.'

Timmy's tail thumped softly on the floor. George ran out of the room and joined the others on the landing. They were having a fine game with Block, who was yelling and wriggling and struggling for all he was worth. He was wrapped up in the curtains like a caterpiller inside a cocoon. His head was completely covered and he could see nothing.

Suddenly Mr Lenoir appeared in the hall below, with a very scared Mrs Lenoir beside him. 'What's all this?' thundered Sooty's stepfather. 'Have you gone mad? How dare you behave like this at this time of night?'

'Sir, we've caught a robber and tied him up,' panted Sooty.

Mr Lenoir ran up the stairs two steps at a time, amazed. He saw the kicking figure on the ground well-tied up in the heavy curtains. 'A robber! Do you mean a burglar? Where did you find him?

'He was hiding behind the curtains, sir!' said Julian. 'We managed to get hold of him and tie him up before he could escape. Could you call the police sir?'

An anguished voice came from inside of the curtains. 'Let me go! I've been bitten! Let me go!'

'Good heavens! You've got Block tied up there!' said Mr Lenoir, in amazement and anger. 'Untie him, quickly.'

'But, sir — it can't be Block. He was hiding behind those curtains at the window,' protested Sooty.

'Do as you're told,' commanded Mr Lenoir,

getting angry. Anne looked at the tip of his nose. Yes, it was turning white, as usual!

The boys reluctantly undid the ropes. Block angrily parted the curtains that enfolded him, and looked out, his usually blank face crimson with rage and fright.

'I won't stand this sort of thing!' he raged. 'Look here, at my leg, sir! I've been bitten. Only a dog could have done that. See my leg?'

Sure enough there were the marks of teeth on his leg, slowly turning purple. Timmy had taken a good nip, and almost gone through the skin.

'There's no dog here,' said Mrs Lenoir, coming timidly up the stairs at last. 'You couldn't have been bitten by a dog, Block.'

'Who bit him, then?' demanded Mr Lenoir, turning fiercely on poor Mrs Lenoir.

'Do you think *I* could have bitten him, sir, in my excitement?' suddenly said Sooty, to the enormous surprise of the others, and to their immense amusement. He spoke very seriously with a worried look on his face. 'When I lose my temper, sir, I hardly know what I do. Do you think I bit him?'

'Pah!' said Mr Lenoir, in disgust. 'Don't talk nonsense, boy! I'll have you whipped if I think you go about biting people. Get up, Block. You're not badly hurt.'

'My teeth do feel a bit funny, now I come to think of it,' said Sooty, opening and shutting his mouth as if to see if they were all right. 'I think I'd better go and clean them, sir. I feel as if I've got the taste of Block's ankle in my mouth. And it isn't nice.'

Mr Lenoir, driven to fury by Sooty's impudence, reached out swiftly to box the boy's ears. But Sooty dodged and ran back up the passage. 'Just going to clean my teeth!' he called, and the others tried to keep from laughing. The idea of Sooty biting anyone was absurd. It was quite obvious, however, that neither Mr nor Mrs Lenoir guessed what had bitten Block.

'Go to bed, all of you,' ordered Mr Lenoir. 'I hope I shall not have to complain of you to your father tomorrow when he comes — or your uncle, as it may be. I don't know which of you are his children, and which not. I'm surprised at you making such a nuisance of yourselves in somebody else's house. Tying up my servant! If he leaves, it will be your fault!'

The children hoped fervently that Block *would* leave. It would be marvellous to have the deaf blank-faced fellow out of the house. He was on the watch for Timmy, they felt sure. He would snoop about till he got Timmy or one of them into trouble.

But Block was still there next morning. He came into the schoolroom with the breakfast, his face almost as blank as usual. He gave Sooty an evil look.

'You look out for yourself,' he said, in a curiously soft voice. 'You look out. Something's going to happen to you one of these days. Yes — and that dog too! I know you've got a dog, see? You can't deceive *me*.'

The children said nothing, but looked at one another. Sooty grinned, and rapped out a gay little tattoo on the table with his spoon.

'Dark, dire, dreadful threats!' he said. 'You look out for yourself too, Block. Any more snooping about, and you'll find yourself tied up again — yes, and I might bite you again too. You never know. My teeth feel quite ready for it this morning.'

He bared his teeth at Block, who made no reply at all, but merely looked as if he had not heard a word. The man went out, and closed the door softly behind him.

487

'Nasty bit of work, isn't he?' said Sooty. But George felt rather alarmed. She feared Block. There was something cold and clever and bad about those narrow eyes of his. She longed with all her heart to get Timmy out of the house.

She got a terrible shock that morning! Sooty came to her, looking agitated. 'I say! What do you think? Your father's going to have *my* room. I've got to sleep with Julian and Dick. Block is taking all my things from my room to theirs this very minute, with Sarah. I hope we shall have a chance to get him out all right, before your father comes!'

'Oh Sooty!' said George, in despair. 'I'll go and see if I can get him at once.'

She went off, pretending to go to Marybelle's room for something. But Block was still in Sooty's room. And there he stayed, cleaning it all morning!

George was very worried about Timmy. He would wonder why she hadn't fetched him. He would miss his walk. She hovered about the passage all morning, getting into Sarah's way as she carried clothes from Sooty's old room to Julian's.

Block gave George some curious looks. He walked with a limp to show that his leg was bad from the bite. He left the room at last and George darted in. But Block returned almost at once and she dashed into Marybelle's room. Again Block left and went down the passage, and again the desperate little girl rushed into Sooty's room.

But Block was back before she could even open the cupboard door. 'What are you doing in this room?' he said, roughly. 'I haven't cleaned it all morning to have children in here messing it up again! Clear out of it!'

George went — and then once more waited for Block to go. He would have to see to the luncheon

488

soon! He went at last. George rushed to the door of Sooty's room, eager to get poor Timmy.

But she couldn't open the door. It was locked — and Block had taken the key!

13

Poor George!

By now George was in despair. She felt as if she was in a nightmare. She went to find Sooty. He was in Julian's room, next to hers, washing his hands ready for lunch.

'Sooty! I shall have to get into the secret passage the way you first took us in,' she said. 'Through that little study-room of your father's — you know, where the sliding panels are.'

'We can't,' said Sooty, looking rather alarmed. 'He uses it now, and he'd half-kill anyone who went in there. He's got the records of all his experiments there, and he's put them ready to show your father.'

'I don't care,' said George, desperately. 'I've got to get in there somehow. Timmy may starve!'

'Not Timmy! He'll live on the rats in the passages!' said Sooty. 'Timmy could always look after himself, I bet!'

'Well, he'd die of thirst then,' said George, obstinately. 'There's no water in those secret passages. You know that!'

George could hardly eat any lunch because she was so worried. She made up her mind somehow to get into that little study-room, and see if she could open the entrance into the wall behind the panels. Then she would slip in and get Timmy. She didn't care what happened; she was going to get Timmy.

'I shan't tell the others, though,' she thought. 'They would only try and stop me, or offer to do it themselves, and I don't trust anyone but myself to do this. Timmy's my dog, and *I'm* going to save him!'

After lunch, everyone went to Julian's room to discuss things. George went with them. But after a few minutes she left them. 'Back in a minute,' she said. They took no notice and went on discussing how to rescue Timmy. It really did seem as if the only way was to raid the study, and try and get into the secret passage without being seen.

'But my stepfather works there now,' said Sooty. 'And I shouldn't be surprised if he locks the door when he leaves the room.'

George didn't come back. After about ten minutes Anne grew puzzled.

'What can George be doing? It must be about ten minutes since she went.'

'Oh, she's probably gone to see if my old room is unlocked yet,' said Sooty, getting up. 'I'll peep out and see if she's about.'

She wasn't. She didn't seem to be anywhere! She wasn't in the passage that led to Sooty's old room; she couldn't be in that room because it was still locked, and she wasn't in Marybelle's room.

Sooty peeped in George's own room, the one she shared with Anne. But that was empty too. He went downstairs and snooped around around a bit. No George!

He went back to the others, puzzled.

'I can't find her anywhere,' he said. 'Where can she be?'

Anne looked alarmed. This was such a queer house, with queer happenings. She wished George would come.

'She's not gone into that little study-room, has she?' said Julian, suddenly. It would be just like George to try and get into the lion's den!

'I didn't think of that,' said Sooty. 'Silly of me. I'll go and see.'

He went down the stairs. He made his way cautiously to his father's study. He stood quietly outside the shut door. There was no sound from inside. Was his father there or not?

Sooty debated whether to open the door and peep in or whether to knock. He decided to knock. Then, if his father answered he could rush back upstairs before the door could be opened, and his father would not know whom to scold for the interruption.

So he knocked, very smartly, Rap-rap.

'Who's that?' came his stepfather's irritable voice. 'Come in! Am I to have no peace?'

Sooty fled upstairs at once. He went to the others. 'George can't be in the study,' he said. 'My stepfather's there, and he didn't sound in too good a temper either.'

'Then *where* can she be?' said Julian, looking worried. 'I do wish she wouldn't go off without telling us where she's going. She must be somewhere about. She wouldn't go very far from Timmy.'

They all had a good hunt over the house, even going into the kitchen. Block was there, reading a paper. 'What do you want?' he said. 'You won't get it, whatever it is.'

'We don't want anything from *you*,' said Sooty. 'How's your poor bad bitten leg?'

492

Block looked so unpleasantly at them that they all retreated from the kitchen in a hurry. Sooty put Julian and Dick on guard, and went up to the staff bedrooms to see if by any chance George had gone there. A silly idea, he knew, but George must be somewhere!

She wasn't there, of course. The children went back gloomily to Julian's room. 'This beastly house!' said Julian. 'I can't say I like it. Sorry to say so, Sooty, but it's a queer place with a queer feeling about it.'

Sooty was not hurt at all. 'Oh, I agree with you,' he said. 'I've always thought the same myself. So has Mother, and so has Marybelle. It's my stepfather that likes it.'

'Where *is* George?' said Anne. 'I keep on and on trying to think. There's only one place I'm certain she's not in — and that's your stepfather's study, Sooty. Even George wouldn't dare to go there while your stepfather was there.'

But Anne was wrong. The study was the very place where George was at that very moment!

The little girl had made up her mind that it was best to try and get in there, and wait for a chance to open the sliding panel. So she had slipped downstairs, gone across the hall, and tried the door of the study. It was locked.

'Blow!' said George, desperately. 'Everything is against me and Timmy. How can I get in? I must, I must!'

She slipped out of the side-door near the study and went into the little yard on to which the study-window looked. Could she get in there?

But the window was barred! So that was no good either. She went back again, wishing she could find the key to unlock the door. But it was nowhere to be seen.

Suddenly she heard Mr Lenoir's voice in the room across the hall. In a panic George lifted up the lid of a big wooden chest nearby, and climbed hurriedly into it. She closed the lid over her, and knelt there, waiting, heart beating fast.

Mr Lenoir came across the hall. He was going to his study. 'I shall get everything ready to show my visitor when he comes,' he called to his wife. 'Don't disturb me at all. I shall be very busy indeed.'

George heard the sound of a key being put into the study door. It turned. The door opened and shut with a click.

But it was not locked again from the inside. George knelt in the dark chest and considered matters. She meant to get into that study. She meant to get through the entrance into the secret passage, where Tim was. That passage led from the study to Sooty's old bedroom, and somewhere in that passage was Timmy.

What she was going to do once she had Timmy she didn't quite know. Perhaps Sooty would take him to someone who could look after him for her, someone on Castaway Hill.

She heard the sound of Mr Lenoir coughing. She heard the shuffling of papers. Then she heard the click of a cupboard being opened and shut. Mr Lenoir was evidently busy!

Then he gave an exclamation of annoyance. He said something in an irritable voice that sounded like 'Now where did I put that?'

Then the door opened very suddenly and Mr Lenoir came out. George had just time to close down the lid, which she had opened to let in fresh air. She knelt in the chest, trembling, as Mr Lenoir passed there and went on across the hall.

George suddenly knew that this was her chance.

Mr Lenoir might be gone for a few minutes and give her time to open that panel in the wall! She lifted the lid of the chest, and jumped out quickly. She ran into the study, and went to the place where Sooty had pressed the panelling.

But before she could even run her fingers over the smooth brown oak, she heard returning footsteps! Mr Lenoir had hardly been half a minute. He was coming back at once.

In a panic poor George looked round for somewhere to hide. There was a large sofa against one wall. George crawled behind it, finding just room to crouch there without being seen. She was hardly there before Mr Lenoir entered the room, shut the door, and sat down at his desk. He switched on a big lamp over it, and bent to look at some documents.

George hardly dared to breathe. Her heart bumped against her ribs and seemed to make a terrible noise. It was very uncomfortable behind the sofa, but she did not dare to move.

She could not think what in the world to do. It would be terrible to be there for hours! What would the others think? They would soon be looking for her.

They were. Even at that moment Sooty was outside the study door, pondering whether to go in or to knock. He knocked smartly — rap-rap — and George almost jumped out of her skin!

She heard Mr Lenoir's impatient voice. 'Who's that? Come in! Am I to have no peace?'

There was no answer. No one came in. Mr Lenoir called again. 'Come in, I say!'

Still no answer. He strode to the door and flung it open angrily. No one was there. Sooty had fled upstairs at once.

'Those tiresome children, I suppose,' muttered Mr Lenoir. 'Well, if any of them comes and knocks again and goes away, I'll punish them properly. Bed and bread and water for them!'

He sounded fierce. George wished she was anywhere but in his study. What would he say if he knew she was only three or four feet away from him?

Mr Lenoir worked for about half an hour, and poor George got stiffer and stiffer, and more and more uncomfortable. Then she heard Mr Lenoir yawn, and her heart felt lighter. Perhaps he would have a nap! That would be good luck. She might creep out then, and try to get into the secret passage.

Mr Lenoir yawned again. Then he pushed his papers aside and went to the sofa. He lay down on it and pulled the rug there over his knees. He settled himself down as if for a good sleep.

The sofa creaked under him. George tried to hold her breath again, afraid that now he was so near to her he would certainly hear her.

Soon a small snore came to her ears. Then another and another. Mr Lenoir was asleep! George waited for a few minutes. The snores went on, a little louder. Surely it would be safe now to creep from her hiding-place?

George began to move, very cautiously and quietly. She crept to the end of the sofa. She squeezed out from behind it. Still the snores went on.

She stood upright and went on tiptoe to the panel that had slid aside. She began to press here and there with her fingers, trying to find the spot that would move the panel to one side.

She couldn't seem to find it. She grew red with anxiety. She cast a glance at the sleeping Mr Lenoir, and worked feverishly at the panel. Where was the spot to press, oh, where was it?

Then a stern voice came from behind her, making

her jump almost out of her skin.

'And what exactly do you think you are doing, my boy? How dare you come into my study and mess about like this?'

George turned round and faced Mr Lenoir. He always thought she was a boy! She didn't know what to say. He looked very angry indeed, and the tip of his nose was already white.

George was frightened. She ran to the door, but Mr Lenoir caught her before she opened it. He shook her hard.

'What were you doing in my study? Was it you who knocked and ran away? Do you think it is funny to play tricks like that? I'll soon teach you that it isn't!'

He opened the door and called loudly. 'Block! Come here! Sarah, tell Block I want him.'

Block appeared from the kitchen, his face as blank as usual. Mr Lenoir wrote something down quickly on a piece of paper and gave it him to read. Block nodded.

'I've told him to take you to your room, lock you in, and give you nothing but bread and water for the rest of the day,' said Mr Lenoir, fiercely. 'That will teach you to behave yourself in the future. Any more nonsense and I'll whip you myself.'

'My father won't be very pleased when he hears you're punishing me like this,' began George in a trembling voice. But Mr Lenoir sneered.

'Pah! Wait till he hears from me how you have misbehaved yourself, and I am sure he will agree with me. Now go, and you will not be allowed out of your room till tomorrow. I will make your excuses to your father, when he comes.'

Poor George was propelled upstairs by Block, who was only too delighted to be punishing one of the children. As she came to the door of the room George shouted to the others who were in Julian's room next door.

'Julian! Dick! Help me! Quick, help me!'

14

A very puzzling thing

Julian, Dick, and the others rushed out at once, just in time to see Block shove George roughly into her room and shut the door. There was a click as he locked it.

'Here! What are you doing?' cried Julian, indignantly.

Block took no notice, but turned to go. Julian caught hold of his arm, and yelled loudly in his ear. 'Unlock that door at once! Do you hear?'

Block gave no sign whether he had or not. He shook off Julian's hand, but the boy put it back again at once, getting angry.

'Mr Lenoir gave me orders to punish that girl,' said Block, looking at Julian out of his cold, narrow eyes.

'Well, you jolly well unlock that door,' commanded Julian, and he tried to snatch the key from Block. With sudden vicious strength the man lifted his hand and struck Julian, sending him half across the landing. Then he went swiftly downstairs to the kitchen.

Julian looked after him, a little scared. 'The brute!' he said. 'He's as strong as a horse. George, George, whatever's happened?'

George answered angrily from the locked bedroom. She told the others everything, and they listened in silence. 'Bad luck, George,' said Dick. 'Poor old girl! Just as you were feeling for the opening to the passage too!'

'I must apologise for my stepfather,' said Sooty. 'He has such a terrible temper. He wouldn't have punished you like this if he had thought you were a girl. But he keeps thinking you're a boy.'

'I don't care,' said George. 'I don't care about any punishment. It's only that I'm so worried about Timmy. Well, I suppose I'll have to stay here now, till I'm let out tomorrow. I shan't eat anything that Block brings me, you can tell him. I don't want to see his horrid face again!'

'How shall I go to bed tonight?' wailed Anne. 'All my things are in your room, George.'

'You'll have to sleep with me,' said little Marybelle, who looked very frightened. 'I can lend you a nightie. Oh dear — what will George's father say when he comes? I hope he will say that George is to be set free at once.'

'Well, he won't,' said George, from behind the locked door. 'He'll just think I've been in one of my bad moods, and he won't mind my being punished at all. Oh dear — I wish Mother was coming too.'

The others were very upset about George, as well as about Timmy. Things seemed to be going very wrong indeed. At tea-time they went to the schoolroom to have tea, wishing they could take George some of the chocolate cake set ready for them.

George felt lonely when the others had gone to tea. It was five o'clock. She was hungry. She wanted Timmy. She was angry and miserable, and longed to escape. She went to the window and looked out.

Her room looked straight down the cliff-side, just as Sooty's old room did. Below was the city-wall that ran round the town, going unevenly up and down as it followed the contours of the hillside.

George knew that she could not jump down to the wall. She might roll off it and fall straight down to the marsh below. That would be horrible. Then she suddenly remembered the rope-ladder that they used when they got down into the pit each day.

It had at first been kept in Marybelle's room, on the shelf in the cupboard, but since the children had been scared by knowing that someone had tried the handle of the door one morning, they had decided to keep the ladder in George's room for safety. They were afraid that perhaps Block might go snooping round Marybelle's room and find it. So George had smuggled it to her own room, and hidden it in her suitcase, which she had locked.

Now, her hands shaking a little with excitement, she unlocked her suitcase and took out the rope-ladder. She might perhaps escape out of the window with it. She looked out again, the rope in her hands.

But windows overlooked the city-wall just there. The kitchen too must be just below, and maybe Block would see her climbing down. That would never do. She must wait till it was twilight.

When the others came back she told them what she was going to do, speaking in a low voice through the door.

'I'll get down on the wall, walk along it for some way, and then jump down and creep back,' she said. 'You get some food for me somehow, and I'll have it.

Then tonight, when everyone has gone to bed I'll get into the study again and find the way through to the secret passage. Sooty can help me. Then I can get Timmy.'

'Right,' said Sooty. 'Wait till it's fairly dark before you go down the ladder, though. Block has gone to his room with a bad headache, but Sarah and Harriet are in the kitchen, and you don't want to be seen.'

So, when the twilight hung like a soft purple curtain over the house, George slid down the rope-ladder out of the window. She only needed to let about a quarter of it out for it was far too long for such a short distance.

She fastened it to the legs of her heavy little oak bed. Then she climbed out of the window and slid quietly down the rope-ladder.

She passed the kitchen window, which fortunately had its blinds drawn down now. She landed squarely on the old wall. She had brought a torch with her so that she could see.

She debated with herself what to do. She did not want to run any risk of coming up against either Block or Mr Lenoir. Perhaps it would be best to walk along the wall till she came to some part of the town she knew. Then she could jump off and make her way cautiously back up the hill, looking out for the others.

So she began to walk along the broad top of the old wall. It was very rough and uneven in places, and many stones were missing. But her torch showed a steady light and she did not miss her footing.

The wall ran round some stables, then round the backs of some quaint old shops. Then it ran round a big yard belonging to some house, and then round the house itself. Then down it went, around some more houses.

George could look into those windows that were

not curtained. Lights shone out from them now. It was queer being able to see into the windows without being seen. A little family sat at a meal in one room, their faces cheerful and happy. An old man sat alone in another, reading and smoking.

A woman sat listening to a radio, knitting, as George silently walked on the wall outside her window. Nobody heard her. Nobody saw her.

Then she came to another house, a big one. The wall ran close against it, for it was built where the cliff ran steeply down to the marsh just there.

There was a lighted window there. George glanced in as she passed. Then she stood still in great suprise.

Surely, surely that was Block in there! He had his back to her, but she could have sworn it was Block. The same head, the same ears, the same shoulders!

Who was he talking to? George tried to see — and all at once she knew. He was talking to Mr Barling, whom everyone said was a smuggler — *the* smuggler of Castaway Hill!

But wait a minute — could it be Block? Block was deaf, and this man evidently wasn't. He was listening to Mr Barling, that was plain, and was answering him, though George could not hear the words, of course.

'I oughtn't to be snooping like this,' said George to herself. 'But it's very strange, very puzzling and very interesting. If only the man would turn round I'd know at once if it was Block!'

But he didn't turn. He just sat in his chair, his back to George. Mr Barling, his long face lighted up by the nearby lamp, was talking animatedly, and Block, if it *was* Block, was listening intently and nodding his head in agreement every now and again.

George felt puzzled. If she only knew for certain that it was Block! But why should he be talking to Mr

503

Barling — and wasn't he stone deaf after all then?

George jumped down from the wall into a dark little passage and made her way through the town, up to Smuggler's Top. Outside the front door, hiding in the shadows was Sooty. He laid his hand on George's arm, making her jump.

'Come on in. I've left the side door open. We've got a fine spread for you!'

The two slipped in at the side door, tiptoed past the study, across the hall, and up to Julian's bedroom. Truly there was a spread there!

'I went and raided the larder,' said Sooty, with satisfaction. 'Harriet was out, and Sarah had run along to the post. Block has gone to bed for a rest, because, he said, he had such an awful headache.'

'Oh,' said George, 'then it couldn't have been Block I saw. And yet I'm as certain as certain can be that it was!'

'Whatever do you mean?' asked the others, in surprise. George sat down on the floor and began to gobble up cakes and tarts, for she was terribly hungry. Between her mouthfuls she told them how she had got out of the window, walked along the city-wall, and found herself unexpectedly by Mr Barling's house.

'And I looked into a lighted window there, and saw Block talking to Mr Barling — and listening to him and answering him!' she said.

The others could not believe this. 'Did you see his face?' asked Julian.

'No,' said George. 'But I'm *certain* it was Block. Go and peep into his room and see if he's there, Sooty. He wouldn't be back yet from Mr Barling's, because he had a glass full of something or other, which would take him some time to drink. Go and peep.'

Sooty vanished. He came back quickly. 'He's in bed!' he said. 'I could see the shape of his body and the dark patch of his head. Are there *two* Blocks then? Whatever does this mean?'

15

Strange happenings

It certainly was very puzzling — most of all to George, who felt so certain it had been Block talking to the well-known smuggler. The others did not feel so certain, especially as George admitted that she had not seen his face.

'Is my father here yet?' asked George, suddenly, remembering that he was supposed to come that evening.

'Yes. Just arrived,' said Sooty. 'Just before you came. I nearly got run over by the car! Just hopped aside in time. I was out there waiting for you.'

'What are our plans?' asked George. 'I'll have to get Timmy tonight, or he'll be frantic. I think I'd better go and climb back through my window again now, in case Block comes along and finds I've disappeared. I'll wait till everyone is in bed and then I'll slip out of the window again, and you must let me into the house, Sooty, please. Then I'll go to the study with you and you must open the secret way for me.

507

Then I'll find Timmy and everything will be all right.'

'I don't see that everything will be all right,' said Sooty, doubtfully. 'But anyway, your plan is the only one to follow. You'd better get back into your room now, if you've had enough to eat.'

'I'll take a few buns back with me,' said George, stuffing them into her pocket. 'Sooty, come and knock at my door when everyone is in bed and I'll know then that it's safe for me to slip out of the window, and come into the house again.'

It wasn't long before George was back in her room once more — just in time too, for Block appeared a little while after with a plate of dry bread and a glass of water. He unlocked the door and put them on the table.

'Your supper,' he said. George looked at his blank face and disliked it so much that she felt she must do something about it. So she took up the water and threw it deftly at the back of his head. It dripped down his neck and made him jump. Block took a step towards her, his eyes gleaming — but Julian and Dick were by the door, and he did not dare to strike her.

'I'll pay you out for that,' he said. 'See? You will never get that dog of yours back again!'

He went out and locked the door. Julian called through as soon as he had gone.

'What did you do that for, you idiot? He's a bad enemy to make.'

'I know. I just couldn't help it somehow,' said George, forlornly. 'I wish I hadn't now.'

The others had to go down to see Mr Lenoir. They left George feeling lonely. It was horrid to be locked up like this, even though she could escape through the window whenever she wanted to. She listened for

508

the others to come back.

They soon did, and reported their meeting with George's father.

'Uncle Quentin is awfully tired and a bit cross, and frightfully annoyed with you for misbehaving,' said Julian, through the door. 'He said you were to be locked up the whole of tomorrow too, if you don't apologise.'

George didn't mean to apologise. She couldn't bear Mr Lenoir, with his false smiles and laughter, and his sudden queer rages. She said nothing.

'We've got to go and have our supper now,' said Sooty. 'We'll save you some of it as soon as Block goes out of the room. Look out for a knocking on your door tonight. It'll be me, telling you everyone's in bed.'

George lay on her bed, thinking. Many things puzzled her. She couldn't get them straight somehow. The signaller in the tower — the queer man, Block — Mr Barling's talk to a man who looked so like Block; but Block was all the time in his bed at home. As she lay thinking, her eyes closed, and she fell asleep.

Anne went to bed with Marybelle, and came to whisper good-night to her. The boys all went into the next room, for Sooty was now to share Julian's and Dick's bedroom. George woke up enough to say good-night and then slept again.

At midnight she awoke with a jump. Someone was knocking softly and impatiently on her door. It was Sooty.

'Coming!' whispered George through the door, and took up her torch. She went to the window and was soon safely down the rope-ladder. She jumped down from the wall, and went to the side door of the house. Sooty was there. She slipped in thankfully.

'Everyone's gone to bed,' whispered Sooty. 'I

thought your father and my stepfather were never going. They stayed talking in the study for ages!'

'Come on. Let's go there,' said George, impatiently. They went to the study door, and Sooty turned the handle.

It was locked again! He pushed hard, but it wasn't a bit of good. It was well and truly locked!

'We might have thought of that,' said George, in despair. 'Blow, blow, blow! What are we to do now?'

Sooty thought for a few moments. Then he spoke in a low voice, in George's ear.

'There's only one thing left to do, George. I must creep into your father's room — my old bedroom — when he is asleep — and I must get into the cupboard there, open the entrance to the secret passage, and slip in that way. I'll find Timmy and bring him back the same way, hoping that your father won't wake!'

'Oh! Would you really do that for me?' said George, gratefully. 'You *are* a good friend, Sooty! Would you rather I did it?'

'No. I know the way up and down that passage better than you do,' said Sooty. 'It's a bit frightening to be all alone there at midnight too. I'll go.'

George went with Sooty up the stairs, across the wide landing, to the door at the end of the passage that led to Sooty's old room, where George's father was now sleeping. When they got there, George pulled his arm.

'Sooty! the buzzer will go as soon as you open the door — and it will wake my father and warn him.'

'Idiot! I disconnected it as soon as I knew my room was to be changed,' said Sooty, scornfully. 'As if I wouldn't think of that!'

He opened the door that led into the passage. He crept up to his old room. The door was shut. He and George listened intently.

510

'Your father sounds a bit restless,' said Sooty. 'I'll wait my chance to creep in, George, and then, as soon as possible, I'll slip into the cupboard and open the secret passage to find Tim. As soon as I've got Timmy I'll bring him along to you. You could wait in Marybelle's room if you liked. Anne's there too.'

George crept into the room next door, where Anne and Marybelle lay fast asleep. She left the door open, so that she might hear when Sooty returned. How lovely it would be to have dear old Timmy again! He would lick her and lick her.

Sooty crept into the room where George's father lay, half-asleep. He made no sound. He knew every creaking board and avoided them. He made his way quietly to a big chair, meaning to hide behind it till he was certain George's father was sound asleep.

For some time the man in the bed tossed and turned. He was tired with his long journey, and his mind was excited with his talk with Mr Lenoir. He muttered now and again, and Sooty began to feel he would never be sound asleep! He grew sleepy himself, and yawned silently.

At last George's father grew quiet and peaceful. No more creaks came from the bed. Sooty cautiously moved out from behind the chair.

Then suddenly something startled him. He heard a sound over by the window! But what could it be? It was a very small sound, like a tiny creak of a door.

The night was rather dark, but the window, its curtains pulled right back, could easily be seen as a square of grey. Sooty fixed his eyes on it. Was someone opening the window?

No. The window did not move. But something queer was happening under it, near the sill.

A big window-seat was built in under the window, wide and comfortable. Sooty knew it well! He had sat

on it hundreds of times to look out of the window. Now, what was happening to it?

It looked as if the top, or lid of the seat was slowly moving upwards, bit by bit. Sooty was puzzled. He had never known it could be opened like that. It had always been screwed down, and he had thought it was just a seat and nothing else. But now it looked as if someone had unscrewed the top, and had hidden himself inside, lifting up the top like a lid when he thought it was safe.

Sooty stared at the upward-moving lid, quite fascinated. Who was in there? Why had he hidden? It was rather frightening, seeing the lid move slowly, bit by bit.

At last the lid was wide open and rested against the window-pane. A big figure cautiously and slowly got out, not making the slightest sound. Sooty felt his hair rising up on his head. He was afraid, terribly afraid. He could not utter a sound.

The figure tiptoed over to the bed. He made a quick and sudden movement, and there was a stifled sound from George's father. Sooty guessed he had been gagged, so that he could not cry out. Still the boy could not move or speak. He had never been so scared in all his life.

The intruder lifted the limp body from the bed, and went to the window-seat. He put George's father into the darkness there. What he had done to make him unable to struggle Sooty didn't know. He only knew that poor George's father was being put down in the window-seat, and couldn't seem to move a hand to help himself!

The boy suddenly found his voice. 'Hi!' he yelled. 'Hi! What are you doing? Who are you?'

He remembered his torch and switched it on. He saw a face he knew, and cried out in surprise. 'Mr Barling!'

Then someone hit him a hard blow on the head and he remembered nothing more at all. He did not know that he was lifted into the window-seat too. He did not know that the intruder followed after him. He knew nothing.

George, awake in the next room, suddenly heard Sooty's voice crying out. 'Hi!' she heard. 'Hi, what are you doing? Who are you?' And then, as she slipped out of bed, she heard the next cry. 'Mr Barling!'

George was extremely startled. What was going on next door? She fumbled about for her torch. Anne and Marybelle were still asleep. George could not find her torch. She fell over a chair and banged her head.

When at last she had found her torch she tiptoed, trembling, to the door. She shone her torch and saw that the door next to hers was a little ajar, just as Sooty had left it, when he had crept inside. She listened. There was absolutely no sound at all now. She had heard a small bumping noise after Sooty's last cry, but she didn't know what it was.

She suddenly put her head round the door of her father's room, and shone her torch again. She stared in surprise. The bed was empty. The room was empty. There was no one there at all! She flashed her torch all round. She opened the cupboard door fearfully. She looked under the bed. She was, in fact, extremely brave.

At last she sank down on the window-seat, frightened and puzzled. Where was her father? Where was Sooty? Whatever had been happening here that night?

16
Next morning

As George sat by the window, on the very seat into which everyone had unaccountably disappeared, though she did not know it, she heard a faint sound from the passage.

Quick as lightning the girl slipped under the bed. Someone was creeping down the long passage! George lay silently on the floor, lifting the valance a little to try and see who it was. What queer things were going on tonight!

Someone came in at the door. Someone stopped there, as if to look and listen. Then someone crept over to the window-seat.

George watched and listened, straining her eyes in the darkness. She dimly saw the someone outlined against the grey square of the window. He was bent over the window-seat.

He showed no light at all. But he made some curious little sounds. First came the sound of his fingers tapping about on the closed lid of the seat.

Then came the clink of something metallic, and a very faint squeaking. George could not imagine what the man — if it was a man — was doing.

For about five minutes the someone worked away at his task in the darkness. Then, as quietly as he had come, he went away. George couldn't help thinking it was Block, though his outline against the dark-grey of the window was too dim to recognise. But he had once given a little cough exactly like Block so often gave. It *must* be Block! But whatever was he doing in her father's room at night, on the window-seat?'

George felt as if she was in a bad dream. The queerest things happened and kept on happening, and they didn't seem to make sense at all. Where was her father? Had he left his room and gone wandering over the house? Where was Sooty, and why had he called out? He wouldn't have shouted out like that, surely, if her father had been asleep in the room!

George lay under the bed, shivering, for a little while longer. Then she rolled out softly and went out of the door. She crept down the long passage to the end. She opened the door there and peeped out. The whole house was in darkness. Little sounds came to George's ears — a window rattling faintly, the creak of some bit of furniture — but nothing else.

She had only one thought in her mind, and that was to get to the boys' room and tell them the mysterious things that had happened. Soon she was across the landing, and had slipped through the door of Julian's bedroom. He and Dick were awake, of course, waiting for Sooty to come with Timmy and George.

But only George arrived. A scared George, with a very very curious story to tell. She wrapped herself in the eiderdown on Julian's bed, and told what had happened, in whispers.

516

They were amazed. Uncle Quentin gone! Sooty disappeared! Someone creeping into the room and fiddling about on the window-seat! What did it all mean?

'We'll come to Uncle Quentin's room with you, straight away now,' said Julian, pulling on a dressing-gown, and hunting about for his slippers. 'I've got a feeling that things are getting pretty serious.'

They all padded off to the other rooms. They went into Marybelle's room and woke her and Anne. Both little girls felt scared. Soon all five children were in the next room, from which George's father and Sooty had so strangely vanished.

Julian shut the door, drew the curtains and switched on the light. At once they all felt better. It was so horrid to grope about in the dark with torches.

They looked round the silent room. There was nothing there to show them how the others had disappeared. The bed was crumpled and empty. On the floor lay Sooty's torch, where it had fallen.

George repeated again what she had thought she had heard Sooty call out, but it made no sense to anyone. 'Why call out Mr Barling's name, when there was only your father in the room?' said Julian. 'Surely Mr Barling wasn't hiding here — that would be nonsense. He had nothing to do with your father, George.'

'I know. But I'm sure it *was* Mr Barling's name that I heard Sooty call out,' said George. 'Do you think — oh yes, do you think Mr Barling could possibly have crept through the secret opening in the cupboard, meaning to do some dirty work or other — and have gone back the same way, taking the others with him because they discovered him?'

This seemed a likely explanation, though not a

517

very good one. They all went to the cupboard and opened it. They groped between the clothes for the secret opening. But the little iron handle set there to pull on the stone at the back, was gone! Someone had removed it — and now the secret passage could not be entered, for there was no way of opening it just there!

'Look at that!' said Julian in astonishment. 'Someone's been tampering with that too. No, George, the midnight visitor, whoever he was, didn't go back that way.'

George looked pale. She had been hoping to go and fetch Timmy, by slipping through the secret opening in the cupboard. Now she couldn't. She longed for Timmy with all her heart, and felt that if only the big faithful dog were with her things would seem much brighter.

'I'm sure Mr Lenoir is at the bottom of all this!' said Dick. 'And Block too. I bet that *was* Block you saw in here tonight, doing something in the dark, George. I bet he and Mr Lenoir are hand in glove with each other over something.'

'Well, then — we can't possibly go and tell them what has happened!' said Julian. 'If they are at the bottom of all these queer happenings it would be foolish to go and tell them what we know. And we can't tell your mother, Marybelle, because she would naturally go to your father about it. It's a puzzle to know what to do!'

Anne began to cry. Marybelle, frightened and puzzled, at once began to sob too. George felt tears pricking the backs of her eyelids, but she blinked them away. George never cried!

'I want Sooty,' wept Marybelle, who adored her cheeky, daring brother. 'Where's he gone? I'm sure he's in danger. I do want Sooty.'

518

'We'll rescue him tomorrow, don't you worry,' said Julian, kindly. 'We can't do anything tonight, though. There's nobody at Smuggler's Top we can possibly get advice or help from, as things are. I vote we go to bed, sleep on it, and make plans in the morning. By that time Sooty and Uncle Quentin may have turned up again. If they haven't, Mr Lenoir will have to be told by someone, and we'll see how he behaves! If he's surprised and upset, we'll soon know if he has had anything to do with this mystery or not. He'll have to do something — go to the police, or have the house turned upside down to find the missing people. We'll soon see what happens.'

Everyone felt a little comforted after this long speech. Julian sounded cheerful and firm, though he didn't feel at all happy, really. He knew, better than any of the others, that something very strange, and probably dangerous was going on at Smuggler's Top. He wished the girls were not there.

'Now listen,' he said. 'George, you go and sleep with Anne and Marybelle next door. Lock your door and keep the light on. Dick and I will sleep here, in Sooty's old room, also with the light on, so you'll know we are quite nearby.'

It was comforting to know that the two boys were so near. The three girls went at last into Marybelle's room, tired out. Anne and Marybelle got into bed again, and George lay down on a small but comfortable couch, pulling a thick rug over her. In spite of all the worry and excitement the girls were soon asleep, quite exhausted.

The boys talked a little, as they lay in Sooty's old bed, where their Uncle Quentin had been asleep some time before. Julian did not think anything more would happen that night. He and Dick fell asleep, but Julian was ready to wake at the slightest noise.

Next morning they were awakened by a most surprised Sarah, who had come in to draw the curtains and bring George's father a pot of early-morning tea. She could not believe her eyes when she saw the two boys in the visitor's bed — and no visitor!

'What's all this?' said Sarah, gaping. 'Where's your uncle? Why are you here?'

'Oh, we'll explain later,' said Julian, who did not want to enter into any details with Sarah, who was a bit of a chatterbox. 'You can leave the tea, Sarah. *We'd* like it!'

'Yes, but where's your uncle? Is he in *your* room?' said the puzzled Sarah. 'What's up?'

'You can go and look in our room if you like and see if he's there,' said Dick, wanting to get rid of the amazed woman. She disappeared, thinking that the household must be going mad. She left the hot tea behind, though, and the boys at once took it into the girls' room. George unlocked the door for them. They took it in turns to sip the hot tea from the one cup.

Presently Sarah came back, with Harriet and Block. Block's face was as blank as usual.

'There's nobody in your room, Master Julian,' began Sarah. Then Block gave a sudden exclamation and stared at George angrily. He had thought she was locked in her room — and here she was in Marybelle's room, drinking tea!

'How did you get out?' he demanded. 'I'll tell Mr Lenoir. You're in disgrace.'

'Shut up,' said Julian. 'Don't you dare to speak to my cousin like that. I believe you're mixed up in this curious business. Clear out, Block.'

Whether Block heard or not, he gave no sign of going. Julian got up, his face set.

'Clear out of this room,' he said, narrowing his

eyes. 'Do you hear? I have a feeling that the police might be interested in you, Block. Now clear out!'

Harriet and Sarah gave little shrieks. The sudden mystery was too much for them. They gazed at Block and began to back out of the room. Fortunately Block went too, casting an evil look at the determined Julian.

'I shall go to Mr Lenoir,' said Block, and disappeared.

In a few minutes along came Mr and Mrs Lenoir to Marybelle's room. Mrs Lenoir looked scared out of her life. Mr Lenoir looked puzzled and upset.

'Now, what's all this?' he began. 'Block has been to me with a most curious tale. Says your father has disappeared, George, and . . .'

'And so has Sooty,' suddenly wailed Marybelle, bursting into tears again. 'Sooty's gone. He's gone too.'

Mrs Lenoir gave a cry. 'What do you mean? How can he have gone? Marybelle, what do you mean?'

'Marybelle, I think I had better take charge of the telling,' said Julian, who was not going to let the little girl give away all the things they knew. After all, Mr Lenoir was probably at the bottom of everything, and it would be foolish to tell him what they suspected about him.

'Julian — tell me what has happened. Quickly!' begged Mrs Lenoir, looking really upset.

'Uncle Quentin disappeared from his bed last night, and Sooty has vanished too,' said Julian, shortly. 'They may turn up, of course.'

'Julian! You are keeping back something,' said Mr Lenoir, suddenly, watching the boy sharply. 'You will tell us *everything*, please. How dare you keep anything back at a moment like this?'

'Tell him Julian, tell him,' wailed Marybelle,

522

Julian looked obstinate, and glared at Marybelle.

The tip of Mr Lenoir's nose went white. 'I am going to the police,' he said. 'Perhaps you will talk to *them*, my boy. They will knock some sense into you!'

Julian was surprised. 'Why — I shouldn't have thought *you* would want to go to the police!' he blurted out. 'You've got too many secrets to hide!'

17

More and more puzzling

Mr Lenoir stared in the utmost amazement at Julian. There was a dead silence after this remark. Julian could have kicked himself for making it, but he couldn't unsay it now.

Mr Lenoir opened his mouth to say something at last, when footsteps came to the door. It was Block.

'Come in, Block!' said Mr Lenoir. 'There seem to have been queer happenings here.'

Block did not appear to hear, and remained outside the door. Mr Lenoir beckoned him in impatiently.

'No,' said Julian, firmly. 'What we have to say is not to be said in front of Block, Mr Lenoir. We don't like him and we don't trust him.'

'What do you mean?' cried Mr Lenoir, angrily. 'What do *you* know about my servants? I've known Block for years before he came into my service, and he's a most trustworthy fellow. He can't help being deaf, and that makes him irritable at times.'

Julian remained obstinate. He caught an angry

gleam in Block's cold eyes, and glared back.

'Well, this is incredible!' said Mr Lenoir, trying not to lose his temper. 'I can't think what's come over everybody — disappearing like this — and now you children talking to me as if I wasn't master in my own house. I insist that you tell me all you know.'

'I'd rather tell it to the police,' said Julian, his eye on Block. But Block showed no trace of expression on his face.

'Go away, Block,' said Mr Lenoir at last, seeing that there was no hope of getting anything out of Julian while the servant was there. 'You'd better all come down to my study. This is getting more and more mysterious. If the police have got to know, you may as well tell me first. I don't want to look a complete idiot in my own house in front of them.'

Julian couldn't help feeling a bit puzzled. Mr Lenoir was not behaving as he had thought he might behave. He seemed sincerely puzzled and upset, and he was evidently planning to get the police in himself. Surely he wouldn't do that if he had had a hand in the disappearances? Julian was lost in bewilderment again.

Mrs Lenoir was now crying quietly, with Marybelle sobbing beside her. Mr Lenoir put an arm round his wife and kissed Marybelle, suddenly appearing very much nicer than he had ever seemed before. 'Don't worry,' he said, in a gentle voice. 'We'll soon get to the bottom of this, if I have to get the whole of the police force in. I think I know who's at the bottom of it all!'

That surprised Julian even more. He and the others followed Mr Lenoir down to his study. It was still locked. Mr Lenoir opened it and pushed aside a great pile of papers that were on his desk.

'Now — what do you know?' he said to Julian

quietly. The children noticed that the top of his nose was no longer white. Evidently he had got over his burst of temper.

'Well, sir — I think this is a queer house, with a lot of queer things happening in it,' said Julian, not quite knowing how to begin. 'I'm afraid, sir, you won't like me telling the police all I know.'

'Julian, don't speak in riddles!' said Mr Lenoir, impatiently. 'You act as if I were a criminal, in fear of the police. I'm not. What goes on in this house?'

'Well — the signalling from the tower, for instance,' said Julian, watching Mr Lenoir's face.

Mr Lenoir gaped. It was clear that he was immensely astonished. He stared at Julian, and Mrs Lenoir cried out suddenly:

'Signalling! What signalling?'

Julian explained. He told how Sooty had discovered the light-flashing first, and then how he and Dick had gone with him to the tower when they had seen the flashing again. He described the line of tiny, pricking lights across the marsh from the seaward side.

Mr Lenoir listened intently. He asked questions about dates and times. He heard how the boys had followed the signaller to Block's room, where he had disappeared.

'Got out of the window, I suppose,' said Mr Lenoir. 'Block's got nothing to do with this, you can rest assured of that. He is most faithful and loyal, and has been a great help to me while he has been here. I have an idea that Mr Barling is at the bottom of all this. He can't signal from his house to the sea because it's not quite high enough up the hill, and is in the wrong position. He must have been using *my* tower to signal from — coming himself to do it too! He knows all the secret ways of this house, better than I do! It would be easy for him to come here whenever he wanted to.'

The children thought at once that probably Mr Barling *had* been the signaller! They stared at Mr Lenoir. They were all beginning to think that he really and truly had nothing to do with the queer goings-on after all.

'I don't see why Block shouldn't know all this,' said Mr Lenoir, getting up. 'It's plain to me that Barling could explain a lot of the queer things that have been happening. I'll see if Block has ever suspected anything.'

Julian pursed his lips together. If Mr Lenoir was going to tell everything to Block, who certainly must be in the plot somehow, he wasn't going to tell him anything more!

'I'll see what Block thinks about everything, and then if we can't solve this mystery ourselves, we'll get in the police,' said Mr Lenoir, going out of the room.

Julian did not want to say anything much in front of Mrs Lenoir. So he changed the subject completely.

'What about breakfast?' he said. 'I'm feeling hungry!'

So they all went to have breakfast, though Marybelle could eat nothing at all, because she kept thinking of poor Sooty.

'I think,' said Julian, when they were alone at the table, 'I rather think we'll do a little mystery-solving ourselves. I'd like a jolly good look round that room of your father's, George, to begin with. There must be some other way of getting out of there, besides the secret passage we know.'

'What do you think happened there last night?' said Dick.

'Well, I imagine that Sooty went there and hid, to wait until it was safe to try and get into the secret passage as soon as Uncle Quentin was asleep,' said Julian, thoughtfully. 'And while he was hiding, someone came into that room from somewhere, to kidnap Uncle Quentin. Why I don't know, but that's what I think. Then Sooty yelled out in surprise, and got knocked on the head or something. Then he and Uncle Quentin were kidnapped together, and taken off through some secret way we don't know.'

'Yes,' said George. 'And it was Mr Barling who kidnapped them! I distinctly heard Sooty yell out "Mr Barling". He must have switched on his torch and seen him.'

'They are quite probably hidden somewhere in Mr Barling's house,' said Anne, suddenly.

'Yes!' said Julian. 'Why didn't I think of that? Why, that's just where they would be, of course. I've a jolly good mind to go down and have a look!'

'Oh, let me come too,' begged George.

'No,' said Julian. 'Certainly not. This is rather a dangerous adventure, and Mr Barling is a bad and dangerous man. You and Marybelle are certainly not to come. I'll take Dick.'

'You are absolutely *mean*!' began George, her eyes flashing. 'Aren't I as good as a boy? I'm going to come.'

'Well, if you're as good as a boy, which I admit you are,' said Julian, 'can't you stay and keep an eye on Anne and Marybelle for us? We don't want them kidnapped too.'

'Oh, don't go, George,' said Anne. 'Stay here with us.'

'I think it's mad to go, anyhow,' said George. 'Mr Barling wouldn't let you in. And if you did get in you wouldn't be able to find all the secret places in his house. There must be as many, and more, as there are here.'

528

Julian couldn't help thinking George was right. Still, it was worth trying.

He and Dick set out after breakfast, and went down the hill to Mr Barling's. But when they got there they found the whole house shut up. Nobody answered their knocking and ringing. The curtains were drawn across the closed windows, and no smoke came from the chimney.

'Mr Barling's gone away for a holiday,' said the gardener who was working in the next door flower-beds. 'Went this morning, he did. In his car. All his servants have got a holiday too.'

'Oh!' said Julian, blankly. 'Was there anyone with him in the car — a man and a boy, for instance?'

The gardener looked surprised at this question, and shook his head.

'No. He was alone, and drove off himself.'

'Thanks,' said Julian, and walked back with Dick to Smuggler's Top. This was queer. Mr Barling had shut up the house and gone off without his captives! Then what had he done with them? And why on earth had he kidnapped Uncle Quentin? Julian remembered that Mr Lenoir had not put forward any reason for that. Did he know one, and hadn't wanted to say what it was? It was all most puzzling.

Meantime George had been doing a little snooping round on her own. She had slipped into Uncle Quentin's room, and had had a really good look round everywhere to see if by chance there was another secret passage Sooty hadn't known about.

She had tapped the walls. She had turned back the carpet and examined every inch of the floor. She had tried the cupboard again, and wished she could get through into the secret passage there and find Timmy. The study door downstairs was again locked, and she did not dare to tell Mr Lenoir about

Timmy and ask his help.

George was just about to leave the quiet room
when she noticed something on the floor near the

window. She bent to pick it up. It was a small screw. She looked round. Where had it come from?

At first she couldn't see any screws of the same size at all. Then her eyes slid down to the window-seat. There were screws there, screwing down the top oaken plank to the under ones that supported it.

Had the screw come out of the window-seat? Why should it, anyway? The others there were all screwed down tightly. She examined one. Then she gave a low cry.

'One's missing. The one in the middle of this side. Now just let me think.'

She remembered last night. She remembered how someone had crept in, while she had hidden under the bed, and had fiddled about by the window, bending over the polished window-seat. She remembered the little noises — the metallic clinks and the tiny squeaks. It was screws being screwed into the seat!

'Someone screwed down the window-seat last night — and in the darkness, dropped one of the little screws,' thought George, beginning to feel excited. 'Why did he screw it down? To hide something? What's in this window-seat? It sounds hollow enough. It never lifted up. I know that. It was always screwed down, because I remember looking for a cupboard under it, like the one we have at home, and there wasn't one.'

George began to feel certain there was some secret about the window-seat. She rushed off to get a screwdriver. She found one and hurried back.

She shut the door and locked it behind her in case Block should come snooping around. Then she set to work with the screwdriver. What would she find in the window-seat? She could hardly wait to see!

18

Curious discoveries

Just as she had unscrewed almost the last screw there came a tapping at the door. George jumped and stiffened. She did not answer, afraid that it was Block, or Mr Lenoir.

Then, to her great relief she heard Julian's voice. 'George! Are you in here?'

The little girl hurried across to the door and unlocked it. The boys came in, looking surprised, followed by Anne and Marybelle. George shut the door and locked it again.

'Mr Barling's gone away and shut up the house,' said Julian. 'So that's that. What on earth are you doing, George?'

'Unscrewing this window-seat,' said George, and told them about the screw she had found on the floor. They all crowded round her, excited.

'Good for you, George!' said Dick. 'Here, let me finish the unscrewing.'

'No, thanks. This is *my* job!' said George. She took

out the last screw. Then she lifted the edge of the window-seat. It came up like a lid.

Everyone peered inside, rather scared. What would they see? To their great surprise and disappointment they saw nothing but an empty cupboard! It was as if the window-seat was a box, with the lid screwed down for people to sit on.

'Well — what a disappointment!' said Dick. He shut down the lid. 'I don't expect you heard anyone screwing down the lid, really, George. It might have been your imagination.'

'Well, it wasn't,' said George, shortly. She opened the lid again. She got right into the box-like window-seat and stamped, and pressed with her feet.

And quite suddenly, there came a small creaking noise, and the bottom of the empty window-seat fell downwards like a trap-door on a hinge!

George gasped and clutched at the side. She kicked about in air for a moment and then scrambled out. Everyone looked down in silence.

They looked down a straight yawning hole, which, however, came to an end only about eight feet down. There it appeared to widen out, and, no doubt, entered a secret passage which ran into one of the underground tunnels with which the whole hill was honeycombed. It might even run to Mr Barling's house.

'Look at that!' said Dick. 'Who would have thought of that? I bet even old Sooty didn't know about this.'

'Shall we go down?' said George. 'Shall we see where it goes to? We might find old Timmy.'

There came the noise of someone trying the handle of the door. It was locked. Then there was an impatient rapping, and a cross voice called out sharply:

'Why is this door locked? Open it at once! What are you doing in there?'

'It's father!' whispered Marybelle, with wide eyes. 'I'd better unlock the door.'

George shut the lid of the window-seat down at once, quietly. She did not want Mr Lenoir to see their latest discovery. When the door was opened Mr Lenoir saw the children standing about, or sitting on the window-seat.

'I've had a good talk to Block,' he said, 'and, as I thought, he doesn't know a thing about all the goings-on here. He was most amazed to hear about the signalling from the tower. But he doesn't think it's Mr Barling. He thinks it may be a plot of some sort against *me*.'

'Oh!' said the children, who felt that *they* would not believe Block so readily as Mr Lenoir appeared to.

'It's quite upset Block,' said Mr Lenoir. 'He feels really sick, and I've told him to go and have a rest till we decide what to do next.'

The children felt that Block would not be so easily upset as all that. They all suspected at once that he would not really go to rest, but would probably sneak out on business of his own.

'I've some work to attend to for a little while,' said Mr Lenoir. 'I've rung up the police, but unluckily the Inspector is out. He will ring me directly he comes back. Now can you keep out of mischief till I've finished my work?'

The children thought that was a silly question. They made no reply. Mr Lenoir gave one of his sudden smiles and little laughs, and went.

'I'm going to pop along to Block's room and see if he really *is* there,' said Julian, as soon as Mr Lenoir was out of sight.

He went to the wing where the staff bedrooms

534

were, and stopped softly outside Block's. The door was a little ajar, and Julian could see through the crack. He saw the shape of Block's body in the bed, and the dark patch that was his head. The curtains were drawn across the window to keep out the light, but there was enough to see all this.

Julian sped back to the others. 'Yes, he's in bed all right,' he said. 'Well, he's safe for a bit. Shall we have a shot at getting down to the window-seat hole? I'd dearly like to see where it leads to!'

'Oh yes!' said everyone. But it was not an easy job to drop eight feet down without being terribly jolted! Julian went first and was very much jarred. He called up to Dick: 'We'll have to get a bit of rope and tie it to something up there, and let it hang down the hole — it's an awful business to let yourself drop down.'

But just as Dick went to find a rope, Julian called up again. 'Oh, it's all right! I've just seen something. There are niches carved into the sides of the hole— niches you can put foot or hand into. I didn't see them before. You can use them to help you down.'

So down went everyone, one after another, feeling for the niches and finding them. George missed one or two, clawed wildly at the air, and dropped down the last few feet, landing with rather a bump, but she was not hurt.

As they had thought, the hole led to another secret passage in the house, but this one went straight downwards by means of steps, so that very soon they went well below the level of the house. Then they came into the maze of tunnels that honeycombed the hill. They stopped.

'Look here — we can't possibly go any farther,' said Julian. 'We shall get lost. We haven't got Sooty with us now, and Marybelle isn't any good at finding the way. It would be dangerous to wander about.'

535

They could hear the hollow sound of footsteps coming from a tunnel to the left of them. They all shrank back into the shadows, and Julian switched off his torch.

'It's *two* people!' whispered Anne, as two figures came out of the nearby tunnel. One was very tall and long. The other — yes, surely the other was Block! If it wasn't Block it was someone the exact image of him.

The men were talking in low voices, answering one another. How could it be Block, though, if he could hear as well as that? Anyway, Block was asleep in bed. It was hardly ten minutes since Julian had seen him there. Were there two Blocks, then, thought George, as she had once thought before.

The men disappeared into another tunnel, and the bright light of their lanterns disappeared gradually. The muffled rumble of their voices echoed back.

'Shall we follow them?' said Dick.

'Of course not,' said Julian. 'We might lose them — and lose ourselves too! And supposing they suddenly turned back and found us following them? We should be in a horrid fix.'

'I'm sure the first man was Mr Barling,' said Anne, suddenly. 'I couldn't see his face because the light of the lantern wasn't on it — but he seemed just like Mr Barling — awfully tall and long everywhere!'

'But Mr Barling's gone away,' said Marybelle.

'*Supposed* to have gone away!' said George. 'It looks as if he's come back, if it *was* him. I wonder where those two have gone — to see my father and Sooty, do you think?'

'Quite likely,' said Julian. 'Come on, let's get back. We simply *daren't* wander about by ourselves in these old tunnels. They run for miles, Sooty said, and cross one another, and go up and down and round about —

even right down to the marsh. We should never, never find our way out if we got lost.'

They turned to go back. They came to the end of the steps they had been climbing, and found themselves at the bottom of the window-seat hole. It was quite easy to pull themselves up by the niches in the sides of the hole.

Soon they were all in the room again, glad to see the sunshine streaming in at the window. They looked out. The marshes were beginning to be wreathed in mist once more, though up here the hill was golden with sunlight.

'I'm going to put the screws back into the window-seat again,' said Julian, picking up the screwdriver, and shutting down the lid. 'Then if Block comes here he won't guess we've found this new secret place. I'm pretty certain that he unscrewed the seat so that Mr Barling could get into this room, and then screwed it down again so that no one would guess what had happened.'

He quickly put in the screws. Then he looked at his watch.

'Almost dinner-time, and I'm jolly hungry. I wish old Sooty was here — and Uncle Quentin. I do hope they're all right — and Timmy too,' said Julian, 'I wonder if Block is still in bed — or wandering about the tunnels. I'm going to have a peep again.'

He soon came back, puzzled. 'Yes, he's there all right, safe in bed. It's jolly funny.'

Block did not appear at lunchtime. Sarah said he had asked not to be disturbed, if he did not appear.

'He does get the most awful sick headaches,' she said. 'Maybe he'll be all right this afternoon.'

She badly wanted to talk about everything, but the children had decided not to tell her anything. She was very nice and they liked her, but somehow they didn't trust anyone at Smuggler's Top. So Sarah got nothing out of them at all, and retired in rather a huff.

Julian went down to speak to Mr Lenoir after the meal. He felt that even if the Inspector of police was not at the police-station, somebody else must be informed. He was very worried about his uncle and Sooty. He couldn't help wondering if Mr Lenoir had made up the bit about the Inspector being away, to put off time.

Mr Lenoir was looking cross when Julian knocked at his study-door. 'Oh, it's you!' he said to Julian. 'I was expecting Block. I've rung and rung for him. The bell rings in his room and I can't imagine why he doesn't come. I want him to come to the police-station with me.'

'Good!' thought Julian. Then he spoke aloud. 'I'll go and hurry him up for you, Mr Lenoir. I know where his room is.'

Julian ran up the stairs and went to the little landing up which the back-stairs went to the staff bedrooms. He pushed open Block's door.

Block was apparently still asleep in bed! Julian called loudly, then remembered that Block was deaf. So he went over to the bed and put his hand rather roughly on the hump of the shoulder between the clothes.

But it was curiously soft! Julian drew his hand away, and looked down sharply. Then he got a real shock.

There was no Block in the bed! There was a big ball of some sort, painted black to look like a head almost under the sheets — and, when Julian threw back the covers, he saw instead of Block's body, a large lumpy bolster, cleverly moulded to look like a curved body!

'*That's* the trick Block plays when he wants to slip

off anywhere, and yet pretend he's still here!' said Julian. 'So it *was* Block we saw in the tunnel this morning — and it *must* have been Block that George saw talking to Mr Barling yesterday, when she looked through the window. He's not deaf, either. He's a very clever — sly — double-faced — deceitful ROGUE!'

19

Mr Barling talks

Meantime, what was happening to Uncle Quentin and Sooty? Many strange things!

Uncle Quentin had been gagged, and drugged so that he could neither struggle nor make any noise, when Mr Barling had crept so unexpectedly into his room. It was easy to drop him down the hole in the window-seat. He fell with a thud that bruised him considerably.

Then poor Sooty had been dropped down too, and after them had come Mr Barling, climbing deftly down by the help of the niches in the sides.

Someone else was down there, to help Mr Barling. Not Block, who had been left to screw down the window-seat so that no one might guess where the victims had been taken, but a hard-faced servant belonging to Mr Barling.

'Had to bring this boy, too — it's Lenoir's son,' said Mr Barling. 'Snooping about in the room. Well, it will serve Lenoir right for working against me!'

The two were half-carried, half-dragged down the

long flight of steps and taken into the tunnels below. Mr Barling stopped and took a ball of string from his pocket. He tossed it to his servant.

'Here you are. Tie the end to that nail over there, and let the string unravel as we go. I know the way quite well, but Block doesn't, and he'll be coming along to bring food to our couple of prisoners tomorrow. Don't want him to lose his way! We can tie the string up again just before we get to the place I'm taking them to, so that they won't see it and use it to escape by.'

The servant tied the string to the nail that Mr Barling pointed out, and then as he went along he let the ball unravel. The string would than serve as a guide to anyone not knowing the way. Otherwise it would be very dangerous to wander about in the underground tunnels. For some of them ran for miles.

After about eight minutes the little company came to a kind of rounded cave, set in the side of a big, but rather low tunnel. Here had been put a bench with some rugs, a box to serve as a table, and a jug of water. Nothing else.

Sooty by now was coming round from his blow on the head. The other prisoner, however, still lay unconscious, breathing heavily.

'No good talking to him,' said Mr Barling. 'He won't be all right till tomorrow. We'll come and talk to him then. I'll bring Block.'

Sooty had been put on the floor. He suddenly sat up, and put his hand to his aching head. He couldn't imagine where he was.

He looked up and saw Mr Barling, and then suddenly he remembered everything. But how had he got here, in this dark cave?

'Mr Barling!' he said. 'What's all this? What did you hit me for? Why have you brought me here?'

'Punishment for a small boy who can't keep his nose out of things that don't concern him!' said Mr Barling, in a horrid sarcastic voice. 'You'll be company for our friend on the bench there. He'll sleep till the morning, I'm afraid. You can tell him all about it, then, and say I'll be back to have a little heart-to-heart talk with him! And see here, Pierre — you do know, don't you, the foolishness of trying to wander about these old passages? I've brought you to a little-known one, and if you want to lose yourself and never be heard of again, well, try wandering about, that's all!'

Sooty looked pale. He did know the danger of wandering about those lost old tunnels. This one he was in he was sure he didn't know at all. He was about to ask a few more questions when Mr Barling turned quickly on his heel and went off with his servant. They took the lantern with them and left the boy in darkness. He yelled after them.

'Hi, you beasts! Leave me a light!'

But there was no answer. Sooty heard the footfalls going farther and farther away, and then there was silence and darkness.

The boy felt in his pocket for his torch, but it wasn't there. He had dropped it in his bedroom. He groped his way over to the bench, and felt about for George's father. He wished he would wake up. It was so horrid to be there in the darkness. It was cold, too.

Sooty crept under the rugs and cuddled close to the unconscious man. He longed with all his heart for him to wake up.

From somewhere there sounded the drip-drip-drip of water. After a time Sooty couldn't bear it. He knew it was only drops dripping off the roof of the tunnel in a damp place, but he felt he couldn't bear it. Drip-drip-drip. Drip-drip-drip. If only it would stop!

542

'I'll have to wake George's father up!' thought the boy, desperately. 'I *must* talk to someone!'

He began to shake the sleeping man, wondering what to call him, for he did not know his surname. He couldn't call him 'George's father!' Then he remembered that the others called him Uncle Quentin, and he began yelling the name in the drugged man's ear.

'Uncle Quentin! Uncle Quentin! Wake up! Do wake up! Oh, won't you please wake up!'

Uncle Quentin stirred at last. He opened his eyes in the darkness, and listened to the urgent voice in his ear feeling faintly puzzled.

'Uncle Quentin! Wake up and speak to me. I'm scared!' said the voice. 'UNCLE QUENTIN!'

The man thought vaguely that it must be Julian or Dick. He put his arm round Sooty and dragged him close to him. 'It's all right. Go to sleep,' he said. 'What's the matter, Julian? Or is it Dick? Go to sleep.'

He fell asleep again himself, for he was still half-drugged. But Sooty felt comforted now. He shut his eyes, feeling certain that he couldn't possibly go to sleep. But he did, almost at once! He slept soundly all through the night, and was only awakened by Uncle Quentin moving on the bench.

The puzzled man was amazed to find his bed so unexpectedly hard. He was even more amazed to find someone in bed with him, for he remembered nothing at all. He stretched out his hand to switch on the reading-lamp which had been beside his bed the night before.

But it wasn't there! Strange! He felt about and touched Sooty's face. What was this beside him? He began to feel extremely puzzled. He felt ill, too. What *could* have happened?

'Are you awake?' said Sooty's voice. 'Oh, Uncle

Quentin, I'm so glad you're awake. I hope you don't mind me calling you that, but I don't know your surname. I only know you are George's father and Julian's uncle.'

'Well — who are you?' said Uncle Quentin, in wonder.

Sooty began to tell him everything. Uncle Quentin listened in the utmost amazement. 'But *why* have we been kidnapped like this?' he said, astonished and angry. 'I never heard of such a thing in my life!'

'I don't know why Mr Barling has kidnapped *you* — but I know he took me because I happened to see what he was doing,' said Sooty. 'Anyway, he's coming back this morning, with Block, and he said he would have a heart-to-heart talk with you. We'll have to wait here, I'm afraid. We can't possibly find our way to safety in the darkness, through this maze of tunnels.'

So they waited — and in due course Mr Barling did come, bringing Block with him. Block carried some food, which was very welcome to the prisoners.

'You beast, Block!' said Sooty, at once, as he saw the servant in the light of the lantern. 'How dare you help in this? You wait till my stepfather hears about it! Unless he's in it too!'

'Hold your tongue!' said Block.

Sooty stared at him. 'So you *can* hear!' he said. 'All this time you've been pretending you can't! What a sly fellow you are! What a lot of secrets you must have learnt, pretending to be deaf, and overhearing all kinds of things not meant for you. You're sly, Block, and you're worse things than that!'

'Whip him, Block, if you like,' said Mr Barling, sitting down on the box. 'I've no time for rude boys myself.'

'I will,' said Block, grimly, and he undid a length of

544

rope from round his waist. 'I've often wanted to, cheeky little worm!'

Sooty felt alarmed. He leapt off the bench and put up his fists.

'Let me talk to our prisoner first,' said Mr Barling. 'Then you can give Pierre the hiding he deserves. It will be nice for him to wait for it.'

Uncle Quentin was listening quietly to all this. He looked at Mr Barling, and spoke sternly.

'You owe me an explanation for your strange behaviour. I demand to be taken to Smuggler's Top. You shall answer to the police for this!'

'Oh no, I shan't,' said Mr Barling, in a curiously soft voice. 'I have a very generous proposal to make to you. I know why you have come to Smuggler's Top. I know why you and Mr Lenoir are so interested in each other's experiments.'

'How do you know?' said Uncle Quentin. 'Spying, I suppose!'

'Yes — I bet Block's been spying and reading letters!' cried Sooty, indignantly.

Mr Barling took no notice of the interruption. 'Now, my dear sir,' he said to Uncle Quentin, 'I will tell you very shortly what I propose. I know you have heard that I am a smuggler. I am. I make a lot of money from it. It is easy to run a smuggling trade here, because no one can patrol the marshes, or stop men using the secret path that only I and a few others know. On favourable nights I send out a signal — or rather Block here does so, for me, using the convenient tower of Smuggler's Top . . .'

'Oh! So it *was* Block!' cried Sooty.

'Then when the goods arrive,' said Mr Barling 'and again at a favourable moment I — er — dispose of them. I cover my tracks very carefully, so that no one can possibly accuse me because they never have any real proof.'

'Why are you telling me all this?' said Uncle Quentin scornfully. 'It's of no interest to me. I'm only interested in a plan for draining the marshes, not in smuggling goods across them!'

'Exactly, my dear fellow!' said Mr Barling, amiably. 'I know that. I have even seen your plans and read about your experiments and Mr Lenoir's. But the draining of the marsh means the end of my own business! Once the marsh is drained, once houses are built there, and roads made, once the mists have gone, my business goes too! A harbour may be built out there, at the edge of the marshes — my ships can no longer creep in unseen, bringing valuable cargoes! Not only will my money go, but all the excitement, which is more than life to me, will go too!'

'You're mad!' said Uncle Quentin, in disgust.

Mr Barling *was* a little mad. He had always felt a great satisfaction in being a successful smuggler in days when smuggling was almost at an end. He loved the thrill of knowing that his little ships were creeping in the mist towards the treacherous marshes. He liked to know that men were making their way over a small and narrow path over the misty marsh to the appointed meeting-place, bringing smuggled goods.

'You should have lived a hundred years or more ago!' said Sooty, also feeling that Mr Barling was a little mad. 'You don't belong to nowadays.'

Mr Barling turned on Sooty, his eyes gleaming dangerously in the light of the lantern.

'Another word from you and I'll drop you in the marshes!' he said. Sooty felt a shiver go down his back. He suddenly knew that Mr Barling really did mean what he said. He was a dangerous man. Uncle Quentin sensed it too. He looked at Mr Barling warily.

'How do I come into this?' he asked. 'Why have you kidnapped me?'

'I know that Mr Lenoir is going to buy your plans from you,' said Mr Barling. 'I know he is going to drain the marsh by using your very excellent ideas. You see, I know all about them! I know, too, that Mr Lenoir hopes to make a lot of money by selling the land once it is drained. It is all his, that misty marsh — and no use to anyone now except to me! But that marsh is not going to be drained — I am going to buy your plans, not Mr Lenoir!'

'Do *you* want to drain the marsh, then?' said Uncle Quentin, in surprise.

Mr Barling laughed scornfully. 'No! Your plans, and the results of your experiments, will be burnt! They will be mine, but I shall not want to use them. I want the marsh left as it is, secret, covered with mist, and treacherous to all but me and my men. So, my dear sir, you will please name your price to me, instead of to Mr Lenoir and sign this document, which I have had prepared, making over all your plans to me!'

He flourished a large piece of paper in front of Uncle Quentin. Sooty watched breathlessly.

Uncle Quentin picked up the paper. He tore it into small pieces. He threw them into Mr Barling's face and said, scornfully: 'I don't deal with madmen, nor with rogues, Mr Barling!'

20

Timmy to the rescue

Mr Barling went very pale. Sooty gave a loud crow of delight. 'Hurrah! Good for *you*, Uncle Quentin!'

Block gave a loud exclamation, and darted to the excited boy. He took him by the shoulder, and raised the rope to thrash him.

'That's right,' said Mr Barling, in a funny kind of hissing voice. 'Deal with him first, Block and then with this — this — stubborn — obstinate — fool! We'll soon bring them to their senses. A good thrashing now and again, a few days here in the dark, without any food — ah, that will make them more biddable!'

Sooty yelled at the top of his voice. Uncle Quentin leapt to his feet. The rope came down and Sooty yelled again.

Then there suddenly came the pattering of quick feet, and something flung itself on Block. Block gave a scream of pain and turned.He knocked the lantern over by accident, and the light went out. There was a sound of fierce growling. Block staggered about trying to keep off the creature that had fastened itself on to him.

'Barling! Help me!' he shouted.

Mr Barling went to his aid, but was attacked in his turn. Uncle Quentin and Sooty listened in amazement and fear. What creature was this that had suddenly arrived? Would it attack them next? Was it a giant rat — or some fierce wild animal that haunted these tunnels?

The fierce animal suddenly barked. Sooty cheered.

'TIMMY! It's you, Timmy! Oh, good dog, good dog! Go for him, then, go for him! Bite him, Timmy, hard.'

The two frightened men could do nothing against the angry dog. Soon they were running down the tunnel as fast as they could go, feeling for the string for fear of being lost. Timmy chased them with much enjoyment, and then returned to Sooty and George's father, rather pleased with himself.

He had a tremendous welcome. George's father made a great fuss of him, and Sooty put his arms round the big dog's neck.

'How did you come here? Did you find your way out of the secret passage you've been in? Are you half-starved? Look, here's some food.'

Timmy ate heartily. He had managed to devour a few rats, but otherwise had had no food at all. He had licked the drops that here and there he had found dripping from the roof, so he had not been thirsty. But he had certainly been extremely puzzled and worried. He had never before been so long away from his beloved mistress!

'Uncle Quentin — Timmy could take us safely back to Smuggler's Top, couldn't he?' said Sooty, suddenly. He spoke to Timmy. 'Can you take us

home, old boy? Home, to George?'

Timmy listened, with his ears cocked up. He ran down the passage a little way, but soon came back. He did not like the idea of going down there. He felt that enemies were waiting for them all. Mr Barling and Block were not likely to give in quite so easily!

But Timmy knew other ways about the tunnels that honeycombed the hillside. He knew, for instance, the way down to the marsh! So he set off in the darkness, with Uncle Quentin's hand on his collar, and Sooty following close behind, holding on to Uncle Quentin's coat.

It wasn't easy or pleasant. Uncle Quentin wondered at times if Timmy really did know where he was going. They went down and down, stumbling over uneven places, sometimes knocking their heads against an unexpected low piece of roof. It was not a pleasant journey for Uncle Quentin, for he had no shoes on his feet, and was dressed only in pyjamas and rugs.

After a long time they came out on the edge of the marsh itself, at the bottom of the hill! It was a desolate place, and the mists were over it, so that neither Sooty nor Uncle Quentin knew which way to turn!

'Never mind,' said Sooty, 'we can easily leave it to Timmy. He knows the way all right. He'll take us back to the town, and once there we'll know the way home ourselves!'

But suddenly, to their surprise and dismay, Timmy stopped dead, pricking up his ears, whined and would go no farther. He looked thoroughly miserable and unhappy. What could be the matter?

Then, with a bark, the big dog left the two by themselves, and galloped back into the tunnel they had just left. He disappeared completely!

'Timmy!' yelled Sooty. 'Timmy! Come here! Don't leave us! TIMMY!'

But Timmy was gone; why, neither Sooty nor Uncle Quentin knew. They stared at one another.

'Well — I suppose we'd better try to make our way over this marshy bit,' said Uncle Quentin, doubtfully, putting a foot out to see if the ground was hard. It wasn't! He drew back his foot at once.

The mists were so thick that it was really impossible to see anything. Behind them was the opening to the tunnel. A steep rocky cliff rose up about it. There was no path that way, it was certain. Somehow they had to make their way round the foot of the hill to the main-road that entered the town — but the way lay over marshy ground!

'Let's sit down and wait for a bit to see if Timmy comes back,' said Sooty. So they sat down on a rock at the entrance to the tunnel and waited.

Sooty began to think of the others. He wondered what they had thought when they had discovered that both he and Uncle Quentin were missing. How astonished they must have been!

'I wonder what the others are doing?' he said, aloud. 'I'd love to know!'

The others, as we know, had been doing plenty. They had found the opening in the window-seat where Mr Barling had taken the captives, and they had gone down it and actually seen Mr Barling and Block on their way to talk to Uncle Quentin and Sooty!

They had found out, too, that Block hadn't been in his bed — he had left a dummy there instead. Now everyone was talking at once, and Mr Lenoir was suddenly convinced that Block had been a spy, put in his house by Mr Barling, and not the good servant he had appeared!

Once Julian felt that he was convinced of this he spoke to him more freely, and told him of the way through the window-seat, and of how they had seen Mr Barling and Block that very day, in the underground tunnels!

'Good heavens!' said Mr Lenoir, now looking thoroughly alarmed. 'Barling must be mad! I've always thought he was a bit queer — but he must be absolutely mad to kidnap people like this — and Block must be, too. This is a plot! They've heard what I've been planning with your uncle — and they've made up their minds to stop it because it will interfere with their smuggling. Goodness knows what they'll do now! This is serious!'

'If only we had Timmy!' suddenly said George.

Mr Lenoir looked astonished.

'Who's Timmy?'

'Well, you might as well know everything now,' said Julian, and he told Mr Lenoir about Timmy, and how they had hidden him.

'Very foolish of you,' said Mr Lenoir, shortly, looking displeased. 'If you'd told me I would have had someone in the town look after him. I can't help not liking dogs. I detest them, and never will have them in the house. But I would willingly have arranged for him to be boarded out, if I'd known you'd brought him.'

The children felt sorry and a little ashamed. Mr Lenoir was a queer, hot-tempered person, but he didn't seem nearly as horrid as they had thought he was.

'I'd like to go and see if I can find Timmy,' said George. 'You'll get the police in now, I suppose, Mr Lenoir, and perhaps we could go and find Timmy? We know the way into the secret passage from your study.'

'Oh — so *that's* why you were hiding there in the afternoon yesterday,' said Mr Lenoir. 'I thought you were a very bad boy. Well, go and try and find him if you like, but don't let him come anywhere near me. I really cannot bear dogs in the house.'

He went to telephone the police-station again. Mrs Lenoir, her eyes red with crying, stood by him. George slipped away to the study, followed by Dick and Julian and Anne. Marybelle stayed beside her mother.

'Come on — let's get into that secret passage and try and find old Timmy,' said George. 'If we all go, and whistle and shout and call, he's sure to hear us!'

They found the way into the passage, by doing the things they had done before. The panel slid back, and then another, larger opening came as before. They all squeezed through it, and found themselves in the very narrow passage that led from the study up to Sooty's bedroom.

But Timmy was not there! The children were surprised, but George soon thought why.

'Do you remember Sooty telling us there was a way into this passage from the dining-room, as well as from the study and Sooty's bedroom? Well, I believe I saw a door or something there, as we passed where the dining-room must be, and it's likely Timmy may have pushed through it, and gone into another passage somewhere.'

They went back, one by one. They came to the dining-room — or rather, they walked behind the dining-room wall. There they saw the door that George had noticed as they passed — a door, small and set quite flat to the wall, so that it was difficult to see. George pushed it. It opened easily, and then flapped shut, with a little click. It could be opened from one side but not from the other.

'That's where Timmy's gone!' said George, and she pushed the door open again. 'He pushed against the door and it opened — he went through, and the door fastened itself so that he couldn't get back. Come on, we must find him.'

They all went through the small door. It was so low that they had to bend their heads to go through, even Anne. They found themselves in a passage rather like the one they had just left, but not quite so narrow. It suddenly began to go downwards. Julian called back to the others.

'I believe it goes down to the passages where we used to take Timmy when we let him down into that pit to go for a walk! Yes, look — we've come to where the pit itself is!'

They went on, calling Timmy, and whistling loudly, but no Timmy came. George began to feel worried.

'Hallo! — surely this is where we came out when we climbed down all those steps from the window-seat passage!' said Dick, suddenly. 'Yes, it is. Look, there's the tunnel where we saw Block and Mr Barling going!'

'Oh — do you think they've done something to Timmy?' said George, in a frightened voice. 'I never thought of that!'

Everyone felt alarmed. It was strange that Block and Mr Barling could go about unmolested by Timmy if Timmy was somewhere near! Could they have harmed him in any way? They had no idea that Timmy was at that very minute with George's father and Sooty!

'Look at this!' said Julian, suddenly, and he shone his torch on to something to show the others. 'String! String going right down this tunnel. Why?'

'It's the tunnel that Mr Barling and Block took!'

said George. 'I believe it leads to where they've taken my father and Sooty! They're keeping them prisoners down here! I'm going to follow the string and find them! Who's coming with me?'

21

A journey through the hill

'I'm coming!' said everyone at once. As if they would let George go alone!

So down the dark tunnel they went, feeling the string and following it. Julian ran it through his fingers, and the others followed behind, holding hands. It would not do for anyone to get lost.

After about ten minutes they came to the rounded cave where Sooty and George's father had been the night before. They were not there now, of course — they were on their way down to the marsh!

'Hallo, look! This is where they must have been!' cried Julian, shining his torch round. 'A bench — with tumbled rugs — and an over-turned lamp. And look here, scraps of paper torn into bits! Something's been happening here!'

Quick-witted George pieced it together in her mind. 'Mr Barling took them here and left them. Then he came back with some sort of proposal to Father, who refused it! There must have been a struggle of some sort and the lamp got broken. Oh —

I do hope Father and Sooty got away all right.'

Julian felt gloomy. 'I hope to goodness they haven't gone wandering about these awful tunnels. Even Sooty doesn't know a quarter of them. I wish I knew what's happened.'

'Someone's coming!' suddenly said Dick. 'Snap out the light, Ju.'

Julian snapped off the torch he carried. At once they were all in darkness. They crouched at the back of the cave, listening.

Yes — footsteps were coming. Rather cautious footsteps. 'Sound like two or three people,' whispered Dick. They came nearer. Whoever was coming was plainly following the tunnel where the string was.

'Mr Barling perhaps — and Block,' whispered George. 'Come to have another talk with Father! But he's gone!'

A brilliant light flashed suddenly round the cave — and picked out the huddled children. There was a loud exclamation of astonishment.

'Good heavens! Who's here? What's all this?'

It was Mr Barling's voice. Julian stood up, blinking in the bright light.

'We came to look for my uncle and Sooty,' he said. 'Where are they?'

'Aren't they here?' said Mr Barling, seeming surprised. 'And is that horrible brute of a dog gone?'

'Oh — was Timmy here?' cried George, joyfully. 'Where is he?'

There were two other men with Mr Barling. One was Block. The other was his servant. Mr Barling put down the lantern he was carrying.

'Do you mean to say you don't know where the others are?' he said, uneasily. 'If they've gone off on their own, they'll never come back.'

Anne gave a little scream. 'It's all your fault,

559

you horrid man!'

'Shut up, Anne!' said Julian. 'Mr Barling,' he said, turning to the angry smuggler, 'I think you'd better come back with us and explain things. Mr Lenoir is now talking to the police.'

'Oh, *is* he?' said Mr Barling. 'Then I think it would be as well for us all to stay down here for a while! Yes, you too! I'll make Mr Lenoir squirm! I'll hold you all prisoners — and this time you shall be bound so that you don't go wandering off like the others! Got some rope, Block?'

Block stepped forward with the other man. They caught hold of George first, very roughly.

She screamed loudly. 'Timmy! Timmy! Where are you? Timmy, come and help! Oh, TIMMY!'

But no Timmy came. She was soon in a corner with her hands tied behind her. Then they turned to Julian.

'You're mad,' Julian said to Mr Barling, who was standing nearby, holding the lantern. 'You *must* be mad to do things like this.'

'Timmy!' shouted George, trying to free her hands. 'Timmy, Timmy, Timmy!'

Timmy didn't hear. He was too far away. But the dog suddenly felt uneasy. He was with George's father and Sooty at the edge of the marsh, about to lead them round the hill to safety. But he stopped and listened. He could hear nothing of course. But Timmy knew that George was in danger. He knew that his beloved little mistress needed him.

His ears did not tell him, nor did his nose. But his heart told him. George was in danger!

He turned and fled back into the tunnel. He tore up the winding passages at top speed, panting.

And, quite suddenly, just as Julian was angrily submitting to have his hands tied tightly together, a furry thunderbolt arrived! It was Timmy!

He smelt his enemy, Mr Barling, again! He smelt Block. Grrrrrrrrrr-rrrrrr!

'Here's that awful dog again!' yelled Block, and leapt away from Julian. 'Where's your gun, Barling?'

But Timmy didn't worry about guns. He leapt at Mr Barling and got him on the floor. He gave him a nip in the shoulder that made him yell. Then he leapt at Block, and got him down, too. The other man fled.

'Call your dog off; call him off, or he'll kill us!' cried Mr Barling, struggling up, his shoulder paining him terribly. But nobody said a word. Let Timmy do what he liked!

It wasn't long before all three of the men had gone into the dark tunnel, staggering about without a light, trying to find their way back. But they missed the string, and went wandering away in the darkness, groaning and terrified.

Timmy came running back very pleased with himself. He went to George and, whining with joy, he licked his little mistress from head to foot. And George, who never cried, was most astonished to find the tears pouring down her cheeks. 'But I'm glad, not sad!' she said. 'Oh, somebody undo my hands! I can't pat Timmy!'

Dick undid her hands and Julian's. Then they all had a marvellous time making a fuss of Timmy. And what a fuss he made of them too! He whined and barked, he rolled over and over, he licked them and butted them all with his head. He was wild with delight.

'Oh Timmy — it's lovely to have you again,' said George, happily. 'Now you can lead us to the others. I'm sure you know where Father is, Timmy, and Sooty.'

Timmy did, of course. He set off, his tail wagging,

George's hand on his collar, and the others behind in a line, holding hands.

They had the lantern with them and two torches, so they could see the way easily. But they would never have taken the right tunnels if Timmy hadn't been with them. The dog had explored them all thoroughly, and his sense of smell enabled him to go the right way without mistake.

'He's a marvellous dog,' said Anne. 'I think he's the best dog in the world, George.'

'Of course he is,' said George, who had always thought that ever since she had had Timmy as a puppy. 'Darling Tim — wasn't it wonderful when he came racing up and jumped at Block just as he was tying Julian's hands? He must have known we needed him!'

'I suppose he's taking us to wherever your father and Sooty are,' said Dick. 'He seems certain of the way. We're going steadily downhill. I bet we'll be at the marshes soon!'

When they at last came to the bottom of the hill, and emerged from the tunnel in the mists, George gave a yell. 'Look! There's Father — and Sooty too!'

'Uncle Quentin!' shouted Julian, Dick and Anne. 'Sooty! Hallo, here we are!'

Uncle Quentin and Sooty turned in the greatest surprise. They jumped up and went to meet the dog and the excited children.

'How *did* you get here?' said George's father, giving her a hug. 'Did Timmy go back for you? He suddenly deserted us and fled back into the tunnel.'

'What's happened?' asked Sooty, eagerly, knowing that the others would have plenty of news to tell him.

'Heaps,' said George, her face glowing. It was so nice all to be together again, Timmy too. She and Julian and Dick began to tell everything in turn, and then her father told his tale, too, interrupted a little by Sooty.

'Well,' said Julian at last, 'I suppose we ought to be getting back, or the police will be sending out bloodhounds to trace us all! Mr Lenoir will be surprised to see us all turning up together.'

'I wish I wasn't in pyjamas,' said his uncle, drawing the rugs about him. 'I shall feel queer walking the streets like this!'

'Never mind — it's awfully misty now,' said George, and she shivered a little, for the air was damp. 'Timmy — show us the way out of this place. I'm sure you know it.'

Timmy had never been out of the tunnel before, but he seemed to know what to do. He set off round the foot of the hill, the rest following, marvelling at the way Timmy found a dry path to follow. In the mist it was almost impossible to see which place was safe to walk on and which was not. The treacherous marsh was all around them!

'Hurrah! There's the road!' cried Julian, suddenly, as they came in sight of the roadway built over the marsh, running up the hill from the salty stretches of mud. They picked their way to it, their feet soaked with wet mud. Timmy tried to take a flying leap on to it.

But somehow or other he slipped! He fell back into the marsh, tried to find a safe foothold and couldn't. He whined.

'Timmy! Oh look, he's in the mud — and he's sinking!' screamed George, in panic. 'Timmy, Timmy, I'm coming!'

She was about to step down into the marsh to rescue Tim, but her father pulled her back roughly. 'Do you want to sink in, too?' he cried. 'Timmy will get out all right.'

But he wasn't getting out. He was sinking. 'Do something, oh, do something!' shouted George, struggling to get away from her father's hold. 'Oh, save Timmy, quick!'

22

Things come right at last

But what could anyone do? In despair they all gazed at poor Timmy, who was struggling with all his might in the sinking mud. 'He's going down!' wept Anne.

Suddenly there came the sound of rumbling wheels along the road to the hill. It was a lorry carrying a load of goods — coal, coke, planks, logs, sacks of various things. George yelled to it.

'Stop, stop! Help us! Our dog's in the marsh.'

The lorry came to a stop. George's father ran his eye over the things it carried. In a trice he and Julian were dragging out some planks from the load. They threw these into the marsh, and, using them as stepping-stones, the two reached poor sinking Timmy.

The lorry-driver jumped down to help. Into the marsh, crosswise on the other planks, went some more wood, to make a safe path. The first lot were already sinking in the mud.

'Uncle Quentin's got Timmy — he's pulling him up! He's got him!' squealed Anne.

George had sat down suddenly at the edge of the road, looking white. She saw that Timmy would now be rescued, and she felt sick with shock and relief.

It was a difficult business getting Timmy right out, for the mud was strong, and sucked him down as hard as it could. But at last he was out, and he staggered across the sinking planks, trying to wag a very muddy tail.

Muddy as he was George flung her arms round him. 'Oh Timmy — what a fright you gave us all! Oh, how you smell — but I don't care a bit! I thought you were gone, poor, poor Timmy!'

The lorry-driver looked ruefully at his planks in the marsh. They were now out of sight beneath the mud. Uncle Quentin, feeling rather foolish in pyjamas and rugs, spoke to him.

'I've no money on me now, but if you'll call at Smuggler's Top sometime I'll pay you well for your lost planks and your help.'

'Well, I'm delivering some coal to the house next to Smuggler's Top,' said the man, eyeing Uncle Quentin's curious attire. 'Maybe you'd all like a lift? There's plenty of room at the back there.'

It was getting dark now, as well as being foggy, and everyone was tired. Thankfully they climbed up into the lorry, and it roared up the hill into Castaway. Soon they were at Smuggler's Top, and they all clambered down, suddenly feeling rather stiff.

'I'll be calling tomorrow,' said the driver. 'Can't stop now. Good evening to you all!'

The little company rang the bell. Sarah came hurrying to the door. She almost fell over in surprise as she saw everyone standing there in the light of the hall-lamp.

'Lands' sakes!' she said. 'You're all back! My, Mr and Mrs Lenoir will be glad — they've got the police hunting everywhere for you! They've gone down secret passages, and they've been to Mr Barling's, and . . .'

Timmy bounced into the hall, the mud now drying on him, so that he looked most peculiar. Sarah gave a scream. 'What's that? Gracious, it can't be a dog!'

'Come here, Tim!' said George, suddenly remembering that Mr Lenoir detested dogs. 'Sarah, do you think you'd have poor Timmy in the kitchen with you? I really can't turn him out into the streets — you've no idea how brave he's been.'

'Come along, come along!' said her father, impatient with all this talk. 'Lenoir can put up with Timmy for a few minutes, surely!'

'Oh, *I'll* have him with pleasure!' said Sarah. 'I'll give him a bath. That's what he wants. Mr and Mrs Lenoir are in the sitting-room, sir. Oh, sir, shall I get you some clothes?'

The little party went in, and made their way to the sitting-room, while Timmy went docilely to the kitchen with the excited Sarah. Mr Lenoir heard the talking and flung open the sitting-room door.

Mrs Lenoir fell on Sooty, tears pouring down her cheeks. Marybelle pawed at him in delight, just as if she was a dog! Mr Lenoir rubbed his hands, clapped everyone on the back, and said: 'Well, well! Fine to see you all safe and sound. Well, well! What a tale you've got to tell, I'm sure!'

'It's a strange tale, Lenoir,' said George's father. 'Very strange. But I'll have to see to my feet before I tell it. I've walked miles in my bare feet, and they're very painful now!'

So, with bits of tales pouring out from everyone, the household bustled round and got hot water for

569

bathing Uncle Quentin's feet, a dressing-gown for him, food for everyone, and hot drinks. It was really a most exciting time, and now that the thrills were all over, the children rather felt important to be able to relate so much.

Then the police came in, of course, and the Inspector at once asked a lot of questions. Everyone wanted to answer them, but the Inspector said that only George's father, Sooty and George were to tell the tale. They knew most about everything.

Mr Lenoir was perhaps the most surprised person there. When he heard how Mr Barling had actually offered to buy the plans for draining the marsh, and how he had frankly admitted to being a smuggler, he sat back in his chair, unable to say a word.

'He's mad, of course!' said the Inspector of Police. 'Doesn't seem to live in this world at all!'

'That's just what I said to him,' said Sooty. 'I told him he ought to have lived a hundred years ago!'

'Well, we've tried to catch him in the smuggling business many and many a time,' said the Inspector, 'but he was too artful. Fancy him planting Block here as a spy, sir — that was a clever bit of work — and Block using your tower as a signalling place! Bit of nerve, that! And Block isn't deaf, after all? That was clever, too — sending him about, pretending he was stone-deaf, so that he could catch many a bit of knowledge not meant for his ears!'

'Do you think we ought to do something about Block and Mr Barling and the other man?' said Julian, suddenly. 'For all we know they're still wandering about in that maze of tunnels — and two of them are bitten by Timmy, we know.'

'Ah yes — that dog saved your lives, I should think,' said the Inspector. 'A bit of luck, that. Sorry you don't like dogs, Mr Lenoir, but I'm sure you'll admit it was a lucky thing for you all that he was wandering about!'

'Yes — yes, it was,' said Mr Lenoir. 'Of course, Block never wanted dogs here, either — he was afraid they might bark at his curious comings and goings, I suppose. By the way — where *is* this marvellous dog? I don't mind seeing him for a moment — though I do detest dogs, and always shall.'

'I'll get him,' said George. 'I only hope Sarah's done what she said, and bathed him. He was awfully muddy!'

She went out and came back with Timmy. But what a different Timmy! Sarah had given him a good hot bath, and had dried him well. He smelt sweet and fresh, his coat was springy and clean, and he had had a good meal. He was feeling very pleased with himself and everything.

'Timmy — meet a friend,' said George to him, solemnly. Timmy looked at Mr Lenoir out of his big brown eyes. He trotted straight up to him, and held up his right paw politely to shake hands, as George had taught him.

Mr Lenoir was rather taken aback. He was not used to good manners in dogs. He couldn't help putting out his hand to Timmy — and the two shook hands in a most friendly manner. Timmy didn't attempt to lick Mr Lenoir or jump up at him. He took away his paw, gave a little wuff as if to say 'How-do-you-do?' and then went back to George. He lay down quietly beside her. 'Well — he doesn't seem like a *dog*!' said Mr Lenoir, in surprise.

'Oh, he *is*,' said George, at once, very earnestly. 'He's a real, proper dog, Mr Lenoir — only much, much cleverer than most dogs are. Could I keep him, please, while we stay here, and get someone in the town to look after him?'

571

'Well — seeing he is such a very fine fellow — and seems so sensible — I'll let you have him here,' said Mr Lenoir, making a great effort to be generous. 'Only — please keep him out of my way. 'I'm sure a sensible boy like you will see to that.'

Everyone grinned when Mr Lenoir called George a boy. He never seemed to realise she was a girl. She grinned, too. She wasn't going to tell him she wasn't a boy!

'You'll never see him!' she said, joyfully. 'I'll keep him right out of your way. Thank you very much. It's awfully good of you.'

The Inspector liked Timmy, too. He looked at him and nodded across to George. 'When you want to get rid of him, sell him to me!' he said. 'We could do with a dog like that in our police force! Soon round up the smugglers for us!'

George didn't even bother to reply! As if she would ever sell Timmy, or let him go into the police force!

All the same, the Inspector had to call on Timmy for help before long. When the next day came, and no one had found Mr Barling and his companions in the maze of tunnels, and they hadn't turned up anywhere, the Inspector asked George if she would let Timmy go down into the tunnels and hunt them out.

'Can't leave them there, lost and starving,' he said. 'Bad as they are we'll have to rescue them! Timmy is the only one who can find them.'

That was true, of course. So Timmy once more went underground into the hill, and hunted for his enemies. He found them after a while, lost in the maze of passages, hungry and thirsty, in pain and frightened.

He took them like sheep to where the police waited for them. And after that Mr Barling and his friends disappeared from public life for quite a long time!

572

'The police must be glad to have got them at last,' said Mr Lenoir. 'They have tried to stop this smuggling for a long time. They even suspected *me* at one time! Barling was a clever fellow, though I still think he was half mad. When Block found out my ideas about draining the marsh, Barling was afraid that once the mists and the marsh were gone, that would be the end of all his excitement — no more smuggling! No more waiting for his little ships to come creeping up in the fog — no more lines of men slipping across the secret ways of the marsh — no more signalling, no more hiding away of smuggled goods. Did you know that the police had found a cave full of them inside the hill?'

It was an exciting adventure to talk about, now that it was all over. The children felt sorry about one thing, though — they were sorry that they had thought Mr Lenoir so horrid. He was a queer man in many ways, but he could be kind and jolly too.

'Did you know we're leaving Smuggler's Top?' said Sooty. 'Mother was so terribly upset when I disappeared, that Father promised her he'd sell the place and leave Castaway, if I came back safe and sound. Mother's thrilled!'

'So am I,' said Marybelle. 'I don't like Smuggler's Top — it's so queer and secret and lonely!'

'Well, if it will make you all happy to leave it, I'm glad,' said Julian 'But *I* like it! I think it's a lovely place, set on a hill-top like this, with mists at its foot, and secret ways all about it. I'll be sorry never to come here again, if you leave.'

'So will I,' said Dick, and Anne and George nodded.

'It's an adventurous place!' said George, patting Timmy. 'Isn't it, Timmy? Do *you* like it, Timmy? Have *you* enjoyed your adventure here?'

'Woof!' said Timmy, and thumped his tail on the floor. Of course he had enjoyed himself. He always did, so long as George was anywhere about.

'Well — now perhaps we'll have a nice peaceful time!' said Marybelle. 'I don't want any more adventures.'

'Ah, but *we* do!' said the others. So no doubt they will get them. Adventures always come to the adventurous, there's no doubt about that!

Enid Blyton

FIVE FALL INTO ADVENTURE

ILLUSTRATED BY JOLYNE KNOX

1

At Kirrin Cottage again

GEORGINA was at the station to meet her three cousins. Timmy her dog was with her, his long tail wagging eagerly. He knew quite well they had come to meet Julian, Dick and Anne, and he was glad. It was much more fun when the Five were all together.

'Here comes the train, Timmy!' said George. Nobody called her Georgina, because she wouldn't answer if they did. She looked like a boy with her short curly hair and her jeans and open-necked shirt. Her face was covered with freckles, and her legs and arms were as brown as a gipsy's.

There was the far-off rumble of a train, and as it came nearer, a short warning hoot. Timmy whined and wagged his tail. He didn't like trains, but he wanted this one to come.

Nearer and nearer it came, slowing down as it reached Kirrin station. Long before it came to the little platform three heads appeared out of one of the windows, and three hands waved wildly. George waved back, her face one big smile.

The door swung open almost before the train stopped. Out came a big boy, and helped down a small girl. Then came another boy, not quite so tall as the first one, with a bag in each hand. He dragged a third bag out, and then George and Timmy were on him.

'Julian! Dick! Anne! Your train's late; we thought you were never coming!'

'Hallo George! Here we are at last. Get down, Timmy, don't eat me.'

'Hallo, George! Oh, Timmy, you darling – you're just as licky as ever!'

'Woof,' said Timmy joyfully, and bounded all round like a mad thing, getting into everybody's way.

'Any trunk or anything?' asked George. 'Only those three bags?'

'Well, we haven't come for long this time, worse luck,' said Dick. 'Only a fortnight! Still, it's better than nothing.'

'You shouldn't have gone off to France all those six weeks,' said George, half-jealously. 'I suppose you've gone all French now.'

Dick laughed, waved his hands in the air and went off into a stream of quick French that sounded just like gibberish to George. French was not one of her strong subjects.

'Shut up,' she said, giving him a friendly shove. 'You're just the same old idiot. Oh, I'm so glad you've come. It's been lonely and dull at Kirrin without you.'

A porter came up with a barrow. Dick turned to him, waved his hands again, and addressed the astonished man in fluent French. But the porter knew Dick quite well.

'Go on with you,' he said. 'Argy-bargying in double-Dutch like that. Do you want me to wheel these up to Kirrin Cottage for you?'

'Yes, please,' said Anne. 'Stop it, Dick. It isn't funny when you go on so long.'

'Oh, let him go on,' said George, and she linked her arms in Anne's and Dick's. 'It's lovely to have you again. Mother's looking forward to seeing you all.'

'I bet Uncle Quentin isn't,' said Julian, as they went along the little platform, Timmy capering round them.

'Father's in quite a good temper,' said George. 'You

579

know he's been to America with Mother, lecturing and hearing other scientists lecturing too. Mother says everyone made a great fuss of him, and he liked it.'

George's father was a brilliant scientist, well-known all over the world. But he was rather a difficult man at home, impatient, hot-tempered and forgetful. The children were fond of him, but held him in great respect. They all heaved a sigh of relief when he went away for a few days, for then they could make as much noise as they liked, tear up and down the stairs, play silly jokes and generally be as mad as they pleased.

'Will Uncle Quentin be at home all the time we're staying with you?' asked Anne. She was really rather afraid of her hot-tempered uncle.

'No,' said George. 'Mother and Father are going away for a tour in Spain – so we'll be on our own.'

'Wizard!' said Dick. 'We can wear our bathing costumes all day long then if we want to.'

'And Timmy can come in at meal-times without being sent out whenever he moves,' said George. 'He's been sent out every single meal-time this week, just because he snapped at the flies that came near him. Father goes absolutely mad if Timmy suddenly snaps at a fly.'

'Shame!' said Anne, and patted Timmy's rough-haired back. 'You can snap at every single fly you like, Timmy, when we're on our own.'

'Woof,' said Timmy, gratefully.

'There won't be time for any adventure these hols,' said Dick, regretfully, as they walked down the lane to Kirrin Cottage. Red poppies danced along the way, and in the distance the sea shone as blue as cornflowers. 'Only two weeks – and back we go to school! Well, let's hope the weather keeps fine. I want to bathe six times a day!'

Soon they were all sitting round the tea-table at Kirrin Cottage, and their Aunt Fanny was handing round plates

580

of her nicest scones and tea-cake. She was very pleased to see her nephews and niece again.

'Now George will be happy,' she said, smiling at the hungry four. 'She's been going about like a bear with a sore head the last week or two. Have another scone, Dick? Take two while you're about it.'

'Good idea,' said Dick, and helped himself. 'Nobody makes scones and cakes like you do, Aunt Fanny. Where's Uncle Quentin?'

'In his study,' said his aunt. 'He knows it's tea-time, and he's heard the bell, but I expect he's buried in something or other. I'll have to fetch him in a minute. I honestly believe he'd go without food all day long if I didn't go and drag him into the dining-room!'

'Here he is,' said Julian, hearing the familiar impatient footsteps coming down the hall to the dining-room. The door was flung open. Uncle Quentin stood there, a news-paper in his hand, scowling. He didn't appear to see the children at all.

'Look here, Fanny!' he shouted. 'See what they've put in this paper – the very thing I gave orders was NOT to be put in! The dolts! the idiots! The . . .'

'Quentin! Whatever's the matter?' said his wife. 'Look – here are the children – they've just arrived.'

But Uncle Quentin simply didn't see any of the four children at all. He went on glaring at the paper. He rapped at it with his hand.

'*Now* we'll get the place full of reporters wanting to see me, and wanting to know all about my new ideas!' he said, beginning to shout. 'See what they've said! "This emi-nent scientist conducts all his experiments and works out all his ideas at his home, Kirrin Cottage. Here are his stack of notebooks, to which are now added two more – fruits of his visit to America, and here at his cottage are his amazing diagrams," and so on and so on.

'I tell you, Fanny, we'll have hordes of reporters down.'

'No, we shan't, dear,' said his wife. 'And, anyway, we are soon off to Spain. Do sit down and have some tea. And look, can't you say a word to welcome Julian, Dick and Anne?'

Uncle Quentin grunted and sat down. 'I didn't know they were coming,' he said, and helped himself to a scone. 'You might have told me, Fanny.'

'I told you three times yesterday and twice today,' said his wife.

Anne suddenly squeezed her uncle's arm. She was sitting next to him. 'You're just the same as ever, Uncle Quentin,' she said. 'You never, never remember we're coming! Shall we go away again?'

Her uncle looked down at her and smiled. His temper never lasted very long. He grinned at Julian and Dick. 'Well, here you are again!' he said. 'Do you think you can hold the fort for me while I'm away with your aunt?'

'Rather!' said all three together.

'We'll keep everyone at bay!' said Julian. 'With Timmy's help I'll put up a notice: "*Beware, very fierce dog*".'

'Woof,' said Timmy, sounding delighted. He thumped his tail on the floor. A fly came by his nose and he snapped at it. Uncle Quentin frowned.

'Have another scone, Father?' said George hurriedly. 'When are you and Mother going to Spain?'

'Tomorrow,' said her mother firmly. 'Now don't look like that, Quentin. You know perfectly well it's been arranged for weeks, and you *need* a holiday, and if we don't go tomorrow all our arrangements will be upset.'

'Well, you might have *warned* me it was tomorrow,' said her husband, looking indignant. 'I mean – I've all my notebooks to check and put away, and . . .'

'Quentin, I've told you heaps of times that we leave on September the third,' said his wife, still more firmly. '*I* want a holiday, too. The four children will be quite all right here with Timmy – they'll love being on their own.

Julian is almost grown-up now and he can cope with anything that turns up.'

Timmy snapped twice at a fly, and Uncle Quentin jumped. 'If that dog does that again,' he began, but his wife interrupted him at once.

'There, you see! You're as touchy and nervy as can be, Quentin, dear. It will do you good to get away – and the children will have a lovely two weeks on their own. Nothing can possibly happen, so make up your mind to leave tomorrow with an easy mind!'

Nothing can possibly happen? Aunt Fanny was wrong of course. *Anything* could happen when the Five were left on their own!

2

A meeting on the beach

IT really was very difficult to get Uncle Quentin off the next day. He was shut up in his study until the last possible moment, sorting out his precious notebooks. The taxi arrived and hooted outside the gate. Aunt Fanny, who had been ready for a long time, went and rapped at the study door.

'Quentin! Unlock the door! You really must come. We shall lose the plane if we don't go now.'

'Just one minute!' shouted back her husband. Aunt Fanny looked at the four children in despair.

'That's the fourth time he's called out "Just one minute",' said George. The telephone shrilled out just then, and she picked up the receiver.

'Yes,' she said. 'No, I'm afraid you can't see him. He's off to Spain, and nobody will know where he is for the next two weeks. What's that? Wait a minute – I'll ask my mother.'

'Who is it?' said her mother.

'It's the *Daily Clarion*,' said George. 'They want to send

a reporter down to interview Daddy. I told them he was going to Spain – and they said could they publish that?'

'Of course,' said her mother, thankfully. 'Once that's in the papers nobody will ring up and worry you. Say, yes, George.'

George said yes, the taxi hooted more loudly than ever, and Timmy barked madly at the hooting. The study door was flung open and Uncle Quentin stood in the doorway, looking as black as thunder.

'Why can't I have a little peace and quiet when I'm doing important work?' he began. But his wife made a dart at him and dragged him down the hall. She put his hat in one hand, and would have put his stick into the other if he hadn't been carrying a heavy despatch case.

'You're not doing important work, you're off on a holiday,' she said. 'Oh, Quentin, you're worse than ever! What's that case in your hand? Surely you are not taking work away with you?'

The taxi hooted again, and Timmy woofed just behind Uncle Quentin. He jumped violently, and the telephone rang loudly.

'That's another reporter coming down to see you, Father,' said George. 'Better go quickly!'

Whether that bit of news really did make Uncle Quentin decide at last to go, nobody knew – but in two seconds he was sitting in the taxi, still clutching his despatch case, telling the taxi-driver exactly what he thought of people who kept hooting their horns.

'Good-bye, dears,' called Aunt Fanny, thankfully. 'Don't get into mischief. We're off at last.'

The taxi disappeared down the lane. 'Poor Mother!' said George. 'It's always like this when they go for a holiday. Well, there's one thing certain – I shall NEVER marry a scientist.'

Everyone heaved a sigh of relief at the thought that

Uncle Quentin was gone. When he was over-worked he really was impossible.

'Still, you simply have to make excuses for anyone with a brain like his,' said Julian. 'Whenever our science master at school speaks of him, he almost holds his breath with awe. Worst of it is, he expects *me* to be brilliant because I've got a brilliant uncle.'

'Yes. It's difficult to live up to clever relations,' said Dick. 'Well – we're on our own, except for Joan. Good old Joan! I bet she'll give us some smashing meals.'

'Let's go and see if she's got anything we can have now,' said George. 'I'm hungry.'

'So am I,' said Dick. They marched down the hall into the kitchen, calling for Joan.

'Now, you don't need to tell me what you've come for,' said Joan, the smiling, good-tempered cook. 'And I don't need to tell you this – the larder's locked.'

'Oh Joan – what a mean thing to do!' said Dick.

'Mean or not, it's the only thing to do when all four of you are around, to say nothing of that great hungry dog,' said Joan, rolling out some pastry vigorously. 'Why, last holidays I left a meat pie and half a tongue and a cherry tart and trifle sitting on the shelves for the next day's meals – and when I came back from my half-day's outing there wasn't a thing to be seen.'

'Well, we thought you'd left them there for our supper,' said Julian, sounding quite hurt.

'All right – but you won't get the chance of thinking anything like that again,' said Joan, firmly. 'That larder door's going to be kept locked. Maybe I'll unlock it sometimes and hand you out a snack or two – but I'm the one that's going to unlock it, not you.'

The four drifted out of the kitchen again, disappointed. Timmy followed at their heels. 'Let's go down and have a bathe,' said Dick. 'If I'm going to have six bathes a day, I'd better hurry up and have my first one.'

'I'll get some ripe plums,' said Anne. 'We can take those down with us. And I expect the ice-cream man will come along to the beach too. We shan't starve! And we'd better wear our shirts and jeans over our bathing costumes, so we don't catch too much sun.'

Soon they were all down on the sand. They found a good place and scraped out comfortable holes to sit in. Timmy scraped his own.

'I can't imagine why Timmy bothers to scrape one,' said George. 'Because he always squeezes into mine sooner or later. Don't you, Timmy?'

Timmy wagged his tail, and scraped so violently that they were all covered with sand. 'Pooh!' said Anne, spitting sand out of her mouth. 'Stop it, Timmy. As fast as I scrape my hole, you fill it up!'

Timmy paused to give her a lick, and then scraped again, making a very deep hole indeed. He lay down in it, panting, his mouth looking as if he were smiling.

'He's smiling again,' said Anne. 'I never knew a dog that smiled like Timmy. Timmy, it's nice to have you again.'

'Woof,' said Timmy, politely, meaning that it was nice to have Anne and the others back again, too. He wagged his tail and sent a shower of sand over Dick.

They all wriggled down comfortably into their soft warm holes. 'We'll eat the plums first and then we'll have a bathe,' said Dick. 'Chuck me one, Anne.'

Two people came slowly along the beach. Dick looked at them out of half-closed eyes. A boy and a man – and what a ragamuffin the boy looked! He wore torn dirty jeans and a filthy jersey. No shoes at all.

The man looked even worse. He slouched as he came, and dragged one foot. He had a straggly moustache and mean, clever little eyes that raked the beach up and down. The two were walking at high-water mark and were obviously looking for anything that might have been cast up by the tide. The boy already had an old box, one wet shoe and some wood under his arm.

'What a pair!' said Dick to Julian. 'I hope they don't come near us. I feel as if I can smell them from here.'

The two walked along the beach and then back. Then, to the children's horror, they made a bee-line for where they were lying in their sandy holes, and sat down close beside them. Timmy growled.

An unpleasant, unwashed kind of smell at once came to the children's noses. Pooh! Timmy growled again. The boy took no notice of Timmy's growling. But the man looked uneasy.

'Come on – let's have a bathe,' said Julian, annoyed at the way the two had sat down so close to them. After all, there was practically the whole of the beach to choose from – why come and sit almost on top of somebody else?

When they came back from their bathe the man had gone, but the boy was still there – and he had actually sat himself down in George's hole.

'Get out,' said George, shortly, her temper rising at once. 'That's my hole, and you jolly well know it.'

'Findings keepings,' said the boy, in a curious sing-song voice. 'It's my hole now.'

George bent down and pulled the boy roughly out of the hole. He was up in a trice, his fists clenched. George clenched hers, too.

Dick came up at a run. 'Now, George – if there's any fighting to be done, I'll do it,' he said. He turned to the scowling boy. 'Clear off! We don't want you here!'

The boy hit out with his right fist and caught Dick unexpectedly on the jawbone. Dick looked astounded. He hit out, too, and sent the tousle-headed boy flying.

'Yah, coward!' said the boy, holding his chin tenderly. 'Hitting someone smaller than yourself! I'll fight that first boy, but I won't fight *you*.'

588

'You can't fight him,' said Dick. 'He's a girl. You can't fight girls – and girls oughtn't to fight, anyway.'

'Ses you!' said the dirty little ragamuffin, standing up and doubling his fists again. 'Well, you look here – *I'm* a girl, too – so I can fight her all right, can't I?'

George and the ragamuffin stood scowling at one

another, each with fists clenched. They looked so astonishingly alike, with their short, curly hair, brown freckled faces and fierce expressions that Julian suddenly roared with laughter. He pushed them firmly apart.

'Fighting forbidden!' he said. He turned to the ragamuffin. 'Clear off!' he ordered. 'Do you hear me? Go on – off with you!'

The gipsy-like girl stared at him. Then she suddenly burst into tears and ran off howling.

'*She's* a girl all right,' said Dick, grinning at the howls. 'She's got some spunk though, facing up to me like that. Well, that's the last we'll see of *her*!'

But he was wrong. It wasn't!

3

Face at the window

THE five curled up in their holes once more. Dick felt his jawbone. 'That ragamuffin of a girl gave me a good bang,' he said, half-admiringly. 'Little demon, isn't she! A bit of live wire!'

'I can't see why Julian wouldn't let me have a go at her,' said George sulkily. 'It was my hole she sat in – she *meant* to be annoying! How dare she?'

'Girls can't go about fighting,' said Dick. 'Don't be an ass, George. I know you make out you're as good as a boy, and you dress like a boy and climb trees as well as I can – but it's really time you gave up thinking you're as good as a boy.'

This sort of speech didn't please George at all. 'Well, anyway, I don't burst into howls if I'm beaten,' she said, turning her back on Dick.

'No, you don't,' agreed Dick. 'You've got as much spunk as any boy – much more than that other kid had. I'm sorry I sent her flying now. It's the first time I've ever hit a girl, and I hope it'll be the last.'

591

'I'm jolly glad you hit her,' said George. 'She's a nasty little beast. If I see her again I'll tell her what I think of her.'

'No, you won't,' said Dick. 'Not if I'm there, anyway. She had her punishment when I sent her flying.'

'Do shut up arguing, you two,' said Anne, and sent a shower of sand over them. 'George, don't go into one of your moods, for goodness' sake – we don't want to waste a single day of this two weeks.'

'Here's the ice-cream man,' said Julian, sitting up and feeling for the waterproof pocket in the belt of his bathing trunks. 'Let's have one each.'

'Woof,' said Timmy, and thumped his tail on the sand.

'Yes, all right – one for you, too,' said Dick. 'Though what sense there is in giving *you* one, I don't know. One lick, one swallow, and it's gone. It might be a fly for all you taste of it.'

Timmy gulped his ice-cream down at once and then went into George's hole, squeezing beside her, hoping for a lick of her ice, too. But she pushed him away.

'No, Timmy. Ice-cream's wasted on you! You can't even have a lick of mine. And do get back into your hole – you're making me frightfully hot.'

Timmy obligingly got out and went into Anne's hole. She gave him a little bit of her ice-cream. He sat panting beside her, looking longingly at the rest of the ice. 'You're melting it with your hot breath,' said Anne. 'Go into Julian's hole now!'

The five of them had a thoroughly lazy morning. As none of them had a watch they went in far too early for lunch, and were shooed out again by Joan.

'How you can come in at ten past twelve for a one o'clock lunch, I don't know!' she scolded. 'I haven't even finished the housework yet.'

'Well – it *felt* like one o'clock,' said Anne, disappointed

592

to find there was so long to wait. Still, when lunch-time came, Joan really did them well.

'Cold ham and tongue – cold baked beans – beetroot – crisp lettuce straight from the garden – heaps of tomatoes – cucumber – hard-boiled egg!' recited Anne in glee.

'Just the kind of meal I like,' said Dick, sitting down. 'What's for pudding?'

'There it is on the sideboard,' said Anne. 'Wobbly blancmange, fresh fruit salad and jelly. I'm glad I'm hungry.'

'Now don't you give Timmy any of that ham and tongue,' Joan warned George. 'I've got a fine bone for him. Coming, Timmy?'

Timmy knew the word 'bone' very well indeed. He trotted after Joan at once, his feet sounding loudly in the hall. They heard Joan talking kindly to him in the kitchen as she found him his bone.

'Good old Joan,' said Dick. 'She's like Timmy – her bark is worse than her bite.'

'Timmy's got a good bite, though,' said George, helping herself to three tomatoes at once. 'And his bite came in useful heaps of times for us.'

They ate steadily, thinking of some of the hair-raising adventures they had had, when Timmy and his bite had certainly come in very useful. Timmy came in after a while, licking his lips.

'Nothing doing, old chap,' said Dick, looking at the empty dishes on the table. 'Don't tell me you've chomped up that bone already!'

Timmy had. He lay down under the table, and put his nose on his paws. He was happy. He had had a good meal, and he was with the people he loved best. He put his head as near George's feet as he could.

'Your whiskers are tickling me,' she said, and screwed up her bare toes. 'Pass the tomatoes, someone.'

'You *can't* manage any more tomatoes, surely!' said Anne. 'You've had five already.'

'They're out of my own garden,' said George, 'so I can eat as many as I like.'

After lunch they lazed on the beach till it was time for a bathe again. It was a happy day for all of them – warm, lazy, with plenty of running and romping about.

George looked out for the ragamuffin girl, but she didn't appear again. George was half sorry. She would have liked a battle of words with her, even if she couldn't have a fight!

They were all very tired when they went to bed that night. Julian yawned so loudly when Joan came in with a jug of hot cocoa and some biscuits that she offered to lock up the house for him.

'Oh, no, thank you, Joan,' said Julian at once. 'That's the man's job, you know, locking up the house. You can trust me all right. I'll see to every window and every door.'

'Right, Master Julian,' said Joan, and bustled away to wind up the kitchen clock, rake out the fire, and go up to bed. The children went up, too, Timmy, as usual, at George's heels. Julian was left downstairs to lock up.

He was a very responsible boy. Joan knew that he wouldn't leave a single window unfastened. She heard him trying to shut the little window in the pantry, and she called down:

'Master Julian! It's swollen or something, and won't shut properly. You needn't bother about it, it's too small for anyone to get into!'

'Right!' said Julian, thankfully, and went upstairs. He yawned a terrific yawn again, and set Dick off, too, as soon as he came into the bedroom they both shared. The girls, undressing in the next room, laughed to hear them.

'*You* wouldn't hear a burglar in the middle of the night, Julian and Dick!' called Anne. 'You'll sleep like logs!'

594

'Old Timmy can listen out for burglars,' said Julian, cleaning his teeth vigorously. 'That's his job, not mine. Isn't it, Timmy?'

'Woof,' said Timmy, clambering on to George's bed. He always slept curled up in the crook of her knees. Her mother had given up trying to insist that George didn't have Timmy on her bed at night. As George said, even if *she* agreed to that, Timmy wouldn't!

Nobody stayed awake for more than five seconds. Nobody even said anything in bed, except for a sleepy good night. Timmy gave a little grunt and settled down, too, his head on George's feet. It was heavy, but she liked it there. She put out a hand and stroked Timmy gently. He licked one of her feet through the bed-clothes. He loved George more than anyone in the world.

It was dark outside that night. Thick clouds had come up and put out all the stars. There was no sound to be heard but the wind in the trees and the distant surge of the sea – and both sounded so much the same that it was hard to tell the difference.

Not another sound – not even an owl hooting to its mate, or the sound of a hedgehog pattering in the ditch.

Then why did Timmy wake up? Why did he open first one eye and then another? Why did he prick up his ears and lie there, listening? He didn't even lift his head at first. He simply lay listening in the darkness.

He lifted his head cautiously at last. He slid off the bed as quietly as a cat. He padded across the room and out of the door. Down the stairs he went, and into the hall, where his claws rattled on the tiled floor. But nobody heard him. Everyone in the house was fast asleep.

Timmy stood and listened in the hall. He knew he had heard something. Could it have been a rat somewhere? Timmy lifted his nose and sniffed.

And then he stiffened from head to tail, and stood as if turned into stone. Something was climbing up the wall of

595

the house. Scrape, scrape, scrape – rustle, rustle! Would a rat dare to do that?

Upstairs, in her bed, Anne didn't know why she suddenly woke up just then, but she did. She was thirsty, and she thought she would get a drink of water. She felt for her torch, and switched it on.

The light fell on the window first, and Anne saw something that gave her a terrible shock. She screamed loudly, and dropped her torch in fright. George woke up at once. Timmy came bounding up the stairs.

'Julian!' wailed Anne. 'Come quickly. I saw a face at the window, a horrible, dreadful face looking in at me!'

George rushed to the window, switching on her torch as she did so. There was nothing there. Timmy went with her. He sniffed at the open window and growled.

'Hark – I can hear someone running quickly down the path,' said Julian, who now appeared with Dick. 'Come on, Timmy – downstairs with you and after them!'

And down they all went – Anne too. They flung the front door wide and Timmy sped out, barking loudly. A face at the window? He'd soon find out who it belonged to!

4

The next day

THE four children waited at the open front door, listening
to Timmy's angry, excited barking. Anne was trembling,
and Julian put his arm round her comfortingly.

'What was this dreadful face like?' he asked her. Anne
shivered in his arm.

'I didn't see very much,' she said. 'You see, I just
switched on my torch, and the beam was directed on the
window nearby – and it lighted up the face for a second. It
had nasty gleaming eyes, and it looked very dark –
perhaps it was a black man's face! Oh, I *was* frightened!'

'Then did it disappear?' asked Julian.

'I don't know,' said Anne. 'I was so frightened that I
dropped my torch and the light went out. Then George
woke up and rushed to the window.'

'Where on earth was Timmy?' said Dick, feeling suddenly surprised that Timmy hadn't awakened them all by
barking. Surely he must have heard the owner of the face
climbing up to the window?

'I don't know. He came rushing into the bedroom when

I screamed,' said Anne. 'Perhaps he *had* heard a noise and had gone down to see what it was.'

'That's about it,' said Julian. 'Never mind, Anne. It was a tramp, I expect. He found all the doors and windows downstairs fastened – and shinned up the ivy to see if he could enter by way of a bedroom. Timmy will get him, that's certain.'

But Timmy didn't get him. He came back after a time, with his tail down, and a puzzled look in his eyes. 'Couldn't you find him, Timmy?' said George, anxiously.

'Woof,' said Timmy, mournfully, his tail still down. George felt him. He was wet through.

'Goodness! Where have you been to get so wet?' she said, in surprise. 'Feel him, Dick.'

Dick felt him, and so did the others. 'He's been in the sea,' said Julian. 'That's why he's wet. I guess the burglar, or whatever he was, must have sprinted down to the beach, when he knew Timmy was after him – and jumped into a boat! It was his only chance of getting away.'

'And Timmy must have swum after him till he couldn't keep up any more,' said George. 'Poor old Tim. So you lost him, did you?'

Timmy wagged his tail a little. He looked very down-hearted indeed. To think he had heard noises and thought it was a rat – and now, whoever it was had got away from him. Timmy felt ashamed.

Julian shut and bolted the front door. He put up the chain, too. 'I don't think the Face will come back again in a hurry,' he said. 'Now he knows there's a big dog here he'll keep away. I don't think we need worry any more.'

They all went back to bed again. Julian didn't go to sleep for some time. Although he had told the others not to worry, he felt worried himself. He was sorry that Anne had been frightened, and somehow the boldness of the burglar in climbing up to a bedroom worried him, too. He must have been determined to get in somehow.

Joan, the cook, slept through all the disturbance. Julian wouldn't wake her. 'No,' he said, 'don't tell her anything about it. She'd want to send telegrams to Uncle Quentin or something.'

So Joan knew nothing about the night's happenings, and they heard her cheerfully humming in the kitchen the next morning as she cooked bacon and eggs and tomatoes for their breakfast.

Anne was rather ashamed of herself when she woke up and remembered the fuss she had made. The Face was rather dim in her memory now. She half wondered if she had dreamed it all. She asked Julian if he thought she might have had a bad dream.

'Quite likely,' said Julian, cheerfully, very glad that Anne should think this. 'More than likely! I wouldn't worry about it any more, if I were you.'

He didn't tell Anne that he had examined the thickly-growing ivy outside the window, and had found clear traces of the night-climber. Part of the sturdy clinging ivy-stem had come away from the wall, and beneath the window were strewn broken-off ivy leaves. Julian showed them to Dick.

'There *was* somebody,' he said. 'What a nerve he had, climbing right up to the window like that. A real cat-burglar!'

There were no footprints to be seen anywhere in the garden. Julian didn't expect to find any, for the ground was dry and hard.

The day was very fine and warm again. 'I vote we do what we did yesterday – go off to the beach and bathe,' said Dick. 'We might take a picnic lunch if Joan will give us one.'

'I'll help her to make it up for us,' said Anne, and she and George went off to beg for sandwiches and buns. Soon they were busy wrapping up a colossal lunch.

'Do for twelve, I should think!' said Joan, with a laugh.

'Here's a bottle of home-made lemonade, too. You can take as many ripe plums as you like as well. I shan't prepare any supper for you tonight – you'll not need it after this lunch.'

George and Anne looked at her in alarm. No *supper*! Then they caught the twinkle in her eye and laughed.

'We'll make all the beds and do our rooms before we go,' said Anne. 'And is there anything you want from the village?'

'No, not today. You hurry up with your jobs and get along to the beach,' said Joan. 'I'll be quite glad of a peaceful day to myself. I shall turn out the larder and the hall cupboards and the scullery, and enjoy myself in peace!'

Anne seemed quite to have forgotten her fright of the night before as they went down to the beach that day, chattering and laughing together. Even if she *had* thought about it, something soon happened that swept everything else from her mind.

The little ragamuffin girl was down on the beach again! She was alone. Her dreadful old father, or whatever he was, was not there.

George saw the girl first and scowled. Julian saw the scowl and then the girl, and made up his mind at once. He led the others firmly to where rocks jutted up from the beach, surrounded by limpid rock-pools.

'We'll be here today,' he said. 'It's so hot we'll be glad of the shade from the rocks. What about just here?'

'It's all right,' said George, half sulky and half amused at Julian for being so firm about things. 'Don't worry. I'm not having anything more to do with that smelly girl.'

'I'm glad to hear it,' said Julian. They had now turned a corner, and were out of sight of the girl. Big rocks ran in an upwards direction behind them, and jutted up all around them. Julian sat down in a lovely little corner, with rocks protecting them from the sun and the wind.

'Let's have a read before we bathe,' said Dick. 'I've got a mystery story here. I simply MUST find out who the thief is.'

He settled himself comfortably. Anne went to look for sea anemones in the pool. She liked the petal-like creatures that looked so like plants and weren't. She liked feeding them with bits of biscuit, seeing their 'petals' close over the fragments and draw them quickly inside.

George lay back and stroked Timmy. Julian began to sketch the rocks around, and the little pools. It was all very peaceful indeed.

Suddenly something landed on George's middle and made her jump. She sat up, and so did Timmy.

'What was that?' said George indignantly. 'Did you throw something at me, Dick?'

'No,' said Dick, his eyes glued to his book.

Something else hit George on the back of the neck, and she put her hand up with an exclamation. 'What's happening? Who's throwing things?'

She looked to see what had hit her. Lying on the sand was a small roundish thing. George picked it up. 'Why – it's a damson stone,' she said. And 'Ping'! Another one hit her on the shoulder. She leapt up in a rage.

She could see nobody at all. She waited for another damson stone to appear, but none did.

'I just wish I could draw your face, George,' said Julian, with a grin. 'I never saw such a frown in my life. Ooch!'

The 'ooch!' was nothing to do with George's frown; it was caused by another damson stone that caught Julian neatly behind the ear. He leapt to his feet too. A helpless giggle came from behind a rock some way behind and above them. George was up on the ledge in a second.

Behind one of the rocks sat the ragamuffin girl. Her pockets were full of damsons, some of them spilling out as she rolled on the rocks, laughing. She sat up when she saw George, and grinned.

'What do you mean, throwing those stones at us?' demanded George.

'I wasn't throwing them,' said the girl.

'Don't tell lies,' said George scornfully. 'You know you were.'

'I wasn't. I was just spitting them,' said the awful girl. 'Watch!' She slipped a stone into her mouth, took a deep breath and then spat out the stone. It flew straight at George and hit her sharply and squarely on the nose.

George looked so extremely surprised that Dick and Julian roared with laughter.

'Bet I can spit stones farther than any of you,' said the ragamuffin. 'Have some of my damsons and see.'

'Right!' said Dick promptly. 'If you win I'll buy you an ice-cream. If I do, you can clear off from here and not bother us any more. See?'

'Yes,' said the girl, and her eyes gleamed and danced. 'But I shall win!'

5

Ragamuffin Jo

GEORGE was most astonished at Dick. How very shocking to see who could spit damson stones out the farthest.

'It's all right,' said Julian to her in a low voice. 'You know how good Dick is at that sort of game. He'll win – and we'll send the girl scooting off, well and truly beaten.'

'I think you're horrible, Dick,' said George, in a loud voice. 'Horrible!'

'Who used to spit cherry-stones out and try and beat me last year?' said Dick at once. 'Don't be so high-and-mighty, George.'

Anne came slowly back from her pool, wondering why the others were up on the rocks. Damson stones began to rain round her. She stopped in astonishment. Surely – surely it couldn't be the others doing that? A stone hit her on her bare arm, and she squealed.

The ragamuffin girl won handsomely. She managed to get her stones at least three feet farther than Dick. She lay back, laughing, her teeth gleaming very white indeed.

'You owe me an ice-cream,' she said, in her sing-song

voice. Julian wondered if she was Welsh. Dick looked at her, marvelling that she managed to get her stones so far.

'I'll buy you the ice-cream, don't worry,' he said. 'Nobody's ever beaten me before like that, not even Stevens, a boy at school with a most enormous mouth.'

'I do think you really are dreadful,' said Anne. 'Go and buy her the ice-cream and tell her to go home.'

'I'm going to eat it here,' said the girl, and she suddenly looked exactly as mulish and obstinate as George did when she wanted something she didn't think she would get.

'You look like George now!' said Dick, and immediately wished he hadn't. George glared at him, furious.

'What! That nasty, rude tangly-haired girl like *me*!' stormed George. 'Pooh! I can't bear to go near her.'

'Shut up,' said Dick, shortly. The girl looked surprised.

'What does she mean?' she asked Dick. 'Am I nasty? You're as *rude* as I am, anyway.'

'There's an ice-cream man,' said Julian, afraid that the hot-tempered George would fly at the girl and slap her. He whistled to the man, who came to the edge of the rocks and handed out six ice-creams.

'Here you are,' said Julian, handing one to the girl. 'You eat that up and go.'

They all sat and ate ice-creams, George still scowling. Timmy gulped his at once as usual. 'Look – he's had all his,' marvelled the girl. 'I call that a waste. Here, boy – have a bit of mine!'

To George's annoyance, Timmy licked up the bit of ice-cream thrown to him by the girl. How *could* Timmy accept anything from her?

Dick couldn't help being amused by this queer, bold little girl, with her tangled short hair and sharp darting eyes. He suddenly saw something that made him feel uncomfortable.

606

On her chin the girl had a big black bruise. 'I say,' said Dick, '*I* didn't give you that bruise yesterday, did I?'

'What bruise? Oh, this one on my chin?' said the girl, touching it. 'Yes, that's where you hit me when you sent me flying. *I* don't mind. I've had plenty worse ones from my Dad.'

'I'm sorry I hit you,' said Dick, awkwardly. 'I honestly thought you were a boy. What's your name?'

'Jo,' said the girl.

'But that's a *boy's* name,' said Dick.

'So's George. But you said she was a girl,' said Jo, licking the last bits of ice-cream from her fingers.

'Yes, but George is short for Georgina,' said Anne. 'What's Jo short for?'

'Don't know,' said Jo. 'I never heard. All I know is I'm a girl and my name is Jo.'

'It's probably short for Josephine,' said Julian. They all stared at the possible Josephine. The short name of Jo certainly suited her – but not the long and pretty name of Josephine.

'It's really queer,' said Anne, at last, 'but Jo *is* awfully like you, George – same short curly hair – only Jo's is terribly messy and tangly – same freckles, dozens of them – same turned-up nose . . .'

'Same way of sticking her chin up in the air, same scowl, same glare!' said Dick. George put on her fiercest glare at these remarks, which she didn't like at all.

'Well, all I can say I hope I haven't her layers of dirt and her sm –' she began, angrily. But Dick stopped her.

'She's probably not got any soap or hair-brush or anything. She'd be all right cleaned up. Don't be unkind, George.'

George turned her back. How *could* Dick stick up for that awful girl? 'Isn't she ever going?' she said. 'Or is she going to park herself on us all day long?'

'I'll go when I want to,' said Jo, and put on a scowl, so

exactly like George's that Julian and Dick laughed in surprise. Jo laughed, too, but George clenched her fists furiously. Anne looked on in distress. She wished Jo would go, then everything would be all right again.

'I like that dog,' said Jo, suddenly, and she leaned over to where Timmy lay beside George. She patted him with a hand that was like a little brown paw. George swung round.

'Don't touch my dog!' she said. '*He* doesn't like you, either!'

'Oh, but he does,' said Jo, surprisingly. 'All dogs like *me*. So do cats. I can make your dog come to me as easy as anything.'

'Try!' said George, scornfully. 'He won't go to *you*! Will you, Tim?'

Jo didn't move. She began to make a queer little whining noise down in her throat, like a forlorn puppy. Timmy pricked up his ears at once. He looked inquiringly at Jo. Jo stopped making the noise and held out her hand.

Timmy looked at it and turned away – but when he heard the whining again he got up, listening. He stared intently at Jo. Was this a kind of god-girl, that she could so well speak his language?

Jo flung herself on her face and went on with the small, whining noises that sounded as if she were a small dog in pain or sorrow. Timmy walked over to her and sat down, his head on one side, puzzled. Then he suddenly bent down and licked the girl's half-hidden face. She sat up at once and put her arms round Timmy's neck.

'Come here, Timmy,' said George, jealously. Timmy shook off the brown arms that held him and walked over to George at once.

Jo laughed.

'See? I made him come to me and give me one of his best licks! I can do that to any dog.'

'How can you?' asked Dick, in wonder. He had never

608

seen Timmy make friends before with anyone who was disliked by George.

'I don't know, really,' said Jo, pushing back her hair again, as she sat up. 'I reckon it's in the family. My mother was in a circus, and she trained dogs for the ring. We had dozens – lovely they were. I loved them all.'

'Where is your mother?' asked Julian. 'Is she still in the circus?'

'No. She died,' said Jo. 'And I left the circus with my Dad. We've got a caravan. Dad was an acrobat till he hurt his foot.'

The four children remembered how the man had dragged his foot as he walked. They looked silently at dirty little Jo. What a strange life she must have led!

'She's dirty, she's probably very good at telling lies and thieving, but she's got pluck,' thought Julian. 'Still, I'll be glad when she goes.'

'I wish I hadn't given her that awful bruise,' thought Dick. 'I wonder what she'd be like cleaned up and brushed? She looks as if a little kindness would do her good.'

'I'm sorry for her, but I don't much like her,' thought Anne.

'I don't believe a word she says!' thought George angrily. 'Not one word! She's a humbug. And I'm *ashamed* of Timmy for going to her. I feel very cross with him.'

'Where's your father?' said Julian at last.

'Gone off somewhere to meet somebody,' said Jo vaguely. 'I'm glad. He was in one of his tempers this morning. I went and hid under the caravan.'

There was a silence. 'Can I stay with you today till my Dad comes back?' said Jo suddenly, in her sing-song voice. 'I'll wash myself if you like. I'm all alone today.'

'No. We don't want you,' said George, feeling as if she really couldn't bear Jo any longer. 'Do we, Anne?'

Anne didn't like hurting anyone. She hesitated. 'Well,' she said at last, 'perhaps Jo *had* better go.'

'Yes,' said Julian. 'It's time you scooted off now, Jo. You've had a long time with us.'

Jo looked at Dick with mournful eyes, and touched the

610

bruise on her chin as if it hurt her. Dick felt most uncomfortable again. He looked round at the others.

'Don't you think she could stay and share our picnic?' he said. 'After all – she can't *help* being dirty and – and . . .'

'It's all right,' said Jo, suddenly scrambling up. 'I'm going! There's my Dad!'

They saw the man in the distance, dragging his foot as he walked. He caught sight of Jo and gave a shrill and piercing whistle. Jo made a face at them all, an impudent, ugly, insolent face.

'I don't like you!' she said. Then she pointed at Dick. 'I only like *him* – he's nice. Yah to the rest of you!'

And off she went like a hare over the sand, her bare feet hardly touching the ground.

'What an extraordinary girl!' said Julian. 'I don't feel we've seen the last of her yet!'

6

What happened in the night?

THAT night Anne began to look rather scared as darkness fell. She was remembering the Face at the Window!

'It won't come again, Ju, will it?' she said to her big brother half a dozen times.

'No, Anne. But if you like I'll come and lie down on George's bed instead of George tonight, and stay with you all night long,' said Julian.

Anne considered this and then shook her head. 'No. I think I'd almost rather have George and Timmy. I mean – George and I – and even you – might be scared of Faces, but Timmy wouldn't. He'd simply leap at them.'

'You're quite right,' said Julian. 'He would. All right then, I won't keep you company – but you'll see, nothing whatever will happen tonight. Anyway, if you like, we'll all close our bedroom windows and fasten them, even if we are too hot for anything – then we'll know nobody can possibly get in.'

So that night Julian not only closed all the doors and windows downstairs as he had done the night before (except the tiny pantry window that wouldn't shut), but he also shut and fastened all the ones upstairs.

'What about Joan's window?' asked Anne.

'She *always* sleeps with it shut, summer and winter,' said Julian, with a grin. 'Country folk often do. They think the night air's dangerous. Now you've nothing at all to worry about, silly.'

So Anne went to bed with her mind at rest. George drew the curtains across their window so that even if the Face came again they wouldn't be able to see it!

'Let Timmy out for me, Julian, will you?' called George. 'Anne doesn't want me to leave her, even to take old Timmy out for his last walk. Just open the door and let him out. He'll come in when he's ready.'

'Right!' called Julian, and opened the front door. Timmy trotted out, tail wagging. He loved his last sniff round. He liked to smell the trail of the hedgehog who was out on his night-rounds; he liked to put his nose down a rabbit-hole and listen to stirrings down below; and he loved to follow the meanderings of rats and mice round by the thick hedges.

'Isn't Timmy in yet?' called George from the top of the stairs. 'Do call him, Ju. I want to get into bed. Anne's half-asleep already.'

'He'll be in in a moment,' said Julian, who wanted to finish his book. 'Don't fuss.'

But no Timmy had appeared even when he had finished his book. Julian went to the door and whistled. He listened for Timmy to come. Then, hearing nothing, he whistled once more.

This time he heard the sound of pattering footsteps coming up the path to the door. 'Oh there you are, Tim,' said Julian. 'What have you been up to? Chasing rabbits or something?'

Timmy wagged his tail feebly. He didn't jump up at Julian as he usually did. 'You look as if you've been up to some mischief, Tim,' said Julian. 'Go on – up to bed with you – and mind you bark if you hear the smallest sound in the night.'

'Woof,' said Timmy, in rather a subdued voice, and went upstairs. He climbed on to George's bed and sighed heavily.

'What a sigh!' said George. 'And what have you been eating, Timmy? Pooh – you've dug up some frightful old bone, I know you have. I've a good mind to push you off my bed. I suppose you suddenly remembered one you buried months ago. Pooh!'

Timmy wouldn't be pushed off the bed. He settled down to sleep, his nose on George's feet as usual. He snored a little, and woke George in about half an hour.

'Shut up, Timmy,' she said, pushing him with her feet. Anne woke up, alarmed.

'What is it, George?' she whispered, her heart thumping.

'Nothing. Only Timmy snoring. Hark at him. He won't stop,' said George, irritated. 'Wake up, Timmy, and stop snoring.'

Timmy moved sleepily and settled down again. He stopped snoring and George and Anne fell sound asleep. Julian woke once, thinking he heard something fall – but hearing Timmy gently snoring again through the open doors of the two rooms, he lay down, his mind at rest.

If the noise had *really* been a noise Timmy would have heard it, no doubt about that. George always said that Timmy slept with one ear open.

Julian heard nothing more till Joan went downstairs at seven o'clock. He heard her go into the kitchen and do something to the kitchen grate. He turned over and fell asleep again.

He was wakened suddenly twenty minutes later by loud screams from downstairs. He sat up and then leapt out of bed at once. He rushed downstairs. Dick followed him.

614

'Look at this! The master's study – turned upside down – those drawers ransacked! The safe's open, too. Mercy me, who's been here in the night – with all the doors locked and bolted, too!' Joan wailed loudly and wrung her hands as she gazed at the untidy room.

'I say!' said Dick, horrified. 'Someone's been searching for something pretty thoroughly! Even got the safe open – and wrenched the drawer out.'

'How did he get in?' said Julian, feeling bewildered. He went round the house, looking at doors and windows.

Except for the kitchen door, which Joan said she had unlocked and unbolted herself as soon as she came down, not a window or door had been touched. All were fastened securely.

Anne came down, looking scared. 'What's the matter?' she said. But Julian brushed her aside. How did that burglar get in? That was what he wanted to know. Through one of the *upstairs* windows, he supposed – one that somebody had opened last night after he had fastened it. Perhaps in the girls' room?

But no – not one window was open. All were fastened securely, including Joan's. Then a thought struck him as he looked into George's room. Why hadn't Timmy barked? After all, there must have been quite a bit of noise, however quiet the thief had been. He had himself heard something and had awakened. Why hadn't Timmy, then?

George was trying to pull Timmy off the bed. 'Ju, Ju! There's something wrong with Timmy. He won't wake up!' she cried. 'He's breathing so heavily, too – just listen to him! And what's the matter downstairs? What's happened?'

Julian told her shortly while he examined Timmy. 'Somebody got in last night – your father's study's in the most awful mess – absolutely ransacked from top to bottom, safe and all. Goodness knows how the fellow got in to do it.'

'How awful!' said George, looking very pale. 'And now something's wrong with Tim. He didn't wake up last night when the burglar came – he's ill, Julian!'

'No, he's not. He's been doped,' said Julian, pulling back Timmy's eyelids. 'So *that's* why he was so long outside last night! Somebody gave him some meat or something with dope in – some kind of drug. And he ate it, and slept so soundly that he never heard a thing – and isn't even awake yet.'

'Oh, Julian – will he be all right?' asked George

616

anxiously, stroking Timmy's motionless body. 'But how *could* he take any food from a stranger in the night?'

'Maybe he picked it up – the burglar may have flung it down hoping that Timmy would eat it,' said Julian. 'Now I understand why he looked so sheepish when he came in. He didn't even jump up and lick me.'

'Oh, dear – Timmy, do, do wake up,' begged poor George, and she shook the big dog gently. He groaned a little and snuggled down again.

'Leave him,' said Julian. 'He'll be all right. He's not poisoned, only drugged. Come down and see the damage!'

George was horrified at the state of her father's study. 'They were after his two special books of American notes, I'm sure they were,' she said. 'Father said that any other country in the world would be glad to have those. Whatever are we to do?'

'Better get in the police,' said Julian, gravely. 'We can't manage this sort of thing ourselves. And do you know your father's address in Spain?'

'No,' wailed George. 'He and Mother said they were going to have a *real* holiday this time – no letters to be forwarded, and no address left till they had been settled somewhere for a few days. Then they'd telegraph it.'

'Well, we'll certainly have to get the police in, then,' said Julian, looking rather white and stern. George glanced at him. He seemed suddenly very grown-up indeed. She watched him go out of the room. He went into the hall and rang up the police station. Joan was very relieved.

'Yes, get in the police, that's what we ought to do,' she said. 'There's that nice Constable Wilkins, and that other one with the red face, what's he called – Mr Donaldson. I'll be making some coffee for them when they come.'

She cheered up considerably at the thought of handing out cups of her good hot coffee to two interested police-men, who would ask her plenty of questions that she

617

would be only too delighted to answer. She bustled off to the kitchen.

The four children stared silently at the ruins of the study. What a mess! Could it ever be cleared up? Nobody would know what was gone till Uncle Quentin came back. How furious he would be.

'I hope nothing very important has been taken,' said Dick. 'It looks as if somebody knew there was something valuable here, and meant to get it!'

'And has probably got it,' said Julian. 'Hallo – that must be the police! Come on – I can see it will be a long time before we get our breakfast this morning!'

7

Policemen in the house

THE police were very, very thorough. The children got tired of them long before lunch-time. Joan didn't. She made them cups of coffee and put some of her home-made buns on a plate and sent Anne to pick up ripe plums. She felt proud to think that it was she who had discovered the ransacked study.

There were two policemen. One was a sergeant, rather solemn and very correct. He interviewed each of the children and asked them exactly the same questions. The other man went over the study bit by bit, very thoroughly indeed.

'Looking for finger-prints, I suppose,' said Anne. 'Oh dear – when can we go and bathe?'

The thing that puzzled everyone, the police included, was – how did the thief or thieves get in? Both policemen went round the house, slowly and deliberately trying every door and window still locked or fastened. They stood and looked at the pantry window for some time.

'Got in there, I suppose,' said one of them.

'Must have been as small as a monkey then,' said the other. He turned to Anne, who was the smallest of the four children. 'Could you squeeze through there, Missy, do you think?'

'No,' said Anne. 'But I'll try if you like.' So she tried – but she stuck fast before she got even half-way through, and Julian had to pull hard to get her down again.

'Have you any idea what has been stolen, sir?' the sergeant asked Julian, who seemed extraordinarily grown-up that morning.

'No, sergeant – none of us has,' said Julian. 'Not even George here, who knows her father's work better than any of us. The only thing we know is that my uncle went to America to lecture a short time ago – and he brought back two notebooks, full of valuable diagrams and notes. He did say that other countries might be very glad to get hold of those. I expect they were in that safe.'

'Well – they'll certainly be gone then,' said the sergeant, shutting his own fat notebook with a snap. 'Pity when people leave such things in an ordinary safe – and then go off without leaving an address. Can't we possibly get in touch with him? This may be terribly important.'

'I know,' said Julian, looking worried. 'We shall have an address in a day or two – but I honestly don't see how we can get in touch before then.'

'Right,' said the sergeant. 'Well – we'll go now – but we'll bring back a photographer with us after lunch to photograph the room – then your cook can tidy it up. I know she's longing to.'

'Coming back *again*!' said Anne, when the two men had solemnly walked down the path, mounted very solid-looking bicycles, and gone sailing down the lane. 'Good gracious! Have we got to answer questions all over again?'

'Well, we'll go down to the beach and take a boat and go rowing,' said Julian, with a laugh. 'We'll be out of reach then. I don't see that we can give them any more help. I must say it's all very peculiar – I wish to goodness I knew how the thief got in.'

George had been very quiet and subdued all the morning. She had worried about Timmy, fearing that he had been poisoned, and not merely drugged, as Julian had said. But Timmy was now quite recovered, except that he seemed a bit sleepy still, and not inclined to gambol round in his usual ridiculous way. He looked extremely sheepish, too.

'I can't think why Timmy looks like that,' said George, puzzled. 'He usually only puts that look on when he's done something he's ashamed of – or got into mischief. He couldn't possibly know, could he, that whatever he picked up and ate last night was something he shouldn't eat?'

'No,' said Dick. 'He's sensible though, I think, not to touch poisoned meat – but he couldn't know if some harmless sleeping powder had been put into anything. It might have no smell and no taste. Perhaps he's just ashamed of being so sleepy!'

'If only he'd been awake!' groaned George. 'He would have heard any noise downstairs at once – and he'd have barked and waked us all, and flown downstairs himself to attack whoever was there! Why, oh why didn't I take him out myself last night as I usually do?'

'It was a chapter of accidents,' said Julian. 'You didn't take him out, so he was alone – and it happened that someone was waiting there with drugged food – which he either found or took from the thief . . .'

'No,' said George. 'Timmy would never, never take anything from someone he didn't know. I've always taught him that.'

'Well, he got it somehow – and slept through the very night he should have been awake,' said Julian. 'What I'm so afraid of, George, is that the thieves have got your father's two American notebooks. They seem to have left most of the stuff – piles and piles of books of all kinds, filled with your father's tiny handwriting.'

Joan came in to say lunch was ready. She told the children that the policemen had eaten every one of her home-made buns. She still felt important and excited, and was longing to get out to the village and tell everyone the news.

'You'd better stay in and give the policemen a good tea,' said Julian. 'They're coming back with a photographer.'

'Then I'd better do another baking,' said Joan, pleased.

'Yes. Make one of your chocolate cakes,' said Anne.

'Oh, do you think they'd like one?' said Joan.

'Not for *them*, Joan – for us, of course!' said George. 'Don't waste one of your marvellous chocolate cakes on policemen. Can you make us up a picnic tea? We're fed up with being indoors – we're going out in a boat.'

Joan packed them a good tea after they had had their lunch and they all set off before the police came back. Timmy was much less sleepy now and did a little caper round them as they walked to the beach. George brightened up at once.

'He's getting better,' she said. 'Timmy, I simply shan't let you out of my sight now! If anyone's going to dope you again they'll have to do it under my very nose.'

They had a lovely time out in George's boat. They went half-way to Kirrin Island and bathed from the boat, diving in and having swimming races till they were tired out. Timmy joined them, though he couldn't swim nearly as fast as they could.

'He doesn't really *swim*,' said Anne. 'He just tries to *run* through the water. I wish he'd let me ride on his back like a sea-dog – but he always slips away under me when I try.'

They got back about six o'clock to find that the policemen had eaten the whole of the chocolate cake that Joan had made, besides an extraordinary amount of scones and buns.

622

Also the study was not tidied up, and a man had come to mend the safe. Everything was safely back there, though the police had told Joan that if there was anything of real value it should be handed to them till George's father came back.

'But we don't know which of all those papers are valuable!' said Julian. 'Well – we'll have to wait till Uncle Quentin cables us – and that may not be for days. Anyway, I don't expect we'll be worried by the thief again – he's got what he wanted.'

The exciting happenings of the day had made them all tired except Julian. 'I'm off to bed,' said Dick, about nine o'clock. 'Anne, why don't you go? You look fagged out.'

'Yes, I will,' said Anne. 'Coming, George?'

'I'm going to take Timmy out for his last walk,' said George. 'I shall never let him go out alone at night again. Come on, Timmy. If you want to go to bed I'll lock up the front door, Ju.'

'Right,' said Julian. 'I'll go up in a minute. I don't fancy staying down here by myself tonight. I'll fasten everything and lock up, except the front door. Don't forget to put up the chain, too, George – though I'm pretty certain we don't need to expect any more burglaries!'

'Or faces at the window,' said Anne, at once.

'No,' said Julian. 'There won't be any more of those either. Good night, Anne – sleep well!'

Anne and Dick went upstairs. Julian finished the paper he was reading, and then got up to go round the house and lock up. Joan was already upstairs, dreaming of policemen eating her chocolate cakes.

George went out with Timmy. He ran eagerly to the gate and then set off down the lane for his usual night walk with George. At a gate in the lane he suddenly stood still and growled as if he saw something unusual.

'Silly, Timmy!' said George, coming up. 'It's only

somebody camping in a caravan! Haven't you seen a caravan before? Stop growling!'

They went on, Timmy sniffing into every rathole and rabbit-hole, enjoying himself thoroughly. George was enjoying the walk, too. She didn't hurry – Julian could always go up to bed if he didn't want to wait.

Julian did go up to bed. He left the front door ajar, and went yawning upstairs, suddenly feeling sleepy. He got into bed quietly and quickly seeing that Dick was already asleep. He lay awake listening for George. When he was half asleep, he heard the front door shut.

'There she is,' he thought, and turned over to go to sleep.

But it wasn't George. Her bed was empty all that night, and nobody knew, not even Anne. George and Timmy didn't come back!

8

Where can George be?

ANNE woke up in the night, feeling thirsty. She whispered across the room:

'George! Are you awake?'

There was no answer, so, very cautiously and quietly Anne got herself a drink from the decanter on the washstand. George was sometimes cross if she was awakened in the middle of the night. Anne got back into bed, not guessing that George hadn't answered because she wasn't there!

She fell asleep and didn't wake till she heard Dick's voice. 'Hey, you two – get up; it's a quarter to eight. We're going for a bathe!'

Anne sat up, yawning. Her eyes went to George's bed. It was empty. More than that, it was all neat and tidy, as if it had just been made!

'*Well!*' said Anne in astonishment. 'George is up already, and has even made her bed. She *might* have waked me, and I could have gone out with her. It's such a lovely day. I suppose she's taken Timmy for an early morning walk, like she sometimes does.'

Anne slipped into her bathing costume and ran to join the boys. They went downstairs together, their bare feet padding on the carpet.

'George has gone out already,' said Anne. 'I expect she woke early and took Timmy; I never even heard her!'

Julian was now at the front door. 'Yes,' he said. 'The door isn't locked or bolted – George must have slipped down, undone it and then just pulled the door softly to. How very considerate of her! Last time she went out early she banged the door so hard that she woke everyone in the house!'

'She may have gone fishing in her boat,' said Dick. 'She said yesterday she'd like to some early morning when the tide was right. She'll probably arrive complete with stacks of fish for Joan to cook.'

They looked out to sea when they got to the beach. There was a boat far out on the water with what looked like two people in it, fishing.

'I bet that's George and Timmy,' said Dick. He yelled and waved his hands, but the boat was too far away, and nobody waved back. The three of them plunged into the cold waves. Brrrr-rrr-rrr!

'Lovely!' said Anne, when they came out again, the drops of sea-water running down their bodies and glistening in the early morning sun. 'Let's have a run now.'

They chased one another up and down the beach, and then, glowing and very hungry, went back to breakfast.

'Where's George?' asked Joan, as she brought in their breakfast. 'I see her bed's made and all – what's come over her?'

'I think she's out fishing with Timmy,' said Dick. 'She was up and about long before we were.'

626

'I never heard her go,' said Joan. 'She must have been very quiet. There you are now – there's a fine breakfast for you – sausages and tomatoes and fried eggs!'

'O-o-o-o-h, lovely,' said Anne. 'And you've done the sausages just how I like them, Joan – all bursting their skins. Do you think we'd better eat George's too? She's still out in the boat. She may not be back for ages.'

'Well, then you'd better eat her share,' said Joan. 'I've no doubt she took something out of the larder before she went. Pity I didn't lock it last night, as usual!'

They finished Goerge's share between them and then started on toast and marmalade. After that Anne went to help Joan make the beds and dust and mop. Julian and Dick went off to the village to do the morning's shopping at the grocer's.

Nobody worried about George at all. Julian and Dick came back from their shopping and saw the little boat still out on the sea.

'George will be absolutely starving by the time she comes back,' said Julian. 'Perhaps she's got one of her moods on and wants to be alone. She was awfully upset about Timmy being drugged.'

They met the ragamuffin Jo. She was walking along the beach, collecting wood, and she looked sullen and dirtier than ever.

'Hallo, Jo!' called Dick. She looked up and came towards them without a smile. She looked as if she had been crying. Her small brown face was streaked where the tears had run through the dirt.

'Hallo!' she said, looking at Dick. She looked so miserable that Dick felt touched.

'What's the matter, kid?' he said, kindly.

Tears trickled down Jo's face as she heard the kindness in his voice. She rubbed them away and smudged her face more than ever.

'Nothing,' she said. 'Where's Anne?'

627

'Anne's at home, and George is out in that boat with Timmy fishing,' said Dick, pointing out to sea.

'Oh!' said Jo, and turned away to go on with her collecting of wood. Dick went after her.

'Hey!' he said. 'Don't go off like that. You just tell me what's wrong with you this morning.'

He caught hold of Jo and swung her round to face him. He looked closely at her and saw that she now had two bruises on her face – one going yellow, that he had given

her when he had sent her flying two or three days before –
and a new one, dark purple.

'Where did you get *that* bruise?' he said, touching it
lightly.

'That was my dad,' said Jo. 'He's gone off and left
me – taken the caravan and all! I wanted to go, too; but he
wouldn't let me into the caravan. And when I hammered
at the door, he came out and pushed me down the steps.
That's when I got this bruise – and I've got another on my
leg, too.'

Dick and Julian listened in horror. What kind of a life
was this that Jo had to live? The boys sat down on the
beach, and Dick pulled Jo down between them.

'But surely your father is coming back?' asked Julian.
'Is the caravan your only home?'

'Yes,' said Jo. 'I've never had another home. We've
always lived in a caravan. Mum did, too, when she was
alive. Things were better then. But this is the first time
Dad's gone off without me.'

'But – how are you going to live?' asked Dick.

'Dad said Jake would give me money to buy food,' said
Jo. 'But only if I do what he tells me. I don't like Jake. He's
mean.'

'Who's Jake?' asked Julian, most astonished at all this.

'Jake's a gipsy fellow. He knows my father,' said Jo.
'He's always turning up for a day or two, and going away
again. If I wait about here, he'll come and give me five
pence or so, I expect.'

'What will he tell you to do?' said Dick, puzzled. 'It all
seems very queer and horrible to me. You're only a kid.'

'Oh, he may tell me to go poaching with him or – or –
well, there's things we do that folks like you don't,' said Jo,
suddenly realizing that Dick and Julian would not at all
approve of some of the things she did. 'I hope he gives me
some money today, though. I haven't got any at all, and
I'm hungry.'

Dick and Julian looked at one another. To think that in these days there should be a forlorn waif like Jo, going in fear of others, and often hungry and lonely.

Dick put his hand in the shopping basket and pulled out a packet of chocolate and some biscuits. 'Here you are,' he said. 'Tuck into these – and if you'd like to go to the kitchen door some time today and ask Joan, our cook, for a meal, she'll give you one. I'll tell her about you.'

'Folks don't like me at kitchen doors,' said Jo, cramming biscuits into her mouth. 'They're afraid I'll steal something.' She glanced up at Dick. 'And I do,' she said.

'You shouldn't do that,' said Dick.

'Well, wouldn't you, if you were so hungry you couldn't even bear to look at a baker's cart?' said Jo.

'No – I don't think so. At least, I hope not,' said Dick, wondering what he really would feel like if he were starving. 'Where's this Jake fellow?'

'I don't know. Somewhere about,' said Jo. 'He'll find me when he wants me. I've got to stay on the beach, Dad said. So I couldn't come to your house, anyway. I dursent leave here.'

The boys got up to go, worried about this little ragamuffin. But what could they do? Nothing, except feed her and give her money. Dick had slipped five pence into her hand, and she had pocketed it without a word, her eyes gleaming.

George was still not home by lunch-time; and now Julian for the first time began to feel anxious. He slipped out to the beach to see if the boat was still at sea. It was just pulling in – and with a sinking heart Julian saw that it was not George and Timmy who were in it, but two boys.

He went to look for George's boat – and there it was, high up on the boat-beach with many others. George had not been out in it at all!

He ran back to Kirrin Cottage and told the others. They

630

were at once as anxious as he was. What *could* have become of George?

'We'll wait till tea-time,' said Julian. 'Then if she's not back we'll really have to do something about it – tell the police, I should think. But she *has* sometimes gone off for the day before, so we'll just wait a bit longer.'

Tea-time came – but no George, and no Timmy. Then they heard someone pattering up the garden path – was it Timmy? They leaned out of the window to see.

'It's Jo,' said Dick, in disappointment. 'She's got a note or something. Whatever does *she* want?'

9

An extraordinary message – and a plan

JULIAN opened the front door. Jo silently gave him a plain envelope. Julian tore it open, not knowing what in the least to expect. Jo turned to go – but Julian put out his hand and caught hold of her firmly, whilst he read the note in complete amazement.

'Dick!' he called. 'Hold on to Jo. Don't let her go. Better take her indoors. This is serious.'

Jo wasn't going to be taken indoors. She squealed, and wriggled like an eel. Then she began to kick Dick viciously with her bare feet.

'Let me go! I'm not doing any harm. I only brought you that note!'

'Stop squealing and being silly,' said Dick. 'I don't want to hurt you, you know that. But you must come indoors.'

But Jo wouldn't stop wriggling and pulling and kicking. She looked scared out of her life. It was as much as Dick and Julian could do to get the little wriggler into the dining-room and shut the door. Anne followed, looking very frightened. Whatever was happening?

'Listen to this,' said Julian, when the door was shut. 'It's unbelievable!' He held out the typewritten note for the others to see as he read it out loud.

'We want the second notebook, the one with figures in, and we mean to have it. Find it and put it under the last stone on the crazy paving path at the bottom of the garden. Put it there tonight.

'We have got the girl and the dog. We will set them free when we have what we want from you. If you tell the police, neither the girl nor the dog will come back. The house will be watched to see that nobody leaves it to warn the police. The telephone wires are cut.

'When it is dark, put the lights on in the front room and all three of you sit there with the maid Joan, so that we can keep a watch on you. Let the big boy leave the house at eleven o'clock, shining a torch and put the notebook where we said. He must then go back to the lighted room. You will hear a hoot like an owl when we have collected it. The girl and the dog will then be returned.'

This amazing and terrifying note made Anne burst into tears and cling to Julian's arm.

'Julian! Julian! George can't have come back from her walk with Timmy last night! She must have been caught then – and Timmy, too. Oh, why didn't we start hunting for her then?'

Julian looked very grim and white. He was thinking hard. 'Yes – someone was lying in wait, I've no doubt – and she and Timmy were kidnapped. Then the kidnappers – or one of them – came back to the house and shut the front door to make it seem as if George was back. And someone has probably been hanging round all day to find out whether we're worried about George, or just think she's gone off for the day!'

'Who gave you the note?' said Dick, sharply, to the scared Jo.

She trembled.

'A man,' she said.

'What sort of a man?' asked Julian.

'I don't know,' said Jo.

'Yes, you do,' said Dick. 'You *must* tell, Jo.'

Jo looked sullen. Dick shook her, and she tried to get away. But he held her far too tightly. 'Go on – tell us what the fellow was like,' he said.

'He was tall and had a long beard and a long nose and brown eyes,' rattled off Jo suddenly. 'And he was dressed in fisherman's clothes, and – he spoke foreign.'

The two boys looked sternly at her. 'I believe you're making all that up, Jo,' said Julian.

'I'm not,' said Jo sulkily. 'I'd never seen him before, so there.'

'Jo,' said Anne, taking Jo's brown little paw in hers, 'tell us truly anything you know. We're so very worried about George.' Tears sprang out of her eyes as she spoke, and she gave a little wail.

'Serve that George-girl right if she's got taken away,' said Jo fiercely. 'She was rude to me – she's crool and unkind. Serve her right, I say. I wouldn't tell you anything – not even if I knew something to tell.'

'You *do* know something,' said Dick. 'You're a bad little girl, Jo. I shan't have anything more to do with you. I felt sorry and unhappy about you, but now I don't.'

Jo looked sullen again, but her eyes were bright with tears. She turned away. 'Let me go,' she said. 'I tell you, that fellow gave me fifteen pence to bring this note to you, and that's all I know. And I'm *glad* George is in trouble. People like her deserve it, see!'

'Let her go,' said Julian wearily. 'She's like a savage little cat – all claws and spite. I thought there might be some good in her, but there isn't.'

634

'I thought so, too,' said Dick, letting go Jo's arm. 'I quite liked her. Well, go, Jo. We don't want you any more.'

Jo rushed to the door, wrenched it open, and fled down the hall and out of the house. There was a silence after she had gone.

'Julian,' whispered Anne. 'What are we going to do?'

Julian said nothing. He got up and went into the hall. He picked up the telephone receiver and put his ear to it, listening for the faint crackling that would tell him he was connected to the exchange. After a moment he put it back again.

'No connection,' he said. 'The wires have been cut, as the note said. And no doubt there's somebody on watch to see we don't slip out to give warning. This is all crazy. It can't be true.'

'But it is,' said Dick. 'Horribly true. Julian, do you know what notebook they want? I've no idea!'

'Nor have I,' said Julian. 'And it's impossible to go and hunt for it, because the safe has been mended and locked – and the police have the key.'

'Well, that's that, then,' said Dick. 'What are we going to do? Shall I slip out and warn the police?'

Julian considered. 'No,' he said at last. 'I think these people mean business. It would be terrible if anything happened to George. Also, you might be caught and spirited away yourself. There are people watching the house, don't forget.'

'But Julian – we can't just sit here and do nothing!' said Dick.

'I know. This will have to be thought about carefully,' said Julian. 'If only we knew where George had been taken to! We could rescue her then. But I can't see how we can find out.'

'If one of us went and hid down the bottom of the garden and waited to see whoever came to take up the notebook –

we could follow the fellow and maybe he'd lead us to where George is hidden,' suggested Dick.

'You forget that we've all got to sit in the lighted front room, so it would easily be spotted if one of us were missing,' said Julian. 'Even Joan has to sit there. This is all very stupid and melodramatic.'

'Does anyone come to the house this evening? Any of the tradesmen, for instance?' asked Anne, again in a whisper. She felt as if people must be all round the house, listening and watching!

'No. Else we could give them a note,' said Julian. Then he gave the table a rap that made the others jump. 'Wait a bit! Yes, of course – the paper-boy comes! Ours is almost the last house he delivers at. But perhaps it would be risky to give him a note. Can't we think of something better?'

'Listen,' said Dick, his eyes shining. 'I've got it! I know the paper-boy. He's all right. We'll have the front door open and yank him in as soon as he appears. And I'll go out immediately, with his cap on, and his satchel of papers, whistling – jump on his bike and ride away. And none of the watchers will know I'm not the boy! I'll come back when it's dark, sneak round the garden at the bottom and hide to watch who comes for the hidden notebook – and I'll follow him!'

'Good idea, Dick!' said Julian, turning it quickly over in his mind. 'Yes – it's possible. It would be better to watch and see who comes rather than tell the police – because if these kidnappers mean business, George would certainly be in trouble once they knew we'd been able to get in touch with the police.'

'Won't the newspaper boy think it's queer?' asked Anne.

'Not very. He's a bit simple,' said Dick. 'He believes anything he's told. We'll make up something to satisfy him and give him such a good time that he'll want to keep visiting us!'

'About this notebook,' said Julian. 'We'd better get some kind of book out of one of the drawers and wrap it up with a note inside to say we hope it's the one. The fellow who comes to collect it will have some kind of parcel to take off with him to give to the kidnappers. It isn't likely he'd undo it and look at it – or even know if it was the right one or not.'

'Go and hunt out a book, Anne,' said Dick. 'I'll be looking out for the newspaper boy. He's not due till half-past seven, but I don't dare to risk missing him – and he may be early, you never know.'

Anne shot off to the study, thankful to have something to do. Her hands were trembling as she pulled out drawer after drawer to look for a big notebook that would do to wrap up in a parcel.

Julian went with Dick to the front door, to help him to deal with the unsuspecting newspaper boy. They stood there, patiently waiting, hearing the clock strike six o'clock, then half-past, then seven.

'Here he comes!' said Dick, suddenly. 'Now – get ready to yank him in! Hallo, Sid!'

10

Sid's wonderful evening

S<small>ID</small>, the paper-boy, was most amazed to find himself yanked quickly through the front door by Julian. He was even more amazed to find his very lurid check cap snatched off his head, and his bag of papers torn from his shoulder.

' 'Ere!' he said feebly. 'What you doing?'

'It's all right, Sid,' said Julian, holding him firmly. 'Just a joke. We've got a little treat in store for you.'

Sid didn't like jokes of this sort. He struggled, but soon gave it up. Julian was big and strong and very determined. Sid turned and watched Dick stride out with his bright check cap sideways on his head, and his paper-bag over his shoulder. He gasped when he saw Dick leap on the bicycle that he, Sid, had left by the gate, and go sailing off up the lane on it.

'What's he doing?' he asked Julian, amazed. 'Funny sort of joke this.'

'I know. Hope you don't mind,' said Julian, leading him firmly into the sitting-room.

'Somebody betted him he wouldn't deliver the papers,
maybe?' said Sid. 'So he's taken the bet on?'

'You're clever, you are, Sid,' said Julian, and Sid
beamed all over his round, simple face.

'Well, I hope he'll deliver them all right,' he said.
'Anyway, there's only two more, up at the farm. Yours is
the last house but one that I go to. When's he coming
back?'

'Soon,' said Julian. 'Will you stay and have supper with
us, Sid?'

Sid's eyes nearly fell out of his head. 'Supper with you folks?' he said. 'Coo! That'd be a rare treat!'

'All right. You sit and look at these books,' said Julian, giving him two or three story books belonging to Anne. 'I'll just go and tell our cook to make a specially nice supper for you.'

Sid was all at sea about this unexpected treat, but quite willing to accept a free meal and sit down. He sat beaming on the couch, turning over the pages of a fairy-story book. Coo! What would his mother say when she heard he'd had supper at Kirrin Cottage? She wouldn't half be surprised, thought Sid.

And now Julian had to tackle Joan, and get her to join in their little plot. He went into the kitchen and shut the door. He looked so grave that Joan was startled.

'What's the matter?' she said.

Julian told her. He told her about the kidnapping of George, and the strange note. He gave it to her to read. She sat down, her knees beginning to shake.

'It's the kind of thing you read in the papers, Master Julian,' she said, in rather a shaky voice. 'But it's queer when it happens to *you*! I don't like it – that's flat, I don't.'

'Nor do we,' said Julian, and went on to tell Joan all they had arranged to do. She smiled a watery smile when he told her how Dick had gone off as the paper-boy in order to watch who took the notebook that night, and described how surprised Sid was.

'That Sid!' she said. 'We'll never hear the last of it, down in the village – him being invited here to supper. He's simple, that boy, but there's no harm in him.

'I'll get him a fine supper, don't you worry. And I'll come and sit with you tonight in the lighted room – we'll play a card game, see? One that Sid knows – he's never got much beyond Snap and Happy Families.'

'That's a very good idea,' said Julian, who had been

wondering how in the world they could amuse Sid all the evening. 'We'll play Snap – and let him win!'

Sid was quite overcome at his wonderful evening. First there was what he called a 'smasher of a supper,' with ham and eggs and chip potatoes followed by jam tarts and a big chocolate mould, of which Sid ate about three-quarters.

'I'm partial to chocolate mould,' he explained to Anne. 'Joan knows that – she knows I'm partial to anything in the chocolate line. She's friendly with my Mum, so she knows. The things I'm partial to I like very much, see?'

Anne giggled and agreed. She was enjoying Sid, although she was very worried and anxious. But Sid was so comical. He didn't mean to be. He was just enjoying himself hugely, and he said so every other minute.

In fact, he was really a very nice guest to have. It wasn't everybody who could welcome everything with so much gusto and say how wonderful it was half a dozen times on end.

He went out to the kitchen after supper and offered to wash up for Joan. 'I always do it for Mum,' he said. 'I won't break a thing.' So he did the washing up and Anne did the drying. Julian thought it was a good thing to give her as much to do as possible, to stop her worrying.

Sid looked a bit taken-aback when he was asked to play games later on. 'Well – I dunno,' he said. 'I'm not much good at games. I did try to learn draughts, but all that jumping over one another got me muddled. If I want to jump over things I'll play leap-frog and do the thing properly.'

'Well – we did think of playing Snap,' said Julian, and Sid brightened up at once.

'Snap! That's right up my street!' he said. And so it was. His habit of shouting snap and collecting all the cards at the same moment as his shout, led to his winning quite a lot of games. He was delighted.

'This is a smasher of an evening,' he kept saying. 'Don't

641

know when I've enjoyed myself so much. Wonder how that brother of yours is getting on – hope he brings my bike back all right.'

'Oh, he will,' said Julian, dealing out the cards for the sixth game of Snap. They were all in the lighted sitting-room now, sitting round a table in the window – Julian, Joan, Anne and Sid. Anyone watching would see them clearly – and would certainly not guess that Sid, the fourth one, was the paper-boy and not Dick.

At eleven o'clock Julian left to put the parcel that Anne had carefully wrapped up under the stone at the bottom of the garden. She had found a big notebook she thought would do, one that didn't seem at all important, and had wrapped it in paper and tied it with string. Julian had slipped a note inside.

Here is the notebook. Please release our cousin at once. You will get into serious trouble if you hold her any longer.

He slipped down the garden and shone his torch on the crazy paving there. When he came to the last stone he found that it had been loosened. He lifted it up easily and put the parcel into a hollow that seemed to have been prepared ready for it. He took a cautious look round, wondering if Dick was hidden anywhere about, but could see no one.

He was back in the lighted sitting-room in under two minutes, yelling 'Snap' with the others. He played stupidly, partly because he wanted the delighted Sid to win and partly because he was wondering about Dick. Was he all right?

An outbreak of owls hooting loudly made them all jump. Julian glanced at Joan and Anne, and they nodded. They guessed that it was the signal to tell them that the parcel had been found and collected. Now they could get rid of Sid, and wait for Dick.

642

Joan disappeared and came back with cups of chocolate and some buns. Sid's eyes gleamed. Talk about an evening!

Another hour was spent in eating and drinking and hearing Sid relate details of all the most exciting games of Snap he had ever played. He then went on to talk of Happy Families and seemed inclined to stay a bit longer and have a game at that.

'Your Mum will be getting worried about you,' said Julian, looking at the clock. 'It's very late.'

'Where's my bike?' said Sid, realizing with sorrow that his 'smasher of an evening' was now over. 'Hasn't that brother of yours come back yet? Well, you tell him to leave it at my house in time for my paper-round tomorrow morning. And my cap, too. That's my Special Cap, that is. I'm very partial to that cap – it's a bit of a smasher.'

'It certainly is,' agreed Julian, who was now feeling very tired. 'Now listen, Sid. It's very late, and there may be bad folks about. If anyone speaks to you, run for your life, and don't stop till you get home.'

'Coo,' said Sid, his eyes nearly falling out of his head. 'Yes, I'll run all right.'

He shook hands solemnly with each of them and departed. He whistled loudly to keep his spirits up. The village policeman came unexpectedly round a corner on rubber soles and made him jump.

'Now then, young Sid,' said the policeman, sternly. 'What you doing out this time of night?'

Sid didn't wait to answer. He fled and when he got home there was his bicycle by the front gate, complete with checked cap and paper-bag. 'That was a bit of all right!' thought Sid.

He glanced in disappointment at the dark windows of his house. Mum was in bed and asleep. Now he would have to wait till morning to tell her of his most remarkable evening.

And now, what had happened to Dick? He had shot out of the house and sailed away on Sid's bicycle, with Sid's dazzling cap on his head. He thought he saw a movement in the hedge nearby and guessed someone was hidden there, watching. He deliberately slowed down, got off his bicycle and pretended to do something to the wheel. Let the watcher see his bag of papers and be deceived into thinking he was without any doubt the paper-boy.

644

He rode to the farm and delivered the two papers there, then down to the village where he left Sid's things outside his house. Then he went into the cinema for a long while – until it was dark and he could safely creep back to Kirrin Cottage.

He set off at last, going a very roundabout way indeed. He came to the back of Kirrin garden. Where should he hide? Was anyone already hidden there? If so, the game was up – and he'd be caught, too!

11

Dick makes a capture

DICK stood and listened, holding his breath. He could hear no sound except for the rustling of the trees around, and the sudden squeak of a field-mouse. It was a dark night and cloudy. Was there anyone hidden nearby, or could he find a hiding-place in safety and wait?

He thought for a few minutes, and decided that there wouldn't be anyone watching the back of the house now that it was dark. Julian and the others would be in full view of any watcher at the front, seated as they were in the lighted sitting-room – there would be no need for anyone to watch the back.

He debated where to hide and then made a quick decision. 'I'll climb a tree,' he thought. 'What about that one just near the crazy paving path? If the clouds clear away I could perhaps catch a glimpse of what the man's like who comes to collect the parcel. Then I'll shin quietly down the tree and stalk him.'

He climbed up into an oak tree that spread its broad

branches over the path. He wriggled down in a comfortable fork and set himself to wait patiently.

What time had that note said? Eleven o'clock. Yes – Julian was to go down at eleven o'clock and put the parcel under the stone. He listened for the church clock to strike. If the wind was in the right direction he would hear it clearly.

It struck just then. Half-past ten. Half an hour to wait. The waiting was the worst part. Dick put his hand into his pocket and brought out a bar of half-melted chocolate. He began to nibble it very gently, to make it last a long time.

The church clock struck a quarter to eleven. Dick finished the chocolate, and wondered if Julian would soon be along. Just as the clock began to chime the hour at eleven, the kitchen door opened and Dick saw Julian outlined in the opening. He had the parcel under his arm.

He saw Julian go swiftly down the path and sensed him looking all about. He dared not give the slightest hint to him that he was just above his head!

He heard Julian scrabble about in the path, and then drop the big stone back into its place. He watched the light of Julian's torch bobbing back up the path to the kitchen door. Then the door shut with a bang.

And now Dick could hardly breathe! Who would come for the parcel? He listened, stiff with excitement. The wind blew and a leaf rustled against the back of his neck making him jump. It felt as if a finger had touched him.

Five minutes went by and nobody came. Then he heard the slightest sound. Was that somebody crawling through the hedge? Dick strained his eyes but could only make out a deeper shadow that seemed to be moving. Then he could most distinctly hear somebody breathing hard as they tugged at the heavy stone! The parcel was being collected as arranged!

The stone plopped back. A shadow crept over to the

hedge again. Whoever had the parcel was now going off with it.

Dick dropped quietly down. He had rubber shoes on and made no noise. He slipped through a big gap in the hedge nearby and stood straining his eyes to find the man he wanted to follow. Ah – there was a shadow moving steadily down the field-path to the stile. Dick followed, keeping close to the hedge.

He kept well behind the moving shadow till it reached the stile, got over it and went into the lane beyond. When it got there it stopped, and a perfect fusillade of loud owl-hoots came to Dick's startled ears.

Of course! That was the signal that the parcel had been collected. Dick admired the excellent imitation of a little owl's loud, excited hooting.

The shadow stopped hooting and went on again. It obviously did not suspect that it might be followed and, although it moved quietly, it did not attempt to keep under cover. Down the lane it went and into a field.

Dick was about to follow when he heard the sound of voices. They were very low, and he couldn't hear a word. He crouched in the shadow of the gate, which was swung right back, leaving an entry into the field.

A loud noise made him jump. Then a brilliant light dazzled him and he felt glad he could duck down behind the gate. There was a car in the field. A car that had just started up its engine and switched on its lights. It was going, moving slowly down to the gate!

Dick tried his hardest to see who was in the car. He could make out only one man, and he was driving. It didn't seem as if anyone else was in the car at all. Where was the other fellow, then – the one who must have collected the parcel and given it to the man in the car? Had he been left behind? If so, Dick had better be care-ful!

The car was soon out in the lane. It gained speed and

then Dick heard it roaring off in the distance. He couldn't stalk a car, that was certain! He held his breath, listening for some movement of the other man who, he felt certain, was still there.

He heard a sniff and crouched lower still. Then a shadow passed quickly through the gate, turned back in the direction of Kirrin Cottage and was lost in the darkness of the lane.

In a trice Dick was after it again. At least he could track down *this* fellow! He must be going somewhere!

Down the lane to the stile. Over the stile and into the field. Across the field and back at the hedge that grew at the bottom of Kirrin Cottage.

Why was this fellow going back there? Dick was puzzled. He heard the shadow creeping through the hedge and he followed. He watched it go silently up the path and peer in at a darkened window.

'Going to get into the house again and ransack it, I suppose!' thought Dick, in a rage. He considered the shadowy figure by the window. It didn't look big. It must be a small man – one that Dick could tackle and bring to the ground. He could yell loudly for Julian, and maybe he could hold the fellow down till Julian came.

'And then perhaps *we* could do a little kidnapping, and a little bargaining, too,' thought Dick grimly. 'If *they* hold George as a hostage, we'll hold one of them, too! Tit for tat!'

He waited till the shadow left the window, and then he pounced. His victim went down at once with a yell.

Dick was surprised how small he was – but how he fought! He bit and scratched and heaved and kicked, and the two of them rolled over and over and over, breaking down Michaelmas daisies in the beds, and scratching legs and arms and faces on rose bushes. Dick yelled for Julian all the time.

'Julian! JULIAN! Help! JULIAN!'

Julian heard. He tore out at once. 'Dick, Dick, where are you? What is it?'

He flashed his torch towards the shouting and saw Dick rolling on top of somebody. He ran to help at once, throwing his torch on the grass so that both hands were free.

It wasn't long before they had the struggling figure firmly in their grips and dragged it, wailing, to the back door. Dick recognized that wailing voice! Good gracious – no, it couldn't be – it couldn't be Jo!

But it was! When they dragged her inside she collapsed completely, sobbing and wailing, rubbing her scratched and bruised legs, calling both boys all the names she could think of. Anne and Joan looked on in complete amazement. *Now* what had happened?

'Put her upstairs,' said Julian. 'Get her to bed. She's in an awful state now. So am I! I wouldn't have lammed her like that if I'd known it was only Jo.'

'I never guessed,' said Dick, wiping his filthy face with his handkerchief. 'My word, what a wild-cat! See how she's bitten me!'

'I didn't know it was you, Dick; I didn't know,' wailed Jo. 'You pounced on me, and I fought back. I wouldn't have bitten you like that.'

'You're a savage, deceitful, double-dealing little wild-cat,' said Dick, looking at his bites and scratches. 'Pretending you know nothing about the man who gave you that note – and all the time you're in with that crooked lot of thieves and kidnappers, whoever they are.'

'I'm not in with them,' wept Jo.

'Don't tell lies,' shouted Dick, in a fury. 'I was up in a tree when you came and took that parcel from under the stone – yes, and I followed you right to that car – and followed you back again! You came back here to steal again, I suppose?'

Jo gulped. 'No, I didn't.'

650

'You did! You'll be handed over to the police tomorrow,' said Dick, still furious.

'I *didn't* come back to steal. I came back for something else,' insisted Jo, her eyes peering through her tangled hair like a frightened animal's.

'Ho! So you say! And what did you come back for? To find another dog to dope?' jeered Dick.

'No,' said Jo, miserably. 'I came back to tell you I'd take you to where George was, if you wouldn't tell on me. My Dad would half kill me if he thought I'd split on him. I know I took the parcel – I had to. I didn't know what it was or anything. I took it to the place I was told to. Jake told me. And then I came back to tell you all I could. And you set on me like that.'

Four pairs of eyes bored into Jo, and she covered her face. Dick took her hands away and made her look at him.

'Look here,' he said, 'this matters a lot to us, whether you are speaking the truth or not. Do you know where George is?'

Jo nodded.

'And will you take us there?' said Julian, his voice stern and cold.

Jo nodded again. 'Yes I will. You've been mean to me, but I'll show you I'm not as bad as you make out. I'll take you to George.'

12

Jo begins to talk

THE hall clock suddenly struck loudly. 'DONG!'

'One o'clock,' said Joan. 'One o'clock in the morning! Master Julian, we can't do any more tonight. This gipsy child here, she's not fit to take you trapesing out anywhere else. She's done for – she can hardly stand.'

'Yes, you're right Joan,' said Julian, at once giving up the idea of going out to find George that night. 'We'll have to wait till tomorrow. It's a pity the telephone wires are cut. I do really think we ought to let the police know something about all this.'

Jo looked up at once. 'Then I won't tell you where George is,' she said. 'Do you know what the police will do to me if they get hold of me? They'll put me into a Home for Bad Girls, and I'll never get out again – because I *am* a bad girl and I do bad things. I've never had a chance.'

'Everyone gets a chance sooner or later,' said Julian gently. 'You'll get yours, Jo – but see you take it when it comes. All right – we'll leave the police out of it if you

promise you'll take us to where George is. That's a
bargain.'

Jo understood bargains. She nodded. Joan pulled her to
her feet and half led, half carried her upstairs.

'There's a couch in my room,' she told Julian. 'She can
bed down there for the night – but late or not she's going
to have a bath first. She smells like something the dog
brought in!'

In half an hour's time Jo was tucked up on the couch

in Joan's room, perfectly clean, though marked with scratches and bruises from top to toe, hair washed, dried, and brushed so that it stood up in wiry curls like George's. A basin of steaming bread and milk was on a tray in front of her.

Joan went to the landing and called across to Julian's room. 'Master Julian! Jo's in bed. She wants to say something to you and Master Dick.'

Dick and Julian put on dressing-gowns and went into Joan's neat room. They hardly recognized Jo. She was wearing one of Anne's old nightgowns and looked very clean and childish and somehow pathetic.

Jo looked at them and gave them a very small smile. 'What do you want to say to us?' asked Julian.

'I've got some things to tell you,' said Jo, stirring the bread round and round in the basin. 'I feel good now – good and clean and – and all that. But maybe tomorrow I'll feel like I always do – and then I wouldn't tell you everything. So I'd better tell you now.'

'Go ahead,' said Julian.

'Well, I let the men into your house here, the night they came,' said Jo. Julian and Dick stared in astonishment. Jo went on stirring her bread round and round.

'It's true,' she said. 'I got in at that tiny window that was left unfastened, and then I went to the back door and opened it and let the men in. They did make a mess of that room, didn't they? I watched them. They took a lot of papers.'

'You couldn't possibly squeeze through that window,' said Dick at once.

'Well, I did,' said Jo. 'I've – I've squeezed through quite a lot of little windows. I know how to wriggle, you see. I can't get through such tiny ones as I used to, because I keep on growing. But yours was easy.'

'Phew!' said Julian, and let out a long breath. He hardly knew what to say. 'Well, go on. I suppose when the men had finished you locked and bolted the kitchen door after them and then squeezed out of the pantry window again?'

'Yes,' said Jo, and put a piece of milky bread into her mouth.

'What about Timmy? Who doped him so that he slept all that night?' demanded Dick.

'I did,' said Jo. 'That was easy, too.'

Both boys were speechless. To think that Jo did that, too! The wicked little misery!

'I made friends with Timmy on the beach, don't you remember?' said Jo. 'George was cross about it. I like dogs. We always had dozens till Mum died, and they'd do anything I told them. Dad told me what I was to do – make friends with Timmy so that I could meet him that night and give him meat with something in it.'

'I see. And it was very, very easy, because we sent Timmy out alone – straight into your hands,' said Dick bitterly.

'Yes. He came to me at once, he was glad to see me. I took him quite a long walk, letting him sniff the meat I'd got. When I gave it to him, he swallowed it all at once with hardly a chew!'

'And slept all night long so that your precious friends could break into the house,' said Julian. 'All I can say is that you are a hardened little rogue. Aren't you ashamed of anything?'

'I don't know,' said Jo, who wasn't really quite certain what feeling ashamed meant. 'Shall I stop telling you things?'

'No. For goodness' sake go on,' said Dick, hastily. 'Had you anything to do with George's kidnapping?'

'I just had to hoot like an owl when she and Timmy were coming,' said Jo. 'They were ready for her with a sack to put over her head – and they were going to bang Timmy on the head with a stick to knock him out – then put him into a sack too. That's what I heard them say. But

I didn't see them. I had to creep back here and shut the front door, so that if nobody missed George till morning they'd just think she'd gone out early somewhere.'

'Which is what we did think,' groaned Dick. 'What mutts we are! The only clever thing we thought of was to stalk the person who collected the parcel.'

'It was only me, though,' said Jo. 'And anyway, I was coming back to tell you I would take you to George. Not because I like her – I don't. I think she's rude and horrible. I'd like her to stay kidnapped for years!'

'What a nice, kind nature!' said Julian to Dick, helplessly. 'What can you do with a kid like this?' He turned to Jo again. 'Seeing that you wish George would stay kidnapped for years, what made you decide to come and tell us where to find her?' he asked, puzzled.

'Well, I don't like George – but I do like *him*!' said Jo, pointing with her spoon at Dick. 'He was nice to me, so I wanted to be nice back. I don't often feel like that,' she added hurriedly, as if being kind was some sort of weakness not really to be admired. 'I wanted him to go on liking me,' she said.

Dick looked at her. 'I shall like you if you take us to George,' he said. 'Not unless. If you deceive us, I shall think you're like one of those sour damson stones – only fit to be spat out as far away as possible.'

'I'll take you tomorrow,' said Jo.

'Where *is* George?' asked Julian, bluntly, thinking it would be as well to know now, in case Jo changed her mind by the morning, and became her wicked little self again.

Jo hesitated. She looked at Dick. 'It would be very nice of you to tell us,' said Dick, in a kind voice. Jo loved a bit of kindness and couldn't resist this.

'Well,' she whispered, 'you know I told you my Dad had gone off and left me to Jake. Dad didn't tell me why – but Jake did. He shut George and Timmy into our caravan, harnessed Blackie the horse, and drove away in the night with them both. And I guess I know where he's gone – where he always goes when he wants to hide.'

'Where?' asked Julian, feeling so astounded at these extraordinary revelations that he really began to wonder if he was dreaming.

'In the middle of Ravens Wood,' said Jo. 'You don't know where that is, but I do. I'll take you tomorrow. I can't tell you any more now.' She began to spoon up her bread and milk very fast indeed, watching the boys through her long eyelashes.

Dick considered her. He felt pretty sure she had told them the truth, though he was equally certain she would have told lies if she could have got more by doing so.

He thought her a bad, cold-blooded, savage little monkey, but he pitied her, and admired her unwillingly for her courage.

He caught sight of her bruises and grazes, and bit his lip as he remembered how he had pounced on her and pummelled her, giving her back kick for kick and blow for blow – he hadn't guessed for one moment it was Jo.

'I'm sorry I hurt you so,' he said. 'You know I didn't mean to. It was a mistake.'

Jo looked at him as a slave might look at a king. 'I don't mind,' she said. 'I'd do anything for you, straight I would. You're kind.'

Joan knocked impatiently at the door. 'Aren't you ready yet, you boys?' she said. 'I want to come to bed. Tell Jo to stop talking, and you come on out too, and go to bed.'

The boys opened the door. Joan took one look at their solemn faces and guessed that what Jo had told them was important. She took the empty basin from the girl's hands and pushed her down on the couch.

'Now you go straight off to sleep – and mind, if I hear any hanky-panky from you in the night I'll get up and give you such a spanking you won't be able to sit down for a month of Sundays,' she said roughly, but not unkindly.

Jo grinned. She understood that kind of talk. She snuggled down into the rugs, marvelling at the warmth and softness. She was already half-asleep. Joan got into bed and switched off her light.

'Two o'clock in the morning!' she muttered as she heard the hall clock strike. 'Such goings-on! I'll never wake up in time to tell the milkman I want more milk.'

Soon only Julian was awake. He worried about whether he was doing right or not. Poor George – was she safe? Would that scamp of a Jo really lead them to the caravan next day – or might she lead them right into the lion's mouth, and get them all captured? Julian simply didn't know.

13

Off to find George

Joan was the only one in the household who woke up reasonably early the next morning – but even she was too late to catch the milkman. She scurried downstairs at half-past seven, an hour later than usual, tying up her apron as she went.

'Half-past seven – what a time to wake up!' she muttered, as she began to do the kitchen fire. She thought of all the happenings of the night before – the queer evening with young Sid, Dick's capture of Jo – and Jo's extraordinary tale. She had had a look at Jo before she went down, half expecting that lively young rogue to have disappeared in the night.

But Jo was curled up like a kitten, her brown cheek on her brown paw, her hair, unusually bright and tidy, falling over her tightly-shut eyes. She didn't even stir when Joan scurried about the bedroom, washing and dressing.

The others were fast asleep, too. Julian woke first, but not till eight o'clock. He remembered immediately all that had happened, and jumped out of bed at once.

He went to Joan's room. He could hear Joan downstairs talking to herself as usual. He peeped round the open door of her bedroom. Thank goodness – Jo was still there.

He went and shook her gently. She wriggled away, turned over and buried her face in the pillow. Julian shook her more vigorously. He meant to get her up and make her take them to where George was as soon as possible!

Most miraculously everyone was down at half-past eight, eating porridge and looking rather subdued. Jo had hers in the kitchen, and the others could hear Joan scolding her for her manners.

'Have you got to stuff yourself like that, as if the dog's going to come and lick your plate before you've finished? And who told you to stick your fingers into the syrup and lick them? I've eyes in the back of my head, so just you be careful what you're doing!'

Jo liked Joan. She knew where she was with her. If she kept on Joan's right side and did what she was told, Joan would feed her well and not interfere too much – but if she didn't, then she could expect something else she understood very well indeed – scoldings and a sharp slap. Joan was good-hearted but impatient, and no child was ever afraid of her. Jo followed her about like a little dog when she had finished her breakfast.

Julian came out into the kitchen at nine o'clock. 'Where's Jo?' he said. 'Oh, there you are. Now, what about taking us to where your father's caravan is? You're sure you know the way?'

Jo laughed scornfully. 'Course I do! I know everywhere round here for miles.'

'Right,' said Julian, and he produced a map, which he spread out on the kitchen table. He put a finger on one spot. 'That's Kirrin,' he said. 'And here's a place called Ravens Wood. Is that the place you mean? How do you propose to get there – by this road, or that one?'

Jo looked at the map. It meant nothing to her at all. She

gazed vaguely at the spot that Julian had pointed to.

'Well?' said Julian, impatiently. 'Is that the Ravens
Wood you mean?'

'I don't know,' said Jo, helplessly. 'The one I mean is a
real wood – I don't know anything about yours on this
map.'

Joan gave a little snort. 'Master Julian, maps are
wasted on her. I don't expect she's ever seen one in her life!
She can't even read!'

'*Can't* she?' said Julian, amazed. 'Then she can't write
either.' He looked questioningly at Jo.

She shook her head. 'Mum tried to learn me to read,'
she said, 'but Mum wasn't very good herself. What's the
good of reading, anyway? Won't help you to trap rabbits
or catch fish for your dinner, will it?'

'No. It's used for other things,' said Julian, amused.

662

'Well – maps are no good to *you*, I can see.' He rolled his map up, looking thoughtful. It was very difficult to know exactly how to deal with a person like Jo, who knew so little of some things and so much of others.

'She'll know the way all right,' said Joan, scraping out a saucepan. 'They're like dogs, these folk – they can smell out any road they want.'

'*Do* you smell out your way like a dog?' asked Anne, curiously. She had come in to see what was going on, and was quite willing to believe that Jo really could smell her way here and there, as Timmy did.

'No, I don't,' said Jo. 'I just know the way I have to go. And I don't go by the roads, either! They take too long to get to a place. I take the shortest way, see?'

'How do you know it's the shortest way?' asked Anne.

Jo shrugged her thin shoulders. All this was very boring to her.

'Where's that other boy?' she said. 'Isn't he coming? I want to see him.'

'She's just crazy on Dick,' said Joan, taking up another saucepan. 'Here he is – now you can go and lick his boots if you want to, young Jo!'

'Hallo, Jo!' said Dick, with one of his amiable grins. 'Ready to take us travelling?'

'Better go at night,' said Jo, staring at Dick.

'Oh, no!' said Dick. 'We're going *now*. We're not going to be put off like that. *Now*, Jo, now!'

'If my Dad sees us coming he'll be mad,' said Jo obstinately.

'Very well,' said Dick, looking at Julian. 'We'll go by ourselves. We've found Ravens Wood on the map. We can easily get there.'

'Pooh,' said Jo, rudely. 'You can get there all right – but it's a big place, Ravens Wood is – and nobody but me and Dad knows where we hide the caravan there. And if Dad wants to keep George quite safe, he'll take her to our hidey-hole in the middle of the wood, see? You can't go without me.'

'Right. Then we'll get the police to take us,' said Julian, quite cheerfully. 'They will help us to comb the wood from end to end. We'll soon find George.'

'No!' cried Jo, in alarm. 'You said you wouldn't! You promised!'

'*You* made a promise too,' said Julian. 'It was a bargain. But I see you're not really to be trusted. I'll just get on my bike and ride down to the police-station.'

But before he could go out of the room Jo flung herself on him and clung to his arm like a cat. 'No, no! I'll take you. I'll keep my promise! But it *would* be best to go at night!'

'I'm not putting things off any more,' said Julian, shaking Jo off his arm. 'If you mean what you say, you'll come with us now. Make up your mind.'

'I'll come,' said Jo.

'Hadn't we better give her another pair of shorts or something?' said Anne, suddenly seeing a tremendous hole in Jo's grubby shorts. 'She can't go out like that. And look at her awful jersey. It's full of holes.'

The boys looked at it. 'She'd smell a bit better if she had clean clothes,' said Joan. 'There's that old pair of shorts I washed for George last week, and mended up. Jo could have those. And there's an old shirt of hers she could have, too.'

In five minutes' time Jo was proudly wearing a pair of perfectly clean, much-mended shorts of George's, and a shirt like the one Anne had on. Anne looked at her and laughed.

'Now she's more like George than ever! They might be sisters.'

'Brothers, you mean,' said Dick. 'George and Jo – what a pair!'

Jo scowled. She didn't like George, and she didn't want to look like her.

'She's even got George's scowl!' said Anne. Jo turned her back at once, and Joan then got the benefit of the scowl.

'My word, what an ugly creature you are!' said Joan. 'You be careful the wind doesn't change – you might get your face stuck like that!'

'Oh, come on,' said Julian, impatiently. 'Jo! Do you hear me? Come along now and take us to Ravens Wood.'

'Jake might see us,' said Jo, sulkily. She was determined to put off going as long as she could.

'Yes, he might,' said Julian, who hadn't thought of that. 'Well – you go on a long way ahead, and we'll follow. We won't let Jake know you're leading us anywhere.'

At last they set off. Joan had packed them up a meal in case they wanted one. Julian slipped the package into a bag and slid it over his shoulder.

Jo slipped out the back way, went down to the bottom of the garden and made her way out to the lane through a little thicket. The others went out of the front gate and walked up the lane slowly, watching for Jo to appear.

'There she is,' said Julian. 'Come on. We must keep the little wretch in sight. I wouldn't be surprised if she gave us the slip even now!'

Jo danced on in front, a good way ahead. She took no notice of the others behind, and they followed steadily.

Then suddenly something happened. A dark figure strode out from the hedge, stood in front of Jo, and said something to her. She screamed and tried to dodge away. But the man caught hold of her and firmly pulled her into the hedge.

'It was Jake!' said Dick. 'I'm sure it was Jake. He was watching out for her. *Now* what do we do?'

14

Simmy's caravan

THEY all hurried up to the place where Jake had caught hold of Jo. There was absolutely nothing to be seen except a few broken twigs in the hedge. No Jake, no Jo. There was not a sound to be heard, either. Not a scream from Jo, not a shout from Jake. It was as if both had faded into the hedge and disappeared.

Dick squeezed through the hedge and into the field beyond. Nobody was there either, except a few cows who looked at him in surprise, their tails whisking.

'There's a little copse at the end of the field,' called back Dick. 'I bet they're there. I'll go and see.'

He ran across the field to the copse. But there was nobody there either. Beyond the copse was a row of huddled-up cottages. Dick looked along the untidy row, exasperated.

'I suppose Jake's taken her to one of those,' he thought, angrily. 'Probably lives there! Well, he won't let her go, that's certain. He most likely guesses that she's in with us now. Poor Jo!'

He went back to the others and they had a low-voiced conference in the lane. 'Let's tell the police now,' begged Anne.

'No. Let's go to Ravens Wood ourselves,' said Dick. 'We know where it is. We wouldn't be able to go the way Jo would have taken us – but at least we can go by the map.'

'Yes. I think we will,' said Julian. 'Come on, then. Quick march!'

They went on up the lane, took a field path and came out eventually on to a road. A bus passed them in the opposite direction to which they were going.

'When we come to a bus stop we'll find out if one goes anywhere near Ravens Wood,' said Julian. 'It would save a lot of time if we caught a bus. We'd be there long before Jake, if he thinks of going to warn Jo's father we're on the way! I bet Jo will tell him. You might as well trust a snake as that slippery little thing.'

'I hate Jo!' said Anne, almost in tears. 'I don't trust her a bit. Do you, Dick?'

'I don't know,' said Dick. 'I can't make up my mind. She hasn't really proved whether she's trustable or not yet. Anyway, she came back to tell us all she knew last night, didn't she?'

'I don't believe she *did* come back for that,' said Anne obstinately. 'I believe she was coming back to pry and snoop.'

'You may be right,' said Dick. 'Look, here's a bus-stop – and a time-table!'

A bus did apparently go quite near Ravens Wood, and was due in five minutes' time. They sat down on the bus-stop seat and waited. The bus was punctual and came rumbling down the road, full of women going to Ravens Market. They all seemed very plump women and had enormous baskets, so it was difficult to squeeze inside.

Everyone got out at Ravens Market. Julian asked his

667

way to Ravens Wood. 'There it is,' said the conductor, pointing down the hill to where trees grew thickly in the valley. 'It's a big place. Don't get lost! And look out for the gipsies. There's usually hordes of them there!'

'Thanks,' said Julian, and the three of them set off down the hill into the valley. They came to the wood.

'It's a proper wood,' said Anne. 'Nothing but trees and trees. I should think it gets very thick in the middle – like a forest.'

They came to a clearing where there was a little gipsy camp. Three rather dirty-looking caravans stood together, and a crowd of brown gipsy children were playing some sort of a game with a rope. Julian took a quick look at the caravans. All had their doors open.

'No George here,' he said in a low voice to the others. 'I wish I knew exactly where to go! I suppose if we follow this broad pathway it would be best. After all, Jo's caravan must have a fairly broad way to go on.'

'Can't we ask if anyone knows if Jo's caravan is any-where about?' said Anne.

'We don't know her father's name,' said Julian.

'But we could say it's a caravan drawn by a horse called Blackie, and that a girl called Jo lives in it with her father,' said Anne.

'Yes. I'd forgotten the horse,' said Julian. He went up to an old woman who was stirring something in a black pot over a fire of sticks. Julian thought she looked very like a witch. She peered up at him through tangled grey hair.

'Can you tell me if there's a caravan in the wood drawn by a horse called Blackie?' he asked politely. 'A girl called Jo lives in it with her father. We want to see her.'

The old woman blinked. She took an iron spoon out of the pot and waved it to the right.

'Simmy's gone down-away there,' she said. 'I never saw Jo this time – but the caravan door was shut so maybe she was inside. What you want with Jo?'

668

'Oh – only just to see her,' said Julian, quite unable to think up a good reason for going to visit a gipsy-child on the spur of the moment. 'Is Simmy her father?'

The old woman nodded and began to stir her pot again. Julian went back to the others.

'This way,' he said, and they went down the rutted path. It was just wide enough for a caravan to go down. Anne looked up. Tree branches waved overhead.

'I should think they brush against the roof of a caravan all the time,' she said. 'What a queer life to live – in a little caravan day in and day out, hiding yourself away in woods and fields!'

They walked on down the path, which wound about through the trees, following the clear spaces. Sometimes the trees were so close together that it seemed impossible for a caravan to go between. But the wheel-ruts showed that caravans did go down the path.

After a time the wood became thicker, and the sunlight could hardly pierce through the branches. Still the path went on, but now it seemed as if only one set of wheel-ruts was marked on it. They were probably the wheels of Simmy's caravan.

Here and there a tree was shorn of one of its branches, and a bush uprooted and thrown to one side.

'Simmy meant to go deep into the wood last time he came,' said Julian, pointing to where a bush lay dying by the side of the path. 'He's cleared the way here and there. Actually we aren't on a proper path any longer – we're only following wheel-ruts.'

It was true. The path had faded out. They were now in a thick part of the wood, with only the ruts of the caravan wheels to guide them.

They fell silent. The wood was very quiet. There were no birds singing, and the branches of the trees were so thick that there was a kind of green twilight round them.

'I wish we had Timmy with us,' half-whispered Anne at last.

Julian nodded. He had been wishing that a long time. He was also wishing he hadn't brought Anne – but when they had started out, they had Jo with them to guide them, and warn them of any danger. Now they hadn't.

'I think we'd better go very cautiously,' he said, in a low voice. 'We may come on the caravan unexpectedly. We don't want Simmy to hear us and lie in wait.'

'I'll go a little way in front and warn you if I hear or see anything,' said Dick. Julian nodded to him and he went on ahead, peering round the trees when he came to any curve in the wheel-rut path. Julian began to think of what they would do when they reached the caravan. He was pretty certain that both George and Timmy would be found locked up securely inside.

'If we can undo the door and let them out, Timmy will do the rest,' he thought. 'He's as good as three policemen! Yes – that's the best plan.'

Dick suddenly stopped and lifted up his hand in warning. He peered round the bole of a big tree, and then turned and nodded excitedly.

'He's found the caravan!' said Anne, and her heart began its usual thump-thump-thump of excitement.

'Stay here,' said Julian to Anne, and went on quietly to join Dick. Anne crept under a bush. She didn't like this dark, silent wood, with the green light all round. She peered out, watching the boys.

Dick had suddenly seen the caravan. It was small, badly needed painting, and appeared quite deserted. No fire burned outside. No Simmy was sitting anywhere about. Not even Blackie the horse was to be seen.

The boys watched intently for a few minutes, not daring to move or speak. There was absolutely no sound or movement from the tiny clearing in which the caravan stood.

Windows and doors were shut. The shafts rested crookedly on the ground. The whole place seemed deserted.

'Dick,' whispered Julian at last, 'Simmy doesn't seem to be about. This is our chance! We'll creep over to the caravan and look into the window. We'll attract George's attention, and get her out as soon as we can. Timmy, too.'

'Funny he doesn't bark,' said Dick, also in a whisper. 'I suppose he can't have heard us. Well – shall we get over to the caravan now?'

They ran quietly to the little caravan, and Julian peered through the dirty window. It was too dark inside to see anything at all.

'George!' he whispered. 'George! Are you there?'

15

Anne doesn't like adventures

THERE was no answer from inside the caravan. Perhaps George was asleep – or drugged! And Timmy, too. Julian's heart sank. It would be dreadful if George had been ill-treated. He tried to peer inside the window again, but what with the darkness of the wood and the dirt on the pane, it really was impossible to see inside.

'Shall we bang on the door?' asked Dick.

'No. That would only bring Simmy if he's anywhere about – and if George is inside and awake, our voices would have attracted her attention,' said Julian.

They went quietly round the caravan to the door at the back. It had no key in the lock. Julian frowned.

Simmy must have got the key with him. That would mean breaking down the door and making a noise. He went up the few steps and pushed at the door. It seemed very solid indeed. How could he break it down, anyway? He had no tools, and it didn't look as if kicking and shoving would burst it in.

He knocked gently on the door – rap-rap-rap. Not a

movement from inside. It seemed very strange. He tried
the round handle, and it turned easily.

It not only turned easily – but the door opened! 'Dick!
It's not locked!' said Julian, forgetting to whisper in his
surprise. He went inside the dark caravan, hardly hoping
now to see George or Timmy.

Dick pushed in after him. There was a nasty sour smell

and it was very untidy. Nobody was there. It was quite empty, as Julian had feared.

He groaned. 'All this way for nothing. They've taken George somewhere else. We're done, now, Dick – we haven't a clue where to go next.'

Dick fished his torch out of his pocket. He flashed it over the untidy jumble of things in the caravan, looking for some sign that George had been there. But there was nothing at all that he could see to show him that either Timmy or George had been there.

'It's quite likely that Jo made the whole story up about her father taking George away,' he groaned. 'It doesn't look as if they've been here at all.'

His torch flashed on to the wooden wall of the caravan, and Dick saw something that arrested his attention. Somebody had written something on the wall!

He looked more closely. 'Julian! Isn't that George's writing? Look! What's written there?'

Both boys bent towards the dirty wall. 'Red Tower, Red Tower, Red Tower,' was written again and again, in very small writing.

'Red Tower!' said Dick. 'What does that mean? *Is* it George's writing?'

'Yes, I think so,' said Julian. 'But why should she keep writing that? Do you suppose that's where they have taken her to? She might have heard them saying something and scribbled it down quickly – just in *case* we found the caravan and examined it. Red Tower! It sounds queer.'

'It must be a house with a red tower, I should think,' said Dick. 'Well – we'd better get back and tell the police now – and they'll have to hunt for a red tower somewhere.'

Bitterly disappointed the boys went back to Anne. She scrambled out from under her bush as they came.

'George is not there,' said Dick. 'She's gone. But she *has* been there – we saw some scribbled writing on the wall of the caravan inside.'

'How do you know it's hers?' said Anne.

'Well, she's written "Red Tower" ever so many times, and the R's and the T's are just like hers,' said Dick. 'We think she must have heard someone talking and say they were taking her to Red Tower, wherever it is. We're going straight back to the police now. I wish we hadn't trusted Jo. We've wasted such a lot of time.'

'Let's have something to eat,' said Julian. 'We won't sit down. We'll eat as we go. Come on.'

But somehow nobody wanted anything to eat. Anne said she felt sick. Julian was too worried to eat, and Dick was so anxious to go that he felt he couldn't even wait to unpack sandwiches! So they started back down the path, following the wheel-ruts as before.

It suddenly grew very dark indeed, and on the leaves of the trees heavy rain fell with a loud, pattering sound. Thunder suddenly rolled.

Anne caught hold of Julian's arm, startled. 'Julian! It's dangerous to be in a wood, isn't it, in a storm? Oh, Julian, we'll be struck by lightning.'

'No, we shan't,' said Julian. 'A wood's no more dangerous than anywhere else. It's sheltering under a lone tree somewhere that's dangerous. Look – there's a little clearing over there; we'll go to that, if you like.'

But when they got to the little clearing the rain was falling down in such heavy torrents that Julian could see that they would immediately be soaked through. He hurried Anne to a clump of bushes, and they crouched underneath, waiting for the storm to pass.

Soon the rain stopped, and the thunder rolled away to the east. There had been no lightning that they could see. The wood grew just a little lighter, as if somewhere above the thick green branches the sun might be shining!

'I hate this wood,' said Dick, crawling out from the

bushes. 'Come on, for goodness' sake. Let's get back to the wheel-rut path.'

He led the way through the trees. Julian called to him. 'Wait, Dick. Are you sure this is right?'

Dick stopped, anxious at once. 'Well,' he said uncertainly. 'I thought it was. But I don't know. Do you?'

'*I* thought it was through those trees there,' said Julian. 'Where that little clearing is.'

They went to it. 'It's not the same clearing, though,' said Anne at once. 'The other clearing had a dead tree at one side. There's no dead tree here.'

'Blow!' said Julian. 'Well – try *this* way, then.'

They went to the left, and soon found themselves in a thicker part of the wood than ever. Julian's heart went cold. What an absolute idiot he was! He might have known that it was madness to leave the only path they knew without marking it in some way.

Now he hadn't the very faintest idea where the wheel-rut way was. It might be in any direction! He hadn't even the sun to guide him.

He looked gloomily at Dick. 'Bad show!' said Dick. 'Well – we'll have to make up our minds which way to go! We can't just stay here.'

'We might go deeper and deeper and deeper,' said Anne, with a sudden little gulp of fear. Julian put his arm round her shoulder.

'Well, if we go deeper and deeper, we shall come out on the other side!' he said. 'It's not an endless wood, you know.'

'Well, let's go straight on through the wood, then,' said Anne. 'We'll *have* to come out the other side some time.'

The boys didn't tell her that it was impossible to go straight through a wood. It was necessary to go round clumps of bushes, to double back sometimes when they came to an impenetrable part, and to go either to the left or

676

right when clumps of trees barred their way. It was quite impossible to go *straight* through.

'For all I know we're probably going round and round in circles, like people do when they're lost in the desert,' he thought. He blamed himself bitterly for having left the wheel-ruts.

They made their way on and on for about two or three hours, and then Anne stumbled and fell. 'I can't go on any further,' she wept. 'I must have a rest.'

Dick glanced at his watch and whistled. Where ever had the time gone? It was almost three o'clock. He sat down by Anne and pulled her close to him. 'What we want is a jolly good meal,' he said. 'We've had nothing since breakfast.'

Anne said she still wasn't hungry, but when she smelt the meat sandwiches that Joan had made she changed her mind. She was soon eating with the others, and feeling much better.

'There's nothing to drink, unfortunately,' said Dick. 'But Joan's packed tomatoes and plums, too – so we'll have those instead of a drink. They're nice and juicy.'

They ate everything, though secretly Julian wondered if it was a good thing to wolf all their food at once. There was no telling how long they might be lost in Ravens Wood! Joan might get worried sooner or later and tell the police they had gone there, and a search would be made. But it might be ages before they were found.

Anne fell asleep after her meal. The boys talked softly over her head. 'I don't much like this,' said Dick. 'We set out to find George – and all we've done is to lose ourselves. We don't seem to be managing this adventure as well as we usually do.'

'If we don't get out before dark we'll have to make up some kind of bed under a bush,' said Julian. 'We'll have another go when Anne wakes – and we'll do a bit of yelling, too. Then if we're still lost, we'll bed down for the night.'But when darkness came – and it came very early in that thick wood, they were still as much lost as ever. They were all hoarse with shouting, too.

In silence they pulled bracken from an open space and piled it under a sheltering bush. 'Thank goodness it's warm tonight,' said Dick, trying to sound cheerful. 'Well – we'll all feel much more lively in the morning. Cuddle up to me, Anne, and keep warm. That's right. Julian's on the other side of you! This is quite an adventure.'

'I don't like adventures,' said Anne, in a small voice, and immediately fell asleep.

16

Visitor in the night

IT took a long time for Julian and Dick to fall asleep. They were both worried – worried about George and worried about themselves, too. They were also very hungry, and their hunger kept them awake as much as their anxiety.

Dick fell asleep at last. Julian still lay awake, hoping that Anne was nice and warm between them. He didn't feel very warm himself.

He heard the whisper of the leaves in the trees, and then the scamper of tiny paws behind his head. He wondered what animal it was – a mouse?

Something ran lightly over his hair and he shivered. A spider, perhaps. Well he couldn't move, or he would disturb Anne. If it wanted to make a web over his hair it would have to. He shut his eyes and began to doze off. Soon he was dreaming.

He awoke very suddenly, with a jump. He heard the hoot of an owl. That must have been what wakened him. Now it would be ages before he slept again.

He shut his eyes. The owl hooted again and Julian

679

frowned, hoping that Anne would not wake. She stirred and muttered in her sleep. Julian touched her lightly. She felt quite warm.

He settled down again and shut his eyes. Then he opened them. He had heard something! Not an owl or the pattering of some little animal's feet – but another sound, a bigger one. He listened. There was a rustling going on somewhere. Some much bigger animal was about.

Julian was suddenly panic-stricken. Then he reasoned sternly with himself. There were no dangerous wild animals in this country, not even a wolf. It was probably a badger out on a nightly prowl. He listened for any snuffling sound, but he heard none, only the rustling as the animal moved about through the bushes.

It came nearer. It came right over to him! He felt warm breath on his ear and made a quick movement of revulsion. He sat up swiftly and put out his hand. It fell on something warm and hairy. He withdrew his hand at once, feeling for his torch in panic. To touch something warm and hairy in the pitch darkness was too much even for Julian!

Something caught hold of his arm, and he gave a yell and fought it off. Then he got the surprise of his life. The animal spoke.

'Julian!' said a voice. 'It's me!'

Julian, his hands trembling, flashed his torch round. The light fell on a dirty dark face, with tangled hair over its eyes.

'Jo!' said Julian. 'JO! What on earth are you doing here? You scared me stiff. I thought you were some horrible hairy animal. I must have touched your head.'

'You did,' said Jo, squeezing in under the bush. Anne and Dick, who had both wakened up at Julian's yell, gazed at her, speechless with surprise. Jo of all people here in the middle of the wood. How had she got there?

'You're surprised to see me, aren't you?' said Jo. 'I got

caught by Jake. But he didn't know you were following behind. He dragged me off to the cottage he lives in and locked me up. He knew I'd spent the night at Kirrin Cottage, and he said he was going to take me to my Dad, who would give me the worst hiding I'd ever had in my life. So he would, too.'

'So that's what happened to you!' said Dick.

'Then I broke the window and got out,' said Jo. 'That

Jake! I'll never do a thing he tells me again – locking me up like that. I hate that worse than anything! Well, then I came to look for you.'

'How did you find us?' said Julian, in wonder.

'Well, first I went to the caravan,' said Jo. 'Old Ma Smith – the one who always sits stirring a pot – she told me you'd been asking for my Dad's caravan. I guessed you'd go off to find it. So along I went after you – but there was the caravan all by itself, and nobody there. Not even George.'

'Where *is* George, do you know?' asked Anne.

'No. I don't,' said Jo. 'Dad's taken her somewhere else. I expect he put her on Blackie, because Blackie's gone, too.'

'What about Timmy?' asked Dick.

Jo looked away. 'I reckon they've done Timmy in,' she said. Nobody said anything. The thought that Timmy might have come to harm was too dreadful to speak about.

'How did you find us here?' asked Julian at last.

'That was easy,' said Jo. 'I can follow anybody's trail. I'd have come quicker, but it got dark. My, you did wander round, didn't you?'

'Yes. We did,' said Dick. 'Do you mean to say you followed all our wanderings in and out and round about?'

'Oh, yes,' said Jo. 'Properly tired me out, you did, with all your messing round and round. Why did you leave the wheel-ruts?'

Julian told her. 'You're daft,' said Jo. 'If you're going somewhere off the path, just mark the trees with a nick as you go along – one here and one there – and then you can always find your way back.'

'We didn't even know we were lost till we were,' said Anne. She took Jo's hand and squeezed it. She was so very, very glad to see her. Now they would be able to get out of this horrible wood.

Jo was surprised and touched, but she withdrew her

hand at once. She didn't like being fondled, though she would not have minded Dick taking her hand. Dick was her hero, someone above all others. He had been kind to her, and she was glad she had found him.

'We found something written on the caravan wall,' said Julian. 'We think we know where George has been taken. It's a place called Red Tower. Do you know it?'

'There's no place called Red Tower,' said Jo at once. 'It's . . .'

'Don't be silly, Jo. You can't possibly know if there's no place called Red Tower,' said Dick, impatiently. 'There may be hundreds of places with that name. That's the place we've got to find, anyway. The police will know it.'

Jo gave a frightened movement. 'You promised you wouldn't tell the police.'

'Yes – we promised that – but only if you took us to George,' said Dick. 'And you didn't. And anyway if you *had* taken us to the caravan George wouldn't have been there. So we'll jolly well have to call in the police now and find out where Red Tower is.'

'*Was* it Red Tower George had written down?' asked Jo. 'Well, then – I *can* take you to George!'

'How can you, when you say there's no place called Red Tower?' began Julian, exasperated. 'I don't believe a word you say, Jo. You're a fraud – and I half-believe you're still working for our enemies too!'

'I'm not,' said Jo. 'I'm NOT! You're mean. I tell you Red Tower isn't a place. Red Tower is a man.'

There was a most surprised silence after this astonishing remark. A man! Nobody had thought of that.

Jo spoke again, pleased at the surprise she had caused. 'His name's Tower, and he's got red hair, flaming red – so he's called Red Tower. See?'

'Are you making this up, by any chance?' asked Dick, after a pause. 'You have made up things before, you know.'

'All right. You can think I made it up, then,' said Jo, sulkily. 'I'll go. Get yourselves out of this the best you can. You're mean.'

She wriggled away, but Julian caught hold of her arm. 'Oh, no, you don't! You'll just stay with us now, if I have to tie you to me all night long! You see, we find it difficult to trust you, Jo – and that's your fault, not ours. But we'll trust you just this once. Tell us about Red Tower, and take us to where he lives. If you do that, we'll trust you for evermore.'

'Will Dick trust me, too?' said Jo, trying to get away from Julian's hand.

'Yes,' said Dick shortly. He felt as if he would dearly like to smack this unpredictable, annoying, extraordinary, yet somehow likeable ragamuffin girl. 'But I don't feel as if I *like* you very much at present. If you want us to like you as well as to trust you, you'll have to help us a lot more than you have done.'

'All right,' said Jo, and she wriggled down again. 'I'm tired. I'll show you the way out in the morning, and then I'll take you to Red's. But you won't like Red. He's a beast.'

She would say nothing more, so once again they tried to sleep. They felt happier now that Jo was with them and would show them the right way out of the wood. Julian hardly thought she would leave them in the lurch now. He shut his eyes and was soon dreaming.

Jo woke first. She uncurled like an animal and stretched, forgetting where she was. She woke up the others, and they all sat up, feeling stiff, dirty and hungry.

'I'm thirsty as well as hungry,' complained Anne. 'Where can we get something to eat and drink?'

'Better get back home for a wash and a meal, and to let Joan know where we are,' said Julian. 'Come on, Jo – show us the way.'

Jo led the way immediately. The others wondered how

in the world she knew it. They were even more astonished when they found themselves on the wheel-rut path in about two minutes.

'Gracious! We were as near to it as that!' said Dick. 'And yet we seemed to walk for miles through this horrible wood.'

'You did,' said Jo. 'You went round in an enormous circle, and you were almost back where you started. Come on – I'll take you *my* way back to your house now – it's much better than any bus!'

17

Off in George's boat

Joan was extremely thankful to see them. She had been so worried the night before that if the telephone wires in the house had been mended, she would most certainly have rung up the police. As it was, she couldn't telephone, and the night was so dark that she was really afraid of walking all the way down to the village.

'I haven't slept all night,' she declared. 'This mustn't happen again, Master Julian. It's worrying me to death. And now you haven't got George or Timmy. I tell you, if they don't turn up soon I'll take matters into my own hands. I haven't heard from your uncle and aunt either – let's hope they're not lost, too!'

She bustled about after this outburst, and was soon frying sausages and tomatoes for them. They couldn't wait till they were cooked, and helped themselves to great hunks of bread and butter.

'I can't even go and wash till I've had something,' said Anne. 'I'm glad you know so many short cuts back here,

686

Jo – the way didn't seem nearly so long as when we came by bus.'

It had really been amazing to see the deft, confident manner in which Jo had taken them home, through fields and little narrow paths, over stiles and across allotments. She was never once at a loss.

They had arrived not long after Joan had got up, and she had almost cried with surprise and relief when she had seen them walking up the front path.

'And a lot of dirty little tatterdemalions you looked,' she said, as she turned their breakfast out on to a big dish. 'And still do, for that matter. I'll get the kitchen fire going for a bath for you. You might all be sister and brothers to that ragamuffin Jo.'

Jo didn't mind remarks of this sort at all. She chewed her bread and grinned. She wolfed the breakfast with no manners at all – but the others were nearly as bad, they were so hungry!

'It's a spade and trowel you want for your food this morning, not a knife and fork,' said Joan, disapprovingly. 'You're just shovelling it in. No, I can't cook you any more, Master Julian. There's not a sausage left in the house nor a bit of bacon either. You fill up with toast and marmalade.'

The bath water ran vigorously after breakfast. All four had baths. Jo didn't want to, but Joan ran after her with a carpet beater, vowing and declaring she would beat the dust and dirt out of her if she didn't bath. So Jo bathed, and quite enjoyed it.

They had a conference after breakfast. 'About this fellow, Red Tower,' said Julian. 'Who is he, Jo? What do you know about him?'

'Not much,' said Jo. 'He's rich, and he talks queer, and I think he's mad. He gets fellows like Dad and Jake to do his dirty work for him.'

'What dirty work?' asked Dick.

'Oh – stealing and such,' said Jo, vaguely. 'I don't really know. Dad doesn't tell me much; I just do what I'm told, and don't ask questions. I don't want more slaps than I get!'

'Where does he live?' said Anne. 'Far away?'

'He's taken a house on the cliff,' said Jo. 'I don't know the way by land. Only by boat. It's a queer place – like a small castle almost, with very thick stone walls. Just the place for Red, my Dad says.'

'Have you been there?' asked Dick, eagerly.

Jo nodded. 'Oh, yes,' she said. 'Twice. My Dad took a big iron box there once, and another time he took something in a sack. I went with him.'

'Why?' asked Julian. 'I shouldn't have thought he'd wanted you messing round!'

'I rowed the boat,' said Jo. 'I told you, Red's place is up on the cliff. We got to it by boat; I don't know the way by road. There's a sort of cave behind a cove we landed at, and we went in there. Red met us. He came from his house on the cliff, he said, but I don't know how.'

Dick looked at Jo closely. 'I suppose you'll say next that there's a secret way from the cave to the house!' he said. 'Go on!'

'Must be,' said Jo. She suddenly glared at Dick. 'Don't you believe me? All right, find the place yourself!'

'Well – it does sound like a tale in a book,' said Julian. 'You're sure it *is* all true, Jo? We don't want to go on a wild-goose chase again, you know.'

'There's no wild goose in my story,' said Jo, puzzled. She hadn't the faintest idea what a wild-goose chase was. 'I'm telling you about Red. I'm ready to go when you are. We'll have to have a boat, though.'

'We'll take George's,' said Dick, getting up. 'Look, Jo – I think we'd better leave Anne behind this time. I don't like taking her into something that may be dangerous.'

688

'I want to come,' said Anne at once.

'No, you stay with me,' said Joan. 'I want company today. I'm getting scared of being by myself with all these things happening. You stay with me.'

So Anne stayed behind, really rather glad, and watched the other three go off together. Jo slipped into the hedge to avoid being seen by Jake, in case he was anywhere about. Julian and Dick went down to the beach and glanced round to make sure the gipsy was nowhere in sight.

They beckoned to Jo, and she came swiftly from hiding, and leapt into George's boat. She lay down in it so that she couldn't be seen. The boys hauled the boat down to the sea. Dick jumped in, and Julian pushed off when a big wave came. Then he jumped in too.

'How far up the coast is it?' he asked Jo, who was still at the bottom of the boat.

'I don't know,' said Jo, with her usual irritating vagueness. 'Two hours, three hours, maybe.'

Time didn't mean the same to Jo as it did to the others. For one thing Jo had no wrist-watch as they had, always there to be glanced at. She wouldn't have found one any use if she had, because she couldn't tell the time. Time was just day and night to her, nothing else.

Dick put up the little sail. The wind was in their favour, so he thought he might as well use it. They would get there all the more quickly.

'Did you bring the lunch that Joan put up for us?' said Julian to Dick. 'I can't see it anywhere.'

'Jo! You must be lying on it!' said Dick.

'It won't hurt it,' said Jo. She sat up as soon as they were well out to sea, and offered to take the tiller.

She was very deft with it, and the boys soon saw that they could leave her to guide the boat. Julian unfolded the map he had brought with him.

'I wonder whereabouts this place is where Red lives,' he said. 'It's pretty desolate all the way up to the next place,

Port Limmersley. If there *is* a castle-like building, it must
be a very lonely place to live in. There's not even a little
fishing village shown for miles.'

The boat went on and on, scudding at times before a
fairly strong wind. Julian took the tiller from Jo. 'We've
come a long way already,' he said. 'Where *is* this place?
Are you sure you'll know it, Jo?'

'Of course,' said Jo, scornfully. 'I think it's round that
far-off rocky cliff.'

690

She was right. As they rounded the high cliff, which jutted fiercely with great slanting rocks, she pointed in triumph.

'There you are! See that place up there? That's Red's place.'

The boys looked at it. It was a dour, grey stone building, and was, as Jo had said, a little like a small castle. It brooded over the sea, with one square tower overlooking the waves.

'There's a cove before you come to the place,' said Jo. 'Watch out for it – it's very well hidden.'

It certainly was. The boat went right past it before they saw it. 'There it is!' cried Jo, urgently.

They took the sail down and then rowed back. The cove lay between two high layers of rock that jutted out from the cliff. They rowed right into it. It was very quiet and calm there, and their boat merely rose and fell as the water swelled and subsided under it.

'Can anyone see us from the house above?' asked Dick, as they rowed right to the back of the cove.

'I don't know,' said Jo. 'I shouldn't think so. Look – pull the boat up behind that big rock. We don't know who else might come here.'

They dragged the boat up. Dick draped it with great armfuls of seaweed, and soon it looked almost like a rock itself.

'Now, what next?' said Julian. 'Where's this cave you were talking about?'

'Up here,' said Jo, and began to climb up the rocky cliff like a monkey. Both the boys were very good climbers, but soon they found it impossible to get any further.

Jo scrambled down to them. 'What's the matter?' she said. 'If my Dad can climb up, surely you can!'

'Your Dad was an acrobat,' said Julian, sliding down a few feet, much too suddenly. 'Oooh! I don't much like this. I wish we had a rope.'

'There's one in the boat. I'll get it,' said Jo, and slithered down the cliff to the cove below at a most alarming rate. She climbed up again with the rope. She went on a good bit higher, and tied the rope to something. It hung down to where Dick and Julian stood clinging for dear life.

It was much easier to climb up with the help of a rope. Both boys were soon standing on a ledge, looking into a curious shaped cave. It was oval-shaped, and very dark.

'In here,' said Jo, and led the way. Dick and Julian followed stumblingly. Where in the world were they going to now?

18

Things begin to happen

Jo led them into a narrow rocky tunnel, and then out into a wider cave, whose walls dripped with damp. Julian was thankful for his torch. It was eerie and chilly and musty. He shivered. Something brushed his face and he leapt back.

'What was that?' he said.

'Bats,' said Jo, 'there's hundreds of them here. That's why the place smells so sour. Come on. We go round this rocky bit here into a better cave.'

They squeezed round a rocky corner and came into a drier cave that did not smell so strongly of bats. 'I haven't been any farther than this,' said Jo. 'This is where me and Dad came and waited for Red. He suddenly appeared, but I don't know where from.'

'Well, he must have come from somewhere,' said Dick, switching on his torch, too. 'There's a passage probably. We'll soon find it.'

He and Julian began to hunt round the cave, looking for a passage or little tunnel, or even a hole that led into the cliff, upwards towards the house. Obviously Red must have come down some such passage to reach the cave. Jo stayed in a corner, waiting. She had no torch.

Suddenly the boys had a tremendous shock. A voice boomed into their cave, a loud and angry voice that made their hearts beat painfully.

'SO! YOU DARE TO COME HERE!'

Jo slipped behind a rock immediately, like an animal going to cover. The boys stood where they were, rooted to the spot. Where did the voice come from?

'Who are you?' boomed the voice.

'Who are *you*?' shouted Julian. 'Come out and show yourself! We've come to see a man called Red. Take us to him.'

There was a moment's silence, as if the owner of the voice was rather taken aback. Then it boomed out again.

'Why do you want to see Red? Who sent you?'

'Nobody. We came because we want our cousin back, and her dog, too,' boomed Julian, making a funnel of his hands and trying to outdo the other voice.

There was another astonished silence. Then two legs appeared out of a hole in the low ceiling, and someone leapt lightly down beside them. The boys started back in surprise. They hadn't expected that the voice came from the roof of the cave!

Julian flashed his torch on the man. He was a giant-like fellow with flaming red hair. His eyebrows were red, too, and he had a red beard that partly hid a cruel mouth. Julian took one look into the man's eyes and then no more.

'He's mad,' he thought. 'So this is Red Tower. What is he? A scientist like Uncle Quentin, jealous of uncle's work? Or a thief working on a big scale, trying to get important papers and sell them? He's mad, whatever he is.'

Red was looking closely at the two boys. 'So you think I

694

have your cousin,' he said. 'Who told you such a stupid
tale?'

Julian didn't answer. Red took a threatening step towards him. 'Who told you?'

'I'll tell you that when the police come,' said Julian,
boldly.

Red stepped back.

'The police! What do they know? Why should they come here? Answer me, boy!'

'There's a lot to know about you, Mr Red Tower,' said Julian. 'Who sent men to steal my uncle's papers? Who sent a note to ask for another lot? Who kidnapped our cousin, so that she could be held till the papers were sent? Who brought her here from Simmy's old caravan? Who . . .?'

'Aaaaaah!' said Red, and there was panic in his voice. 'How do you know all this? It isn't true! But the police – have they heard this fantastic tale, too?'

'What do you suppose?' said Julian, wishing with all his heart that the police *did* know, and that he was not merely bluffing. Red pulled at his beard. His green eyes gleamed as he thought quickly and urgently.

He suddenly called loudly, turning his head up to the hole in the celing. 'Markhoff! Come down!'

Two legs were swung down through the hole, and a short burly man leapt down beside the two startled boys.

'Go down the cliff. You will find a boat in the cove, somewhere – the boat we saw these boys coming in,' said Red sharply. 'Smash it to pieces. Then come back here and take the boys to the yard. Tie them up. We must leave quickly, and take the girl with us.'

The man stood listening, his face sullen. 'How can we go?' he said. 'You know the helicopter is not ready. You *know* that.'

'Make it ready, then,' snapped Red. 'We leave tonight. The police will be here – do you hear that? This boy knows everything – he has told me – and the police·must know everything too. I tell you, we must go.'

'What about the dog?' said the man.

'Shoot it,' ordered Red. 'Shoot it before we go. It's a brute of a dog. We should have shot it before. Now go and smash the boat.'

The man disappeared round the rocky corner that led

into the cave of bats. Julian clenched his fist. He hated to think of George's boat being smashed to bits. Red stood there waiting, his eyes glinting in the light of the torches.

'I'd take you with us too, if there was room!' he suddenly snarled at Julian. 'Yes, and drop you into the sea!

'You can tell your uncle he'll hear from me about his precious daughter – we'll make an exchange. If he wants her back he can send me the notes I want. And many thanks for coming to warn me. I'll be off before the police break in.'

He began to pace up and down the cave, muttering. Dick and Julian watched in silence. They felt afraid for George. Would Red really take her off in his helicopter? He looked mad enough for anything.

The sullen man came back at last. 'It's smashed,' he said.

'Right,' said Red. 'I'll go first. Then the boys. Then you. And boot them if they make any trouble.'

Red swung himself up into the hole in the roof. Julian and Dick followed, not seeing any point in resisting. The man behind was too sulky to stand any nonsense. He followed immediately.

There had been no sign of Jo. She had kept herself well hidden, scared stiff. Julian didn't know what to do about her. He couldn't possibly tell Red about her – and yet it seemed terrible to leave her behind all alone. Well – she was a sharp-brained little monkey. Maybe she would think up something for herself.

Red led the way through another cave into a passage with such a low roof that he had to walk bent almost double.

The man behind had now switched on a very powerful torch, and it was easier to see. The passage sloped upwards and was obviously leading to the building on the cliff. At one part it was so steep that a hand-rail had been put for the climber to help himself up.

697

Then came a flight of steps hewn out of the rock itself – rough, badly-shaped steps, so steep that it was quite an effort to climb from one to the next.

At the top of the steps was a stout door set on a broad ledge. Red pushed it open and daylight flooded in. Julian blinked. He was looking out on an enormous yard paved with great flat stones with weeds growing in all the crevices and cracks.

In the middle stood a helicopter. It looked very strange and out-of-place in that old yard. The house, with its one tall square tower, was built round three sides of the yard. It was covered with creeper and thick-stemmed ivy.

A high wall ran along the fourth side, with an enormous gate in the middle. It was shut, and from where he stood Julian could see the huge bolts that were drawn across.

'It's almost like a small fort,' thought Julian, in astonishment. Then he felt himself seized and taken to a shed nearby. His arms were forced behind him and his wrists were tightly tied. Then the rope was run through an iron loop and tied again.

Julian glared at the burly fellow now doing the same to Dick. He twisted about to try to see how the rope was tied, but he couldn't even turn, he was so tightly tethered.

He looked up at the tower. A small, forlorn face was looking out of the window there. Julian's heart jumped and beat fast. That must be poor old George up there. He wondered if she had seen them. He hoped not, because she would know that he and Dick had been captured, and she would be very upset.

Where was Timmy? There seemed no sign of him. But wait a minute – what was that lying inside what looked like a summer-house on the opposite side of the yard? *Was* it Timmy? Surely he would have barked a welcome when he heard them coming into the yard, if it *was* Timmy!

'Is that my cousin's dog?' he asked the sullen man.

The man nodded. 'Yes. He's been doped half the time,

he barked so. Savage brute, isn't he? *Ought* to be shot, I reckon.'

Red had gone across the yard and had disappeared through a stone archway. The sullen man now followed him. Julian and Dick were left by themselves.

'We've muddled things again,' said Julian, with a groan. 'Now these fellows will be off and away, and take George with them – they've been nicely warned!'

Dick said nothing. He felt very miserable, and his bound wrists hurt him, too. Both boys stood there, wondering what would happen to them.

'Pssssst!'

What was that? Julian turned round sharply and looked in the direction of the door that led from underground into the yard. Jo stood there, half-hidden by the archway over the door. 'Pssssst! I'll come and untie you. Is the coast clear?'

19

Jo is very surprising

'Jo!' said the boys together, and their spirits lifted at once. 'Come on!'

There was no one about in the yard. Jo skipped lightly across from the doorway and slipped inside the shed.

'There's a knife in my back pocket,' said Julian. 'Get it out. It would be quicker to cut these ropes than to untie them. My word, Jo – I was never so pleased to see anyone in my life!'

Jo grinned as she hauled out Julian's sturdy pocket-knife. She opened it and ran her thumb lightly over the blade. It was beautifully sharp. She set to work to saw the blade across the thick rope. It cut easily through the fibres.

'I waited behind,' she said, rapidly. 'Then I followed when it was safe. But it was very dark and I didn't like it. Then I came to that door and peeped out. I was glad when I saw you.'

'Good thing the men didn't guess you were there,' said Dick. 'Good old Jo! I take back any nasty thing I've ever said about you!'

Jo beamed. She cut the last bit of rope that bound Julian, and he swung himself away from the iron loop and began to rub his stiff, aching wrists. Jo set to work on Dick's bonds. She soon had those cut through, too.

'Where's George?' she asked, after she had helped Dick to rub his wrists and arms.

'Up in that tower,' said Julian. 'If we dared to go out in that yard you could look up and see her. And there's poor old Tim, look – half-doped – lying in that summer-house place over there.'

'I shan't let him be shot,' said Jo. 'He's a nice dog. I shall go and drag him down into those caves underground.'

'Not now!' said Julian, horrified. 'If you're seen now, you'll spoil everything. We'll *all* be tied up then!'

But Jo had already darted over to the summer-house and was fondling poor old Timmy.

The slam of a door made the boys jump and sent Jo into the shadows at the back of the summer-house at once. It was Red, coming across the yard!

'Quick! He's coming over here!' said Dick, in a panic. 'Let's get back to the iron loops and put our hands behind us so that he thinks we're still bound.'

So, when Red came over to the door of the shed, it looked exactly as if the boys still had their hands tied behind them. He laughed.

'You can stay here till the police come!' he said. Then he shut the shed door and locked it. He strolled over to the helicopter and examined it thoroughly. Then back he went to the door he had come from, opened it, and slammed it shut. He was gone.

When everything was quiet Jo sped back from the summer-house to the shed. She unlocked the door of the shed. 'Come out,' she said. 'And we'll lock it again. Then nobody will know you aren't here. Hurry!'

There was nothing for it but to come out and hope there

was nobody looking. Jo locked the shed door after them and hurried them back to the door that led underground. They slipped through it and half-fell down the steep steps.

'Thanks, Jo,' said Dick.

They sat down. Julian scratched his head, and for the life of him could not think of anything sensible to do. The police were *not* coming because they didn't know a thing about Red, or where George was or anything. And before long George would be flown off in that helicopter, and Timmy would be shot.

Julian thought of the high square tower and groaned. 'There's no way of getting George out of that tower,' he said aloud. 'It'll be locked and barred, or George would have got out at once. We can't even get to her. It's no good trying to make our way into the house – we'd be seen and caught at once.'

Jo looked at Dick. 'Do you badly want George to be rescued?' she said.

'That's a silly question,' said Dick. 'I want it more than anything else in the world.'

'Well – I'll go and get her, then,' said Jo, and she got up as if she really meant it.

'Don't make jokes now,' said Julian. 'This really is serious, Jo.'

'Well, so am I,' retorted Jo. 'I'll get her out, you see if I don't. Then you'll know I'm trustable, won't you? You think I'm mean and thieving and not worth a penny, and I expect you're right. But I can do some things you can't, and if you want this thing, I'll do it for you.'

'How?' said Julian, astonished and disbelieving.

Jo sat down again.

'You saw that tower, didn't you?' she began. 'Well, it's a big one, so I reckon there's more than one room in it – and if I can get into the room next to George's I could undo her door and set her free.'

702

'And how do you think you're going to get into the room next to hers?' said Dick, scornfully.

'Climb up the wall, of course,' said Jo. 'It's set thick with ivy. I've often climbed up walls like that.'

The boys looked at her. 'Were you the Face at the Window by any chance?' said Julian, remembering Anne's fright. 'I bet you were. You're like a monkey, climbing and darting about. But you can't climb up that great high wall, so don't think it. You'd fall and be killed. We couldn't let you.'

'Pooh!' said Jo, with great scorn. 'Fall off a wall like that! I've climbed up a wall without any ivy at all! There's always holes and cracks to hold on to. That one would be easy!'

Julian was quite dumbfounded to think that Jo really meant all this. Dick remembered that Jo's father was an acrobat. Perhaps that kind of thing was in the family.

'You just ought to see me on a tight-rope,' said Jo earnestly. 'I can dance on it – and I never have a safety-net underneath – that's baby-play! Well, I'm going.'

Without another word she climbed the steep steps lightly as a goat and stood poised in the archway of the door. All was quiet. Like a squirrel she leapt and bounded over the courtyard and came to the foot of the ivy-covered tower. Julian and Dick were now at the doorway that led into the yard, watching her.

'She'll be killed,' said Julian.

'Talk about pluck!' said Dick. 'I never saw such a kid in my life. There she goes – just like a monkey.'

And, sure enough, up the ivy went Jo, climbing lightly and steadily. Her hands reached out and tested each ivy-stem before she threw her weight on it, and her feet tried each one, too, before she stood on it.

Once she slipped when an ivy-stem came away from the wall. Julian and Dick watched, their hearts in their mouths. But Jo merely clutched at another piece of stem and steadied herself once. Then up she went again.

Up and up. Past the first storey, past the second, and up to the third. Only one more now and she would be up to the topmost one. She seemed very small as she neared the top.

'I can't bear to look and I can't bear not to,' said Dick, pretending to shield his eyes and almost trembling with nervousness. 'If she fell now – what should we do?'

'Do shut up,' said Julian, between his teeth. 'She won't fall. She's like a cat. There – she's making for the window next to George's. It's open at the bottom.'

Jo now sat triumphantly on the broad window-sill of the room next to George's. She waved impudently to the boys far below. Then she pushed with all her might at the window to open it a little more. It wouldn't budge.

So Jo laid herself flat, and by dint of much wriggling and squeezing, she managed to slip through the narrow space between the bottom of the window-pane and the sill. She disappeared from sight.

Both boys heaved heartfelt sighs of relief. Dick found that his knees were shaking. He and Julian retired into the underground passage below the steep steps and sat there in silence.

'Worse than a circus,' said Dick at last. 'I'll never be able to watch acrobats again. What's she doing now, do you suppose?'

Jo was very busy. She had fallen off the inside window-sill with a bump, and bruised herself on the floor below. But she was used to bruises.

She picked herself up and shot behind a chair in case anyone had heard her. Nobody seemed to have heard anything, so she peeped cautiously out. The room was furnished with enormous pieces of furniture, old and heavy. Dust was on everything, and cobwebs hung down from the stone ceiling.

Jo tiptoed to the door. Her feet were bare and made no sound at all. She looked out. There was a spiral stone stairway nearby going downwards, and on each side was a door – there must be four rooms in the tower then, one for each corner, two windows in each. She looked at the door next to the room she was in. That must be the door of George's room.

There was a very large key in the lock, and a great bolt

705

had been drawn across. Jo leapt across and dragged at the bolt. It made a loud noise and she darted back into the room again. But still nobody came. Back she went to the door again, and this time turned the enormous key. It was well oiled and turned easily.

Jo pushed open the door and put her head cautiously round. George was there – a thin and unhappy George, sitting by the window. She stared at Jo as if she couldn't believe her eyes!

'Psssst!' said Jo, enjoying all this very much indeed. 'I've come to get you out!'

20

The adventure boils up

GEORGE looked as if she had seen a ghost. 'Jo!' she whispered. 'It can't really be you.'

'It is. Feel,' said Jo, and pattered across the room to give George quite a hard pinch. Then she pulled at her arm.

'Come on,' she said. 'We must go before Red comes. Hurry! I don't want to be caught.'

George got up as if she was in a dream. She went across to the door. She and Jo slipped out, and stood at the top of the spiral staircase.

'Have to go down here, I suppose,' said Jo. She cocked her head and listened. Then she went down a few steps and turned the first spiral bend.

But before she had gone down more than a dozen steps she stopped in fright. Somebody was coming up!

In panic Jo ran up again and pushed George roughly into the room she had climbed into first of all.

'Someone's coming,' she panted. 'Now we're finished.'

'It's that red-haired man, I expect,' said George. 'He comes up three or four times a day and tries to make me tell him about my father's work. But I don't know a thing. What are we to do?'

The slow steps came up and up, sounding hollowly on the stone stairs. They could hear a panting breath now, too.

An idea came to Jo. She put her mouth close to George's ear. 'Listen! We look awfully alike. I'll let myself be caught and locked up in that room – and you take the chance to slip down and go to Dick and Julian. Red will never know I'm not you – we've even got the same clothes on now, because Joan gave me old ones of yours.'

'No,' said George, astounded. 'You'll be caught. I don't want you to do that.'

'You've *got* to,' whispered Jo, fiercely. 'Don't be daft. I can open the window and climb down the ivy, easy as winking, when Red's gone. It's your only chance. They're going to take you off in that helicopter tonight.'

The footsteps were now at the top. Jo pushed George well behind a curtain and whispered fiercely again: 'Anyway, I'm not really doing this for you. I'm doing it for Dick. You keep there and I'll do the rest.'

There was a loud exclamation when the man outside discovered the door of George's room open. He went in quickly and found nobody there. Out he came and yelled down the stairs.

'Markhoff! The door's open and the girl's gone! Who opened the door?'

Markhoff came up two steps at a time, looking bewildered. 'No one! Who could? Anyway, the girl can't be far off! I've been in the room below all the time since I locked her in last time. I'd have seen her if she's gone.'

'Who unlocked the door?' screamed Red, quite beside himself with anger. 'We've *got* to have that girl to bargain with.'

'Well, she must be in one of the other rooms,' said Markhoff, stolidly, quite unmoved by his master's fury.

He went into one on the opposite side to the room where Jo and George crouched trembling. Then he came into their room, and at once saw the top of Jo's head showing behind the chair.

He pounced on her and dragged her out. 'Here she is!' he said, and didn't seem to realize that it was not George at all, but Jo. With their short hair, freckled faces and their similar clothes they really were alike. Jo yelled and struggled most realistically. Nobody would have guessed that she had planned to be caught and locked up!

George shook and shivered behind the curtain, longing to go to Jo's help, but knowing that it wouldn't be of the least use. Besides – there might be a chance now of finding Timmy. It had almost broken George's heart to be parted from him for so long.

Jo was dragged yelling and kicking into the room and locked in again. Red and Markhoff began to quarrel about which of them must have left the door unlocked.

'You were there last,' said Red.

'Well, if I was, I tell you I didn't leave the door unlocked,' Markhoff raged back. 'I wouldn't be so fat-headed. That's the kind of thing *you* do.'

'That'll do,' snapped Red. 'Have you shot that dog yet? No, you haven't! Go down and do it before *he* escapes too!'

George's heart went stone-cold. Shoot Timmy! Oh *no*! Dear darling old Timmy. She couldn't let him be shot!

She didn't know what to do. She heard Red and Mark- khoff go down the stone stairway, their boots making a terrific noise at first, and then gradually becoming fainter.

She slipped down after them. They went into a nearby room, still arguing. George risked being seen and shot past the open door. She came to another stairway, not a spiral one this time, and went down it so fast that she almost lost her footing. Down and down and down. She met nobody at all. What a very strange place this was!

She came into a dark, enormous hall that smelt musty

and old. She ran to the great door at the front and tried to open it. It was very heavy, but at last it swung slowly back.

She stood there in the bright sunlight, peering out cautiously. She knew where Timmy was. She had been able to see him sometimes, flopping queerly in and out of the summer-house. She knew that because of his continual barking he had been doped. Red had told her that when she had asked him. He enjoyed making her miserable. Poor George!

She tore across the courtyard and came to the summer-house. Timmy was there, lying as if he were asleep. George flung herself on him, her arms round his thick neck.

'Timmy, oh Timmy!' she cried, and couldn't see him for tears. Timmy, far away in some drugged dream, heard the voice he loved best in all the world. He stirred. He opened his eyes and saw George!

He was too heavy with his sleep to do more than lick her face. Then his eyes closed again. George was in despair. She was afraid Markhoff would come and shoot him in a very short time.

'Timmy!' she called in his ear. 'TIMMY! Do wake up. TIMMY!'

Tim opened his eyes again. What – his mistress still here! Then it couldn't be a dream. Perhaps his world would soon be right again. Timmy didn't understand at all what had been happening the last few days. He staggered to his feet somehow and stood swaying there, shaking his head. George put her hand on his collar. 'That's right, Tim,' she said. 'Now you come with me. Quick!'

But Timmy couldn't walk, though he had managed to stand. In despair George glanced over the couryard, fearful that she would see Markhoff coming at any moment.

She saw somebody else. She saw Julian standing in an

archway opposite, staring at her. She was too upset about Timmy even to feel much astonishment.

'Ju!' she called. 'Come and help me with Timmy. They're going to shoot him!'

In a trice Julian and Dick shot across the courtyard to George. 'What happened, Jo?' said Julian. 'Did you find George?'

'Ju – it's me, George!' said George, and Julian suddenly saw that indeed it was George herself. He had been so certain that it was still Jo that he hadn't known it was George!

'Help me with Timmy,' said George, and she pulled at the heavy dog. 'Where shall we hide him?'

'Down underground,' said Dick. 'It's the only place. Come on!'

How they managed it they never quite knew, but they did drag the heavy, stupid Timmy all the way across the yard and into the archway. They opened the door and shoved him inside. Poor Timmy fell over and immediately rolled down the steep steps, landing at the bottom with a frightful thud. George gave a little scream.

'He'll be hurt!'

But astonishingly enough Timmy didn't seem to be hurt at all. In fact the shaking seemed to have done him good. He got up and looked round him in rather a surprised way. Then he whined and looked up at George. He tried to climb the steep steps, but wasn't lively enough.

George was down beside him in a moment, patting him and stroking him. The two boys joined in. Timmy began to feel that things might be all right again, if only he could get rid of the dreadful, heavy feeling in his head. He couldn't understand why he kept wanting to lie down and go to sleep.

'Bring him right down to the caves,' said Dick. 'Those men are sure to hunt for him and for us too when they find Timmy gone, and us not in the shed.'

So down the narrow passages and into the little cave with the hole in the roof they all went, Timmy feeling as if he didn't quite know which of his legs to use next.

They all sat down in a heap together when they got there, and George got as close to Timmy as she could. She was glad when the boys switched off their torches. She badly wanted to cry, and as she never did cry it was most embarrassing if anyone saw her.

She told the boys in a low voice all that had happened with Jo. 'She *made* me stay hidden so that she could be caught,' she said. 'She's wonderful. She's the bravest girl I ever knew. And she did it all even though she doesn't like me.'

'She's a queer one,' said Dick. 'She's all right at heart, though – very much all right.'

They talked quickly, in low voices, exchanging their news. George told them how she had been caught and taken to the caravan with Timmy, who had been knocked out with a cudgel.

'We saw where you had written Red's name,' said Dick. 'That gave us the clue to come here!'

'Listen,' said Julian, suddenly. 'I think we ought to make a plan quickly. I keep thinking I hear things. We're sure to be looked for soon, you know. What can we *do*?'

21

A few surprises

As soon as Julian had said that he kept hearing noises, the others felt as if they could hear some, too. They sat and listened intently, George's heart beating so loudly that she was certain the boys would be able to hear it.

'I think perhaps it's the sound of the sea, echoing in through the caves and the tunnels,' said Julian at last. 'In the ordinary way, of course, we wouldn't need to bother to listen – Timmy would growl at once! But, poor old chap, he's so doped and sleepy that I don't believe he hears anything.'

'Will he get all right again?' asked George, anxiously, fondling Timmy's silky ears.

'Oh, yes,' said Julian, sounding much more certain than he really felt. Poor Timmy – he really did seem ill! There wasn't even a growl in him.

'You've had an awful time these last few days, haven't you, George?' asked Dick.

'Yes,' said George. 'I don't much want to talk about it. If I'd had Timmy with me it wouldn't have been so bad, but at first, when they brought me here, all I knew of Timmy was hearing him bark and snarl and bark and snarl down below in that yard. Then Red told me he had doped him.'

'How did you get to Red's place?' asked Julian.

'Well, you know I was locked in that horrible-smelling caravan,' said George. 'Then suddenly a man called Simmy – he's Jo's father, I think – came and dragged us out. Timmy was all stupid with the blow they'd given him – and they put him in a sack and put us both on the caravan horse and took us through the wood and along a desolate path by the coast till we came here. That was in the middle of the night.'

'Poor old George!' said Julian. 'I wish Tim was himself again – I'd love to set him loose on Red and the other fellow!'

'I wonder what's happening to Jo,' said Dick, suddenly remembering that Jo was now imprisoned in the tower room where George had been kept so long.

'And do you suppose that Red and Markhoff have discovered that we've got out of that shed, and that Timmy has disappeared, too?' said Julian. 'They'll be in a fury when they do discover it!'

'Can't we get away?' said George, feeling suddenly scared. 'You came in a boat, didn't you? Well, can't we get away in that and go and fetch help for Jo?'

There was a silence. Neither of the boys liked to tell George that her beloved boat had been smashed to pieces by Markhoff. But she had to know, of course, and Julian told her in a few short words.

George said nothing at all. They all sat silently for a few minutes, hearing nothing but Timmy's heavy, almost snoring, breathing.

'Would it be possible, when it's dark, to creep up into the courtyard, and go round the walls to the big gate?' said Dick, breaking the silence. 'We can't escape anywhere down here, it's certain – not without a boat, anyhow.'

'Should we wait till Red and Markhoff have gone off in the helicopter?' said Julian. 'Then we'd be much safer.'

'Yes – but what about Jo?' asked Dick. 'They think she's George, don't they? – and they'll take her away with them, just as they planned to do with George. I don't see how we can try to escape ourselves without first trying to save Jo. She's been a brick about George.'

They talked round and round the idea of trying to save Jo, but nobody could think of any really sensible plan at all. Time went on, and they all felt hungry and rather cold. 'If only we could *do* something, it wouldn't be so bad!' groaned Dick. 'I wonder what's happening up at the house.'

Up at the grey stone house with its big square tower, plenty was happening!

To begin with, Markhoff had gone to shoot Timmy, as Red had ordered. But when he got to the summer-house there was no dog there!

Markhoff stared in the greatest amazement! The dog had been tied up, even though he was doped – and now, there was the loose rope, and no dog attached to it!

Markhoff gazed round the summer-house in astonishment. Who could have loosed Timmy? He darted across to the locked shed where he had tied Julian and Dick with rope to the iron staples. The door was still locked, of course – and Markhoff turned the key and pushed it open.

'Here, you . . .' he began, shouting roughly. Then he stopped dead. Nobody was there! Again there was loose rope – this time cut here and there, so that it lay in short pieces – and again the prisoners had gone. No dog. No boys.

Markhoff couldn't believe his eyes. He looked all round the shed. 'But it was locked from the outside!' he muttered. 'What's all this? Who's freed the dog and the boys? What will Red say?'

Markhoff looked at the helicopter standing ready for flight in the middle of the yard, and half decided to desert Red and get away himself. Then, remembering Red's mad tempers, and his cruel revenges on anyone who dared to let him down, he changed his mind.

'We'd better get off now, before it's dark,' he thought. 'There's something queer going on here. There must be somebody else here that we know nothing about. I'd better find Red and tell him.'

He went in through the massive front door, and in the hall he came face to face with two men waiting there. At first he couldn't see who they were, and he stepped back hurriedly. Then he saw it was Simmy and Jake.

'What are you doing here?' shouted Markhoff. 'Weren't you told to keep watch on Kirrin Cottage and make sure the police weren't told anything?'

'Yes,' said Jake, sulkily. 'And we've come to say that that cook – woman called Joan – went down to the police this morning. She had one of the kids with her – a girl. The boys don't seem to be about.'

'No. They're here – at least, they were,' said Markhoff. 'They've disappeared again. As for the police, we've heard they're on the way, and we've made our plans. You're a bit late with your news! Lot of good you are, with your spying! Clear off now – we're taking the girl off in the helicopter before the police come. How did anyone know where the girl was? Have you been spilling the beans?'

'Pah!' said Simmy, contemptuously. 'Think we want to be messed up with the police? You must be mad. We want some money. We've done all your dirty work, and you've only paid us half you promised. Give us the rest.'

'You can ask Red for it!' growled Markhoff. 'What's the good of asking me? Go and ask *him*!'

'Right. We will,' said Jake, his face as black as thunder. 'We've done all he told us – took the papers for him, took the girl – and that savage brute of a dog too – see where he

717

bit me on my hand? And all we get is half our money! I reckon we've only just come in time, too. Planning to go off in that there heli-thing and do us out of our pay. Pah!'

'Where's Red?' demanded Simmy.

'Upstairs,' said Markhoff. 'I've got some bad news for him, so he won't be pleased to see you and your ugly mugs. Better let me find him for you and say what I've got to say – then you can chip in with your polite little speeches.'

'Funny, aren't you?' said Jake, in a dangerous voice. Neither he nor Simmy liked Markhoff. They followed him up the broad stairway, and then up again till they came to the room that lay below the spiral staircase.

Red was there, scanning through the papers that had been stolen from the study of George's father. He was in a black temper. He flung down the papers as Markhoff came in.

'These aren't the notes I wanted!' he began, loudly. 'Well, I'll hold the girl till I get . . . why, Markhoff, what's up? Anything wrong?'

'Plenty,' said Markhoff. 'The dog's gone – he wasn't there when I went to shoot him – and the two boys have gone too – yes, escaped out of a locked shed. Beats me!

'And here are two visitors for you – they want money! They've come to tell you what you already know – the police have been told about you.'

Red went purple in the face, and his strange eyes shone with rage. He stared first at Markhoff, then at Simmy and Jake. Markhoff looked uneasy, but Simmy and Jake looked back insolently.

'You – you – you *dare* to come here when I told you to keep away!' he shouted. 'You've BEEN paid. You can't blackmail me for any more money.'

What he would have said next nobody knew because from up the spiral stairs there came yells and screams and the noise of someone apparently trying to batter down a door.

718

'That's that girl, I suppose,' muttered Markhoff. 'What's up with her? She's been quiet enough before.'

'We'd better get her out now and go,' said Red, his face still purple. 'Jake, go and get her. Bring her down here, and knock some sense into her if she goes on screaming.'

'Fetch her yourself,' said Jake, insolently.

Red looked at Markhoff, who immediately produced a revolver.

'My orders are always obeyed,' said Red in a suddenly cold voice. '*Always*, you understand?'

Not only Jake scuttled up the stairs then but also Simmy! They went to the locked and bolted room at the top and unlocked the door. They pulled back the bolt and door. Simmy stepped into the room to deal with the imprisoned girl.

But he stopped dead and gaped. He blinked, rubbed his eyes and gaped again. Jake gaped too.

'Hallo, Dad!' said Jo. 'You *do* seem surprised to see me!'

22

Jo is very smart

'Jo,' said Simmy. 'Well, of all the . . . well . . . *JO!*' Jake recovered first. 'What's all this?' he said, roughly, to Simmy. 'What's Jo doing here? How did *she* get here? Where's the other kid, the one we caught?'

'How do *I* know?' said Simmy, still staring at Jo. 'Look here, Jo – what are you doing here? Go on, tell us. And where's the other kid?'

'Hunt round the room and see if you can find her!' said Jo, brightly, keeping on her toes in case her father or Jake was going to pounce on her. The two men looked hurriedly round the room. Jake went to a big cupboard.

'Yes – she might be in there,' said Jo, enjoying herself. 'You have a good look.'

The two bewildered men didn't know what to think. They had come to get George – and had only found Jo!

But how – why – what had happened? They didn't know what to do. Neither of them wanted to go back and tell Red. So they began to search the room feverishly,

720

looking into likely and unlikely places, with Jo jeering at them all the time.

'Better take the drawers out of that chest and see if she's here. And don't forget to look under the rug. That's right, Jake, poke your head up the chimney. Mind George doesn't kick soot into your eyes.'

'I'll lam you in a minute!' growled Jake, furiously, opening a small cupboard door.

An angry voice came up the stairway. 'Jake! What are you doing up there? Bring that kid down.'

'She's not here!' yelled back Jake, suddenly losing his temper. 'What have you done with her? She's gone!'

Red came tearing up, two steps at a time, his eyes narrow with anger. The first thing he saw in the room was Jo – and, of course, he thought she was George.

'What do you mean – saying she's not here!' he raged. 'Are you mad?'

'Nope,' said Jake, his eyes narrow too. 'Not so mad as you are, anyway, Red. This kid isn't that fellow's daughter – the scientist chap we took the papers from – this is Simmy's kid – Jo.'

Red looked at Jake as if he had gone off his head. Then he looked at Jo. He could see no difference between Jo and the absent George at all – short hair, freckles, turned-up nose – he couldn't believe that she was Simmy's daughter.

In fact, he didn't believe it. He thought Jake and Simmy were suddenly deceiving him for some strange reason.

But Jo had a word to say, too. 'Yes, I'm Jo,' she said. 'I'm not Georgina. She's gone. I'm just Jo, and Simmy's my Dad. You've come to save me, haven't you, Dad?'

Simmy hadn't come to do anything of the sort, of course. He stared helplessly at Jo, completely bewildered.

Red completely lost his temper. As soon as he heard Jo's voice he realized she was not George. Somehow or other he had been deceived – and seeing that this was Simmy's daughter, then it must be Simmy who had had a hand in the deception!

He went suddenly over to Simmy and struck him hard, his eyes blazing. 'Have you double-crossed me?' he shouted.

Simmy was sent flying to the floor. Jake came up immediately to help him. He tripped up Red, and leapt on him.

Jo looked at the three struggling, shouting men, and shrugged her shoulders. Let them fight! They had forgotten all about her, and that suited her very well. She ran to the door and was just going down the stairs, when an idea came into her sharp little mind. With an impish grin she turned back. She pulled the door to quietly – and then she turned the key in the lock, and shot the bolt.

The three men inside heard the key turn, and in a trice Jake was at the door, pulling at the handle.

'She's locked us in!' he raged. 'And shot the bolt, too.'

'Yell for Markhoff!' shouted Red, trembling with fury. And Markhoff, left down in the room at the bottom of the stairs, suddenly heard yells and shouts and tremendous hammerings at the door! He tore up at once, wondering what in the world had happened.

Jo was hiding in the next room. As soon as Markhoff went to the door and shot back the bolt she slipped out and was down the spiral stairway in a trice, unseen by Markhoff. She grinned to herself and hugged something to her thin little chest.

It was the big key belonging to the door upstairs. Nobody could unlock that door now – the key was missing. Jo had it!

'Unlock the door!' shouted Red. 'That kid's gone.'

'There's no key!' yelled back Markhoff. 'She must have taken it. I'll go after her.'

But it was one thing to go after Jo and quite another to find her. She seemed to have disappeared into thin air.

722

Markhoff raged through every room, but she was no-where to be seen. He went out into the courtyard and looked round there.

Actually she had made her way to the kitchen and found the larder. She was very hungry and wanted something to eat. There was nobody in the kitchen at all, though a fine fire burned in the big range there.

She slipped into the larder, took the key from the outer side of the door and locked herself in. She saw that there was a small window, and she carefully unfastened it so that she could make her escape if anyone discovered that she was locked in the larder.

Then she tucked in. Three sausage rolls, a large piece of cheese, a hunk of bread, half a meat pie and two jam tarts went the same way. After that Jo felt a lot better. She remembered the others and thought how hungry they must be feeling, too.

She found a rush bag hanging on a nail and slipped some food into it – more sausage rolls, some rock-buns, some cheese and bread. Now, if only she could find the others, how they would welcome her!

Jo put the big key at the bottom of the rush basket. She was feeling very, very pleased with herself. Red and Simmy and Jake were all nicely locked up and out of the way. She didn't fear Markhoff as much as Red. She was sure she could get away from him.

She wasn't even sorry for her father, Simmy.

She had no love for him and no respect, because he was everything that a father shouldn't be.

She heard Markhoff come raging into the kitchen and she clambered quickly up on the larder shelf, ready to drop out of the window if he tried the door. But he didn't. He raged out again, and she heard him no more.

Jo unlocked the door very cautiously. There was now an old woman in the kitchen, standing by the table, folding some clothes she had brought in from the clothes line in the yard. She stared in the greatest surprise at Jo peeping out of the larder.

'What . . .?' she began, indignantly; but Jo was out of the room before she had even got out the next word. The old dame waddled over to the larder and began to wail as she saw all the empty plates and dishes.

Jo went cautiously into the front hall. She could hear Markhoff upstairs, still tearing about. She smiled delightedly and slipped over to the door.

She undid it and pulled it open. Then, keeping to the wall, she sidled like a weasel to the door that led underground. She opened it and went through, shutting it softly behind her.

Now to find the others. She felt sure they must be down in the caves. How pleased they would be with the food in her bag!

She half-fell down the steep steps, and made her way as quickly as she could down the slanting passage. She had no torch and had to feel her way in the dark. She wasn't in the least afraid. Only when she trod on a sharp stone with her bare foot did she make a sound.

The other three – Julian, Dick and George – were still sitting crouched together with Timmy in the centre. Julian had been once up to the door that led into the yard and had cautiously peered out to see what was to be seen – but had seen nothing at all except for an old woman hanging out some clothes on a line.

The three had decided to wait till night before they did anything. They thought maybe Timmy might have recovered a little then, and would be of some help in protecting them against Red or Markhoff. They half-dozed, sitting together for warmth, enjoying the heat of Timmy's big body.

Timmy growled! Yes, he actually growled – a thing he hadn't done at all so far. George put a warning hand on him. They all sat up, listening. A voice came to them.

'Julian! Dick! Where are you? I've lost my way!'

'It's Jo!' cried Dick, and switched on his torch at once. 'Here we are, Jo! How did you escape? What's happened?'

'Heaps,' said Jo, and came gladly over to them. 'My, it was dark up in those passages without a torch. Somehow I went the wrong way. That's why I yelled. But I hadn't gone far wrong. Have a sausage roll?'

'*What?*' cried three hungry voices, and even Timmy lifted his head and began to sniff at the rush basket that Jo carried.

Jo laughed and opened the basket. She handed out all the food and the three of them fell on it like wolves. 'Jo, you're the eighth wonder of the world,' said Dick. 'Is there anything left in the basket?'

'Yes,' said Jo, and took out the enormous key. 'This, look! I locked Red and Jake and Simmy into that tower room, and here's the key. What do you think of *that*?'

23

Markhoff goes hunting

GEORGE took the big key and looked at it with awe. 'Jo! Is this really the key – and you've locked them all in? Honestly, I think you're a marvel.'

'She is,' said Dick, and to Jo's enormous delight he gave her a sudden quick hug. 'I never knew such a girl in my life. Never. She's got the pluck of twenty!'

'It was easy, really,' said Jo, her eyes shining joyfully in the light of the torch. 'You trust me now, Dick, don't you? You won't be mean to me any more, any of you, will you?'

'Of course not,' said Julian. 'You're our friend for ever!'

'Not George's,' said Jo at once.

'Oh yes you are,' said George. 'I take back every single mean thing I said about you. You're as good as a boy.'

This was the very highest compliment that George could ever pay any girl. Jo beamed and gave George a light punch.

'I did it all for Dick, really,' she said. 'But next time I'll do it for you!'

'Goodness, I hope there won't *be* a next time,' said

George, with a shiver. 'I can't say I enjoyed one single minute of the last few days.'

Timmy suddenly put his head on Jo's knee. She stroked him. 'Look at that!' she said. 'He remembers me. He's better, isn't he, George?'

George carefully removed Timmy's head from Jo's knee to her own. She felt decidedly friendly towards Jo now, but not to the extent of having Timmy put his head on Jo's knee. She patted him.

'Yes, he's better,' she said. 'He ate half the sausage roll I gave him, though he sniffed at it like anything first. I think he knows something has been put into his food and now he's suspicious of it. Good old Timmy.'

They all felt much more lively and cheerful now that they were no longer so dreadfully empty. Julian looked at his watch. 'It's getting on towards evening now,' he said. 'I wonder what all those fellows are doing?'

Three of them were still locked up! No matter how Markhoff had tried to batter in the door, it held. It was old and immensely strong, and the lock held without showing any sign of giving way even an eighth of an inch. Two other men had been called in from the garage to help, but except that the door looked decidedly worse for wear, it stood there just the same, sturdy and unbreakable.

Simmy and Jake watched Red as he walked up and down the tower room like a caged lion. They were glad they were two against one. He seemed like a madman to them as he raged and paced up and down.

Markhoff, outside with the other two men he had brought up to help, was getting very worried. No police had arrived as yet (and wouldn't either, because Joan hadn't been able to tell them anything except that she knew Julian and Dick had gone to see a man called Red – but where he lived she had no idea!).

But Red and Markhoff didn't know this – they felt sure that a police ambush was somewhere nearby. If only they could get away in the helicopter before anything else happened!

'Markhoff! Take Carl and Tom and go down into those underground caves,' ordered Red at last. 'Those children are sure to be there – it's the only place for them to hide. They can't get out of here because the front gate is locked and bolted, and the wall's too high to climb. Get hold of the kids and search them for the key.'

So Markhoff and two burly fellows went downstairs and out of the door. They crossed the yard to the door that led to the caves.

They got down the steep steps and were soon stumbling along the narrow, slanting passage, their nailed boots making a great noise as they went. They hung on to the hand-rail when they came to the difficult stretch of tunnel, and finally came out into the cave that had the hole in the floor.

There was nobody there. The children had heard the noise of the coming men, and had hurriedly swung themselves down through the hole into the cave below.

They ran through into another cave, the sour smelling one where bats lived and slept. Then round the rocky corner into the first cave, the curious oval-shaped one that led out to the ledge of rock overlooking the steep cliff.

'There's nowhere to hide,' groaned Julian. He looked back into the cave. At least it was better in there than out on this ledge, outlined by the daylight. He pulled the others back into the cave, and shone his torch up and down the walls to find some corner that they could squeeze behind.

Half-way up the wall was a shelf of rock. He hoisted George up there, and she dragged Timmy up too. Poor Timmy – he wasn't much use to them; he was still so bemused and so very sleepy. He had growled at the noise made by the coming men, but had dropped his head again almost immediately.

Dick got up beside George. Julian found a jutting-out rock and tried to hide behind it, while Jo lay down in a hole beside one wall and covered herself cleverly with sand. Julian couldn't help thinking how sharp Jo was. She always seemed to know the best thing to do.

But as it happened, Jo was the only one to be discovered! It was quite by accident – Markhoff trod on her. He and the other two men had let themselves down through the hole into the cave below, had then gone into the cave of bats, seen no sign of anyone there, and were now in the cave that led to the cliff.

'Those kids aren't here,' said one of the men. 'They've gone to hide somewhere else. What a horrible place this is – let's go back.'

Markhoff was flashing his torch up and down the walls to see if any of the children were crouching behind a jutting rock – and he trod heavily on Jo's hand. She gave an agonized yell, and Markhoff almost dropped his torch!

In a trice he had pulled the girl out of her bed of sand and was shaking her like a rat. 'This is the one we want!' he said to the others. 'She's got the key. Where is it, you little rat? Give it to me or I'll throw you down the cliff!'

Julian was horrified. He felt quite certain that Markhoff really would throw Jo down the cliff, and he was just about to jump down to help her, when he heard her speak.

'All right. Let me go, you brute. Here's the key! You go and let my Dad out before the police come! I don't want him caught!'

Markhoff gave an exclamation of triumph, and snatched a shining key out of Jo's hand. He gave her a resounding box on the ear.

'You little toad! You can just stay down here with the others, and it'll be a very, very long stay! Do you know what we're going to do? We're going to roll a big rock over the hole in that other cave's roof – and you'll be prisoners!

729

'You can't escape upwards – and you won't be able to escape downwards. You'll be dashed on the rocks by the sea if you try to swim away. That'll teach you to interfere!'

The other two men guffawed. 'Good idea, Mark,' said one. 'They'll all be nicely boxed up here and nobody will know where they are! Come on – we've no time to lose. If Red isn't unlocked soon he'll go mad!'

They made their way into the heart of the cliff again, and the listening children heard their footsteps getting fainter. Finally they ceased altogether, as one by one the men levered themselves up through the hole in the roof of the last cave, and disappeared up the narrow, low-roofed tunnel that led to the courtyard.

Julian came out from his hiding-place, looking grim and rather scared. 'That's done it!' he said. 'If those fellows really do block up that hole – and I bet they have already – it looks as if we're here for keeps! As he said, we can't get up, and we can't escape down – the sea's too rough for us to attempt any swimming, and the cliff's unclimbable above the ledge!'

'I'll go and have a look and see if they *have* blocked up that hole,' said Dick. 'They may be bluffing.'

But it hadn't been bluff. When Julian and Dick shone their torches on to the hole in the roof, they saw that a great rock was now blocking it up.

They could not get through the hole again. It was impossible to move the rock from below. They went soberly back to the front cave and sat out on the ledge in the light of the sinking sun.

'It's a pity poor Jo was found,' said George. 'And an even greater pity she had to give up the key! Now Red and the others will go free.'

'They won't,' said Jo, surprisingly. 'I didn't give them the key of the tower room. I'd another key with me – the key of the kitchen larder! And I gave them that.'

'Well, I'm blessed!' said Julian, astounded. 'The things

you do, Jo! But how on earth did you happen to have the key of the *larder*?'

Jo told them how she had taken it out and locked herself in when she was having a meal there.

'I had to unlock the door to get out again, of course,' she said. 'And I thought I'd take that key, too, because, who knows? – I might have wanted to get into that larder again and lock myself in with the food!'

'No one will ever get the better of you, Jo,' said Dick with the utmost conviction. 'Never. You're as cute as a bagful of monkeys. So you've still got the right key with you?'

'Yes,' said Jo. 'And Red and my Dad and Jake are still locked up in the tower room!'

But suddenly a most disagreeable thought struck Dick. 'Wait a bit!' he said. 'What's going to happen when they find they've got the *wrong* key? They'll be down here again, and my word, what'll happen to us all then!'

24

A grand surprise

THE thought that the men might soon return even angrier than they had been before was most unpleasant.

'As soon as Markhoff tries the key in the door of the tower room he'll find it won't unlock it, and he'll know that Jo has tricked him!' said George.

'And then he'll be in such a fury that he'll tear down here again, and goodness knows what will happen to us!' groaned Julian. 'What whall we do? Hide again?'

'No,' said Dick. 'Let's get out of here and climb down the cliff to the sea. I'd feel safer there than up here in this cave. We might be able to find a better hiding-place down on the rocks in that little cove.'

'It's a pity my boat's smashed,' said George, with a sigh for her lovely boat. 'And, I say – how are we going to get old Timmy down?'

There was a conference about this. Timmy couldn't climb down, that was certain. Jo remembered the rope still hanging down the side of the cliff to the ledges below – the one she had tied there to help Julian and Dick climb up the steep sides of the cliff.

'I know,' she said, her quick mind working hard again. 'You go down first, Julian, then Dick. Then George can go – each of you holding on to the rope as you climb down, in case you fall.

'Then I'll haul up the rope and tie old Timmy to it, round his waist – and I'll lower him down to you. He's so sleepy still, he won't struggle. He won't even know what's happening!'

'But what about you?' said Dick. 'You'll be last of all. Will you mind? You'll be all alone up on this ledge, with the men coming behind you at any minute.'

'No, I don't mind,' said Jo. 'But let's be quick.'

Julian went down first, glad of the rope to hold to as his feet and hands searched for crevices and cracks. Then came Dick, almost slipping in his anxiety to get down.

Then George climbed down, slowly and anxiously, not at all liking the steep cliff. Once she glanced down to the sea below, and felt sick. She shut her eyes for a moment and clung with one hand to the rope.

It was a dreadful business getting Timmy down. George stood below, anxiously waiting. Jo found it very difficult to tie Timmy safely. He was big and heavy, and didn't like being tied up at all, though he really seemed hardly to know what was going on. At last Jo had got the knots well and securely tied, and called out to the others.

'Here he comes. Watch out that the rope doesn't break. Oh, dear – I wish he wouldn't struggle – now he's bumped himself against the cliff!'

It was not at all a nice experience for poor Timmy. He swung to and fro on the rope as he was slowly let down, and was amazed to find that he was suspended in mid air. Above him Jo panted and puffed.

'Oh, he's so awfully heavy! I hope I shan't have to let go. Look out for him!' she screamed.

The weight was too much for her just at the last, and the rope was let out with rather a rush. Fortunately Timmy was only about six feet up then, and Julian and George managed to catch him as he suddenly descended.

'I'm coming now,' called Jo, and without even holding the rope, or looking at it, she climbed down like a monkey, seeming to find handholds and footholds by magic. The others watched her admiringly. Soon she was standing beside them. George was untying Timmy.

'Thanks awfully, Jo,' said George, looking up gratefully at Jo. 'You're a wonder. Tim must have been frightfully heavy.'

'He was,' said Jo, giving him a pat. 'I nearly dropped him. Well – what's the next move?'

'We'll hunt round this queer little cove a bit and see if there's any place we can hide,' said Julian. 'You go that way, George, and we'll go this.'

They parted, and began to hunt for a hiding-place. As far as Julian and Dick could see there was none at all, at least on the side they were exploring. The sea swept into the cove, swelling and subsiding – and just outside the great waves battered on to the rocks. There was certainly no chance of swimming out.

There was suddenly an excited shriek from George. 'JU! Come here. Look what I've found!'

They all rushed round to where George was standing, behind a big ledge of rock. She pointed to a great mass of something draped with seaweed.

'A boat! It's covered with seaweed – but it's a boat!'

'It's *your* boat!' yelled Dick, suddenly, and began to pull the fronds of seaweed madly off the hidden boat. 'Markhoff *didn't* smash it! It's here, perfectly all right. He couldn't find it – it was hidden so well with seaweed – so he just came back to Red and told him a lie.'

'He didn't smash it!' shouted Jo, and she, too, began to pull away the seaweed. 'It's quite all right – there's nothing wrong with it. He didn't smash it!'

The four children were so tremendously surprised and

734

joyful that they thumped each other ridiculously on the back, and leapt about like mad things. They had their boat after all – George's good, sound boat. They could escape, hip hip hurrah!

A roar from above made them fall silent.

They gazed up, startled. Markhoff and the other two men were on the ledge far above, shouting and shaking their fists.

'You wait till we get you!' yelled Markhoff.

'Quick, quick!' said Julian, urgently, pulling at the boat. 'We've got just a chance. Pull her down to the water, pull hard!'

Markhoff was now coming down the cliff, and Jo wished she had untied the rope before she herself had climbed down, for Markhoff was finding it very useful. She tugged at the boat with the others, wishing it wasn't so heavy.

The boat was almost down to the water when something happened. Timmy, who had been gazing at everything in a most bewildered manner, suddenly slid off the ledge he was on and fell straight into the sea. George gave a scream.

'Oh, Timmy! He's in the water, quick, quick – he's too doped to swim! He'll drown!'

Julian and Dick didn't dare to stop heaving at the boat, because they could see that Markhoff would soon be down beside them. George rushed to Timmy, who was splashing around in the waves, still looking surprised and bemused.

But the water had an amazing effect on him. It was cold and it seemed to bring him to his senses quite suddenly. He became much more lively and swam strongly to the rock off which he had slipped. He clambered out with George's help, barking loudly.

The boat slid into the water, and Julian grabbed at George. 'Come on. In you get. Buck up!'

Jo was in the boat and so was Dick. George, trying to

clutch at Timmy, was hauled in, too. Julian took a despairing look at Markhoff, who was almost at the end of the rope, about to jump down. They just wouldn't get off in time!

Timmy suddenly slipped out of George's grasp and tore madly over to the cliff barking warningly. He seemed to be perfectly all right. The sudden coldness of the sea had washed away all his dopeyness and sleepiness. Timmy was himself again!

Markhoff was about five feet above the ledge when he heard Timmy barking. He looked down in horror and saw the big dog trying to jump up at him. He tried to climb up quickly, out of Timmy's reach.

'Woof!' barked Timmy. 'Woof, woof, woof! Grrrrrrr!'

'Look out – he'll have your foot off!' yelled one of the men above on the ledge.

'He's mad – angry – he's savage. Look out, Mark!'

Markhoff *was* looking out! He was terrified. He clambered up another few feet, and then found that Timmy was making runs at the cliff to try and get up after him. He went up a bit further and clung to the rope with one hand, afraid of falling and being pounced on by the furious Timmy.

'Come on, Timmy!' suddenly cried George. 'Come on!'

The four of them had now got the boat on the waves, and if only they had Timmy they could set off and row round the rocks at the cave entrance before Markhoff could possibly reach them.

'Timmy! Timmy!'

Timmy heard, cast a last regretful look at Markhoff's legs, and bounded across to the boat. He leapt right in and stood there, still barking madly.

Markhoff dropped down the rope to the ledge – but he was too late. The boat shot out to the entrance of the cove and rounded it. In half a minute it had disappeared round the rocky corner and was out at sea.

Julian and Dick rowed steadily. George put her arms round Timmy and buried her face in his fur. Jo did the same.

'He's all right again, quite all right,' said George, happily.

'Yes, falling into the cold water did it,' agreed Jo, ruffling up his fur. 'Good old Timmy!'

Timmy was now snuffling about in the bottom of the boat joyfully. He had smelt a lovely smell. Jo wondered what he had found. Then she knew.

'It's the packet of sandwiches we brought with us in the boat and never ate!' she cried. 'Good old Timmy – he's wolfing the lot!'

'Let him!' said Julian, pulling hard at the oars. 'He deserves them all! My word, it's nice to hear his bark again and see his tail wagging.'

And wag it certainly did. It never stopped. The world had come right again for Timmy, he could see and hear properly again, he could bark and caper and jump – and he had his beloved George with him once more.

'Now for home,' said Julian. 'Anne *will* be pleased to see us. Gosh, what a time we've had!'

25

Everything okay

IT was getting dark as George's boat came into Kirrin Bay. It had seemed a very long pull indeed, and everyone was tired out. The girls had helped in the rowing when the boys had almost collapsed from exhaustion, and Timmy had cheered everyone up by his sudden high spirits.

'Honestly, his tail hasn't stopped wagging since he got into the boat,' said George. 'He's so pleased to be himself again!'

A small figure was on the beach as they came in, half-lost in the darkness. It was Anne. She called out to them in a trembling voice.

'Is it really you? I've been watching for you all day long! Are you all right?'

'Rather! And we've got George and Timmy, too!' shouted back Dick, as the boat scraped on the shingle. 'We're fine!'

They jumped out, Timmy too, and hauled the boat up the beach. Anne gave a hand, almost crying with joy to have them all again.

'It's bad enough being in the middle of an adventure,' she said, 'but it's much, much worse when you're left out. I'll never be left out again!'

'Woof,' said Timmy, wagging his tail in full agreement. He never wanted to be left out of adventures either!

They all went home – rather slowly, because they were so tired. Joan was on the look-out for them, as she had been all day. She screamed for joy when she saw George. 'George! You've got George at last! Oh, you bad children, you've been away all day and I didn't know where and I've been worried to death. George, are you all right?'

'Yes, thank you,' said George, who felt as if she was about to fall asleep at any moment. 'I just want something to eat before I fall absolutely sound asleep!'

'But where have you been all day? What have you been doing?' cried Joan, as she bustled off to get them a meal.

'I got so worked up I went to the police – and what a silly I felt – I couldn't tell them where you'd gone or anything. All I could say was you'd gone to find a man called Red, and had rowed away in George's boat!'

'The police have been up and down the coast in a motor-boat ever since,' said Anne. 'Trying to spot you, but they couldn't.'

'No. Our boat was well hidden,' said Dick. 'And so were we! So well hidden that I began to think we'd stay hidden for the rest of our lives.'

The telephone bell rang. Julian jumped. 'Oh, good – you've had the telephone mended. I'll go and 'phone the police when you've answered this call, Joan.'

But it was the police themselves on the telephone, very pleased to hear Joan saying excitedly that all the children were back safely. 'We'll be up in ten minutes,' they said.

In ten minutes' time the five children and Timmy were tucking into a good meal. 'Don't stop,' said the police sergeant, when he came into the room with the constable the children had seen before. 'Just talk while you're eating.'

So they talked. They told about every single thing. First George told a bit, then Jo, then Dick, then Julian. At first the sergeant was bewildered, but then the bits of information began to piece themselves together in his mind like a jigsaw puzzle.

'Will my father go to prison?' asked Jo.

'I'm afraid so,' said the sergeant.

'Bad luck, Jo,' said Dick.

'I don't mind,' said Jo. 'I'm better off when he's away – I don't have to do things he tells me then.'

'We'll see if we can't fix you up with a nice home,' said the sergeant, kindly. 'You've run wild, Jo – you want looking after.'

'I don't want to go to a Home for Bad Girls,' said Jo, looking scared.

'I shan't let you,' said Dick. 'You're one of the pluckiest kids I've ever known. We'll none of us let you go to a Home. We'll find someone who'll be kind to you, someone like – like . . .'

'Like *me*,' said Joan, who was listening, and she put her arm round Jo and gave her a squeeze. 'I've got a cousin who'd like a ragamuffin like you – a bad little girl with a very good heart. Don't you fret. We'll look after you.'

'I wouldn't mind living with somebody like you,' said Jo, in an offhand way. 'I wouldn't be mean any more then, and I daresay I wouldn't be bad. I'd like to see Dick and all of you sometimes, though.'

'You will if you're good,' said Dick, with a grin. 'But mind – if I ever hear you've got in at anyone's pantry window again, or anything like that, I'll never see you again!'

Jo grinned. She was very happy. She suddenly remembered something and put her hand into the little rush basket she still carried. She took out an enormous key.

741

'Here you are,' she said to the sergeant. 'Here's the key to the tower room. I bet Red and the others are still locked up there, ready for you to catch! My, won't they get a shock when *you* unlock the door and walk in!'

'Quite a lot of people are going to get shocks,' said the sergeant, putting away his very full notebook. 'Miss Georgina, you're lucky to get away unharmed, you and your dog. By the way, we got in touch with a friend of your father's, when we tried to find out about those papers that were stolen. He says your father gave him all his important American papers before he went – so this fellow Red hasn't anything of value at all. He went to all his trouble for nothing.'

'Do you know anything about Red?' asked Julian. 'He seemed a bit mad to me.'

'If he's the fellow we think he is, he's not very sane,' said the sergeant. 'We'll be glad to have him under lock and key – and that man Markhoff too. He's not as clever as Red, but he's dangerous.'

'I hope he hasn't escaped in that helicopter,' said Dick. 'He meant to go tonight.'

'Well, we'll be there in under an hour or so,' said the sergeant. 'I'll just use your telephone, if I may, and set things going.'

Things were certainly set going that night! Cars roared up to Red's house, and the gate was broken in when no one came to open it. The helicopter was still in the yard – but alas! it was on its side, smashed beyond repair. The children were told afterwards that Markhoff and the other two men had tried to set off in it, but there was something wrong – and it had risen some way and then fallen back to the yard.

The old woman was trying to look after the three hurt men, who had crawled from their seats and gone to bathe their cuts and bruises. Markhoff had hurt his head, and showed no fight at all.

'And what about Red?' the sergeant asked Markhoff. 'Is he still locked up?'

'Yes,' said Markhoff, savagely. 'And a good thing, too. You'll have to break that door down with a battering-ram to get him and the others out.'

'Oh no, we shan't,' said the sergeant, and produced the key. Markhoff stared at it.

'That kid!' he said. 'She gave me the key of the larder. Wait till I get her – she'll be sorry.'

'It'll be a long wait, Markhoff,' said the sergeant. 'A long, long wait. We'll have to take you off with us, I'm afraid.'

Red, Simmy and Jake were still locked up, and were mad with rage. But they saw that the game was up, and it wasn't long before all of them were safely tucked away in police cars.

'A very, very nice little haul,' said the sergeant to one of his men. 'Very neat, too – three of them all locked up ready for us!'

'What about that kid, Jo?' said the man. 'She seems a bad lot, and as clever as they make them!'

'She's going to have a chance now,' said the sergeant. 'Everybody has a chance sometimes, and this is hers. She's just about half-and-half, I reckon – half bad and half good. But she'll be all right now she's got a chance!'

Jo was sleeping in Joan's room again. The rest were in their own bedrooms, getting ready for bed. They suddenly didn't feel sleepy any more. Timmy especially was very lively, darting in and out of the rooms, and sending the landing mats sliding about all over the place.

'Timmy! If you jump on my bed again I'll slam the door on you!' threatened Anne. But she didn't, of course. It was so lovely to see old Timmy quite himself once more.

The telephone bell suddenly rang, and made everyone jump.

'*Now* what's up?' said Julian, and went down in the hall to answer it. A voice spoke in his ear.

'Is that Kirrin 011? This is Telegrams. There is a cable for you, with reply prepaid. I am now going to read it.'

'Go ahead,' said Julian.

'It is from Seville in Spain,' said the voice, 'and reads as follows:

"HERE IS OUR ADDRESS PLEASE CABLE BACK SAYING IF EVERYTHING ALL RIGHT – UNCLE QUENTIN".'

Julian repeated the message to the others, who had now crowded round him in the hall. 'What reply shall I give?' he asked. 'No good upsetting them now everything is over!'

'Not a bit of good,' said Dick. 'Say what you like!'

'Right!' said Julian, and turned to the telephone again. 'Hallo – here is the reply message, please. Ready?

"HAVING A MOST EXCITING TIME WITH LOTS OF FUN AND GAMES EVERYTHING OKAY – JULIAN".'

'Everything okay,' repeated Anne, as they went upstairs to bed once more. 'That's what I like to hear at the end of an adventure. Everything okay.'